AN INCH OF TIME

AN INCH OF TIME

Ian Weston Smith

The Book Guild Ltd
Sussex, England

This book is a work of fiction. The characters and situations in this story are imaginary. No resemblance is intended between these characters and any real persons, either living or dead.

This book is sold subject to the condition that it shall not, by way of trade or otherwise, be lent, re-sold, hired out, photocopied or held in any retrieval system or otherwise circulated without the publisher's prior consent in any form of binding or cover other than that in which this is published and without a similar condition including this condition being imposed on the subsequent purchaser.

The Book Guild Ltd
25 High Street,
Lewes, Sussex

First published 1994
© Ian Weston Smith 1994

Set in Meridien

Typesetting by Raven Typesetters,
Ellesmere Port, South Wirral

Printed in Great Britain by
Antony Rowe Ltd.
Chippenham, Wiltshire.

A catalogue record for this book is available from the British Library

ISBN 0 86332 959 4

An inch of time cannot be bought with an inch of gold

Chinese proverb

1

The cupboard was empty, and that was a boon because space for investigation was important for a man whose girth had noticeably increased since July '44.

With the pencil torch from his camera case he searched the underside of the staircase for the horizontal crack two feet from the floor which would tell him that Tom Preston's device for concealing the tunnel entrance was undisturbed. It was no more than an outside chance; thirty seven years is a long time for a hinged piece of plywood and plasterboard. On the other hand, from its general condition of dust and smell he guessed the cupboard had been little used, if at all.

Forbes wriggled into the confined space and fingered the door shut from inside. He had seen the crack. He pushed firmly at the plasterboard flap where it rested on the concrete floor, and sure enough it moved. He pushed harder and there, in his torchlight, was the pseudo-concrete manhole cover and, above it, the bottom inside treads of the stairs.

The staircase to the first floor had been long enough for Preston to drop the lining behind the stair treads to an angle which gave him two clear feet on the ground behind the treads. Hence the hinged flap opening upwards and giving access to the manhole cover and the tunnel's vertical shaft.

The idea of the flap hinging upwards to give access

hadn't been Tom Preston's only good idea. The tunnel itself was the product of his many years' experience in designing London's underground. We felt confident with Tom, Forbes remembered.

A business trip to Germany had given him an opportunity to visit the prison camp where he'd spent a year, some of it digging a tunnel. More important, he had driven around the country and the villages where he and James had spent ten very active and often frightening days after their escape in April '45. But there *seemed* to be something else. Something which got in the way of those simple, enjoyable memories. His mind kept trying to side-track itself. It had done so since he had presented himself that morning and asked if he could walk round what was now an immaculate police cadet training centre. *Ja, aber natürlich* – the familiar words. And take photographs, perhaps? *'Bestimmt.'*

So he'd spent the morning undisturbed, taking outdoor shots – the *lagerstrasse*, the canteen building, the main blocks of the original barracks, which looked out across the sports field to the river beyond, and the road beyond that, which the US Tomahawks had strafed early that April morning in '45. Then they had wheeled and, for good measure, strafed 2,000 Allied prisoners already marshalled on the upper road for the long march to Hitler's 'redoubt' south of the Danube. Forbes had been lying beside Phil Denison when he got a cannon shell in his backside. He would have died there and then but for Ansbach, the interpreter, who got stretcher-bearers from nowhere. As it was, he died six days later in the camp hospital.

'But enough of all that,' Forbes said aloud, 'or you'll get stuck in this fucking manhole of Tom Preston's and not be found for weeks.'

He lifted the manhole cover, having wedged the

hinged flap with a convenient piece of broken broom handle. With the light from the torch he looked down into what he remembered as a deepish shaft. Well, there's plenty of time, he thought. The police cadets had shown no interest in him, and when he had infiltrated the ground floor of the second of the three main barrack blocks, where he and fifteen others had spent those last twelve anxious months of World War II, their indifference had been almost palpable. Too many old Kriegies wandering round, he thought. They don't bat an eyelid. It had been disconcerting, however, to find that the central entrance to the building and the lobby space had been converted to a shower and locker-room. The area behind the staircase itself however was happily undisturbed – an unlikely place for anyone to come looking on a Saturday afternoon.

His memory was having another go now, trying to say something. Some trick, some damn nonsense, now come on, Forbes – get on with it, clear your mind, take a look, perhaps just a flashlight glimpse and then call it a day.

The air was fusty; of course, the original air extraction system would have collapsed. Now he must turn himself round and drop down the vertical shaft feet first, using what was left of the firebars which had been cemented into the chimney foundations as ladder rungs. To a hand pull, the top two seemed OK – and anyway they would suffice to get him up if the shaft was about ten feet deep, as he dimly remembered.

Forbes sank to his knees as soon as his feet touched the bottom, and fished out the torch. First he examined the rungs. They were firm, carefully cemented into the brickwork of the chimney's base, very rusty but well able to bear his weight.

The chamber was, as he remembered it, about five

feet by four, and four feet high – space enough for a man to crouch for a four-hour stint, filling bags made from battle-dress trousers with earth from the wooden toboggan which he periodically pulled from the tunnel. Then the face-worker would wriggle out backwards and the next shift would take over. The full length of the tunnel to the opening in the vegetable plot across the road outside the camp must have been about a hundred feet, sloping gently upwards to a final short vertical shaft, with working chambers about every twenty feet or so. Only room enough for a man's shoulders, plus space to hack at the stony soil with a short crowbar. Bloody claustrophobic, Forbes remembered, and only just enough air from Preston's air-extraction system of dried-milk tins piped together in the curvature of the roof.

But why sit here thinking about the dimensions of the bloody thing, he thought, when there it is in front of you with a bit of rotten looking sacking propped across it with two sticks?

He moved nearer and took the sticks away, and the canvas dropped to the crumbled soil where the tunnel mouth had partly fallen away. The gasp of astonishment became 'Jesus Christ' as his torch caught the dull, unmistakable glimmer of neatly stacked gold ingots, so neatly stacked that he immediately noticed the gap in the centre – a gap the size of an ingot!

'My God,' said Forbes aloud. 'How far back do they go?'

He sank back on his haunches, the torch playing on the ingot ends. It was gold all right. The fascination was there too; he could feel it taking over as he put a hand out to scratch the surface. Momentarily as he did so there was a glint somewhere by his right knee. Then it was gone. A piece of glass? Or rusty tin, more likely, from the old collapsed ventilation pipe? Jagged, no doubt, so take it slowly, he told himself, or it could pierce his knee. Blood stains on a trouser leg wouldn't look good walking through the police cadet Headquarters on his way out. There was the glint again, dully brassy – OK, grab it, get it out from under the trouser leg. Something attached to it dragged in the soft soil. He held it up, peering in the torchlight. A coin attached to a chain? He rubbed it with his gritty fingers, then on his shirt-sleeve – a gold St Christopher, worn but in good condition, a small nick out of one edge. He tried hard not to believe. It was his own, given to him by Zulka and he had been wearing it yesterday!

Now he knew what had happened to him. Now he knew why this morning he had found his nails so beautifully clean. Someone had kidnapped him.

Yesterday's meeting with Oberdorf in Eichstätt *had* been a dream. Someone had brought him here, drugged presumably. The missing ingot. God – the implications! Somehow his abductors had planted in his mind the recollection of a lunch and a business meeting so as to account for the missing hours he'd spent leading them to the tunnel and the gold. His mind whirled. By sheer chance he had repeated the visit. By sheer chance he now knew what it was quite possibly going to be very dangerous to know. He also knew that someone had made a bloody fool of him, that there would be embarrassing consequences with Oberdorf, and his boss. Other possible consequences also flitted through his mind. He didn't care for any of them.

One thing was quite certain – nothing he said would be believed.

2

Forbes sat in his Wimbledon garden trying to do Saturday morning homework. It was warm, early April. He'd had three weeks to digest and explain. Digestion had been easy because there was no food for his thoughts. The gold had become a mirage. Explanation had been hellish difficult. Forbes's boss had been amazingly sympathetic but equally firm. 'You loused up a perfectly good deal with Oberdorf, and I'm going to have an explanation. Go to Germany. Take time over it. Take a couple of airline tickets if you want them but, within one month, explain to me why an experienced man, who knows Germany well, disappears completely for seven hours on a Friday afternoon.'

Forbes had said nothing about the gold. He wouldn't have been believed. He didn't believe it himself. What he did believe was that his new-found business career was on a cliff edge.

He now reflected – giving way to a nasty bout of introspection, which was most unusual for him. At the same time, his Intelligence training told him to take a firm grip on the process of analysis. It wasn't easy because his mind kept slipping back to his present predicament – the prospect of losing a hard-won job in industry which he'd managed to find after three lousy years of unemployment, preceded by eight hilarious but disastrous years' hotel-keeping in Austria – a marvellous and joyous relief after sixteen years with British Intelligence which had nearly wrecked his marriage.

His boss in the service – Brockles Fitzherbert – had been mentor and friend. Yes, friend; not an easy one – a tricky one, in fact, and a boss friend is always tricky – but they'd worked well together. In retrospect it had been a successful relationship. Forbes' aptitude for languages, the fact that Brock had been his wartime company commander, Forbes's post-war background and the Army ski school in Austria (where he'd first met Zulka) and the British Military Mission in Prague, where he'd made some good Czech friends, had all helped.

Still sixteen years had been too long, despite the foreign postings, and Zulka had been right to dig him out, but he'd learnt a lot – a helluva lot.

What he *hadn't* learnt was what to do when your memory refuses to acknowledge that you've gone missing for seven critical hours and that *someone* has engineered it, someone who wanted that gold.

Zulka hadn't been a lot of help. Instinct and experience had suffused her mind with the idea that there was a girl mixed up in it somewhere.

'You met some girl on the aeroplane, Archie, and then you offer to drive her around this romantic part of Bavaria where you and James had done your escaping and then you take her somewhere for lunch.' The eyebrows had become very expressive. Zulka's eyebrows could arch themselves in good-humoured surprise, giving a wealth of meaning to an unfinished sentence. In thirty three years of marriage they had often played a useful part in bringing Forbes back to earth after one of what he called his 'romantic peccadilloes'.

'I am not the biggest fool in Christendom,' he'd said crossly, 'I had it all fixed with Oberdorf. I arranged to go directly to Eichstätt in the hire-car, where he would join me for lunch, leaving the afternoon and evening to finalise the agreement. I never showed up. He waited for two hours and then drove off in a fury, thinking this was a tactic to wreck the agreement. He is still fuming; so is everyone else. There *was* no bloody girl; how could there be?' He slammed out of the room.

That their marriage had been a fair success – despite Forbes's peccadilloes – was largely due to Zulka's immense resilience, a resilience born in the Warsaw ghetto in 1944, where her mother, Countess Ratocka, was shot by the Germans for helping a Jewish family. She and her English governess had been trapped in the Ratocki town house and so they joined the resistance – almost *force majeure*. At sixteen it had been a horrifying experience, which made her an adult in three months. They had arranged somehow to get out just before the collapse, and made their way via Palestine to find her father, who was fighting for General Anders in Italy. Major Ratocki was thrilled and horrified when his daughter came up one day with the rations. He quickly got her into uniform and pushed her into 8th Army HQ as an interpreter, where she was invaluable because Anders and Oliver Leese were having fearful communication difficulties. The governess, Miss Summerskill, found herself in the Hadfield Spears Ambulance Unit, where she had a tough but lovely war.

Father and daughter returned to England with Anders but it wasn't long before Zulka had winkled some travel documents out of the Polish Corps and set off on a swan round Continental Europe. What she was looking for she had no idea, but at the British Army ski school above Klagenfurt she had found Archie Forbes.

Zulka was a wonderful skier and a beautiful Slav. Archie's romantic nature and the *Berggeist* – the spirit of the mountains – did the rest.

Papa had mounted opposition, largely on grounds of Zulka's youth, and Brock had urged Forbes to accept a posting to the Military Mission in Prague, which he knew would be useful training for what he had in mind for Forbes when he left the Army.

It was almost a disaster. Zulka followed him to Prague in a mood of jealous possessiveness, and found her untrustworthy beloved dallying with fashionable ladies who had progressively transferred their favours from German to British officers via American diplomats. Sanity was restored only when she and Forbes had spent twenty-four hours incarcerated in a frontier post, having wandered into Poland in a snowstorm while trying to find a ski-hotel. After that, marriage, and Brock, had gobbled them up.

During those sixteen years, many of them *en poste* in half a dozen different countries, Forbes had done well, or anyway reasonably well. His gift for quenching incipient hostility had turned some tricky situations into enduring success. It was this ability, she knew, he felt had let him down painfully in the Oberdorf imbroglio. He had competence too – despite the romanticism – albeit sporadic. Competence of a kind which got the job finished just before his enthusiasm ran out and he started to cut the odd corner.

Then the Ratocki jewels – or anyway some of them – managed to somehow slip into Switzerland and the money they produced realised their dream of running a ski-hotel in Austria. Forbes had always seen Zulka as the Slav princess on a sleigh in a Nielsen drawing, but reality had come quickly. They had worked like demons. It had all been fun but the money ran out. The hotel was too small and they couldn't borrow enough to enlarge it.

Then, for Forbes, three years of unemployment – save for some odd 'special' jobs for David Stirling in what Archie had elegantly called The Gulf protection racket – while the capital from the hotel sale dwindled on school and grocers' bills. Agony for them both; 'Famous Grouse' had made it a threesome.

Finally came the job offer. Forbes's languages of course were just what they needed, and possibly Brock played a part? It hadn't been easy; at fifty three high-technology industry isn't; you don't flop into it like a duck to water. There are jealousies, tensions, curious nuances of language, addiction to jargon, suspicion of good English and above all 'competitor security', in addition to all the other kinds. But it had all been working, he had been settling down, the track record had started to write itself.

Zulka could see him on the terrace, slumped in a chair. She went out and said, 'I'm going to do some shopping.'

Silence.

In a placatory tone – 'I suppose when you woke in the morning you were convinced that the Oberdorf meeting had in fact taken place and the agreement was put to bed?'

Without looking up – 'I was damn certain of it – until I found my St Christopher.'

3

The telephone rang. 'Mr Forbes?'
'Yes.'
The voice was calm, cool almost. 'I would like to try to explain what happened to you in Germany three weeks ago.'
Forbes liked the 'try to'. He said, 'Are you in London?'
'Yes.'
'The bridge, then, in St James's Park. Tomorrow morning at 10.30.' His voice had the crispness of his S.I.S training. 'Yes, of course.' He put down the telephone and wondered for the thousandth time why Germans always said 'Yes, of course.'
Damn the woman, he thought. It was the coolness which had irritated him.
Forbes approached the bridge some ten minutes early and slowed up to get a good look. The girl was early too. He liked the calves and the ankles, and the suit was smart, if perhaps not a perfect cut; figure not bad. The hair was darkish bronze, if there is such a colour, and the nose had a touch of Roman about it. That was all he could see before their eyes met. Dark Slav eyes – like Zulka; this is not one of your Wiesbaden fräuleins.
'Mr Forbes?' Her voice had the faintest American twang, the accent more French than German. She held

out a hand, and her eyes were friendly, if hesitant. 'I am the daughter of von Heimann, whom perhaps you remember from Eichstätt?'

The English was very precise and the voice had that inevitable lilt on the final syllable, making Eichstätt sound like rather a nice place.

'Also, Josel Buchowitz was my grandmother and she often told me about you.'

Forbes thought, if this social introduction is to put me at a disadvantage, she's bloody well succeeding.

Of course he remembered Josel Buchowitz; Prague in the spring of '47 was not easily forgotten. But her father? OK, so she must be the daughter of the security officer at Eichstätt who had helped James and him to escape from the night march in April 1945. Very much helped, at that. All this went through his mind as he piloted her in silence to a bench facing the lake. It was a perfect April morning; there seemed to be green everywhere, in the sky and on the ground, huge beds of tulips blazed with colour and the Horse Guards looked fresh and clean.

Funny how when you sit on a bench you always look first at a girl's ankles, he mused. Perhaps you're meant to. Then the eye travels up rather quickly and almost too soon there are, once more, the eyes.

'I suppose you used a drug?' he said, unsmiling.

'No, hypnosis,' was the reply, with a very steady gaze.

'It must be powerful stuff.' There was more than a touch of resentment in his voice. 'So now perhaps you'll explain all these coincidences, your father, Josel Buchowitz, my visit to Germany and, of course, the gold?'

'I am also called Josel,' she said, 'and first I want to apologise. To kidnap you was terrible. Simply, we thought it was unavoidable. Perhaps we made a mistake.'

'I am here out of curiosity,' said Forbes.

They talked, or rather Forbes listened, for two hours and then for two more hours over lunch at the Cavalry Club. Finally, soon after four, he had dropped Josel at London Airport for her flight to Munich.

The final exchanges were to the point.

'Without you we couldn't find the gold. Now, without you, our plan for the future of Germany must nearly certainly come to – nothing.'

'Well, I'd like to meet Willi Ansbach again – that I've always wanted to do – and your father too. They helped us a lot, and damn risky it must have been for them – *damn* risky.' And he thought about the SS battalion which had fought such a tough defensive battle just south of Eichstätt. A German officer helping British prisoners to escape would have struck them as conduct most unbecoming. He could see now a grim-faced SS platoon officer as he marched his men up the Böhmfeld village street, their Spandaus ready to hold off an American battalion.

They were nearing the terminal when Forbes said, 'How were you so sure the hypnosis would work?'

'I was taught by the Malgache – I used to live in Madagascar. They've never known it to fail.'

Forbes breath hissed a little as he asked, 'And then I suppose I became a zombie and said "Yes" to everything?'

'Certainly not, you behaved perfectly normally in every way. We simply asked you most politely to show us the tunnel. You went down, told my father you could see the gold and, at his request, handed him up one bar.'

'Then it was all over,'' said Forbes.

'Exactly – straight back to your hire-car.'
'Just outside Böhmfeld,' said Forbes.
'Yes.'
They were at the terminal now, and as the car drew up Forbes saw Josel studying his hands on the wheel.

'Yes,' he said, 'that was the best manicure I've ever had,' and this time his laugh was genuine.

He heard the door open, felt a quick kiss on his cheek, and watched the trim figure with the shoulder-bag disappear through the entrance doors.

That was to remind me that I'm old enough to be her father, he chuckled. Josel Buchowitz – well, I'll be damned!

It was a slow drive home. If this is an escapade, he thought, fifty five years of age is too long in the tooth. 'Battle for the soul of Germany' (wasn't that the phrase she'd used?). Well, that's high-sounding by any standard.

On the other hand, Ansbach and Helmut von Heimann were not foolish men. He had known von Heimann hardly at all, but Ansbach very well indeed, from the time the tunnel had 'blown' and Forbes had been taken on as adjutant for the other ranks, with Ansbach as his interpreter. A thinking man, only in the Interpreter Corps because of poor health, Ansbach had spent a year from May '45 in an American POW camp and subsequently joined the Bavarian Freedom Party. They had later corresponded, and Forbes could well believe that Willi Ansbach had built up a fairly strong movement.

A link with the Kremlin? Two men murdered? And they'd sent the girl with the whole story, without knowing that he had been back to the tunnel on his own account and found the gold for the second time? Amazing. She'd said that without help from him they were now scuppered. In fact they were scuppered already; he had only to tell the old department the bare bones, and the escapade would be well and truly over and the soul of Germany, like John Brown's body, would have to go marching on alone. But how would his boss feel if he were told that, on an important, well-prepared business trip, he just happened to get himself hypnotised by some people (old friends as it turned out!) who wanted him to lead them to some gold hidden in a tunnel in an old POW camp?

Aelred Jones, his immediate superior, tinged with Welsh romanticism, might rather like it – could even believe it – but the head boy? The one who had never much liked Forbes's track record? It was asking too much. The thought of job-hunting at fifty five sent a shiver down his spine.

Hell, now, he must go to Germany and find something, anything, which would restore his credibility. Zulka would have to go on being patient; God knew, he'd taxed her patience enough; but isn't that what patience is for?

Forbes picked up the telephone.

4

Willi Ansbach sat reflectively; watching Hans Detleffson's car disappear down the hill into Kufstein. There was no rancour in his mind, and that was as well because the conversation had been almost civilised and not unbusinesslike. He simply felt two things: one was finality and the other regret. Hans's father, 'Daddy' Detleffson, as the British officers had called him, had been a lifelong friend. The British had seen him as the archetypal 'decent' German officer, the one who kept his extreme colleagues at bay, the one whose normally expressionless pug face occasionally betrayed a twinkle. To the normal ramrod mentality of the German officer class, a twinkle was an unforgivable sin. To Ansbach it was a sign that all was not inhumanly lost in war-time Germany.

Ansbach had returned to Germany in early '39 after a year in England. Wounded near Calais as an under officer, the interpreter posting to the prison camp at Eichstätt had been ideal. It had allowed him to keep in touch with the anti-Nazi faction in Munich and to court the lovely Elli on weekend leaves at her parents' house near Kufstein, just over the Austrian border. At the end of the war he and Detleffson had both spent some months in an American POW camp; and then he had quietly slipped back into civilian life, Detleffson to his small law practice in Eichstätt.

Ansbach had fought his way into journalism, achieving the editorship of *Die Erweckung*, with offices in Munich, Frankfurt and Bonn. He had also made progress with his fledgling Bavarian Freedom Party and was well-known in German liberal circles.

He and Detleffson had always kept in touch, despite the fifteen-year age difference. He had helped the older man re-establish his law firm and more recently had battled to help keep his younger son out of trouble. The boy, Hans, had been hopelessly spoilt as a child. His elder brother had been killed in a Munich air raid, and the Detleffsons had lavished attention on Hans. The disasters followed one another in a wearisome catalogue, the most recent being the seemingly inevitable drug-trafficking. His parents had virtually bought him back, using all their resources, from the drug barons. Ansbach had helped. Hans's wife, a good country girl, had done her best. There were no children.

And now blackmail. Since his father's death six months before and his mother's soon afterwards, Hans had given up his Munich flat and moved into the Eichstätt family home. Things had got better: there was a small-holding and Hans had seemed to enjoy it.

'I've come to see you about the gold', Hans had said. 'In my opinion you have taken advantage of my father's trust in you. He told you about the gold.'

'You know, Hans, from long experience, that I would not do that. So what exactly are we talking about?'

Hans looked crafty, a saddeningly familiar expression. 'The Englishman has led you to the gold, has he not? I am now asking for my share.'

Ansbach gazed steadily at the young man.

'Your father told me that after the evacuation of the camp in April '45 the SS battalion, which was delaying the American advance in the area, cordoned off the camp and brought in some trucks by night. Your father had stayed late in the camp hospital, and as he passed the trucks on the way out he caught a glimpse; in other words, he was convinced he saw gold ingots. In the morning two members of the Headquarters staff were shot by the SS. Your father presumed they had known something about the shipment. Your father knew no more than I have told you.'

'But the Englishman did,' said Hans. 'My friends in the police cadet barracks say he has paid two visits in the last week.'

Ansbach lent forward and said with emphasis, 'Hans, *should* any gold be extracted from those barracks – and it certainly won't be if you keep gossiping with your friends in the police cadet force – you will receive, depending on the quantity, the handsome reward which would have been your father's. That is all I can say.'

Hans's sneer curled not just his lip but his whole face.

'So you speak to me of largesse. Crap on your largesse.' His voice rose, his fingers were scrabbling on the table. 'It is the Englishman, isn't it, the man who was your friend; you helped him to escape and he was one of those who worked on the tunnel, the tunnel which was never dug out. So you think I am stupid? The gold is in the tunnel and the Englishman has shown you the undiscovered tunnel! It is so, it must be so, and now I am not warning you, Willi, old friend of my father – I am *telling* you. You are going to put into my account immediately one million Deutschmarks, and then I will receive one-third of the value of all gold extracted – and I will be supervisor of the extraction team so as to ensure what you English lovers call "fair play"! Otherwise Willi, my dear Willi, who has patronised me all the years I can remember, I am going to the police. Yes, because there will be a big reward for a hoard of Nazi gold. And then the publicity; *Der Spiegel* will pay me big money for a series – "Son of POW camp officer finds Nazi gold in old escape tunnel." Of course, television too perhaps?'

Ansbach took a deep breath. 'I will think about the publicity angle, Hans.'

'No you won't,' said Hans. 'You have seven days for that money to be in my bank account, Willi.'

Then he was down the terrace steps and the car door slammed.

Elli came out of the kitchen. 'There are good slams and bad slams,' she said.

'That was a bad slam,' he answered. 'A very bad slam.'

He sat reflectively, finality uppermost but also regret – much, much more regret.

He had already telephoned Wolfmannis.

5

Wolfmannis arrived the following evening from Düsseldorf, well before Helmut von Heimann, who had only the short journey from Munich. He had brought caviar and vodka, and they sat on the terrace and waited for von Heimann. As they looked at the mountains and clinked their glasses, Wolfmannis looked across at Elli and said, 'How was your skiing this year?'

'I am a little bit old now for the steep runs, but it was wonderful as always.'

'*Du Wunderschönes Alpenland,*' said Wolfmannis, and they all smiled.

'*Mein Heimatland Tyrol.*' Yes,' she said, 'the mountains have brought great happiness to Willi and me.'

They had known Wolfmannis for about four years. Ansbach had met him at a 'defection' Bavarian Freedom Party meeting soon after his defection from the KGB. The defection had come as little surprise to anyone. In fact, although detested by the hard men of the KGB, it was the closest thing to an unofficial ambassadorship, with East–West trade as its apparent prime object. For Wolfmannis it had been the ambition of a lifetime.

Born in Riga and brought up by his grandmother, his aunt and two cousins, Juris Wolfmannis was a prime target for KGB recruiters. They threatened to assassinate his parents, who had escaped to Paris at the end of the war. There were inducements too. By twenty five he was climbing the ladder of preferment, opportunistically sending some old school-mates to labour camps to gain promotion, but successfully protecting his immediate family. He recognised that it was a lousy existence.

Ultimately the Baltic States would again be free, but before or after the collapse of the Bolshevik experiment? That was the question which dominated his mind. From outside, he could help to architect, even become *the* architect of the freedom of the Baltic States. But to get into that positon required a very special form of defection, connived at by both West and East, which would protect his family.

In 1977 came the opportunity. His immediate boss had summoned him to Moscow for what purported to be a briefing on Cocom, the Western allies' system of restricting high-technology exports to the USSR.

'It is working too well for the West. We must find ways of teaching the Germans how to evade these controls.'

'Do we know that they want to evade these controls?'

'German industrialists *always* like to evade controls which hamper closer technological links with the Soviet Union, because *one day* – this with great emphasis – it will be possible for German industry to rejuvenate the Soviet economy. I want you, Wolfmannis, to "defect" – this with a hearty but nervous laugh – 'and become the "first architect" of that rejuvenation process. Do you understand what I am saying?'

They were walking in Gorky Park and Wolfmannis allowed himself ten paces before answering. 'I understand very well that one day I may hear that you have been shot for treachery.'

The older man stopped, turned Wolfmannis by his arm to face him and said, 'You are right, but just remember that if that should happen there are many more here in Moscow who think and act in the same way as me. The alternative is the collapse of the entire Soviet Union. Russia has always been more important than Communism.'

After three weeks' holiday in Paris with his parents, Juris Wolfmannis had moved to Bonn to establish himself under that all-purpose flag of convenience 'East–West trade'.

When he first met Ansbach and von Heimann, it was soon clear to all three that their philosophies were in harmony. The meeting had been completely fortuitous. Wolfmannis gatecrashed a meeting in Munich of the Bavarian Freedom Party. 'One of the best ways of spying,' he had said afterwards – over huge steins of beer – 'is though the front door'. They had discussed, they had argued, they had demurred. They had visited Wolfmannis' parents in Paris, where his mother, steely-eyed, in response to a question had said, 'Petersburg, I do not *wish* to remember Petersburg.'

'Why not?' they asked on the way home.

'Oh, I suppose because my grandfather was treated so badly. He kept a St Petersburg factory going until 1927, often paying the workers with soap. The English owners wanted their dividends, so he cast small gold ingots for them to carry away in their specially designed waistcoats. Finally he was tortured and murdered. There are so many things my mother doesn't want to remember about her childhood.'

Eventually Wolfmannis told them that there was a growing section of opinion in the Kremlin which, to the fury of the Red Army, and most of the KGB, shared the belief of Ansbach and von Heimann that to eliminate –

or at any rate drastically to reduce – the risk of a third European war, the reunification of Germany was an essential preliminary. This belief encompassed two massive and challenging assumptions. The first was that the basic tenet of Marxism-Leninism – that capitalism in its death throes would launch an attack on Mother Russia – no longer had the faintest credibility. The second, that Germany had abandoned the concept of the *Drang nach Osten* (her drive for the east) except in terms of a huge market for her technology. For finding the courage to make two such daunting assumptions, Germany's reward would be to prevent the Soviet economy from sliding into chaos.

'As for the dream of world revolution – well, could we leave that for another time, my friends? Perhaps it is still there, but does it have any greater prospect than that faced by the Catholic faith after the Reformation?'

'Of course,' said Wolfmannis, on one occasion, 'it is only because these thoughts are stirring in the Kremlin that I am here. I am more of an ambassador than a defector. My Kremlin masters want to sow the seeds of an irreversible accord with the West. All the eggs are not in one basket, of course; some other recent defectors have similar terms of reference. For that you must, for the moment, take my word. Of course, the time is not yet come, the Brezhnev regime is still far too powerful.'

The conversations between the three men covered a long span of time. They examined many aspects of history. Very often von Heimann was the interrogator. His hard, incisive questioning, came from his pre-war legal training and his wartime experiences. Badly wounded in Yugoslavia, he had escaped the partisans by spending five days straddling the axle of a goods wagon. No longer fit for active service, and because of his good English, he had been seconded to the Sicherheitdienst and despatched to the Eichstätt POW camp to crack the exploding black market. This he had done in exactly three weeks in September '44. He had caught German sentries throwing loaves of bread from their sentry boxes as he waited below. In the morning he had sent them to the Russian front irrespective of their medical category.

Forbes he had known because the British other ranks, who were under Forbes's wing, had naturally shown great restlessness at the prospect of losing their own private black market in the form of food brought into the camp from the farms where they worked daily. It was von Heimann's first experience of a British meaningless compromise. He had suggested that the British other ranks should retain their so-called 'right' to bring in farm produce on condition they did not resell to British officers and so re-create what von Heimann dismantled. Forbes had agreed, knowing only too well that virtually no order issued by him or his RSM would be obeyed. He also knew that it was unnecessary – the other ranks had no intention of supplying officers with food. It was not from hostility; by this stage of captivity, they were a race apart.

Ansbach had worn a wry smile at the end of that particular discussion. He knew what had been passing through Forbes's mind, he knew that von Heimann couldn't win, but it didn't worry him because he also knew that October '44 had brought all three of them on to the same side. He admitted as much soon afterwards when he offered to supply Forbes and his room mates with black market food 'from my own personal sources'.

After that they had seen a great deal of each other, the under-officer interpreter and the young second lieutenant taken prisoner in Italy in the spring of '44.

For weeks after his arrival Forbes had dug and carted earth from David Stirling's tunnel. Finally it was agreed that only nine could safely go out, and Forbes had lost in the ballot. He felt a mixture of relief and groaning disappointment – how could there ever be another chance?

He had then settled down to a prosaic mixture of law studies and the ineffectual administration which von Heimann and Ansbach (and sometimes rebellious British other ranks themselves) occasionally made more interesting.

As he drove from Munich to Kufstein to answer Willi Ansbach's summons, von Heimann considered the possibilities. He knew that Juris Wolfmannis would be there and that a crisis had blown up, from the reference on the telephone to Hans Detleffson. Detleffson would spell trouble. He always spelt trouble. Well, they would just have to handle any amount of trouble as far as the gold was concerned, because without it their plan was dead. Intellectually conceived and pragmatically hammered into workable shape, it was ambitious, visionary even, and given *their* projection of history, very nearly immediately workable. He corrected himself – no, not immediately, but as soon as the Kremlin could bring to themselves to hear Louis XVI's cryptic message of *'le déluge'*; as soon, in fact, as Brezhnev's total incapacity was recognised.

Thoughts of the gold turned his mind to Forbes. His daughter Josel's idea had been brilliantly simple: a pretty girl, a broken-down motor car – and Forbes was a romantic. 'They all are, the English,' Josel Buchowitz had said. 'We Slavs are supposed to be but we can't hold a candle to the English public schoolboy; Robert Louis

Stevenson I suppose. Von Heimann had wondered how she knew about Robert Louis Stevenson.

Forbes had not disappointed them. He and Ansbach had kept vaguely in touch over the years, so a sneaky call to Forbe's office had bamboozled his secretary into giving the date and destination of the Oberdorf mission.

Josel had followed the hire-car out of the airport and then nipped in front just south of Böhmfeld. Forbes had come upon the open BMW ('Thank God for a fine warm morning,' she'd thought) half in the ditch, and Josel, looking distraught, with a sad story about the power steering. She'd told her father later that she felt awful because 'he'd been so damned nice about everything'.

Von Heimann had been surprised by Josel's enthusiasm for the plan which she, Ansbach, Wolfmannis and he had put together. From a different generation without any 'Nazi war guilt', (those words haunted him), he guessed she had come to it all as a kind of therapy for the sickening disaster of her marriage to Jean Louis and her humiliation by the Malgache witches. Her ideas and her consoling femininity when the three men had had their periodic bouts of *angst* had been of immense value. He just hoped the therapy had been mutual. His mind clouded over at that thought; he was running late thanks to that damned court official, and something, something was seriously awry. Willi Ansbach was not a man for false alarms.

Juris Wolfmannis was at the gate when he arrived, getting into his car. Getting *into* his car? What on earth was he doing? He shouted, 'How are you, Juris? What goes on?' Wolfmannis slammed the door, lowered the window and said, 'Willi will tell you, Helmut. I must go now, I need the daylight.'

As the car moved off, von Heimann stared at his

face. The narrow dark features had a look of intense preoccupation, a sombre, resigned expression round the eyes, but the thin mouth, which von Heimann had never altogether liked, was drawn down in a determination which could have been self-dislike.

'What is the matter with Juris, Willi?' he shouted, and then he saw his friend's face as he came down the path.

Germans have a strong sentimentality which some of their enemies believe enables them to mask their feelings while they do unpleasant but 'necessary' things. Willi Ansbach wore an expression of priestlike solemnity, the resignation of a parent who has tried every solution many times. His face was without self-pity. It took very few words. 'Hans Detleffson has gone too far?' said von Heimann.

'Yes,' came the answer, 'and Juris will do it well.'

Neither man had any squeamishness about death; war had cauterised any such feeling. Von Heimann could remember in March '45 being asked by a British officer, 'Is there any truth in the camp rumour about the "Fleisch Machine"?' (POW jargon for summary execution). His reaction was more indignation that the Wehrmacht *might* be ordered to do such things, than disbelief that it *could* happen. No, the execution of Hans Detleffson cast a black shadow, but only because it put in both their minds the unspoken question, How many more will there have to be?

6

Von Heimann had gone by morning. Just as well, thought Ansbach as he saw his old friend Erich Vogler get out of an unmarked car at eight o'clock and walk up the path. Vogler, chief of the Special Branch of the Munich police, had always kept a friendly eye on the activities of the Bavarian Freedom Party – Ansbach half suspected that in political thought they were not very far apart.

'I have bad news for you, Willi my friend,' he said. 'Your friend Hans Detleffson is dead, murdered. A Munich policeman has no business here in Austria, but it is better for you to know sooner rather than later. Also in the house, and also dead, were the wife of Detleffson and a gentleman whom I believe you know – Herr Juris Wolfmannis?'

Willi Ansbach thought he had arranged his rather inexpressive features to register shock, horror and sadness. Now his rehearsed reaction simply disappeared; he realised that he was standing with his mouth wide open and no sound coming from it. After some seconds, he managed to call out, 'Elli, some coffee for Erich Vogler, please,' and, taking the policeman's arm, he walked him up to the house.

Elli's expression, when they got to the house and told her, was one of total disbelief. He knew she had been very fond of Wolfmannis and, more than that, had admired his competent, unfussed coolness.

'What happened?' she said, holding on to what just passed for composure.

'From the reports I have had, only by telephone, of course, it seems that Hans and his wife were killed by the same heavy-calibre automatic pistol which was found beside Wolfmannis. He had been killed by two shots from a double-barrelled shotgun which was found on the kitchen floor beside Detleffson's wife.'

'And what does your man think actually happened?'

'I'll tell you what *I* think happened,' said Vogler, stirring his coffee. 'As you and I remember only too well, Detleffson had been involved very dangerously and expensively with drugs and was therefore chronically short of money. I don't know how or when he met Wolfmannis' – the look he was giving Willi said very clearly *perhaps through you* – but he *might* have thought that a little blackmail would go a very long way.'

'Blackmail?'

'Yes, Willi, blackmail. Please don't act the innocent. You must have known that Wolfmannis wasn't entirely what he seemed. The East–West Trade Mission is highly respectable, but you and I know the Russians wouldn't put a first-class man in charge who couldn't help them in other ways. Come come, Willi, you *know* the man.' The policeman's broad face was glistening.

Elli moved slightly in her chair. 'Why were they *all* killed?' she said.

Vogler took a deep draft of coffee. 'Possibly Detleffson had *succeeded* in blackmailing Juris Wolfmannis. Despite the drugs the boy had an ingenious mind. Perhaps Wolfmannis decides he must silence both the Detleffsons and leave some evidence implicating one of the Munich drug gangs. He shoots Hans in the back in the sitting-room and turns and shoots Frieda through the hatchway to the kitchen, where she is standing behind the table. What he hasn't noticed is the shotgun on the kitchen table where Hans left it when he came in from shooting pigeon. There are two cartridges in the breach; Frieda closes it and pulls the trigger as she goes down. Her body steadies the gun.'

The policeman was looking happier now. He quite evidently liked his theory and would do his best to persuade the coroner to like it too. He got up to go.

Willi Ansbach's mind was erupting with thoughts but his voice did not seem to respond to any of them.

'Yes, it was a single-trigger gun,' was all he managed to whisper. His mind was full of the horror of that kitchen.

Later he telephoned von Heimann.

7

Von Heimann and Ansbach spent the evening, and for that matter, the night, in von Heimann's flat in Munich. Von Heimann's wife, Dashka, gave them an excellent supper. She had inherited little of her mother's Slav ebullience and she kept a watchful eye on her husband's, from her point of view, rather wild ambitions. Strange perhaps for the daughter of a Czech princess, but then her mother, Josel, had been born a peasant with all a peasant's caution.

The two men slaughtered the night. It was painful for Willi; he had always found Helmut's interrogation difficult to take completely in his stride. Necessary - yes most certainly; essential if they were to recover their poise and confidence. Yes, it was a mistake to send Wolfmannis, he had never been a professional assassin. To risk their vital ally even on such a critical mission was amateurish. The Kremlin liberals who had taken such trouble to get him in place might take it so badly as to withdraw altogether from *Operation Awakening*, as they had designated their scheme. In any event how willing would they be to replace Wolfmannis and how long would it take?

Eventually Dashka intervened.

'Perhaps it *was* a little rash to assume that *only* a powerful ally from the benign Kremlin faction could enable the *Erweckung* to take shape. Your Kremlin friends, if they still exist, will be very cautious now; the invasion of Afghanistan will have seen to that. So why not look for help from the Americans? The Jean Kirkpatrick Americans, I mean, the ones who are always preoccupied with Latin America and firmly believe that Europe should shoulder the burden of her own defence and allow the American Army to come home. You always have to remember that America seldom has less than three foreign policies at any one time.'

With a twinge of resentment at the role of scapegoat, Willi said, 'And where should we look for these influential Americans who will enjoy helping us to poison their own soldiers with drugs?'

'Never underestimate American ruthlessness,' said Dashka, half to herself.

Helmut had been reflective for some moments, his long face visible evidence of a mind hard at work.

'The British,' he said, finally, with a chuckle, 'the British and their famous Military Intelligence!'

By midnight a calmer atmosphere prevailed. They had rationalised and accepted that Wolfmannis' contribution had been largely philosophical and intellectual, invaluable in persuading their industrial friends at two-day seminars that Central Europe must be re-architected, revitalised and given the role of buffer state, while a re-unified Germany geared herself up as the engine room of a Soviet economic miracle. The hard practical business of undermining the American NATO garrison would never have been his forte. Even more important was the dawning realisation in their minds that the spectre of Vietnam would actually be welcome in some sectors of American opinion if, and only if, handled with a high degree of skill and well-placed collusion. The spectre, that is, of American soldiers once more drug-addicted.

Willi Ansbach's tensions had vanished as the evening wore on and it was he who picked up von Heimann's mocking reference to British Intelligence with a cool, 'Well, we could consult Forbes.'

Danska's eyebrows were raised more in admiration than surprise. 'He has access to them, of course, as Juris has confirmed through his channels, but why on earth would he want to lift a finger? We kidnapped this man and sent him back to England looking a perfect fool. You say he has a Polish wife, and this was done to him by Germans!' Dashka shuddered.

'Wait,' said Willi and they listened, partly because he knew Forbes well, and partly because it was late, they were dog tired and *some* line of action had to be hammered out. 'It could be in Forbes's interest to see us and even to help us because we *might* – in his mind – be able to give him some acceptable reason for his seven-hour disappearance during his important business trip.' 'Forbes was in Intelligence at one time – as we know – and so he has access.' 'Were he to go to his old boss and persuade him to establish liaison with some "crackpot" (the English love that adjective) Germans, who think they can, with the help of some German industrialists, solve Germany's future, would not that old boss, with one telephone call to Forbes's employer, get him completely reinstated – even make him more valuable?'

'And then *we* persuade British Intelligence to arrange for our collaboration with what you call Kirkpatrick Americans?' said von Heimann.

'And no mention of drugs?' said Dashka.

'If possible, no,' said Ansbach. 'Not an idea these English public schoolboys would easily understand.'

The two men laughed with relief and tiredness. Dashka didn't join in.

8

Forbes had the light step of the reprieved as he boarded the aircraft. He even felt no irritation when the Lufthansa stewardess replied in English to his excellent German.

Zulka had taken it well, as she had taken a great many things well throughout their marriage, which was no less than a miracle, as Slav blood is no tolerator of the human failings of which Forbes had done so little to rid himself.

'You go and see your damn Germans,' she had said, 'and make them give you a bloody good alibi and a couple of those gold bars while they're in such a helpful mood!' But there was a twinkle in her voice and she had not forgotten to add, 'And don't forget it's not your blue eyes, it's Brock they're after.'

Or, in other words, thought Forbes, don't get drawn into anything and especially be careful with the girl. Oh, he'd be careful all right; at his age, with every sort of mistake behind you, carefulness was the centre of life. He had not needed Aelred Jones's sharp reminder, 'This is *serious*, Archie, 'when he had flippantly said, 'I think I will weekend in Munich and look for Rip Van Winkle!'

He thought with gratitude of Zulka as he tucked in to a second gin and tonic. Perhaps awful husbands nearly always marry really nice women? But then Zulka had no reforming zeal – bred out of her, perhaps, because Poles *are* awful husbands, something that girls learn to ignore or accept at their mother's knee. But thinking kind thoughts about Zulka wouldn't help him prepare for the meeting in Munich, he decided, and so he tried to wrench his mind to the two Germans who had played their parts so impeccably in those critical early days of April '45.

After six months fighting in the Italian campaign, a night attack had gone wrong and he had found himself, just nineteen, in a German POW camp in Bavaria, where the sensible thing was to learn German and start digging in David Stirling's tunnel.

When the tunnel was blown in July '44 and the nine who escaped were rounded up (several had managed twelve or thirteen days of freedom), the Germans ordered that it be dug out by British other ranks, but only from the exit on the far side of the road back to just within the wire. Thus they had not bothered to trace it under the barrack wall and find the access within the building. Sloppy of them, but in the late summer of that year, German minds had been on other things, notably the daylight streams of Flying Fortresses heading for Munich. RAF night bombing had been equally bad for the nerves.

Forbes wriggled in his seat – what about his present mission? But it didn't work – his mind was back in those last months of '44–'45. Trigger-happy guards, two or three officers shot for watching the Fortresses, food all but zero as the OKW suddenly assumed that prisoner-of-war camps would become bases for Allied parachutists, an SS battalion storming in to remove all mattresses as a reprisal for something, or was it to stop the parachutists from having a kip?

March '45 had been rife with rumours – Allied

officers were to be herded into a redoubt near Berchtesgaden and used as hostages; prisoners were being shot; the Russian front was collapsing; Russian troops were wilder than wild beasts, and rape was routine. The news that they were all to march south – albeit with sinister implications – nevertheless came as a relief. Ducking off the column at 1.0 a.m. with James Mahon had come as a happy diversion, much stimulated by very practical help in the form of maps and a compass from Ansbach and von Heimann.

After that his three more years in the Army had been carefree; conscientious soldiering of course, but lots of skiing – snow and water – and girls. No thought for the future, he had lived on his pay, just, and on that oblivion which the fighting man uses to mop up the memories of fear. Well could he understand the Wild Geese, the Catholics who, after the Battle of the Boyne, had flighted out to fight in the armies of Hesse, France and the Czar, returning home only long enough to marry and breed.

Zulka had appeared just before his honeymoon with youth came to an end, and their marriage was seventh heaven; marred occasionally by Forbes's leanings towards Lucifer.

OK – a deep breath – he was at last going to unravel his motives for coming to Munich.

First, his job. If no alibi was forthcoming it was finished. Oberdorf would see to that; they were in such a high technology and security category that any whiff of irregularity would mean the withdrawal of his credentials (so far only suspended), and that meant the sack. Aelred Jones couldn't employ him anywhere else; he knew that. Jones had only taken him on because of his excellent German, and, to an extent, his Intelligence background had helped as a kind of insurance policy.

His Intelligence background! How he wished he had resisted Brock's persuasions to join. A steady job in one of Britain's strong export firms, unspectacular promotion perhaps but safe and sound, that was the sane and sensible course for him to pursue. But the war-hero Ulsterman had won the day. Zulka had never liked it because of possible Polish ramifications, but when had he ever considered Zulka? Love was one thing, consideration another. So he'd joined 'the firm' and he had done well. Too well in some respects; it had led to over-confidence and, combined with long absences, to indiscretions. Only with girls, of course, nothing else, but it got noticed, and sure enough one day he went a step too far. He'd always had a light-hearted appeal for women, partly from his physical confidence, mostly the product of a jokey, happy nature. Nothing lasting or passionate – ships that pass, that sort of thing. Well, he'd got entangled eventually, and all the tact and diplomacy in the world weren't going to prevent resignation, nor did they.

Hell, what am I doing down *this* memory lane? he thought. Am I trying to work out the simple reason for being on this aircraft, and it *is* damn simple and obvious, or am I trying to forestall some idiotic male menopausal caper with that Josel Heimann?

He had grabbed himself another gin and tonic and, as the landing gear rumbled down, he knocked it back, thinking, almost audibly, I expect I'm just a poor man's Hemingway.

They had arranged to meet in the bar of the Vierjahreszeiten, and all three came forward to greet him as he walked into the cavernous gloom. The girl hung back smiling as the two men advanced with an eagerness which made them seem awkward, formal

German courtesy struggling to keep control. Business suits, of course, for Friday lunch-time, surmounted by faces which were wholly unrecognisable except for the moon shape of Willi Ansbach's. But the hand clasps and the grip on the shoulder had unmistakable exuberance, and Forbes felt an astonishing lump in his throat. Helmut Heimann he had last seen standing on a moon-drenched road near Böhmfeld – not thirty miles from where they now were – saying altogether too loudly for comfort (there were a dozen German soldiers in earshot) 'Why haven't you gone Herr Leutenant? I can't tell them not to shoot, you know.' They'd scarpered soon after that.

And Willi Ansbach? His sharpest memory had been Ansbach helping him to give Phil Denison some kind of comfort after he'd had an American cannon shell in his backside, fired from the Tomahawk fighter which mistook the British POWs for a German column. The stern, resolute expression on the face of the young under officer as he sped off saying, 'I will tell the Oberst that he *must* put everyone back into the camp for safety,' had seemed the strangest reversal of roles. German under-officers did *not* question orders, and yet here was one who was going a whole lot further: he was issuing them.

The gin was fuzzing Forbes's brain – was this a reunion, or had he come to meet the men who had kidnapped him for a thirty-foot tunnel full of gold bars and then dumped him, in almost the worst predicament of his life? He was so pleased to see them he didn't care.

Lunch took a very long time. There was so much to be said about 1945. The memories were crystal clear. The occasional shadow passed over the faces of the three men, but bursts of reminiscence were punctuated by laughter and pauses while memories were searched for more. Josel was entranced. The tall, Englishman with the thin face and humorous mouth seemed to bring a kind of intransigent schoolboy fun to recollections of a war – admittedly the end of a war – in which they had been on opposite sides. It could almost be, she thought, that old enemies have more in common than old allies.

She followed as best she could. At one moment Willi and her father would be describing in general the last six months of the war, referring to Albert Speer's autobiography as an authentic record of the break up of Hitler's authority and the efforts Speer had made to preserve the infrastructure of the Reich. Then they would quiz Forbes about the ten days he'd spent with his brother officer, James Mahon, in the Waltinger Forst south of Eichstätt and the anxious moments which had been all too frequent and often not funny.

'For some crazy reason,' she heard Forbes say, 'after we had liberated ourselves by finding an American column and taken one of their Jeeps back to the hospital in Eichstätt to see Phil Denison, we returned to Böhmfeld to see what we could do for our French POW friends who had looked after us so marvellously. Believe it or not, the village was in an uproar, preparing for an attack from an SS battalion as reprisal for the handing over to the Americans of their local Nazis. We had ourselves seen the SS moving up to Hofsteffen, a couple of miles north, so we were in no doubt. That night, barricaded in the bistro with fifteen Frenchmen, we had prepared to take them on!'

'Weapons – you had weapons?' said von Heimann his voice rising slightly with incredulity.

'Yes, an assortment of shotguns and game rifles from the Forstmeister's office, and one pistol from the

Americans. But sadly no discipline – our French allies were all asleep by 3.0 a.m.!'

Once or twice Forbes looked at Josel with a twinkle as much as to say, This is great fun for me but it won't go on for ever!

But it was not the end, not that soon, because with lunch finished they got into Ansbach's Mercedes (Was I kidnapped in this car? Forbes asked himself as he caught Josel's eye) and drove around the villages of Böhmfeld, Hofstetten and Schumbach which had so occupied the minds of Forbes and James Mahon exactly thirty six years before. Nostalgia had taken hold. Of course there was nothing special to look at except the barn at Böhmfeld where they had spent six or seven nights expecting hourly to be invaded by a column of Russian POWs or German troops looking for billets as they withdrew across the Danube. No point, he thought, in visiting Frau Blobb, the farmer's wife who had so willingly provided their shelter, and trying to explain why he now had two Germans and a pretty girl for company! Only the Waltinger Forst – as he stood in the Summe Strasse, the fifty-yard-wide ride – brought a pricking to his eyes and a tightening of the fists. He could feel Josel standing beside him, and for the moment was glad she was half Czech, not wholly German, for the memory of first freedom was overpowering. Not a hundred yards away, in the wood, he and James Mahon had spent their first two nights – until they ran out of water – simply anaesthetised by the sense of freedom. Standing there in silence he could recapture it. Soon it would be gone.

In the car again on the way to Eichstätt, where von Heimann had decided they should stay the night – evocative and intelligent of him, Forbes had thought – he told them, rather light-heartedly, how for the final two days, when SS intervention had been expected at any minute, he had, as the senior of the two Brits, found himself in command of a German guard company of fifty sentries who had arrived unannounced from Ingoldstätt with their German officer and 350 French POWs. Hauptmann Fischbach had surrendered formally. 'There couldn't have been many Allied officers commanding German soldiers complete with weapons in April '45!'

Then he began to feel that he was rubbing it in, getting some of his own back perhaps for the faintly patronising atmosphere of the last two hours. But for these two Germans, he and Mahon *might* not have made their moonlight dash. On the other hand, but for the French, they would certainly have been recaptured and probably shot. It was gratitude for the French which had dominated their thoughts for the final forty eight hours, the French who had hugely enjoyed seeing British officers in command of the erstwhile sentries. The whole reminiscence, reflected Forbes, had probably been conjured up to soften him for an evening's hard talking. Well, to hell with that, he had enjoyed himself.

He found himself thinking again about Josel and the conversation in London which had brought him here. What *had* she told him, in fact, beyond an outline of her father's philosophy for Germany's future and the oft-repeated insistence that the gold was essential to their project, that the project was *now* critically endangered by the violent deaths of two men and that Forbes *could* be of immense assistance and, at the same time extricate himself from the embarrassing consequences of being kidnapped? About herself she had told him very little. He remembered that Josel Buchowitz had escaped from the Communist regime in Prague in 1948 to join her daughter in Paris, having married a young English officer for the sake of a British passport. A passionately eccentric lady; Forbes could happily remember her famous cellar parties when he had been on the British Military Mission in 1947. She had clearly kept alive in her granddaughter a keen interest in the history of Central Europe, so that might account for young Josel's enthusiasm for 'the battle for the soul of Germany', as von Heimann and Ansbach so grandly described their project. Or, on the other hand, he thought, it might not.

Other things puzzled him. Why had they expected him to accept their invitation? How much did they know of the importance of the high-tech industrial agreement he had been sent to negotiate and therefore the degree of embarrassment his disappearance had caused? How did they assess the risk that he might listen to everything and simply return to London and grass to British Intelligence, where, of course, they must have known he had once been employed? They must have immense confidence in Josel as an appraiser of character – especially as he himself was by no means certain why he had come.

As the project was gently unfolded over dinner in the Gasthaus, his doubts seemed more than fully justified. He raised his hand as Ansbach was speaking and said, 'But why do you trust me with all this?'

'Because we have no alternative,' said von Heimann

There was a long silence. Josel sat with her mouth slightly open. Forbes thought she looked less attractive like that. She hesitated. 'I told you about the two men?'

'Yes.' said Forbes. She looked guilty and unsure of herself. 'I'd better know the rest,' he said.

9

Forbes had drunk two glasses of schnapps, so to awake at four o'clock was almost inevitable. The moon was pouring over the *platz* as he pulled the curtains right back and leaned out of the window into the cold night air. The same cold night air and the same moonlight in which they had bathed, thirty-six years before, standing in the Waltinger Forst, wondering which side of the ride to choose and how deep they should go to find a hiding-place. Not that the forest wasn't one huge hiding-place, a world of Fairy-land-soft turf under silver moonlight.

Despite the astonishing plan he'd heard that evening from the two Germans, his mind was still full of his 36-year-old memories, of the villages – Schumbach, Böhmfeld, Hofstetten, Gamersheim – only a few miles away, of German farmers and shepherds, Frau Blobb in particular, of the French (the Bistro Commando, as they'd called Abel and René), who had looked after them until the roles had to be reversed as the SS began to take an unhealthy interest in avenging the local Nazis. He thought of James Mahon, red-haired Jimmy, and his unflagging sense of humour and teeth-gritting determination to grasp the dialect, critical enough when Farmer Maurer had said, 'I forget I've seen you,' and the Yugoslav farm worker hissed, 'That means he's off to telephone. How fast and how far can you run?' He could see the old sentry clanking along the momentarily deserted piece of road just before they ran for dear life, and the platoon of 16-year-old (they looked) SS going up to Hofstetten to hold the American advance, the outstretched hand with the packet of cigarettes and the feeling of shame at the generosity and Mahon's muttered *'danke, wir haben'*. He could see the back of the SS 'werewolf' sniper in civilian clothes sitting on the bonnet of the American Jeep, his hands behind his head as they drove back to Eichstätt, and hear the sickening sound of the firing-squad executing him in front of the villagers of Hofstetten. 'For God's sake learn,' they had said to the first American officer of any seniority they could find, 'that the SS will shoot a hundred POWs when the grapevine tells them of this.'

He thought of the goodbyes, the temporary goodbyes which, with the exception of Frau Blobb, had become permanent – the goodbyes which were so muddled up in French minds with excitement and apprehension, excitement at the prospect of France and apprehension at leaving their German mistresses to face the music. From some of the faces it had seemed that a little more war would be rather welcome.

Memories, he thought, are like a box of old toys, taken out, wondered at and then soundlessly put away.

But there was movement in the *platz* below, in the bright moonlight a shadowy figure. Instinct, more than recognition, took him swiftly down the stairs, and a careful easing of bolts had him in the square and looking for what he expected to see – Josel. Muffled in a huge camel-hair coat and fur hat she was pacing in the cold night air and he fell in beside her for a long silence before he spoke.

'Are we asking ourselves the same question?' he said quietly.

For a moment he thought the look on her face was hostile, then he realised her features were etched by moonlight, giving them a look of severity.

'You mean, what are we both doing here in the *platz*? Or why are we all discussing my father's *erweckung* plan? Please make yourself clear' – this rather severely.

Forbes took a deep breath. 'The project is crazy by any standard: to undermine the morale of the US Army in Germany with a drug-addiction campaign so that American voters demand its return and thus leave Germany free to join up with the DDR. That idea makes a whole raft of assumptions. Then Willi and your father are also persuaded by Juris that the Kremlin liberals, of whom so far there has been no visible sign, would dismantle the Warsaw Pact so as to achieve a neutral Germany. Where is there a scrap of evidence?'

'In any case, what is a nice girl like you doing in this set-up? You should be married to a good man and bringing up children.'

This time the jaw certainly stiffened, with a sharp intake of breath. Forbes could see that his blurted remark had caused much more offence than he felt the half-jocular words deserved. Without a word she turned and made for the Gasthaus.

He found her sitting beside the hot stove in the little lounge, coat off, hunched and, he thought, shivering.

'I'm sorry,' he told her. 'I said too much.' He took her hand. It was cold, passive, without reaction, but it stayed. 'I have thought endlessly about my own motives, and they somehow got mixed up with yours. To keep my job I need an alibi; to get an alibi I must interest British Intelligence in your venture. They might even send me to talk to what you call the Kirkpatrick Americans, a tough, sceptical bunch, always on the look-out for clever European tricks. But

I'm *not* convinced. If Juris were alive I might be, but I'm not. Can you understand? To me the whole scheme is a sentimental longing for a unified Germany dreamed up by two old men with a complex about the legacy of Nazi guilt.'

The hand had gone, not even taken away, just gone. The set of the mouth and the face turned towards him had a sort of quiver of seriousness.

'In Germany *everyone* has a complex about Nazi guilt. It is very nice for you self-righteous English to pat yourselves on the back and say, We won the war, let's make sure Germany is partitioned for ever in order to keep the Russians quiet and happy and – oh yes! – as a punishment for falling in love with Hitler! But you forget two things – one that the Soviet economy really *is* in a mess. It cannot provide the people with even basic necessities, and as the population and the memories grow older, the young people say, 'Why do we need armaments for a war which will never come? "Butter before guns" – 'that you can remember,' she said, with a short, dry laugh. 'And the other thing you like to forget – that nuclear weapons destroy the will to fight; if you cannot win why should you want to fight? "Conventional" war would be nuclearised too, because someone's bombs will hit the nuclear power stations.'

There was a sadness in her voice which was not all to do with nuclear war, he thought.

'Let's go back to my other question,' he said. 'Why are *you* involved in all this – daughterly love, passionate conviction, or a tender trap for the impressionable Forbes?' He realised that his tone had become that of the interrogator but he couldn't help it.

'A mixture of all three, I suppose,' and the laugh was spontaneous, the smile came and went but tried to stay.

'When my marriage to Jean Louis Morsaing broke up in '78 I went to work in my father's office, and so I was drawn into his talks with first Willi and then Juris. It was Juris who thought the drugs could be stored in Madagascar – he had been there on a trade mission. It is conveniently en route from Asia – and therefore *not* under the control of drug barons. Jean Louis suggested the crocodiles as custodians and the graphite shipments as the route into Germany.'

'Why did your marriage break up?'

'Because the Malgache women poisoned me. I would have died if I had stayed. Jean Louis had warned me – it is an old Malgache custom to poison the foreign usurper and hand the man back to the native girls. They call the process *fanafouté*, using untraceable herbal poisons. They turn the man away from his foreign wife. We tried to fight it with modern drugs and prophylactics but we failed. It was the end of our marriage but somehow we went on with a kind of loving.'

The interrogator in him persisted. 'So Jean Louis is on the team, as the Americans say?'

'Yes' – again that smile; it seemed to be growing friendlier – 'and now there's the one more thing you'd better know' – the tone was businesslike – 'since you are such an unbeliever. Your conversation with British Intelligence should not be too difficult because Juris – how do you say – "paved the way" some weeks ago.'

'Did he now,' said Forbes, 'and they will have played him for a sucker for all they're worth. I don't know whether to laugh or cry.'

There were footsteps on the stairs, and Ansbach caught the last words as he opened the door.

'Always better to laugh, Archie,' he said as he beamed at Josel.

'Your briefing last night left out the most important bit, Willi,' said Forbes aggressively.

'So you've told him about Juris making the first approach?' said Willi to Josel, who nodded. 'Well, of course, we hoped last night that our arguments would be strong enough to convince you on their own.'

'He's a pig-headed Englishman,' said Josel in a voice which managed to make the words sound vaguely flattering.

The fräulein had come in with coffee and clatter, and in the long silence Josel studied demurely the green baize, looking crisp and elegant in shirt and long skirt despite her long moonlight walk. Von Heimann was more aquiline than usual, Archie thought, and Ansbach more pudding-faced. Perhaps it was the heat in the little breakfast room.

'Perhaps we drink some coffee and then I tell you what Juris said to the British precisely.' Willi's German accent was sounding very faintly aggressive.

'The man he saw is called Wheway, and Juris told him of the whole plan –'

'Except, of course, for the crocodiles,' hissed Josel.

'And asked to be put in touch with the liberal-minded wing of the CIA, the existence of which has long been known to the Kremlin. He was sure that neither the British nor the Americans would – how you say? – tell tales, because and this for three reasons. It is always easier to listen and then be told more; anyone they might think of warning would not believe it and would not dare to take precautions because precautions would leak, cause scandal and have the very effect on US voters that the plan is designed to achieve; and lastly collaboration, even fake collaboration, gives a measure of control.'

'Why go to the British, why not straight to the CIA?

The KGB have always had plenty of contacts there. Why trust the British?'

Ansbach shot an amused glance at von Heimann. 'Much more practical, it was an insurance policy in case your kidnap went wrong. Don't underestimate yourself, Archie. Your old employers would have come to the rescue if we had made a mess of it and got you entangled with the German police.'

'How about a CIA plant? Did you think of that?' said Forbes, wishing he could flinch the confidence of these men who had thought out, with such care, a role for him.

'A plant?'

'Yes, the American double agent with impeccable credentials.'

'Who would do what?'

'Knock off you two would be enough. No, no, don't tell me – the British will always see fair play!'

The two Germans beamed as if at a pupil learning fast.

'So if I persuade the Brits – in exchange for my alibi – to pass the message that Juris is dead but that nothing has changed, what is it you want those American liberals (who could be a figment of your imagination) actually to do?'

'We want them to re-establish our links with Juris's friends in the KGB and reassure them, and then of course to organise political and press reaction in the US *when* we are operational.'

'What's the timing now that Juris is gone?'

'That depends on the KGB and, of course, the programme running smoothly.'

'And there's one other thing in your minds, isn't there,' said Forbes, looking, he hoped, as if an afterthought had struck him. 'The possibility that the KGB

55

have already investigated Juris's death and are not entirely happy with the German police cock-and-bull story; that, if the hard-liners have discovered what Juris was up to, you could both be marked men. At worst you would just like to know. Is that it?'

Von Heimann's face went frosty. Forbes could just glimpse Josel biting her lip. Ansbach's pasty countenance, hitherto benign, had parted lips which closed soundlessly.

'There were always going to be risks,' von Heimann murmured.

'So the hostage goes forth to parley!' Forbes put a brightness into his voice and saw the tension slide from their faces. 'Some detailed briefing, please, and then I'll be off.'

'A reluctant ally but a friendly hostage.' Willi's voice had a confident, not an enquiring ring.

An hour later Josel appeared with the car. 'How do we get in touch?' she said, after he had settled himself into what seemed to her an unhelpful silence.

'Willi should ring my office one week from tomorrow, saying that he will be in London on the fifteenth of April and would I please call his hotel. This call will be assumed to be from our Munich agents and my office will either say, "Fine, we'll tell Mr Forbes," *or*, "The next London visit would be more convenient." This will be said *only* if my friends in Intelligence need more time. If the answer is, "Fine," then *you* should be in the Serpentine Gallery the following day, the sixteenth of April, at three o'clock.

'OK,' she said, and there was more silence. Eventually – 'How does your wife feel about all this?'

He shot a glance but all he saw was a firm profile, eyes on the road.

'I'm an untidy character,' he said. 'I used to get into

what we English call "scrapes", so Zulka has a certain sense of foreboding.'

'You mean, worse to come?' This time her eyes came off the road and she looked at him – kindly, he thought. 'With scepticism there must always be that feeling. Sceptiscm about a unified Germany in particular; it's not a happy thought for a Pole. But possibly a neutralised Russia. The Poles and the Czechs (remember my grandmother) would like that. A Russia at last fulfilling the dream of Peter the Great, a Russia modernised by a peaceful *Drang nach Osten*, fear of the Red Army backlash gone for ever. A unified Germany is not a big price to pay for that!' The questioning sound had gone from her voice – her fingers were tattooing on the steering wheel, her eyes searching the road for encouragement. 'And don't forget, when you speak of a monstrous concept, self-righteous Englishman, that that's not how the Americans see it. They've already licensed their Panama friend Noriega to deal in drugs as the price for shipping arms to the rebels in Nicaragua. And where are those drugs going? Not to grown-up American soldiers but to ghetto kids in the big cities.'

She was laughing at him now and he was enjoying it. The enjoyment was still there as they waved each other goodbye at the airport concourse.

Forbes slumped into his aircraft seat. Some twenty four hours that had been. Nostalgia used to great effect, not to mention moonlight and a pretty girl. Yes, a very attractive, intelligent, in the might-have-been category of lady. Good with her arguments too; pity Brock was not susceptible to females. Pity you *are*, he told himself as sleep claimed her due.

10

Brockles FitzHerbert wiped away a tear as he waved at a waiter for more sherry, only to be shaken by another gust of laughter.

'It would have to be you, Archie,' he said, 'of all people. But I'm blowed if I know why I find it so funny.'

'I can't see the joke either, Brock, but if it helps, I'll keep trying.'

They had met at the Guards Memorial and walked twice round the lake before repairing to Brock's club. The man was as large as ever. The chalk-stripe suit, with cuffs half-way down his hands and cabochon sapphire links, was worn like a uniform. The bowler and umbrella completed the contrast with nondescript passers-by.

'I was Wheway,' Brock had said when Forbes had embarked on the Juris saga, and he made it sound like a non-committal passing reference. 'I'm retired now but Gordievski thought I was the man for Juris to talk to. Of course, Gordievski had been consulted on Juris's credentials, which were, incidentally, impeccable. Your German friends were on firm ground with him.'

'Who's Gordievski?'

'A *very* senior KGB man. He's been with us for a long time. The less you know about him the better.'

The snub was as stinging as Brock had meant it to be. Forbes, who hadn't seen the man since the hotel venture had collapsed, felt the exact wave of irritation which had been an essential ingredient of those long years working with him.

Brockles FitzHerbert, or Brock of Ages, as they, like schoolboys, used to call him in those early days in the department, had been an efficient boss, thorough in everything, a first-class wartime product with all the right experience, but not affectionately regarded. One kept at arm's length. There was always something vaguely unsatisfactory, almost slippery, about the man, completely belied by his reputation but there just the same. How Forbes had, in the end, come to look upon him as a friend, he had never quite understood.

Meanwhile the eyes had been hard at work. Then had come the questions.

Forbes had forgotten how they could penetrate, double back, come in from a half-forgotten angle, probe for motive while apparently checking facts, sometimes menacing with half-finished suggestions beginning with 'I suppose you've considered?'

This man may be retired, he thought, but the brain isn't, nor the imagination, nor the instinct to rationalise, simplify and often attribute mean and dishonourable purposes. He had more than welcomed that first glass of sherry.

Now, of course, they were in purdah for an hour or more; smoking-rooms and club dining-rooms are for small talk and occasional glances round to see who is lunching with whom. Forbes couldn't afford club life so he knew he wouldn't be recognised. After lunch, in a corner of the library perhaps, he would get his answer – or some sort of answer. He hadn't seen Brock for five years or more, but the old relationship had firmly reasserted itself and he knew the form. The form included a decent house claret and what seemed like a beaker of vintage port.

'Well, Archie.' The blue eyes were twinkling over the rim of the glass and for a moment another explosion of mirth seemed imminent. 'I can't give you a final verdict until our American friends have assimilated the possible consequences of Juris's death, but in *broad* terms there *are* matching philosophies, and I'll tell you why. The liberals in the CIA (no one ever thought there could be such a thing as a liberal in the CIA but Vietnam changed many things) are not at all comfortable with the Evil Empire syndrome, especially coupled with the invasion of Afghanistan. Now that sounds like a contradiction, so let's digress for a moment. The Red Army can't win the Afghan war because it's a guerrilla war, and guerrilla wars are won by guerrillas. But Evil Empire talk and the US defence programme for more sophisticated weapons gets the Red Army (a "State within a State" you remember Kissinger called it) all steamed up about West Germany and NATO, so their thinking becomes "How about a pre-emptive strike?" Not so daft as one might think, because they *know* the Soviet economy is crumbling and to have West Germany as a vassal state to take over the management of Soviet industry could mean its salvation.'

'Whose thinking is this, CIA liberals'?'

'Yes, but hold on, let's look at the Juris scenario and stop me when I go wrong. It goes something like this . . . Failure in Afghanistan means collapse of morale and appalling loss of face, so a blitzkrieg on Germany to achieve by force the rebuilding of the Soviet economy is seen as the greatest prize since May '45 – thus argues the Red Army. After two or three days of so-called conventional war, the Americans, who dominate NATO, use a nuclear weapon. American public opinion can't face casualties, so the nuke is inevitable. Then the German population panics – they're not facing another Bomber Harris scenario – and Helmut Schmidt sues for peace. The Red Army has taken the trick.'

'So, with no American troops in Germany it makes the surrender that much easier?'

'I'll come to that word "surrender" in a minute, Archie. Just concentrate on Juris's argument and remember that he claimed to interpret the philosophy of German industry. When the drug scandal forces the withdrawal of US troops because of the ghosts of Vietnam, the German industrialists can push Schmidt into a deal with the Kremlin which spells, in fact, the economic conquest of Russia in exchange for a neutral unified Germany. At *last* the German dream, the *Drang nach Osten, and* the war guilt wiped out by unification.'

'And the bonus for the Americans' – Forbes took up the theme – 'is *one*: they can finally escape the imbroglio of a third European war. *Two* – they can concentrate on Latin America and the Pacific. *Three* – they can spend more of their defence budget on high profit and high tech, rather than on GIs. *Four* – it reduces the Kremlin's temptation to meddle in the Third World.'

'You've forgotten the cleansing of the American conscience, Archie. They can at last lay down the millstone of the Kennedy philosophy, "bear any burden, pay any price." The nuclear weapon has removed from our vocabulary words like "surrender" and "victory"; that's the hardest part of the message.'

It was tea-time now, with a faint rattle of crockery. 'So I'll hear from you, Brock, how soon? My German friends are somewhat edgy.'

'Today week, dear boy, ten o'clock at the same place. Meanwhile, I'll fix your alibi, and *possibly* think of something you could do for me.' The eyes were watching like a hawk's.

'You've got the Juris philosophy word-perfect, Brock, and your Washington analysis is not bad either, but what are your own convictions?'

'Kind of you, dear boy.' He felt his arm being patted and wondered if Anno Domini made one immune to mild sarcasm. 'Remember what Lenin said – "Every time you are faced with a choice between doctrine and reality, choose reality."' Forbes was down the steps by now and into St James's, and as he returned the wave he thought, Not bad for a parting shot.

Aelred Jones received him with a beaming smile. 'Well done, Archie,' he chuckled with a conspiratorial glee. 'I always suspected it was engineered, that little escapade, so not another word, except, between you and me, although nothing will be *said*, your reputation will be enhanced!'

Forbes murmured grateful thanks which were genuine, and wondered if Brock had slightly overplayed his hand. Then with a twinge he remembered the words '. . . think of something you could do for *me*.' Sufficient unto, he thought and basked in Jones's approval.

In Zulka's approval too – a great deal more important because Zulka had unfathomable instincts and they were by no means always flattering to her husband. 'Be careful of Brock,' she said, 'he's always had tricks up his sleeve. He's had time to think, and the role he is planning for you will be devious. You are not a fool, Archie, but you *think* you are cleverer than you are. Don't get drawn in, and watch out for the girl. They know your weakness.' The eyebrows spoke again. Zulka always managed to leave the room or answer the telephone at that stage; wonderful timing and accurate as ever.

'Let's recapitulate, Brock,' he said as they got into their stride, flickering their eyes to take in tulip beds, pretty girls, wildfowl and bursting greenery. 'There you are in retirement, and a "feeler" called Juris calls you up and says, "Please listen, Mr Wheway." You grasp this feeler.'

'One always does, Archie boy, that's what we retired folk are for, and a feeler can have an arm at the end. Don't forget we checked his credentials.'

'So Juris expounds a possible Red Army plan to blitzkrieg West Germany and make it a vassal economic power-house for the rejuvenation of Russia. All this Juris has picked up from his Red Army sources, and you and he between you have sold the package to the "liberal" Americans. My German friends see in this scenario the one opportunity to save Germany from what they call the victims' war, but it's a foul deed, Brock, because, leave aside the morality, the risk of drug addiction, the use of corruption – Noriega or no Noriega – it's the death throes for NATO, the lynchpin of our security.'

'It's the crack of doom for – for our self esteem?' interjected Brock. 'You put it better than I could, Archie; almost as well as Juris himself, better perhaps than your German friends because they feel guilt, I imagine, at planning to escape a repetition, much *more* than a repetition of '44 and '45. You can remember those Fortresses going over and the *thump-thump*, day and night, of their bombs, can't you? We all cheered like mad then, didn't we? Germany getting it at last.'

'So what happens now?' said Forbes rather tersely. 'How have your Americans reacted to Juris's death?'

'They are practical people. Juris's work was done. It's a new chapter and new men will appear.'

'What new men?'

'First there's Bradley, an American CIA man, who was with John Vann in Vietnam. He will turn up at the US Consulate in Frankfurt and get in touch with your German pals. Next time we meet I'll give you the full briefing on him. Juris's successor will turn up in Bonn as Assistant Military Attaché – name of Melkov, grandson of a cavalry soldier who was stationed in the Ukraine in October '17. He was a soldier servant whose officer slipped away and rode west when the troops mutinied. The soldier went as far as the Polish frontier and then said, "My future is with the Revolution," and turned his horse round.'

Forbes interrupted, 'So now you're going to tell me that the grandson has turned *his* horse?'

'You always were a sarcastic bugger, Archie, but roughly speaking that was it. He was a good KGB man up to five years ago, and an ex-soldier to boot. He's an even better one now that his horse is pointing west!'

'Two new boys on top of Juris's murder means rumours and leaks.'

'There are always rumours and leaks, Archie. You know that. You also know that I can cope with them while you cope with Madagascar.'

Brock had produced a crumpled paper bag from the pocket of his tidy blue overcoat and was throwing bits of bread at the ducks. The ducks could have been rumour-mongers as they bobbed and swerved.

'Get you off to Madagascar, Archie, and check the set-up there. We Brits are going to control this situation whether the Yanks like it or not, and you're my man on the spot, aren't you, dear boy?'

He crumpled the empty bag and threw it in a bin.

'And supposing I say you can stuff the whole thing, as I've told you in the past on occasion?'

'Your boss wouldn't like that, Archie, now would he?'

Catkins in Spring, it said beneath the painting. They were in the Serpentine Gallery, and Archie and Josel stood side by side like children on an art outing.

'So now you're Brock's hostage?' she said, in a voice which, he thought had a hint of apology in it.

'Let's go and drink coffee,' he said. 'I can't look at any more pictures.'

They sat in a long moody silence. 'I have got you into a mess, haven't I?' Josel said.

'Yes, *and* it's going to be a long business. Brock doesn't give up easily, especially when he's in the driving seat, and with two new boys joining the team he's very much in the driving seat.'

'And your wife?' said Josel.

Forbes looked up from the table. 'Is far from calm and peaceful in her very resilient mind. She sees me as a romantic who half *wants* to be drawn into a crazy scheme which involves all the people she has good reason to like least in the world – Germans, ex-Nazis (not too much 'ex' in her mind), KGB and Brock; the last possibly most. He's always disapproved of her *and* admired her in a rather spooky way.'

He got up suddenly, paid for the coffee, and came back, leaning over her, his eyes intense, his body stiff although at an angle.

'I'll do my best to help,' she said. She was wearing a red and white striped shirt with a thin gold chain round her neck and a dark woollen skirt; a pullover and silk scarf were in her lap. For a day trip, all she had needed. He thought she looked beautiful, which increased his sense of helplessness.

'I'll see you on Friday week at the Hôtel Colbert – tea-time.'

'Yes, Englander, tea-time at the Hôtel Colbert.' Her smile had a mocking warmth.

11

Alex Bradley groaned as he hit the ball, and the groan did nothing for the shot – too much height, not enough length; now he couldn't be sure of being on the green in two. But he could always think better on the golf course, so what the hell.

It was still lunch-time and the course was empty. Symington he had dropped at the airport after an early sandwich, so now he could play two rounds if necessary, go back to his office around 4.30, deal with the mail and then go home and talk it all through with Susannah.

Talk it all through? That meant he was going to say yes, didn't it? He steadied himself for a long putt and tried to think about the undulations. What had Symington said? 'Susannah will enjoy a year in Europe and she needn't know you're organising a drug run.' Needn't know? Jesus, the day Susannah joined the needn't know brigade he would be collected by men in white coats – sent by Symington probably.

But there were *some* attractions, above all the feeling that this assignment could exorcise, finally exorcise, the horrors of Vietnam. He gloomily teed up his ball, thinking that that word 'exorcise' alone could wreck a whole round of golf. Christ, how many times had he and Susannah invoked it, and how many times had it jeered back at him, usually from the last inch in a bottle of Scotch. The jeering had stopped when they had reached what they had reckoned was eighty per cent success, but then the whispering had started. The whisper had said, 'You would be out of trouble now, you bum, if you hadn't turned down the psychos, the stress relievers, the therapists; you arrogant sod, you wanted to do it all by yourself – "complete cure has to be self-cure", that was the slogan, wasn't it, you pathetic little man?'

The ball hit the ground and shot forward, for all the world looking as if it had been struck a second time. It was a perfect run-up to the green and gave him every chance of being pin-high with three. Pathetic? – nothing pathetic about that now was there?

He polished off his birdie and thought, To hell with Symington – let's take this golf game seriously. It didn't work. The next hole was a long one and he gave it a brilliant slice. Watching the ball curve elegantly away over some low pines, he kicked the golf trolley and capitulated to the urge for a long sit by a brook where there could be dragon-flies. It was early summer in North Carolina, the perfect setting for saying to hell with Europe, Commies, Krauts, the lot. His grandmother was German, but so what? It was '81 not '73, Vietnam was a long time ago, he was cured at last of the 'Viet-vet' malaise. It had been a hard fight, but thanks to Susannah and – yes – Symington, he had won. Symington? Damn the man. It was the CIA now saying, Come on now, pay the debt; you came back a piece of 'Nam wreckage, we put you out to grass, fixed you up with a job with the Brits in North Carolina, world-wide company, promotion opportunities, a main board directorship even? 'All you have to do, Alex,' Symington had said, 'is take a year off, sabbatical it's called, and we fix it with your British chairman. The project is right up your street; it calls for the exact skills you built up in Vietnam, and the battle you lost there is the one you can win now in Europe. You want a good reason? OK, because this time you'll be on the other side, not drug-busting, Alex, but drug-*running*.' And Symington's face had crinkled into an ominous grin.

Alex Bradley's Vietnam secondment had been one of John Vann's great successes. He had been the sidekick, the number two, the man who got things done, in action or out of action. If Vann had been awarding the medals, Bradley would have been heavily decorated. But after the 'Tet' offensive it had all gone wrong. Vann had put him in charge of a unit to seek out the drug pushers and wind them up. After the 'Tet' the GIs had been a soft target for the pushers and too many – far too many – had fallen prey.

Bradley's job had been to find the top men and snuff them out. He had done well to begin with, too well perhaps, and then he'd fallen into a classical blackmail trap and had had to be pulled out by Vann and shipped home to the US. Given leave, he'd sulked around his grandmother's farm in Iowa, staring moodily at the Mississippi and tipping a half-bottle of bourbon. Susannah in time had put all that right. She'd come from her home in self-confident Pasadena to study the river for her Ph.D. They had worked together to find and rebuild his self-confidence. It hadn't been easy.

Bradley squinted at the dragon-flies. What had Symington said? 'Look at it this way, Alex: you'll be saving the US Army in Europe from the casualties of a Soviet blitzkrieg at the cost of a few hundred drug victims, and don't forget *this* blitzkrieg *would* go nuclear. Also remember that we only trigger the whole business when our KGB friends are confident that Honecker and his gang can be run out of town by well-orchestrated demonstrations and that the Bonn government can then reunite Germany.'

'KGB friends,' Bradley had said, 'you mean Gordievski?'

'Yes, and others; one of them will be seeing you in Frankfurt from time to time. As the Soviet Assistant Military Attaché he will be especially well placed.'

'You really want me to believe this, don't you?' Bradley had said.

'Yes, I do, because this is 1981 and Afghanistan is the death sentence for the Red Army; they know they can't fight a genuine war with those pathetic conscripts, but they *could* launch a blitzkrieg to make West Germany a vassal state. And they just *might* try. Get it into your head, Alex, that *both* sides want out of this Warsaw Pact/NATO log-jam. Our project simply architects a scandal which then becomes the pretext they both need. Then they can start to build the New Europe, based on a united Germany, "from the Atlantic to the Urals". (Never tell anyone, by the way, that I quoted de Gaulle!) All *we* do is provide the excuse, the face-saver, and you bet your life we'll make sure it works. We'll make sure the US media lights a fire under every peacenik in the States; the cry will be, "Bring the boys home" and it will come from every mother's heart.'

'Sure, and then you get the double-cross – am I right? NATO in disarray, and so the Red Army can launch its blitzkrieg?'

'No, no, Alex – wrong, wrong. The KGB takes out Honecker; that's the signal for us to set in motion the drug business – '

'– and then Bonn picks up the telephone,' Bradley had finished for him.

'That's much better, Alex. I was getting worried about you.'

Bradley had pressed on. 'What part do these three Germans have to play?'

'They ship in the drugs, pay for them and help you set up the drug line.'

'So where is control?'

'Control is the CIA and the KGB in partnership.'

'And the enemy?'

'The hard-liners on both sides, and there are plenty of them, as you must know. The Pentagon and the Kremlin are stuffed with them. They are the perennial war party, the guys who always think that a quick war will settle something – you know, "to the victor the spoils".'

'Hi,' said the voice. 'You looking for a ball or something?' Bradley stared up at a man, a very large man, in red shorts and blue check shirt. He vaguely recognised him as the truck depot manager in Raleigh. He scrambled to his feet, grinning. 'No, just day-dreaming after a good lunch; got bored playing golf against myself. Please go through, I'm due in the office now anyway.'

He drove back to the endless cups of coffee that Shoobach, his black secretary, would brew for him while his mind flogged away at the final question-and-answer session he'd had with Symington. He'd had another go at the 'window of opportunity' for the would-be blitzkriegers. 'If an engineered East German collapse is the curtain-raise for your Kremlin liberals, and for Bonn and the German barons to sign up a rejuvenation deal for the Soviet economic system, why is it not *also* the signal for the Red Army to have a bash? And why make it easier for them by sapping US morale?

'Alex, the United States was *never* going to fight a land battle in Europe. The ground-force divisions, armour and infantry, are only a symbol. The real power is the US Air Force and the tactical nuclear weapons. This the Red Army knows all too well.'

'So if it's only a symbol and they know it, why pull it out?'

'Because it's a way of saying that we won't attack the Warsaw Pact; a virtual guarantee. Remember your history: Napoleon, Hitler, Leningrad, Stalingrad, the paranoia of Mother Russia – an attack from the west. It's the one *genuine* visceral fear they all share – Commies and non-Commies.'

All the way to the airport Bradley had slugged away at these questions. He wanted to believe in the answers and at the same time he knew it would suit him much better to disbelieve them – Susannah and he were tucked away happily in their semi-British enclave; Vietnam and its drug barons, Europe and its divided Germans, the nightmare scenario of a World War III were all far away.

'Yes, yes,' his German grandmother would say. 'You are a typical Midwesterner, Alex Bradley, you just want those goddam Europeans to do something for themselves for a change. But Europe will never go away, Alex; the world is too small.' And if he *was* a typical Midwesterner, what had he been doing in the CIA, for God's sake?

Paradoxically it had been Latin America which had drawn him in. After college, an aptitude for Spanish had taken him there on a long trip, and a perilous curiosity had taught him almost too much about the drug traffic. One day on a bus journey in the Aburré valley in Colombia he had spotted a boy at the back of the bus in a blood-stained T-shirt. He had been wounded in a gun-fight and was badly shaken. Bradley had got him to talk. The boy came from Manrique and was one of the motor-cycle cartel assassins, the deliverers of the *definitivo adios* from the pillions of their souped-up bikes. They were the lethal cavalry of the drug war. Bradley had taken the boy back to his home and stayed and talked to his mother and sisters. He had arranged to meet other teen-aged gunmen, he had talked to the police, the priests, finally the CIA. The subject absorbed and fascinated him. He had been the ideal recruit.

'You sound convinced enough,' he'd said to Symington in the airport lounge, and got the answer – with a ferocious grin – 'And so should you be, Alex. OK, there's a high-risk poker game in all this, but not any higher than it has been for the best part of thirty years and, if it's the casualties you still mind about, then ask yourself – what's a few more druggies if we're at last getting shot of World War III?' The grin was getting infectious, cold-blooded though it was.

'Just why should I do it?' Bradley had heard himself say as he saw the boarding light flashing 'Last call'.

'Because you're a CIA man with a bad conscience, that's all.'

He sat hunched in his office brooding on that answer, forgetting that Susannah had people coming in for mint juleps on their terrace. He got a very curious look from her when he wandered in late, and so he wasn't surprised when she walked him down the lawn after the guests had gone and turned him quietly round to look at the perfect Carolina moon.

'Someone's been at you, Alex,' she said in a low, not-too-serious voice. The shadows of the oleanders were looking like bears waiting for a signal.

'Yeah, that's about it,' came with a sigh.

'So you want to do it – whatever it is?'

'Not without a lot of thinking and talking.'

'You get the barbecue going, Alex, and I'll bring out

steaks and salad' – this as she disappeared in a businesslike way into the house.

Susannah's grandparents had emigrated – that was the word they had used – from Boston to California soon after Pearl Harbor and had worked in the fast-expanding aircraft industry. Her grandfather had then set up an aircraft components business on his own and made a good deal of money until a premature investment in the development of carbon fibre in the early seventies had set him back to more ordinary millionaire status. Susannah's father was an academic, a lecturer in physics, who had encouraged his daughter's studies and her travels on vacation. The result was a mature mind, well informed and able to cope with her husband's rather more impetuous approach to the difficulties of what she sometimes felt was an ill-chosen career.

The steak spat happily from the barbecue, the salad and the home-made bread were almost invisible in the moonlight, and the Californian red wine in their glasses had a sombre blackness. Susannah's spectacles gave her an owlish look of wisdom.

Bradley began. 'What I am now telling you is the CIA story, supported, it seems, by London's MI, the KGB's liberal wing (if you can believe in such a thing) as represented by Gordievski and a little Latvian, a Soviet commercial counsellor in Bonn (de facto KGB), who was recently murdered in a private vendetta over gold bars. These unlikely – to say the least – allies have been brought together by two German ex-officers born and bred in the old German liberal tradition and with an almost religious conviction that Germany can be – once unified – the saviour of Europe. This group have convinced themselves after careful research that the Soviet economy has only five or six years before total collapse, and that if we wait for total collapse the Red Army will make a last desperate attempt to enslave West Germany by force. This would make nuclear war inevitable. So what is required is a deal, a deal which enables Germany to reunify and harness her enormous technological resources to the rejuvenation of the Soviet economy. But it has to be a deal which the Red Army can swallow without complete loss of face. There is the rub. I must now digress.'

'Europe has reached the stage when the presence of US troops, as opposed to our Air Force that is, has become a provocation because, in the even of attack, it guarantees the use of nuclear weapons. So the solution is to remove US ground forces and eliminate the provocation – a constructive sell out, in other words. The withdrawal of what many Germans and many more Russians see as an army of occupation thus opens the doors to German reunification and the resurrection of the Soviet economy; also, and by no means least, it finally breaks the Cold War log-jam.'

There was now a tremor in his voice and Susannah knew that whatever logic she might bring to bear, the emotions of Vietnam were once again taking charge. Funny, she thought, how strong a hold missionary zeal had on most of her countrymen and women; hideously dangerous, responsible for dreadful mistakes and even more dreadful misunderstandings – but without it could they ever have built such a country? She thought of the Civil War and shuddered.

'So what is the pretext to be? You spoke a while back about a pretext.'

The moon was much lower now and Alex's head bobbed about in front of it as he explained how drug-pushers would be organised to create a major scandal, a scandal which would be magnified by hysteria in the

US media and make the withdrawal of US troops inevitable.

'And that's when you get the Red Army double-cross?' interposed Susannah.

'Just what I said to Symington.'

'And so?'

'And so the answer is – if that were to happen, I say if it *were* to happen, the Germans would throw in the towel and say, "Walk right in." They are not going to face becoming a battleground, and *this* battle would be conventional for about forty eight hours. It's the doctrine of self-preservation, Susannah, as simple as that. Hitler did for *Kampfgeist* (the German army's fighting spirit) what Vietnam did to our GIs; and as far as the Red Army's concerned, look at Afghanistan – do you want any more proof than that? The hotheads might *start* an *Anschluss* and that's about all.'

She took his hand. 'It's getting dark,' she said. Somehow they both knew that the decision didn't have to be put into words.

12

Forbes settled into his first-class seat on the Johannesburg flight (the Eichstätt gold was coming in handy for air tickets, he thought) and automatically ordered a drink and eyed the Russian hostesses' figures. He had thought the Aeroflot flight from Moscow would fit rather well in his cover plan.

Then he forced himself to remember all that Zulka had said after she'd heard his full account in a pained silence. It wasn't rebuke, just an accurate analysis. He was too old for romantic adventures, the scheme was hare-brained *and* morally indefensible: sabotage of the NATO alliance, two old Germans, over-excited by finding some gold, wanting to play a game of power politics.

'Germans always look for intrigues and conspiracies, Archie, look at von Trott and von Stauffenberg and what happened to them for their attempt to kill Hitler' – he knew, in fact, that she had admired them greatly; but never expect logic from a Slav – 'and if your friends *are* decent fellows, they are all the more certain to fail. Only the château-bottled brigade could hope to get away with a scheme like this.'

Zulka's English was perfect, but sometimes her choice of idiom – 'decent fellows' and 'château-bottled brigade' (for awful shits) – *made* him catch her eye, and they would both dissolve in laughter.

The tirade – except that, in fairness, it hadn't *been* a tirade – had ended with, 'You're caught up in it now, Archie, and you're too damned old.'

No mention of the girl, but Zulka had done so once, and that, she knew, was enough.

He got out his documents and scanned them to rehearse what he *might* say if the Malgache trade department (if there was such a thing) had decided to have him met at the airport.

There was the imposing letter from the Red Star Crucible Factory in Leningrad (his name had been inserted by Wolfmannis' secretary at Ansbach's behest) inviting Mr Archibald Forbes to visit the graphite workings (*gisement*) in Madagascar of Monsieur Jean Louis Morsaing to discuss supplies of graphite under long-term contract.

But what were the qualifications of Mr Forbes as a buyer of graphite? Certainly not the fact that, in order to justify the ex-Madame Morsaing as his interpreter, he must pretend to know no French. Perhaps his very English appearance might stifle curiosity, the English being so well known for sending their eccentrics to Africa for a multitude of ambiguous reasons, and, of course, Madagascar graphite *had* been a very English development at the beginning of the century.

There was no Malgache official waiting for him so he took a taxi to the Hôtel Colbert and found Josel. She clapped hands for tea. There's something about khaki slacks on a woman, he thought, which flatters the hips, not that Josel's needed much flattering. She looked tired, but who wouldn't after a long flight? He felt dreadfully tired himself and stared in disbelief when she said they would fly north at seven in the morning to Antsiranana, where they would pick up a camionette. It was important, she said, to leave Tananarive without delay because gossip and rumour would sparkle.

'Where the hell are we going anyway?' he asked crossly.

'We'll tell you in the aeroplane.'

'Why not now?'

'Because Henri Challois and Jean Louis are joining us here for dinner and we'll stick to generalities. Meanwhile, I have two things to report; one – the gold is now all safely in Switzerland, and two – the new American has made a visit to my father. Incidentally, Jean Louis has all the kit you will need, so just pack a small holdall please.'

This is German competence all right, Forbes thought, but maybe just as well, and anyway it's a cover-up for her feelings on seeing Jean Louis again – he would have met her aeroplane. But the travel instructions did nothing to blunt his longing for some decent whisky. He could have spoken aloud because she was clapping her hands again.

'How do you like my cover plan?' he said after a first long draught of whisky, 'An Englishman who speaks no French negotiating on behalf of a Russian crucible factory for a long-term contract for graphite, a material about which he knows almost nothing?'

She grinned mischievously. 'If you can get away with that you can get away with anything! But be careful with Henri Challois. Henri knows everybody and everything that happens in Madagascar. His father pioneered the development of the graphite deposits at the beginning of the century, so he has a sort of droit de seigneur. We thought it best to see him and tell him the – how do you say? – cock-and-bull story ourselves, and so perhaps reduce exaggeration. He won't believe it, but it may be good enough because we won't be coming back and, after all, Jean Louis *will* be shipping graphite to the Red Star Crucible Factory, thanks to Juris and, of course, to you!'

She twinkled; she was in good form despite the journey.

'You *might* say – why come at all if Jean Louis is perfectly competent to handle the drug shipments and hide the stuff?' Forbes asked.

'Well, only so that you can satisfy your English spymaster that the whole scheme is not a figment of someone's imagination, a confidence trick to make off with a large pile – it was a *very* large pile, Archie – of Nazi gold. But I think very soon you will be satisfied, more than satisfied, although even you and I won't know *precisely* where the heroin will be hidden – that, fortunately, is not possible. Jean Louis will show you why it's not possible, but that's just as well for both of us, isn't it? We both know only too well what unscrupulous people can achieve by using unfair means of persuasion!'

She was laughing at him, teasing him *and* looking damned attractive. The white wine she was drinking had brought colour to her cheeks and sparkle to her eyes. She swung one foot gently from crossed knees; it seemed to mock him. Despite the whisky he felt intense irritation and longed to bend her over his knee. He knew perfectly well he was being childish, but the irritation was too much for him.

'I've never really understood *why* you got mixed up in this whole business – Jean Louis, I suppose?'

She nodded, almost imperceptibly; it was more a movement of the eyelids, but the laughter in her eyes had gone.

After a shower and what Forbes admitted to himself was quite a lot more whisky in his room, they were once more in the lounge as Challois and Jean Louis arrived together, laughing.

They looked rather as he had expected – but more so. Challois, much the elder, was slight, not very tall, a little stooping, with short grey hair and large extremely lively eyes in a face of humour and awareness. Jean Louis was taller than Challois, and given another inch in height would have been an Adonis. It was the build of the man, the graceful movement and the sparkling dark eyes in the heavily bearded face. No wonder Josel had fallen for him, no wonder parting from him had been such an agony, no wonder she had embraced her father's crusade – a way of stilling the voices in her head crying out that surely there was *some* drug the doctors had overlooked, *some* medication for the hideous, slow, painful *fanafouté* with which the Malgache witch-doctors (yes, witch-doctors – he knew about the '46 rebellion when the natives faced the French machine-guns with the conviction that only the 'golden bullet' could bring them down) had wrecked their marriage.

What is their relationship now? Forbes wondered. Jean Louis had the key role – the importing of the drugs, their concealment on the island and finally their conveyance in sacks of graphite to West Germany. So much (too much?) depended on him. Brock had said *too* much. Brock had taken a deal of persuading. 'Convince yourself Forbes,' he had said. 'Go there, case the joint' – Brock's American jargon put his teeth on edge – 'make sure.'

So Jean Louis was going to show Forbes where on the island the heroin would be hidden; that's when trust would begin.

They ate roasted baby blue pigeon with a decent Bordeaux, and before that the forbidden hearts of raffia (*'marché noir pour les étrangers'* hissed Challois at Forbes). The conversation was almost entirely reminiscences from Challois, with just the occasional sharp question at Forbes, who was desperate to sustain his ignorance of the French language.

'*Votre première visite, monsieur?*' came in a sharp sideways jab.

'*Ah oui, certainement.*' Forbes thought he could go that far, in what he hoped was an English schoolboy accent.

The difficulty was in looking either blank or glancing hopefully at Josel for translation as Challois wound his way through story after story. But it was fun. Jean Louis and Josel were laughing with each other happily as the picture of Challois *père* was sketched skilfully by his son – the first journey from the coast to the central plateau and Tananarive had meant walking two hundred miles. Thereafter, he and Bergheim, who had come out from England to help pioneer the graphite mining for the manufacture of foundry crucibles, had used either the pirogue (hollowed tree trunk) or the *filanzan* (sedan chair) to explore and exploit the deposits. That had been soon after 1900. By 1920 a number of French Army *sous-officiers* had decided, after their garrison duty, to stay on. Jean Louis's father had been one. They had prospered, or at any rate most of them had, with private aeroplanes and frequent trips to their apartments in Paris, where their children were schooled.

Morsaing *père* had been the exception; his *gisement* had been too small and remote, and so Jean Louis had grown up with the Malgache – among the alien corn. All this Forbes had gathered from Josel; she had seemed anxious for him to absorb Jean Louis's background. He was beginning to understand her purpose. When he saw Henri Challois bunching his fingers and leaning forward to say, '*Je suis né ici*', it began to sink in that this island was like no other place; it had an effect on its adopted peoples which was in a way mesmeric. Its very size, its isolation, its history of the immigrant settlers from Polynesia, Malaysia, Arabia and Africa, the sinister primitive religion of the cult of the dead, and ultimately the quasi-civilising influence in the 1840s of Jean Laborde, the French entrepreneur, all had compounded to create strange relationships between the people and the land itself.

Forbes had practically sunk into reverie (they had reached the stage of brandy and coffee) when Challois tapped him lightly on the knee, saying, *'Eh bien, monsieur, vous êtes ici à part des Russes, n'est ce pas?'*

'A part des Russes?' said Forbes, looking at Jean Louis and kicking himself for simulating difficulty with such an easy question.

'Et Madame Morsaing ici, notre vieille amie, est votre patronne n'est ce pas?' he continued, with a sly look at Jean Louis, whose riposte was firm and to the point.

'Monsieur Forbes vient ici pour examiner le possibilité d'un contract entre moi et la Société Etoile Rouge de Leningrad pour les embarquements de graphite.'

'Oui, oui, oui, naturellement il faut examiner les possibilités' – this with a strong shrug of inevitability and a self-pitying expression.

'Nous colons sont imbéciles de rester ici avec ces salles Communistes.' The voice was lowered to a whisper as the head jerked the eyes round the room. *'C'est une maison de verre, cette Colbert.'*

Challois had sung for his supper. He had been entertaining. He could, and might, scotch rumours simply by being the author of them, and graphite for Leningrad was perfectly feasible, even probable. There was, of course, from such a man a parting shot which made them wince, but which *could* provide a double alibi – *'Je devine peut-être une renaissance de votre* rapport n'est ce pas?' he said, almost but not quite leering at Josel. '*Vous avez aussi le rôle de Cupid, je crois, Monsieur Forbes.*' He patted the Englishman lightly on the knee. Then he was gone.

Josel lay awake, her mind in turmoil. Was the plan holding together? How big was the risk that Forbes and Jean Louis would remain distant and cool, 'correct', as the French would say? How could she manage her feelings for Jean Louis and his for her? Why had she joined her father's crusade? Was it not the dream of an old man who, brave as he had been, had hated the war and wanted somehow to expiate the guilt of Germany? Had she thought she could bury the memories of Jean Louis, Madagascar, the *fanafouté*, the awful illness and the humiliating divorce? Humiliating because French culture, French medicine, the Catholic religion, had all been powerless, worse than powerless, in the face of primitive prehistoric witchcraft. Why had Jean Louis never mentioned the possibility? Because love triumphs, it's nothing but old wives' tales? The Paris doctors had said the same, hinted at subconscious incompatibility, asked whether her Parisian upbringing in contrast with *la vie coloniale* had perhaps induced a psychosomatic illness.

Jean Louis had done his best. The son of a second marriage, his mother had arrived *enceinte* from Paris and the taboo does not apply to pregnant women. No, he had never believed the stories or heeded old wives' warnings: *Take a native girl into your bed, and her family appoint themselves guardians watchful for the day you bring to the island a French wife.* Then they prepare her food, and the process of debilitation begins. No trace of poison, nothing which Western laboratories can isolate, analyse, just steady deterioration in physique, in mental awareness, alertness, and most perceptibly a waning of the husband's interest, affection, protection.

So Jean Louis had made no great effort to resist Josel's mother's insistence on divorce on medical grounds. It had not been easy to steer such a case through the French courts. The result was the cleaving to her father's cause, and putting thoughts of men and marriage from her mind.

But now? Jean Louis was as attractive as ever. Joining her father's crusade to bury memories, if that had been the reason, was the craziest thing of all. They had met originally in her grandmother Josel Buchovitz' apartment when Jean Louis was serving with the French Army on his tour of duty. The eyes, the darkness of skin and the muscular tautness of his movements had fascinated her. They had wandered down the Champs Elysées, his romantic idea of Paris, and she had told him of Maréchal Lyautey's instruction to Malagary, his chief engineer in Morocco – *'Je désire que vous construissiez un boulevard pour l'approche à Fez, mais dix centimetres moins large que les Champs Elysées comme compliment à la France.'*

He had laughed and laughed – *'C'est un geste très coloniale!'*

So they had loved, and assumed, as love will always assume, that all would be well.

It was her grandmother who had told her father of the young British officer on the Military Mission in Prague in '47 who had talked so often of 'our tunnel' at Eichstätt, and this had led to their targeting Forbes as the man to lead them to the gold.

'Archie Forbes,' she mused, 'So far, all is well; he has reacted predictably, with humour and obstinacy, both good English characteristics, with intelligence and sensitivity too, not bad for a soldier of fortune now in his fifties.'

But much, *too* much, she thought, now depended on his relationship with her and, despite his buccaneering background, he had a moral sticking point, the English liberal conscience. Would he overcome his repugnance for introducing drugs to the American Army even if, by doing so, a Red Army blitzkrieg and its nuclear response could be stillborn? What *was* his motive in joining them? Self-protection, to keep his job, as he claimed, with a powerful element of blackmail from Brockles? Or something else besides? An interest in her? She had noticed the glances.

Jean Louis's motives too . . . . Guilt? To absolve himself for the *fanafouté*? Certainly not a European patriotism, still less *'pour la belle France'*?

And what a task he'd volunteered for: the clandestine import of large amounts of heroin, hiding it in the crocodile caves and shipping it on a given signal in sacks of graphite to the crucible manufacturers in Germany.

Of course, he had many advantages. Most of the drug-smuggling into France had, for years, been organised by French NCOs who had served in Indo-China, friends of his father, to whom he had easy access. His hiding-place, the crocodile caves in the north of the island where they were going tomorrow, would be more secure than Fort Knox. They would need to be. Then, of course, *if* there should be trouble from Soviet Military Intelligence, the GRU, Jean Louis could rely on his upbringing *en brousse*. He could simply fade away, leaving his *gisement* in the hands of his excellent foreman and live a maquis existence. There would always be plenty of warning. Russians in Madagascar stuck out like sore thumbs.

They had had a lot of happiness together until the poisons had started to work. Was she still in love with him? Were she and Jean Louis both somehow looking for a way out of an impasse, an impasse they were now re- inventing?

She went to sleep thinking about Jean Louis. But curiously Archie Forbes occupied her dreams. She woke refreshed and smiling.

13

Archie Forbes woke with a hangover plus the uneasy feeling of a bad day ahead. All he knew from Jean Louis was that, after flying north to Antsiranana (the old Diego Suarez), they would drive south about sixty miles to the village of Matsaborimanga and there pick up a bullock cart for the last leg of the journey to their campsite. He put on the cotton boiler suit supplied by Jean Louis, filled his water bottle and tried on his sun-hat. In the mirror he looked horrible, red-faced and bleary-eyed.

There was silence in the taxi to the airport and again in the aircraft itself, mostly due to engine noise but perhaps they all felt dispirited; it was very early in the morning.

Forbes concentrated on the view. It was spectacular. So this, he thought, is the Great Red Island; probably uninhabited until two thousand years ago when the first settlers arrived by boat from Indonesia; now ten million people of extraordinary cultural diversity. Yes, he'd done his guidebook homework and hoisted in that there were tropical rain forests in the east (where the graphite deposits were), a sharp contrast to the south-western deserts. He knew about the ancestor worship (the cult of the dead) and the concept of *fady* (taboo), which he had vaguely begun to hope might be helpful in discouraging crocodile-hunters. He also knew about the lemur, the little known aye-aye with its bat ears and beaver-like teeth and the slender elongated middle finger with which it extracts insects from wood. The thought of meeting one began to cheer him up. But in the meantime – the view!

The green of the foliage and the red of the earth were swept over by a sky of delphinium blue flecked with cloud like an English June. But the heat was beginning to change the colour; it was becoming a copper blue, empty of cloud, with thick visible heat rising from the rivers whose banks were of such dark green they seemed black to the eye. He could see a far horizon of traveller's trees on a cascade of hills falling to the Indian Ocean. A world of frangipani, poinsettia, and endless varieties of bougainvillea; no wonder the early Portuguese explorers had seen it as the garden of Eden.

But Jean Louis was gently tapping his forearm. He had drifted off to sleep and they were about to land.

There was a heavily loaded Mercedes camionette waiting for them at the airport, with a beaming Malgache driver who greeted Jean Louis as an old friend. They piled in. Josel looked cool, Jean Louis looked as if he and the Malgache enjoyed the same body temperature, Forbes felt hot and prickly; it was the hangover at last coming to heel.

Once again it was a largely silent journey (because of the Malgache driver, Forbes imagined) with only brief instructions from Jean Louis on setting up camp and some rather jolly botanical waffle from Josel about the island's thousand species of endemic orchids. Forbes drifted off again.

Three hours later they were in the bullock cart – No kipping in this, he decided, and concentrated on what confronted him; the Massif of Ankarana. Josel had done some briefing in English on the truck journey, so he knew roughly what to expect. 'The first thing you'll see,' she had said, 'is the north-western edge of the Massif itself which is a huge cliff, the Ankarana Wall, nine hundred feet in places. This wall, and the sheer canyons which divide the Massif, which is about 130 square miles, are fearful barriers to both animal and human movement. Within the canyons is dense forest or tangled scrub, which again is very difficult. There are some old logging trails, but access to the centre is only by climbing over the limestone, known as *tsingy*. Jean Louis will explain in more detail this evening.'

They lunched in the bullock cart off wild honey and dried banana, and made camp in the early afternoon. Then Jean Louis took Forbes off for a walk in order to work in his Foreign Legion boots and brief him in detail on their early morning start for the River Styx and the caves – the famous crocodile caves.

'Recently hunters have killed some crocodiles – eleven, it was said, in one night – and so the natives have brought back *fady*, the taboo, which I think will be effective,' he said with a smile.

'At your instigation, I imagine,' said Forbes.

Jean Louis's smile broadened.

'What do they eat?'

'Oh, fish, crabs, shrimps, crayfish and, we think, the big eels which are often four feet long. Don't imagine that we'll *see* any crocs, Archie. There are sixty miles of cave passages in the Massif, and this is the dry season when they escape the drought by retreating into the *very* remote caves of the River Styx where we are going tomorrow. But their very existence will be sufficient protection, because of native superstition. Even *without* crocodiles to guard them, Archie, these drugs will be hard to find. You will discover that in the morning.'

'But *you* are vulnerable, Jean Louis, and if the KGB got you into one of those clinics . . .?'

'Archie, they have to find me first. In this island, *en brousse*, as we say, information about strangers reaches me very quickly. I can become your Scarlet Pimpernel. This with a reassuring hand on the arm. 'In any case, the Malgache have a herbal potion which makes one insensitive to pain; one feels nothing. They used it when they rebelled against the French after the war.'

'And many were killed,' Forbes murmured. 'Supposing you *are* killed – who can find the drugs?'

'Josel knows where to look for the clues. She was my wife, you remember.' He turned away. Forbes found himself liking the man.

They dined superbly. Fresh meat and vegetables cooked by the Malgache driver, rice, tomatoes and dried banana washed down by a red Rhône wine which had travelled badly, resenting the heat, but which to Forbes was nectar.

Then it was early into the hammocks and the bivi bags which eliminated the need for tents. The hammocks had two sticks at either end to hold them out and allow sleeping on one's side. The night was quite cold and the moon poured down. They rigged the mosquito nets, mostly as extra protection against scorpions; biting insects (*Les bibs*, the Malgache called them) were apparently rare.

They were up well before first light, Jean Louis having warned that the *tsingy* becomes uncomfortably hot to the touch by midday.

Everything – the Avon inflatable, the outboard, the camera gear, petzl lighting units and helmets – was laid out for loading up when Forbes heard a sharp cry from Josel and saw her drop to one knee, sucking a finger.

'Scorpion,' she said, looking frightened. 'Look.' She tipped out the bag she had been rummaging in. *Grosphus palpator* – the nasty one with small claws. I'll take some morphine tablets and lie down. Perhaps I should have a hydrocortisone injection.'

From the corner of his eye Forbes could see Jean Louis already preparing the syringe.

'Crush the scorpion,' he said, 'and rub the remains on the place where he stung.'

Forbes did as he was told and realised that Josel was pouring with sweat and rigid with pain.

'Drink water and take morphine tablets,' commanded Jean Louis. 'Archie and I must go now. Christian,' he said to the Malgache, *'vous restez ici avec madame.'*

'Bien sur, monsieur.'

'Archie, we can just about carry this junk between us. At least we can try!'

They staggered as the weight settled on the carrying straps. *'En piste,'* said Jean Louis.

Forbes heard the mocking note and thought, I'll show the bugger.

The next two hours were unmitigated torture. But for the scorpion, they would have had Josel and Christian to help carry. Forbes never knew how they made it over the steadily hotter *tsingy* to the Styx. Jean Louis was young, taut, muscular, and his knowledge of the terrain was superb in finding the easiest going; but even he was showing signs of strain as they unpacked the inflatable, blew it up with the gas bottles and mounted the engine. At long last Forbes's groans could be given voice, drowned by engine noise as they chugged into the dark in the slowly moving water.

At about 9.30 sunlight reached the water and they saw lemurs slipping over boulders worn smooth by their frequent passage, to drink. Then it was back into darkness with helmet lamps, searching for signs of a cave; the humidity made it difficult to see. Forbes was wringing wet inside his boiler suit. The river, he thought, was well named. Then suddenly, there was a cave, its entrance some 60 yards wide and 50 yards high. This narrowed to a huge passage, 30 yards high and 20 yards wide, which quickly became a long canal with no dry land visible for almost half a mile. There was not a sign of life. Another mile of chugging and they came to a huge boulder blockage.

'Finish,' said Jean Louis. 'That is, if you have enough photographs for your *chef-en-chef*, Monsieur Brockles' he chuckled. They chugged back to where they'd started, tucked up the inflatable and left it behind. 'I shall be back soon I hope.'

They set off for the camp, taking turns carrying the outboard engine over the limestone, which was cooling now. They could watch crowned lemurs, ignoring the boot-wrecking sharpness as they travelled to the next forest patch and browsed on the tiny fleshy fruits of noronhia, ficus and pandanus.

As they neared the camp, Christian came running out beaming and a faint cry, *'Tout va bien'*, came from Josel's bivi. 'I still feel lousy but I am not going to die. I have a sensation of rain falling on me, and anything my skin touches feels cold. I opened my mouth to drink some coconut milk and screamed with the pain in my jaw. Maybe I shouldn't have sucked out the poison.'

They stayed another night so that Josel could gather strength and, selfishly – because her pain came back and she had to take more morphine – they dined well and drank the last two bottles of the travel-weary Rhône red. Forbes listened and learnt a lot about Madagascar.

As the wine went down and the cool air seemed to make the moon shine brighter, Forbes asked at last, 'What's the motive, Jean Louis? This drug business is already dangerous; what lies ahead could turn very nasty. It is clear why I am involved – and I'm reluctant. What about you – for the *beaux yeux* of Josel?' – this with a softening of his tone.

Jean Louis looked away and said, 'You English love to simplify. I will just tell you that I was brought up by my father on this island, but also to have some feeling for France. He was *just* in the First World War and he used to say, "We colons, we can do nothing now for France, but it is still our country, we owe her something." France did not die in 1940, Archie, despite all the unkind words, and somehow this crazy alliance of you, me, two Germans and a half-Czech girl seems to spell the sort of new Europe our ancestors would be happy about. Sentimentality is what you English call it; we try to hide it with our cynicism but we often fail. Besides, I like to pit my wits, and I was brought up to know crocodiles better than you know your English shooting dogs!'

On the aeroplane back to Tananarive, Forbes looked down at the Betsiboka river, a slash of red water through the dark jungle as a hundred tributaries poured earth into it, and thought that something *so* primitive perhaps could make one love France more.

Jean Louis drove Josel – stiff-armed but much recovered – and Forbes to the airport for the Paris flight. It was a fond farewell, warm and smiling as if they were all three saying, we have no complications in our lives, all is well.

The travellers went through emigration, the currency check and so on, tired and inattentive until suddenly a Malgache official beamed at Forbes – all teeth and gums – and said in high-pitched pidgin English, 'Mistah Forbes fly Paris not Moscow. Your graphite business now no good perhaps?'

'What did you make of that graphite crack?' he said to Josel as they settled down to wait for the flight to be called.

Tired, tense and still shaky, she replied, 'As we expected Challois has been talking.'

14

Forbes carefully negotiated the Place de la Concorde and then strolled, wasting time, so welcoming were the May morning sun and the chestnut trees in the Champs Elysées.

He'd spent the night at the Hôtel de Suède in the Rue de Bac, where he'd meditavely dined alone, knowing that Josel and her father were ensconced in the Buchowitz apartment which Josel had bequeathed to her grandaughter.

So here he was, heavily briefed by Brock, to meet the new CIA ally, Alex Bradley, check him through (oh God – Brock's American jargon again) the whole scenario, introduce him to Josel, von Heimann and Ansbach and tell him as much as they all thought he ought to know, not necessarily the same quantity or quality as Brock had in mind. Why not? Because Americans, in the eyes of Germans, girls with Czech grandmothers, or Englishmen with Polish wives, did not automatically qualify for special relationships. They had to work their passage; nothing could be taken for granted. Why not? A damned hard question to answer. Their passion for over-simplification? Their urge to analyse, to communicate? Their intense striving for the perfect world? Were these the urges which made them such naive bedfellows? Not that he had had much to do with them.

Brock had said as much. 'Take it gently, Archie. Get to know him well, let him see you as the archetypal Englishman, keep his hands off the girl and don't let him *too* close to Melkov when he comes in,' (from the cold, Forbes had muttered; these Brocks love their clichés). Well, those weren't exactly easy instructions, and now the bugger was only ten minutes away on the steps of the Petit Palais. Forbes straightened the magenta bow-tie and unrumpled, as best he could, the ancient seersucker suit he'd unearthed for this rendez-vous. He couldn't be missed, and at least he'd look more like an art-dealer than an ageing queer.

Brock had been rather difficult, when the Bradley briefing was over, about the Madagascar trip. 'So they took you all that way and didn't show you where the heroin is to be hidden? Come, come, Archie, you know the basic rule: there has to be back-up, come the day when you, JL and the girl all get "blown away" – to coin an expression – he added hastily, 'someone has to know.'

'No, Brock, not this time. JL is a man of mystery. It's called trusting your ally, Brock; not always easy as you and I have learned together.'

The atmosphere hadn't been made any easier by the suggestion that at some stage Brock FitzHerbert would like to come over and, as he put it, 'meet the cast'.

'Hell no,' said Forbes. 'They're nervous enough already, and the last thing they want is you appearing as a bloody ringmaster. Don't forget they've just lost their favourite double agent; they blame themselves for that, and now they're facing the arrival of *two* new boys, and there'll be plenty of hissing and sucking in of breath before the new team settles down without you gatecrashing the party.'

For a moment he thought he'd overdone it, but the

twitch of Brock's nose and the 'let's get on with the briefing' in a good-humoured tone, reassured him.

'Alex Bradley was John Vann's right-hand man in the early days of the Vietnam war. He saw at first hand all the mistakes the Americans made and how they made all the mistakes that were to be made! He has no starry-eyed ideas about the American Army, nor does he think the CIA is God-wonderful. The last few years he has been on secondment with a British firm in North Carolina. He's a Californian, around forty four, very bright wife, and – dare I say it to an Englishman, he's got a sense of humour? Speaks good German too, Archie. I reckon you could use him in an active role – if you wanted to,' he murmured.

Now he was only yards away from the Petit Palais, so he ran quickly through the rendezvous drill. A slow stroll through the whole exhibition, which, except for students, at this early hour would not be crowded, and then a longish close study of Van Gogh's *Peasant Woman Seated* (on loan from Den Bosch in Holland). At that point, Bradley was to appear and address him as an art-dealer. Good straightforward stuff; and so it was.

He saw the tall, typically American figure from the corner of his eye and fingered his catalogue. The throat was cleared. 'I'm looking, excuse me, sir,' (Americans always use that bogus 'sir', he thought irritably) 'for an art-dealer who could tell me about the other Impressionists in the Den Bosch.' The tone was light-hearted, almost jocular; it was a 'so if you're not the guy so what' tone. Forbes thought it was about right.

'I might be able to help; are you thinking of a visit to Holland?' he said, and looked carefully at a tanned face with very slightly screwed-up eyes which suggested a lot of sailing, they were brown, humorous but calm. Dark hair, brown or black, he couldn't tell, and a longish face with a strong nose, 'a good nose', Zulka would have called it.

'Well, well,' the American laughed, 'I think this is Brock's leg-pull, don't you? He said there was a pretty girl mixed up in the business, but this sure isn't one! Perhaps he really meant her!' He jerked his head towards Manet's *Berthe Morisot*.

They meandered through the rooms, enjoying themselves, letting the atmosphere do the work, then out into the Champs Elysées, where the brilliance of the morning made conversation staccato.

As they reached the Travellers' Club ('My club in New York gives me a temporary membership,' Bradley explained) Forbes said, 'Let's talk more over lunch, but keep it pretty general, I suggest.'

'You mean like how good-looking is the girl and is that going to complicate things?' grinned Bradley.

'With you around it might easily.' Both men laughed as if a new friendship had begun.

They took their drinks into the little courtyard and Forbes said, 'OK, fire all the other questions.'

'Well,' drawled Bradley, 'we meet at seven this evening for drinks in the Ritz Bar, but that's just to give our new Russian friend the creeps. I can tell you about him from my sources – not that he won't tell you his personal history himself – born '47, in '65 went to Higher Military School, 1970 joined GRU Volga Military District, which controlled the 13th Army Spetsnatz. After Military Diplomatic Academy he and his wife spent five years in Geneva, whence he defected in '78. Bear in mind, Archie, that in Sergei's case the word "defect" includes the corollary "stays in place". He is now Assistant Military Attaché in Bonn. He has an intimate knowledge and understanding of GRU technical espionage; more importantly, he knows how the Red Army spy system works!

'So how does Sergei Melkov become the ideal replacement for Juris Wolfmannis – at least in the eyes of our German friends?'

'I'll tell you after lunch,' said Bradley as he led the way up the rococo staircase which made Forbes exclaim with admiration for the French, something he normally found hard to do.

They talked in the deserted smoking-room long into the afternoon, and Forbes began to see how Bradley's experiences with John Vann in Vietnam were going to be valuable. He had learnt how to interpret the confusing behaviour of the South Vietnamese generals. Now he and Melkov were going to have to perform the same service with respect to the Red Army; in particular the special sabotage and terrorist units which were integrated throughout the complete Soviet military, naval and intelligence network, units of special purpose forces reporting directly to the central intelligence staff which would be activated well in advance of any Red Army main attack.

'But even more important than that, Archie, in the short run, is the virtual certainty that, if the hard-liners *have* been watching Juris and if his death *could* have somehow led them to us, Spetsnatz (the special force I'm talking about) would be given the rub-out job, and Melkov would be well ahead of the game with his warning.'

'You're a great comfort,' said Forbes. 'Tell me what else Melkov can do.'

'Essentially, keep our friends in the Kremlin calm and happy; nervous friends are almost as bad to have around as enemies. *Most* important of all is his ability to read those Red Army generals. As you know, our timing is crucial. If something should trigger the Red Army before we're in place, and US public opinion starts clamouring for the boys to come home, then we're up that creek and no mistake – and don't our Kremlin friends know it!'

'Would they dump us?'

'Well, you know, Archie, that the world is full of people who will take all the help you can give and then throw you off the train. Yes, they might, but more likely just fold their tents, I guess. In any case, we're some way off that scenario; the Red Army's got its hands full, prestigewise, with those Afghan guerrillas.'

Brock had planned this meeting well; they had all the time in the world and Paris had its May-time smile. They walked down the Faubourg St Honoré, appreciating, in not quite equal measure, shop windows and girls and turned left for the Place Vendôme and then left again into the Rue Cambon.

As they approached the side entrance to the Ritz, Forbes said, 'A funny place to meet a Russian military attaché, – rather conspicuous?'

Bradley laughed. 'You Limeys are all the same – side-streets and filthy raincoats! The Ritz Bar is *in*conspicuous, it's for tourists, business men and freeloaders, and when it's Paris Air Show the military attachés are here every day!'

As he spoke a taxi drew up and von Heimann, Ansbach and Josel got out. Forbes made the introductions, having briefed each of them on the telephone the previous evening, and was rewarded with beaming smiles. Josel smiled sweetly at the American, and they filed into the darkened room – which was all too empty, Forbes thought – to see a shortish cropped-haired figure rise to his feet from a corner sofa.

Bradley introduced them all (where he and Melkov had met, Forbes had forgotten to ask) and the atmosphere stayed stiffly correct until the whiskies gave

Bradley the moment to lean forward, tap the Russian on the knee and say, 'Tell them about your grandfather, Sergei, and his Cossack general.' The place was filling up and the noise clearly made any story-telling an impossibility but the ice – if there had been any – was broken and Melkov's raised glass, beaming smile and series of bows was proof enough. Ansbach slipped out and ordered taxis.

Von Heimann had chosen the little restaurant in the Rue de Bac because he and Josel were well known there. He had ordered *moules marinière* and *selle d'agneau*, a Sancerre followed by a Beychevelle '75. They would not often dine together!

Forbes sat beside Josel and observed Bradley and Melkov. They seemed to get on; the Russian did much laughing and seemed genuinely amused and slightly, or politely, amazed by the American's stories about his native California, especially the one about meeting a friend of his father's in the early fifties who could remember, as a boy, seeing his grandfather shot by an Indian arrow.

This reminiscence was, of course, designed to produce Melkov's story about *his* grandfather and the Cossack brigade commander in the Ukraine in 1917. News had travelled slowly in those days and so it was December before the garrison had heard of the revolution. The general made a rapid departure with his soldier servant – Melkov's grandfather – and only when they reached the Polish frontier did the trooper take out his carbine and say, 'General, I am taking you to Kiev for trial.' Whereupon the officer drew his sabre, shouting, 'I will cut you down for mutiny.' The next thing either of them knew was they had thrown down their weapons and opened a bottle of wine. 'My grandfather become a good old-fashioned Communist,' said Sergei.

'And good Communists are good soldiers,' said von Heimann 'We met them at Stalingrad.'

There were some silent glances and von Heimann raised his glass. Forbes caught his breath and wondered, Could these feelings be genuine? and then saw Josel smile, looking at her father. It was a smile of wonder and admiration. It was a glimpse of the future which made him tuck his cynicism away.

After coffee they went separately to the Rue de l'Assomption to the apartment Josel had recently inherited from her grandmother. There was more coffee and brandy, and von Heimann conducted what he called an 'order group'.

'A good British Army expression, eh, Archie?' he said, grinning at Forbes, whose brandy glass was being refilled by Josel with a slightly reproachful expression. Forbes was beginning to enjoy himself or, to be more accurate, his recollection of Bradley's vivid description of Spetsnatz was beginning to fade.

'If you say so, Helmut,' Forbes replied with a grin.

'I will go quickly through some points. First, this flat will not normally be used for meetings, it is too sensitive. Second, there will be very few meetings. If any of you want to meet in Paris, may I suggest the Museum Rodin, in the Rue de Varennes. It has a very nice garden. Third, we have rented a house in Provence until the end of October. It is remote and can be used for detailed briefings and by Jean Louis when he comes to France to organise distribution. Fourth, I will now describe the functions of various people:

'Willi and I are getting on in years, so we do not propose to be men of action. In consequence we, with Josel, will look after money and administration. Josel lives here in this apartment and Willi and I will be at our homes. Only Willi will normally communicate with

Sergei. Archie will liaise with Brockles. I hope one day to meet him, Archie,' he added in his most formal tone, belied by a twinkle which made Forbes guffaw. 'Also with Josel, who is, of course, in touch with Jean Louis.'

'Got anything for me, Helmut?' Bradley asked in a voice of lazy innocent enquiry.

'Very certainly,' came the reply. Forbes noticed the English was getting a little stilted and wondered about those generous glasses of Beychevelle. 'You are the drug-runner-in-chief, of course.'

'Oh sure, choose a CIA man for that job – makes perfect sense,' came the rather affected drawl.

Von Heimann kept going. 'Your first job will be to work out a deal with the manager of the crucible factory in Germany to which the graphite will be consigned by Jean Louis. Josel will make the introductions. Any questions, anyone?'

Forbes sat in wonderment. Twenty-four hours before, the Russian and the American had been total strangers to each other, as well as to the tunnel team (as he thought of the others), and here they were behaving as if the whole evening was routine, and comfortable routine at that. It said a lot for the meticulous briefings of Brock and von Heimann respectively, and, for that matter, for Bradley and Melkov. He began to feel a stirring of what could only be described as confidence; not a feeling which had been at all familiar since the moment he'd found himself staring in disbelief at his St Christopher medal.

He rose rather unsteadily to his feet. The brandy had cleared a path in his brain. He was not altogether certain it was the right path, but down it he would go. 'Most of you, probably all of you, know that I am here' – he intercepted a look of amazed disapproval from Josel – 'of necessity rather than from conviction, but

I'm bound to say that if anyone can bring it off it's Jean Louis and the people in this room.' He swayed a little, aiming what he hoped was an atrocious wink at Josel. But her chair was empty; she was speaking on the telephone in the next room, in French, audibly.

'That was Jean Louis,' she said when she came back, looking what Forbes called green about the gills. 'He has had a visit from a Russian trade official who came to the *gisement* to ask about a contract negotiated by an Englishman for the Red Star Crucible Company in Leningrad. The official knew, thanks to Juris, that Archie had been accredited by Red Star, but clearly he wasn't happy and was asking awkward questions, such as, Was Forbes some kind of specialist in graphite applications, otherwise why choose him?'

'What did Jean Louis do?' – this in a very calm voice from Melkov, and Alex noticed that he used the verb 'do' and not 'say'.

'He got him drunk and next day took him up to Nossi bé for the weekend with two girls.'

'Where there was an accident,' said Sergei in a voice without a question mark.

'Yes, how did you know?'

'I only know it wasn't Spetsnatz because Spetsnatz doesn't get drunk. From my briefing I know that Jean Louis understands crocodiles, so he would certainly understand a Russian trade official.'

'But it wasn't a crocodile,' said Josel, her sense of humour deserting her, 'it was a shark.'

So the fairy story they'd spun for Challois, thought Archie Forbes, had been too clever by half. Perhaps, after all, they *were* just a bunch of amateurs. He helped himself to more brandy under Josel's disapproving stare.

15

Despite the absence of any reference to *his* responsibilities Archie Forbes was only too clear what his role was going to be. Brock had nagged him to be his 'eyes and ears' and that of course meant snooping; not, he reflected unhappily, a wholly unaccustomed role, he had often been Brock's man behind the arras. But he felt a respect for Josel which sometimes wandered into the sentimental, and that made the task unusually distasteful. Josel would be handling the purse strings, Bradley and Jean Louis the deal; Forbes the supernumerary snooper would therefore make his appearance short and hopefully sweet.

But there was another reason for a touch of the old arm's-length relationship. He knew that Jean Louis had another even more crucial deal to make while in France – the distribution plan, the network which would get the stuff into the hands (the arms, more likely, Forbes thought wryly) of the US Army in Germany. A foolproof, blackmail-proof, KGB-proof network to be unquestioningly controlled by one of the old army friends of Morsaing *père*. This man, who had so far been barely mentioned, was the rarest of birds, a narcotics boss who was a straight dealer. And, rarer still in the underworld of drugs, a lover of France. All this Forbes had learnt from Jean Louis over the red wine under those Malgache stars.

Strenca, the son of Morsaing *père's sous-officier* at Verdun, was a Corsican and a *pied noir*. Brought up in Algiers, he had found himself, aged twelve, after the North African landings in 1942, running messages for the British Army with a boundless enthusiasm which had clearly marked him to join the Foreign Legion. After Dien Bien Phu, the Algerian war had brought some of them, including Emile Strenca, into conflict with de Gaulle. They finished in French jails, with death sentences – just to concentrate their minds. In Strenca's case it had meant exile to South Africa, where he had prospered. Then had come the offer to restore his French passport and the temptation to quit the wearying world of growing racial hatred. The Paris underworld had received him with open arms. In their university of life he was fully qualified.

All these and a jumble of other thoughts raced through Forbes' mind as he fumbled with the lift and wondered about a taxi, only to find Alex Bradley waiting in one outside the front door.

'Come on, Archie old boy.' (The 'old boy' was delivered with a touch of hauteur to show he was pulling the English leg.) 'Let's have a nightcap so we can fix a date to meet *chez* Moulin, or whatever you call it. I guess the party's going to be fun.'

Forbes forgot to wonder what party he had in mind. He felt he could work with Alex Bradley and the night was young. In the darkness of the *boîte* they fended off several female advances, barely noticing the strange glances the rejections earned.

Bradley got straight to the point. 'Josel has said she will fix it with Jean Louis for me to have introductions to all the German crucible makers to which he supplies graphite. It's about three. He will indicate which managers he thinks *could* be venal, and I will go to work. But I need a fool proof plan – do you have any ideas?'

Forbes had been thinking rather hard about a girl sitting at a table six feet away and wondering why an extremely rare evening in a Paris night-club should be spent discussing a long-winded plan with his new American friend. Also the brandy was making him belligerent.

'It's my guess that in this case all you need is a warehouse foreman who would like a few nice presents for his wife in exchange for swallowing a cock-and-bull story which, given its African origins, might just be true.' He swallowed his drink, looking hard at Bradley.

'OK, Limey, I guess you know the score. How would you do it?' Alex's face, in the almost pitch darkness, had what looked like a good-natured grin.

Archie Forbes drew in his breath, hoping the brandy hadn't turned from friend to enemy, and his voice rasped. Grossalmerode isn't a big place, so it should be simple enough to find a warehouse foreman prepared to "mislay" a dozen sacks of graphite once it had been explained to him that they would contain samples of let's say poached ivory, smuggled from Maputo and specially marked to be used as evidence in a court case in the US in which the CIA has a special interest. Very flattering, all that, and clinched, I would guess, by a present of some very nice pieces of carved ivory for his wife. Of course, the first marked sacks would have to contain some ivory to satisfy his curiosity, and Jean Louis could doubtless sew them in such a way that we could check whether they had been opened. If *not* tampered with then "honest Joe" foreman lets the next batch be collected (by Willi, I would guess) with the heroin safe inside.'

'OK.' The word was long drawn out, thoughtful and tinged with admiration.

As Forbes's glass was refilled he mused that behind Alex Bradley's cultivated façade of amused laziness he was quick-witted and could bring a very experienced track record quickly to work. After all, that was why he was on the team, wasn't it? 'One of the best, if not *the* best, of their ex-Vietnam boys,' Brock had said, 'Knows the working of the US Army at platoon level, battalion level, staff level and general level; he and John Vann, between them, rescued a good many situations and reputations in the US officer corps, as well as fighting at Da Nang like Kilkenny cats. Bradley earned a very high security clearance – how high I'm not allowed to tell you.'

Typical patronising Brock, Forbes had thought, but even so, he'd been impressed.

The dark red EXIT sign behind Forbes's shoulder had started to flicker very slightly on Bradley's sun-browned Californian face. What the hell is a 'Californian face'? he was asking himself as the flicker gave it a demonic look. He wasn't completely sure that his speech had been intelligible, but he felt encouraged by his companion's good humour.

As he decanted at the Hôtel Suède he heard Bradley's soft 'OK, Archie boy, I'll play it your way, I guess.' And then, 'See you a couple of weeks from now in Isle-sur-la-Sorgue.'

On balance (which wasn't very good at the moment) it had been a useful evening.

In the morning his memory was clearer – 10 a.m. in the church in Isle-sur-la-Sorgue on Thursday week.

16

Archie Forbes meandered in the church of Isle-sur-la-Sorgue, having happy thoughts of churches in Bohemia where chickens, geese and turkeys had seemed to wander at will. Here, in the darkness flickered by innumerable candles and speared by shafts of sunlight from high windows, there seemed to be only black-clad crones shuffling and muttering, and the occasional determined-looking young woman whose demeanour seemed to hint at a marriage ceremony. Then came the light touch on the arm, followed swiftly by Alex Bradley's grin. Forbes wondered if that grin was going to irritate him slightly as the weeks went by; not that there was anything wrong with the face behind it, it was a likeable open face, a sort of grown-up Huckleberry Finn face, Forbes thought, strong-jawed, with a mouth full of humour.

'How was your trip?'

'Fine,' said Forbes. 'I took the sleeper at Avignon and my hire-car is parked out beyond the main bridge.

'Right next to mine, I expect,' said Bradley, putting on a phoney conspiratorial look. 'I guess we might wander through that market out there and have coffee at the café with the river running through the middle of it. Josel is around somewhere and Jean Louis arrives this evening.'

Sounds like a house party, thought Forbes. Well, it *is*

a house party, he corrected himself, and let's hope it's a productive one. He had a fading memory of Zulka's eyebrows.

They wandered through the bustle of the stalls, chatting, admiring, picking up and putting down, occasionally asking a price, feeling comfortable with each other.

'I fixed that crucible warehouse guy,' said Bradley, 'and he's happy because his wife's even happier, thought it was a great joke to be playing a part in a CIA versus the baddies set-up. Josel checked with Jean Louis that some chunks of ivory could be put in the test shipment, and I think we're now on good ground with this arrangement – thanks, Archie.'

'What's the main item on the agenda this weekend at the Moulin?' asked Forbes, who felt he was learning how to settle into the second-string role.

'Timing – mostly timing. Jean Louis will give us a run-down on the logistics. My job is to tell you all how I see the political atmosphere in the States, and then we have Sergei with his little old appreciation of how the Red Army thinks and feels these days. Let's not forget to check with Willi how much enthusiasm and pressure can be exerted by his industrialist friends. What we're in fact doing is destroying America's will to fight, and there mustn't be a vacuum between that happening and German industry pushing its government into a démarche.'

'Delicate timing, in other words,' said Forbes.

They were browsing at a stall of rather nice wooden candlesticks. In fact, they were buying a pair as a house present for Josel and laughed happily at discovering simultaneously what they were about. They meandered on to the café, and there at a table by the river, sipping coffee and reading a newspaper, was Josel.

'I thought you would both – how you say? – turn up here,' she said.

The water sparkled in the sunshine, someone took their order for coffee, and the house party weekend had begun.

'Bernice, my grandmother's cook from Paris, who was born in Provence, has taken over at the Moulin, so at least we should eat well. What do you think Sergei likes best of all to eat?'

'Blinis,' said Bradley, grinning. 'All Russians love blinis best of all.'

'Not in Provence,' said Josel, with her slow 'I-know-you-pull-my-leg smile, but we'll think of some good ideas, Bernice and I.'

They had a lazy lunch. The candlesticks were a great success, and Forbes managed to suppress a scoffing hiss as he saw the happy smile on Josel's face when Bradley came out with the expected 'I think we'll make a great team' as he emptied the second wine bottle. Forbes consoled himself by thinking, We're in Dornford Yates country, and almost uttered the words before realising he was the only one old enough to remember.

They retrieved their hire-cars and set off at twenty-minute intervals for the Moulin, Josel first. Archie dallied in Gordes just to spy out a restaurant, and began to fall in love with red earth and blue sky. Jean Louis, he thought, will like it too.

The three of them were sitting on the terrace under a canopy of plumbago when Jean Louis and Melkov arrived, almost together. There was some nervous laughter as Jean Louis told his story about the weekend at Nossi bé and Melkov looked thoughtful.

'There should be no consequence, the Russian assured them. 'It sounds like a bureaucratic excuse for a trip, but please contact me if you have some anxiety. If there *should* be another visit, that would be to kill Jean Louis.'

The flatness of this statement wiped the grins from all our faces, thought Forbes. 'Would that mean,' he asked, 'that they could have rumbled the whole scheme – silly question, I suppose?'

'No it wouldn't,' answered Melkov. 'For them, murder is the reflex of the smallest quiver of suspicion when it is clearly too difficult to interrogate.'

They dined on the lower of the two patios, where Bernice produced a magnificent cassoulet and salad, followed by cheese and *fraises de bois en bateaux*. She had given Melkov some pretty mean looks until Josel explained that he was an official from the Czech embassy come to discuss the expropriation of some of her grandmother's erstwhile property in Bohemia.

'Then why give him such a good time?' Bernice had grumbled.

'Because it's a form of bribery,' Josel had said, 'and there are one or two pieces of jewelry I would love to get my hands on!'

Melkov, having been told all this, did a placatory fetching and carrying.

After supper, it was back to the other patio for what Forbes happily called the board meeting. The evening sun was soon going to do its Mediterranean dive, and shadows were already distorting the garden below.

A local builder had found the Moulin hanging in a ruin from the steep hillside down which the water cascaded from springs. It was a clever and not overambitious restoration. The mill-wheel could still be heard turning and grumbling, loud enough to drown the approach of any vehicle on the long, winding drive. Where they sat now was a large cavernous stone-flagged space, under the first floor of the house, with stone mangers set in the walls at intervals and a huge stone mill-wheel on straddles in the centre, from which they served themselves with drinks and coffee. There seemed to be plenty of bedrooms; it would be ideal for a French family for the summer, especially the pool, which was huge and hung with vast curtains of bougainvillaea. Too far from the sea? 'Pouf,' the agent had said, 'those beaches are becoming *déclassés*. From here you can explore the whole of Provence. *Le pays de Van Gogh*, he had added superfluously.

As Bradley and Forbes (and evidently the others) had expected, Josel took charge of the discussion, and once again her coolness and composure impressed Forbes, who had been just beginning to doubt whether the absence of Ansbach and von Heimann was altogether wise.

'Sergei will not be staying long,' she said, 'because of discretion. So let us begin by discussing the timing of our operation from his point of view.'

Melkov took a deep breath and looked at each in turn; not, because of the shadows, a very penetrating look, but enough to rivet attention.

'I want to emphasise that my sources are generally very good but occasionally contradictory. This is because the Red Army is, by its very nature, contradictory. It does not have a smooth pattern of thought processes, rather it reacts to events and sometimes to the absence of events. At present, for example, it is preoccupied with Afghanistan. From the generals' point of view the campaign is satisfactory but please remember that Russian generals are not particularly concerned with the welfare of their soldiers, and the Russian soldiers in Afghanistan are beginning to discover that they must win *every* engagement, because failure means death or mutilation – and frequently death *after* mutilation. Often the officers have to shoot soldiers who have been severely mutilated by the mujahideen. Morale deteriorates as the soldiers' families begin to understand the horror of the casualties and of the conscript recruits waiting in dread for the ambushes. The generals cannot play with their high-technology weapons and so become disenchanted. Finally, when *that* war *is* over the Red Army will look for a morale-boosting, quick results, high-technology campaign. Even *before* Afghanistan is finished, they could use Germany as an excuse, an opportunity, to break it off in favour of the blitzkreig. And, of course, the withdrawal of the US NATO contingent as a result of Vietnam-style hysteria in the US would make the opportunity irresistible. So I don't need to tell you how important it is that West Germany should be very ready for negotiations towards unification, and that US opinion should react quickly to the scandal of the drugs.'

'Will there be any advance signs or indications of Red Army intentions towards the West?' This from Bradley. 'And I don't mean the intelligence services; when you work for an intelligence outfit you get to learn just how goddam inaccurate they can be.'

'Yes,' said Melkov, 'the Spetsialnoye Naznacheniye – who are special purpose forces. They are sabotage and terrorist units who are programmed and trained to assassinate leading politicians, military commanders, police chiefs. Each battalion of "Spetsnatz" could field forty five groups of saboteurs. In my present job, because I have worked with these people in the past, I *should* be able to pick up some very faint signals of intention; but please remember that if that stage is reached it will be already dangerously late for the neutrality negotiations to succeed.'

Bradley looked out at the moon and wondered if the temperature had dropped or was it just the effect of Melkov's words? Forbes got up and poured drinks and thought that the moon made Josel's turquoise shirt look dark and sombre. Jean Louis had said nothing. There was desultory chat about the morning. Melkov said he would leave before breakfast and Jean Louis that he would make his report and leave after lunch so as to meet Strenca in Paris on Saturday.

'That will give you a morning in the pool,' said Bradley.

'Yes, and we can talk.'

'Sure.'

The two men, surprisingly alike in many physical ways, had chatted through dinner about the Vietnam jungle compared with the Malgache jungle, and about natives and the effect of colonisation.

'The Malgache had the French civilisation from 1896, then Vichy in 1940 and the British in 1942; we survived all that! And you in Vietnam, you had Graham Greene!' Bradley had liked that.

Melkov and Jean Louis said their good nights and murmured about long journeys. Forbes poured himself another drink and sat down in the chair next to Josel. Bradley did the same, and all three murmured with laughter, the mood of their luncheon still with them. It was a good moment to say it, and so Bradley spoke.

'I can track Pentagon thinking pretty well, I guess, in my present job, but there will be some confusing signals. Brock wants all that fed back to him, which is OK by me, and I presume, Archie, that you will drop by Frankfurt on a business trip and hear what I have to tell you. I have fixed with Willi that he will have the graphite sacks shipped to Strenca. Just to go back to those confusing signals for a moment – you have to remember that there is a war party in the Pentagon, just as there's a war party in the Kremlin and, with the Red Army, that makes three. So you may hear more Evil Empire speeches and be tempted to think that the liberals (and remember that's a dirty word in the US) have taken to the hills. They will not do so; but please don't keep asking me for reassurances, because there's going to be no proof of what I say. We'll all just have to get used to being highly nervous from time to time.'

He lit a cigarette and the light sparkled on Josel's ring – a pink beryl, the Madagascar jewel, Forbes remembered. The moonlight was pouring down now and he thought of how it had lit up the *Platz* in Eichstätt.

'Time for my bed, Josel, I think,' and he stood up.

There were smiles and friendly movements of the hands as Forbes made for the stone steps. He didn't look back, but he realised that Bradley was looking out into the valley of shadows and hadn't stirred.

It was some time before he got to sleep, and he was vaguely aware that the terrace below his room was in silence save for the scrape of a chair.

17

Alex Bradley sat in his Frankfurt office in front of a pile of neglected paperwork. Helga, his crisp little German secretary, had flagged the items which screamed for attention. Bradley loathed paperwork and more than once had found himself in serious trouble for neglecting it. Frankfurt, being a new assignment, was full of unfamiliar and baffling routines. Happily, Helga had got the measure of it, more or less, so Bradley told himself to stop grumbling and attack the stack of red tabs. An hour later they were mounting in the out basket and his coffee was cold and forgotten.

There was a buzz on the intercom and Helga's voice came through with a twang which made him think she was trying to talk like an American. 'I have a Mr' – and then a jumble of vowels – 'here to see you, Mr Bradley,' followed by the familiar give-it-some-thought-before-you-react click of the intercom.

Bradley bounded to his feet. He'd had enough; any excuse to stop. He flung open the door and found himself confronted by a grinning Vietnamese. 'Van Cai,' he almost shouted, and the grin got wider, if that was possible. 'Gee, am I glad to see you, you little devil.' Helga was clicking her teeth in wonderment as Bradley swung his guest round and took him into his office saying, 'Coffee please, Helga – coffee.'

German efficiency slipped quietly into *Jawohl*,

bestimmt,' as Helga forgot to be American in her astonishment at the warmth of the greeting.

They drank their coffee in the speechless pleasure of being together again. Bradley's mind flooded into memories, especially of that last Vietnam battle of Easter '72 when honest, fearless and devoted Cai had alternated with him in John Vann's Jetranger as they made sortie after sortie from Vo Dinh to pitch out on Fire Base Delta what had seemed endless cases of M-16 ammunition, grenades, claymore mines, flares, water and medical supplies for the beleaguered Saigon paratroopers. Huynh Van Cai could have been the role model of what Vann had hoped the South Vietnam Army would turn out to be. After eight months as a platoon officer, he had become the trusted aide.

'Come on Cai,' Bradley said, 'let's go and drink some beer.'

In the clatter and hum of the bierkeller they grinned at each other over huge steins, and Bradley wondered if Cai was also remembering the Soviet T54s at the Tan Canh compound being blasted by 105 mm howitzers from the Spectre C130 gunships. 'They were "striking the head of the snake",' he suddenly said aloud, and Cai dissolved into tears of laughter and rocked backwards and forwards in his chair.

'Same memories, Alex, always same memories.'

Finally Bradley thought to ask him what he was doing in Frankfurt, and Cai's face, still crinkled with laughter, became very serious. 'I have come to see you, Alex, from Truong Chinh, with some important ideas. Truong Chinh believes that these important ideas, already being discussed with your CIA, could interest you very much. Truong Chinh also would like some help from you, Alex. I am here to explain.'

Bradley remembered Truong Chinh as one of a group

of 'Marxist Mandarins' from scholar-gentry families. He had been a senior theoretician of the party, but fell from grace in 1956. 'So Chinh is once again with power and influence,' he said under his breath. 'But why me?' Vietnam had gone away. it was in the past. For years he hadn't even thought of Vo Dinh and Tan Canh and the battles which had led to Kissinger's Paris agreement of '73 and the final humiliation of the US.

'You come to ask *me* to help Truong Chinh?' he said, as he saw Cai's face beginning to crumble with disappointment at his long silence.

'Not to help Truong Chinh, Alex, to help American prisoners.'

'Are you telling me there are American prisoners *alive* in Vietnam?'

'I am telling you that there are almost seventeen hundred, Alex, and that Truong Chinh already has the beginnings of a deal with the CIA, but we need some help from you.'

Bradley noticed the 'we'. He got up. 'We need a quieter place, Cai. Let's get in my car.'

He drove north-east out of Frankfurt, making for the Vogelsberg, along the line of the river and the railway. He knew he could think and talk better on high ground, and the long, brilliant June day was going to give him time. He needed time. It was the memory of one special colleague that needed time.

He had been the tall, cheerful Foreign Service officer fluent in Vietnamese, seconded in 1965 to John Vann as assistant for the Reinstate pacification plan for Han Nghia province. In January '66 he was ambushed and captured by the Viet Cong while trying to deliver emergency rations to some refugees. Because he had been in plain clothes, in a civilian car, armed with an automatic rifle and carrying a large sum of money with which to pay a building contractor, the Viet Cong assumed he was a member of the detested CIA. In consequence he had spent seven years of purgatory in the Annamite rain forest, most of the time chained to a tree, crippled by beriberi and malaria – the Falciparum variety which attacks the brain. All this he, Bradley, had taken years to piece together.

His friend's suffering had been the direct consequence of being *thought* to be a CIA man. The Viet Cong had seen the CIA as a Gestapo, complete with its full equipment of horror. Bradley was CIA. He had no personal feelings of guilt, but he knew that the link would be exploited, nicely by Cai, not so nicely by Truong Chinh.

'So what's the deal, Cai?' he asked as they left the car and started up the ride between the belts of pines. 'What kind of help is Chinh looking for from me?'

Cai cleared his throat apologetically. 'The deal is very ambitious, Alex; it is an attempt – a very brave attempt I must say – to wipe out the past.'

Alex Bradley stopped and stared at him; the brown eyes were puckered with friendly anxiety, the smile hovered, a small hand, the same one he'd seen hurling those boxes of M16 ammo, was laid on his sleeve.

'It's difficult to be generous after a war, even many years after a war. Sometimes longer time makes even more difficulties for both peoples.' His English was slipping a little as emotion charged his voice.

'OK, Cai, just give me the outline; we can sit and look at the blick. If we could focus for forty miles we would see the wire, the East German frontier, the symbol of another war, Cai.'

'You will remember there was nearly a deal with Nixon; now we build on that foundation, the result will be very good for both countries. I explain as follows.'

Bradley listened. It took some time because Van Cai spoke very carefully. Bradley almost felt like taking notes, and his mind raced on as he assimilated and condensed the basic elements. Vietnam would at last return the prisoners, and the US would cease the covert war still being waged against Hanoi. The US would offer a war reparations programme of several billion dollars, which would bring Vietnam into the capitalist fold and to its people finally justify the war. All drug shipments from Vietnam would cease. Finally, on a somewhat banal note, 'Can you lunch with Truong Chinh in Paris on Friday?'

'Yes, Cai, I can. But first tell me what help *I* can give if this deal is already under way?'

'Truong Chinh knows that you are CIA and have the right influence in Washington. There are many voices in Washington, and many ears to listen; your good offices are important.'

'And more specifically, Cai – more specifically?'

The brown eyes searched his face. 'There has been a very large shipment of heroin to Madagascar. It must be intended for Europe, and if it were to arrive there it would wreck the deal.'

'Because?'

'Because no one in America or Vietnam would then believe there could ever be peace between our two countries; drugs are weapons of war.'

'Drugs come to Europe from many parts of South East Asia.'

'Yes,' said Cai, 'and the enemies of this deal would make very sure that it was known that this *very* large shipment was in fact from Vietnam.'

It was a hot glorious afternoon, hazy towards the east; not the only haze hereabouts, thought Bradley.

They dined together that evening in Frankfurt, and through the reminiscences Bradley's mind beat a tattoo of questions and half-answers. Yes, of course, such a deal – if it came off – would enormously benefit the US administration. Reparations, coupled with the returning of many of the Viet-Kieu (the Vietnamese who had escaped to the States), would turn the country into a market economy; and the resentment over the prisoners, felt by *both* sides, would finally evaporate. But the poison of the drug shipments? A large shipment to *Europe* would look as if the US was saying, And if you *have* to go on with the narcotics trade, flood the *European* market – be our guests. The ultimate in cynicism?

On his way into Paris he thought about Truong Chinh. He well knew that motives in Vietnam were always a mixture of personal relationships, graft and politics. From anyone other than one of the Marxist Mandarins a plan such as this was doomed to failure. But Chinh was of the tiny minority, long-sighted, determined, capable of seeing the formula which would lay to rest the agonies of the war. A paradoxical solution in a sense, similar to Ho Chi Minh's embrace of Communism as a means to rid his country of colonial rule, but a solution nevertheless. He also thought of the drugs embargo. No drugs on the European market must be *known* to have come from Vietnam or through Vietnamese agencies; from Laos, Cambodia, Thailand, of course – but from Vietnam, no. The American people (the Europeans themselves probably wouldn't care) would not stand for that. They had tiptoed down that path before.

Cai and Chinh were sitting in the long foyer of the Ritz overlooking the courtyard. They both got up to greet him, and so, for a moment, as he straightened, Bradley could take in Vietnam's elder statesman's physical appearance. He was small, dressed in the familiar darkish green uniform, the collar of which was a little generous for his neck – advancing years, thought Bradley. The face, genial with a smile which showed not much in the way of teeth, reminded him of Deng Xiaoping. The eyes were scrutinising him in a kindly but beady way.

There were no aperitifs; they went straight into the dining-room and sat down. Some white wine was brought immediately and poured out. They discussed the menu. Conversation was in French, which Alex could handle reasonably well, but it didn't exactly flow, Chinh contenting himself with a few banal observations about how much he hoped to visit the United States. Then, with his mouth full of a particularly rich fruit salad, he patted Bradley's wrist and said, '*J'espère, mon ami, que vous pouviez faire une étude de nos propositions.*'

It was more a question than a statement and rather what Bradley had expected, so he replied, '*Certainement, monsieur, aussi je propose d'ouvrir une discussion bientôt avec mes collegues à Washington.*'

Chinh smiled with satisfaction and signalled to the waiter to bring more wine, a gesture which suggested to Bradley's mind a certain naivety.

Bradley turned to Cai. 'I don't want to ask too much of my French, so would you please tell the minister that, while I find the grand design most attractive – as I'm sure does the White House – I see some practical difficulties in effecting a complete embargo on narcotics shipments from Vietnam to, for example, France; that is to say, without the use of violence. That is one question; the other is, why should *I* be able to help, why, to put it bluntly, should I even want to help, given that you are already talking to Washington and receiving, it seems, a helpful response, perhaps even an enthusiastic response? To lay the war and its memories at last to rest is a splendid goal. It deserves to succeed.'

With profuse apologies for doing so, the two men had a rapid exchange in Vietnamese before Cai turned again to Bradley.

'There are three reasons why we come to you, Alex. They are – *not* in order of importance – first, that you understand our country and our customs. Very few Americans can understand who in Vietnam is to be trusted – who is dealing from the top of the pack. Second, you are very important in the CIA, perhaps because of your Vietnam experience' – which is, of course, why no one in Washington has consulted me about this, thought Bradley as he sipped at his glass of Meursault – 'and therefore you could perhaps help to persuade your colleagues that the covert war from Cambodian bases which they now support with money and arms can never succeed, any more than similar adventure-movie heroics in Latin America.' Cai was waxing, laying it on a bit, Alex thought, but never mind, they'd been over this ground together the other evening. 'Third, your position in Frankfurt, with access to European intelligence agencies, makes it possible – we think – for you to find out which organisation is planning to distribute the very large Madagascar shipment. We would, of course, pay to have it destroyed.'

Yes, with US reparations dollars, thought Bradley.

There was a very long silence while the waiter brought coffee. '*Un cognac, m'sieur?*'

'*Oui, s'il vous plaît.*'

Chinh was scrutinising him carefully; some of the bonhomie seemed to have evaporated. They were good mind-readers, these boys. The conversation returned to banalities, and Chinh's puckish face once more radiated good humour.

Bradley took his leave with a firm 'I'll be in touch' to Cai, made for the Travellers' and some telephone calls, and then for Charles de Gaulle and the earliest available flight for Washington. God, he thought, Susannah and the kids will soon be arriving in Frankfurt.

18

Reynolds Frobisher, although ten years older than Bradley, was a buddy. They had worked together in Latin America, where great respect and a lot of humour had grown up between them. Bradley knew he had to play the game according to the extraordinary CIA rules, based on the concept of 'need to know'. He was well aware that Reynolds, who now had the South East Asia desk, would be wholly ignorant – although very senior in the CIA – of his real mission in Europe. He was further comforted by the knowledge that he was also protected by what was never admitted to be a special presidential interest. So he knew the rules and he didn't expect Frobisher to tell him anything, but there were such things as eyebrows.

Frobisher's office was in a small, comfortable house in Georgetown, its atmosphere evocative of England. Frobisher was Ivy League; his suit and his shoes said so and the good-humoured intelligent face hammered it home. Was he glad to see Bradley?

'Well, well! This is a really good "accident"? (Alex had used the word 'accident' on the telephone; it was an old code they had used in Nicaragua) 'which brings you here, Alex. Just tell me how long for and I'll set up some dinner and get the spare room ready, if that's what you want?'

'That would be just fine, Rey. I have to get back to

Frankfurt tomorrow because I've only got ten days before Susannah gets over for the school holidays.'

'OK, so tell me about the "accident" and we'll talk.'

In a dozen crisp sentences Bradley outlined Cai's visit and his lunch with Truong Chinh as he watched the half-humorous eyes of his attentive friend. He allowed pauses, but there were no questions and the face was as uncommunicative as a New England face could be. (He's getting better at it, thought Bradley; there used to be the odd very quiet sucking-in of breath.) When he'd finished, the silence was positively oriental. It went on and on.

At long last Rey Frobisher put his fingertips together and said quietly, 'Even *your* security clearance doesn't mean you can come to me for comment on a story like that, Alex.'

Bradley stayed silent until what seemed minutes later he heard the words, spoken in a kind of sleep-walking voice, 'Those prisoners loom large in our thoughts.'

Later that evening, as the malt whisky went down, Rey Frobisher said, 'So Chinh believes that Vann's prophecy could come true, that the only effective philosophy for Vietnam is colonialism, as long as its *dollar* colonialism!'

19

One of the telephone calls from the Travellers' had been to Willi Ansbach, asking him to call an urgent meeting at the Moulin. 'An order group, Willi, that's what the Brits call it. And with skates on, Willi, please – if you'll forgive the expression.'

Forbes sighed when he got the message. How Americans love to dramatise, he thought. Still, it would be good to see Josel again – a thought which almost brought another sigh. And the pool would be nice; it was getting hot in London, that early July heat with murmurings of thunder. A quick word with Brock? Heavens no, keep the old bugger at arm's length – he might try and sneak down there himself and 'meet the team', perish the thought. He went out and bought himself some swimming shorts.

Josel flustered a bit. She had just told Bernice she could return to Paris for a week to look after her mother, who'd had a fall. So she was going to have to do the cooking for six of them herself. Thank God there was just time for Bernice to do some shopping and leave a first course already prepared for supper. She too wondered about the American sense of drama.

But forty eight hours later, when the hire-cars had all gathered at the Moulin and Alex had told them in a few brief sentences the burden of his conversation with Truong Chinh, all thoughts that Bradley might have been crying wolf swiftly vanished. There were questions, many questions, but von Heimann stayed the flood by ordering everyone into the pool while Josel and Melkov set about producing a light and very late lunch. Swimming and food did their soothing work and coffee triggered another bout of rather calmer questioning. It went on until more swimming was needed, and so they continued until Bradley and Forbes brought drinks on to the terrace and the analysis began in disciplined earnest.

Von Heimann summarised his thoughts with a question, 'So, what we now have is an ultimatum, yes? These Vietnamese are saying that Jean Louis's heroin must not arrive in Europe, that Alex must find some way of stopping the shipments, and in fact they believe that he can and will ask his CIA friends to stop Jean Louis, or more plainly to kill him. Am I correct?'

'Yes,' said Bradley, 'you are correct, but before that stage is reached they believe that perhaps I can persuade someone to *persuade* Jean Louis that the heroin should stay in Madagascar – anyway for time enough to get a prisoner–reparations deal into the works. In their minds Jean Louis is just another drug-dealer who wants a big profit. When they say they'll pay for the drugs, of course they mean buy him off.'

'And why,' said Forbes, with a touch of hostility in his voice, 'should they imagine that you even know Jean Louis, leave alone well enough to offer him a bribe?'

'You can cut the acid, Archie. Vietnamese firmly believe there is nothing beyond the resources of the CIA, that they have a directory with every drug-dealer's name in it, *and* that they could *instruct* me to go visit Jean Louis and tell him where to jump. Truong knows that I understand the mentality of both the Vietnamese and the CIA. So, from his point of view, who better than me to block any double games? In *his* mind, once Bradley is convinced, Jean Louis's heroin will not leave Madagascar.'

There was a chilly silence. Forbes's thoughts switched – with his eyes – to the faces.

'Hell,' said Bradley, 'don't tense up on me. Chinh doesn't know you people exist!'

The silence grew longer.

Finally Helmut said, 'Of course Jean Louis must be told immediately; he runs the greatest risk. But we should decide *now* how *we* are to deal with this threat, and then give Jean Louis the casting vote.'

'No decisions *or* casting votes, Father, until we have eaten dinner, which I have to cook. Now, who will volunteer to help with the *filets mignons flambés*?'

Sergei was smiling at her side before she finished speaking and they disappeared into the kitchen. Forbes shrugged and got up to pour more drinks.

'A lot depends on Reagan, doesn't it?' He said, 'If we *could* assume that he is privy to *both* schemes then he might make up his mind where the advantage lies as far as the US is concerned.'

'But we can't assume any such thing, Archie,' countered Bradley. 'The CIA tells the President what they think he needs to know, and that's not very much. They know his heart's in Latin America – Communism in his backyard, the nightmare scenario. Then he's a Californian of the "blue water" school, which thinks the eastern seaboard is soft on Europeans. There are plenty of Senator Glenns around who say, "Time these goddam Europeans paid for their own defence." All presidents think most of the time about the American voter, and those missing-in-action boys coming home from Vietnam could swing a lot of votes.'

'Your friends could talk to Jean Louis themselves,' said Forbes. 'They know he bought the heroin, the quantity and who from.'

'Yes they could.' The placatory grin was back on Bradley's face. 'But they reckon a CIA man has more clout.'

Willi asked if anyone thought that seventeen hundred US POWs, *if* still alive, could weigh in the balance against a nuclear response to a Red Army attack in Europe.

Bradley said he thought that American public opinion might attach, because emotional, much greater importance to the prisoner legacy of one war than to the maybe of nuclear weapons in another.

Melkov up to now had remained silent. His slightly oriental cast of feature seemed to give him added authority. 'There is, I think, something of what you call irony in all this. If the American public were told that at last there is a deal which brings Americans home from Vietnam, they would become very emotional, as you say. Also they could become extremely sensitive about US soldiers generally, and clamour very loudly indeed for their army in Europe to be brought home once they realise it has become infected with drugs. All those memories of drug-addicted GIs in Vietnam would come – how do you say? – home to roost. If Truong Chinh knew all this he *might* suppose that his deal and our programme had in essence something in common. But of course that risk cannot be taken.'

'Certainly not,' said Forbes rather sharply, wondering if he had seen a flicker of interest in Bradley's eye, and went back to watching Josel's ankles as she brought more drinks. He thought they looked even more attractive under her cotton skirt than at the end of the long sun-gold legs in the swimming-pool.

'Chinh,' Bradley was saying, 'credits me with the ability to head off the CIA from any kind of clever games my colleagues might be dreaming up – such as the ideas I guess you're half trailing Sergei.'

Archie tried again. 'But on the big wide canvas, Alex, Germany and the future of Europe, peaceful and united, *must* count for more than Vietnam.'

'It's your goddam colonial history makes you say that, Archie boy. Leave the natives to do the best they can, just shove in a garrison and a governor, that's all that's needed to stop the buggers killing each other, old boy' – this last in a fair imitation of a public-school accent. 'We think differently – give the Vietnamese a taste of the American dream (and the war *did* raise their standard of living, believe it or not) and it's next stop China!'

Josel stood in the doorway, eyes sparkling, arms akimbo, in a huge striped apron. 'Ten minutes to the first course, and keep the arguments for after dinner; Papa, keep the peace between these two or they'll start their eighteenth-century war again – or was it a revolution?'

She was looking more attractive by the hour, Forbes thought, more confident, assertive and somehow surprisingly unconcerned at having just heard that one way for *someone* to solve the problem was to kill Jean Louis. Without him, that heroin stayed where it was, guarded by crocodiles and inaccessible, no longer menacing either the US Army of Europe or the MIAs. He went upstairs to put on a silk shirt and linen trousers, and as he did so he teased all the discussions through his mind, including what he knew would follow after dinner. The Germans would like a good excuse to leave NATO, if only to reduce the risk of their country again being a battleground; to be bribed by reunification with the eastern provinces, plus the enormous opportunities for German industry to modernise the Soviet economy, would be irresistible. Then American high-tech investment would follow and eventually, as de Tocqueville had foretold a hundred years ago, the United States and Russia would find in each other natural allies. Chilling? Quite possibly, but if the other scenario (that Kissinger word again) took us to nuclear war, there was no choice. The contribution of the *Erweckung* group was to light the fuse – the Americans would like their army out of Europe, as Bradley had so clearly put it, but hadn't quite found the excuse. A systematic, well-organised programme to hook US garrison troops on drugs, so well publicised that it outraged the American public with echoes of the Vietnam war, was all that was needed.

'Archie!' (Oh God, it was Josel again.) 'What *are* you doing? The first course is on the table and you are in charge of the wine!'

He sped for the stairs which were polished oak, came down fast to where she stood at the bottom and, partly from slipping, mostly by inclination, caught her by the waist and kissed her quickly on the cheek. She slapped his face, laughingly, and disappeared into the kitchen. Forbes poured out the cool Cépage for the first course of *aubergine à la turque* and uncorked – rather late in the day – several bottles of Vacqueras to keep them going throughout what he thought would be a long evening. Ansbach, von Heimann and Bradley filed on to the terrace, glancing a shade apprehensively at gathering clouds. The heat was intense. Despite Josel's efforts conversation faltered; they were all too deep in thought. Someone asked where Melkov was and Josel said, 'Warming up teaspoons of brandy for the *filets mignons*,' and slipped out to join him.

He was dealing with the tomatoes and fried potatoes. 'No need,' he said, 'no need,' smiling, 'we Georgians understand vegetables. One thing please, Josel,' he added quickly. 'If Alex goes to see Jean Louis, as certainly he must, I shall propose to go with him.' And then, as he saw her puzzled look, 'I am quite ignorant of Vietnam but I do know something about murder.' The amused look had gone from his face.

The discussion, or argument, or simply thoughts put into words, swayed round the terrace as the distant storm grew nearer and thunder sporadically drowned the voices. Cheese was followed by *pêches Eugénie* with their topping of golden sabayon, then coffee and much more talk.

Bradley recalled the effects of drugs on the US combat troops in '69, stoned to the edge of mutiny and using their weapons and grenades 'accidentally' against their own officers and non coms. Was it *really* necessary to reduce men to such a shameful mess in order to get the US Army out of Germany? Was there no other way of firing up the American voter?

Forbes had not neglected the whisky bottle before dinner, nor had his wineglass been empty for long. Leaning forward he said, 'You Yanks are always looking for an easy way of doing things. I think that our plan stinks to high heaven on moral grounds but I can see it's the only way, and, however much I hate it, the stakes are high enough to salve anyone's conscience. And you, Alex Bradley had better get yours salved pretty damn quick because first you have to put it fair and square to Jean Louis, and next you have to make sure, with your PR hat on, that American public opinion *does* hit the roof when the time comes. Oh, and one more thing – just make sure that *your* CIA pals don't somehow foul everything up by crossing wires with Chinh's CIA friends.' A roaring crash of thunder drowned the last two words and as it died away, Ansbach expelled his breath with a sigh.

Josel could see, in the flickering candle-light – they had dined absurdly late – Bradley's fingers tightening on his glass and thought he would certainly throw it; but then the whiteness of his knuckles lessened as the studied (and it was *very* studied) drawl made a sort of searching cadence down the table.

'Guess we Americans like to talk things through, look at all points of view, examine the options – you know the jargon – never see things quite so clear cut as you Limeys. It's not having had an empire, I suppose. Funnily enough, you Brits were fighting Ho Chi Minh in 1945 to reinstall the French and, strangest of all, alongside the Japanese! That *must* have been a clear-sighted decision.'

The drawl was jocular now and Josel found herself pressing Forbes's hand, hoping to get the tension out of him. But while the words were slowly finding the good humour in which they ended, Bradley's thoughts were elsewhere.

'Who does the goddam Englishman think he is? What does he know about MIAs who have been kept in sickening conditions for anything up to sixteen years? How does his six months in the British Italian campaign compare with the '68 Tet offensive on Saigon? He was locked up for under a year in a German POW camp; OK, he escaped, but it was easy and he talks about it too much. He's been foisted on us by British Intelligence because he used to work for them – dirty tricks department, I can well imagine,' And here the humour crept back. 'Now he's almost a lush and keeps eyeing the girl. Yes sir, leave him be, he's not worth coming the acid with, leave alone a glass of good wine.'

'Can we now sum up the position?' It was the calm voice of von Heimann and there was just time to catch Forbes's 'Sorry Alex – went too far' before the next crash of thunder made the glasses shiver.

'Alex,' von Heimann continued, 'I think you are probably going to see Jean Louis?'

'Yes, Helmut, tomorrow.'

'And I will meet you out there, Alex,' said Sergei, 'because at least I can bring a pistol in my diplomatic bag.' He smiled at Josel. 'Does Jean Louis have a gun?'

'A hunting rifle is all I can remember.'

'All this means, I think,' said Willi, 'that we are resolved?' There was a murmur of assent and a raising of glasses.

'With the casting vote for Jean Louis,' murmured Bradley, 'and on that casting vote Truong Chinh gets his answer – no deal.'

This time it was von Heimann. 'And why should they believe you, Alex? Will they not go and see for themselves? What *is* this huge importance they attach to the CIA?'

'They believe the CIA to be all-powerful and they think, bless their hearts, my influence to be far-reaching and conclusive. But when they get the message that the merchandise is not for sale they *will* go and see for themselves.'

Josel shivered and, as if in answer, the wind dropped and the rain cascaded down. They all found themselves scuffling up the stone steps to the hall-cum-sitting-room, carrying their brandy and coffee as best they could. Some more coffee appeared. Melkov seemed to have an instinct for this sort of thing. It was pitch-dark outside and blowing again.

Forbes walked across the room to Bradley and said, 'When I get to London I'll find out from Brock if he's picked anything up on *his* CIA grape-vine.'

'OK, Archie, but say nothing about my trip to Washington. It never happened – remember?'

After more brandy, Forbes stumbled off to bed, as did they all, the rain sheeting down now with the sound of thunder dying away and only the occasional distant flicker of lightning. Not a night, he thought, for sitting on terraces and looking at the moon – you old spoil-sport! Time for him to get back to London and that other old cramper of style – the Guru from Ulster, Brockles FitzHerbert.

20

Save Bradley and Josel, they were all gone by nine o'clock on what was a brilliant rain-washed and much cooler morning. Josel and Melkov had given them coffee and baguettes by the pool after early dips, and slowly the hire-cars wound their way down the long drive.

Bradley looked up at Josel from the telephone and said, 'They can get me on a flight early in the morning to Rome, where I pick up the UTA plane for Tananarive. I should get to Nice this evening, so how about a picnic?' He had the map open in front of him. 'I guess Ventoux looks a bit bare, but there's some wild looking country beyond Sisteron. We could find a place to swim – what say you?'

Josel let her head go back as she laughed. It was very attractive, he thought. 'You Americans are never short of ideas – especially for what the English call "polishing the shining hour"! A picnic sounds lovely; I'll find some food and you can look for some wine.'

They lost their way several times, but that didn't matter because they didn't have any way to lose. As the sun grew hotter they dallied more, hoping for a place to swim. Eventually they spotted a cluster of trees under a rock face which promised no more than a longish hot walk. So out of the car they lugged the picnic basket, happy with excitement and the thought of putting brave faces on what could be a hot disappointment.

'This picnic basket's damn heavy,' said Bradley. 'It's the wine.'

'Well, let's drink some,' Josel suggested, and they collapsed in laughter under a solitary Corsican pine. 'Cool and delicious,' she said.

'Like you,' Bradley said.

'Alex, remember we are business partners.' This came out a trifle too severely and they both laughed again.

'You bet,' said Bradley.

They went on, and soon there was the pool with a stream gushing out of the rock above it and heavenly shade all round. 'A swim before lunch!' the words zipped out and in seconds the skirt and shirt had gone and the striped bikini was plunging into the pool with hissing gasps of *'quelle froideur'*. The water was crystal but not deep, so Bradley could only manage a shallow dive under an overhanging rock. There was just enough room in the pool for brisk swimming with feet scratching gravel on the bottom, or floating to watch the wasps and bees hunting with darting movements.

Bradley was out of the water first. He towelled vigorously, then battled with the wine bottle, having pushed the cork in too far. Josel came up the short slope, towel round her waist. Her shirt was on but it was damp and clinging. He abandoned the wine to put up a hand, pulling her down on top of him, their moist bodies welding together. The air of resignation and somehow innocence which he had so often noticed, was gone – this was a Josel with a very different smile. There was a sob, which gave way to a wild gust of joy.

She felt as if a whole coven of witches had just taken wing, together with all their spells, locked inside her by the *fanafouté*, horrors which had seemed to be for all time.

Alex struggled again with the wine bottle, and they splashed each other with it and laughed, hesitant at first, but happier and happier as the birds seemed to dart closer in curiosity. Bradley wished he could remember for ever the mixture of smells, shadows, sunlight, and the gentleness of Josel's touch.

Late that night, from her bed, Josel could see the witches riding across the moon. She shivered, for a moment wondering, Would they come back? But no, they were going even faster and higher and away and away.

21

Bradley and Melkov made their rendezvous at the Hôtel Colbert, Bradley having flown by UTA from Rome and Melkov by Aeroflot from Moscow, as befitted a representative from the Red Star Crucible Factory on a visit to inspect the *gisement* of his new graphite supplier.

They lost no time in hiring a four-wheel-drive vehicle, Josel having telephoned the French embassy with a message for Jean Louis – to be passed on by short-wave radio – to meet at the river jetty *two* Red Star representatives. Jean Louis would be surprised, she thought, but not for long. Not the only thing which would surprise him – her mind wandered back to the picnic and her escape from the witches. That would delight him too. His feelings about Alex Bradley? Well none, probably; they had got on well together at the Moulin – as well as an American and a Frenchman could ever get on! They had common love of wild country and simple people. Enough – she didn't want to think of Alex Bradley; the expulsion of the memory of the *fanafouté* was all that mattered for the moment.

Bradley felt reassured by Melkov's matter-of-factness, which almost reached a disregard for his surroundings. It wasn't long however before the endless change of light and colour brought an exclamation of wonderment, as he grasped the steering-wheel the more firmly in order to look about him. 'Red earth, blue and white sky and every green a painter has ever dreamed of!' Then came a gust of laughter. 'And to think we're here on *business*!'

Jean Lous was at the jetty with his canoe. Bradley quickly explained their mission and got barely more than a shrug in reaction. 'We had better get moving and talk at the *gisement*, the outboard engine is too noisy for talking on the river.' So they chugged in silence, watching the colours change as the sun gave and took away light and life. Twice a raft came sweeping past them downstream, laden with fruit, coconuts and brightly clothed people sparkling with waves and smiles. They kept their course with broad sweeps, and great shouts of laughter rippled across the water.

'They stick to the mid-stream despite their shallow draft because there are always crocodiles near the banks. They go down twice a year to trade and buy clothes and above all hats, and then they walk home through the *brousse* – ten days sometimes.' Jean Louis smiled. It was a nice smile, Bradley thought, a sharing-of-pleasure smile which crinkled the dark eyes and made the beard look like a friendly conspirator.

They tied up at Jean Louis's jetty, got out their hand packs and walked up the 300-yard hill to Jean Louis's house. Although the cool season, it was hot enough. Jean Louis's face crinkled again as he said, 'It's time, I think, for some cold white wine,' and clapped his hands, releasing a scuffle of bare feet belonging to someone clearly listening in the portico. Beaming Malgache faces almost instantly surrounded them, and as Bradley saw the movements of the hips and shoulders of the girls in their multicoloured dresses, he felt a flicker of the magic which had defeated Josel.

Then came a magnificent omelette full of mysterious

fungi and hearts of palm, accompanied by cheese, fruit, red wine and talk. It didn't take long for Jean Louis to say he wasn't interested in Truong Chinh's offer. He just seemed puzzled that an offer should have been made.

'They know I have the drugs because the dealer in Vietnam will have told them that I was the buyer. So why not just come straight here and kill me? Why the warning? Why the bribe?'

'Because,' said Bradley, 'they couldn't be sure that *all* the heroin is still here. Your collaboration would have given them names and destinations in Europe. Also they have an exaggerated idea of the power and competence of the CIA. Had I gone back to them with the offer of a deal, they would have expected my CIA section to *help* them shut down the distribution networks.'

Jean Louis filled their glasses. 'So, my friends, you have come a long way to tell me that if I do not wish to *jouer le jeu*, I can expect to have some difficulty in remaining in good health; *c'est bien que*' – his voice had dropped a little and the smile had become serious – '*le terrain, et peut-être certains des animaux, sont mes alliés*.'

'I brought you this,' said Melkov, a trifle awkwardly, fishing out a useful-looking automatic pistol. 'Josel said you didn't have much in the way of weapons.'

'Thank you very much, *and* thanks also to your diplomatic bag.' He was thumbing the safety-catch and opening the breech in a reassuring way. 'Let's go and practise, I'll get my other pistol.'

They walked into the house for the first time and Bradley felt his eyes widen with surprise and pleasure. This was Josel's house, and it delighted him. The main room, where Jean Louis was scuffling in a chest for his pistol, was immensely high and astonishingly cool.

There was a balcony of dark wooden rails in front of small windows running round two of the walls, which gave the room a subdued light and a faintly cloistered atmosphere belied by the startling colours of the huge cushions on the white-washed stone benches and the Van Gogh and Picasso reproductions on the walls. Bradley didn't feel quite certain that they were *all* reproductions.

They walked out on to another large terrace which was a small forest of stone pillars whose tops were laced and interwoven with a creeper which dangled datura-like flowers in the heavy shade. Then they went out further into sunlight which poured cascades of colour from three or even four stone terraces above the house, bougainvilleas of orange, yellow and snow-white, frangipani with huge spreading yellow-eyed white flowers, scarlet morning glory with yellow throats, and then more pillars, shorter than those on the terrace, entwined with jasmine and the orange trumpets of datura. Altogether it was 'colour in operatic confusion' – as Monet once said of his Rouen façade. And, of course, there were the butterflies – in little circles like over-large haloes. Their movement was almost imperceptible; like airborne ballet-dancers they were an effortless diadem of colour. Josel had talked about them. She had talked a lot about the garden she had left behind.

Jean Louis walked past, towards the hill behind the terraces, a target in one hand and a long-barrelled pistol dangling from the other. He was grinning. Melkov followed, holding his automatic pistol. He waved it encouragingly at Bradley, who fell in behind. Jean Louis was pinning the target to a tree at what seemed to Bradley forty yards away. He called out, 'What's that gun you've got there, Jean Louis?' and heard the faint reply from the striding figure.

'You mean you don't recognise the gun that won the West? Your very own beloved Colt .45!'

'Good grief – where in hell did you get that? I've never seen one before. The long-barrel Colt .45!' He took the pistol from Jean Louis and balanced it in one hand.

'I got it from an American friend who had had some replicas made – exact replicas. It shoots well; try it.'

Bradley cocked and fired – no recoil, or anyway virtually none. He fired again and walked forward to the target. Two neat holes, not bull's-eyes but certainly inners, and he had held the pistol in one hand.

'No wonder John Wayne hit so many of those Indians,' he said, and walked back to the terrace, leaving Melkov to give Jean Louis a lesson on the Russian automatic.

He stretched out on a low bamboo chair and wondered if his host would think it odd if he dozed off. He looked at the dark comforting green of the low hills round whose contours water channels carried the graphite down to the simple refinery of mechanised sieves below Jean Louis's house.

He was damned if he would think any more about Josel.

They woke him up with some ribald stuff about CIA men falling asleep at the switch. It was dark, with a rising moon partially obscured by cloud. There was a cacophony of insects. Sergei and Jean Louis dropped into chairs one either side of him, still chuckling like schoolboys. In the near distance there was laughter and voices, girls' voices and the swishing sounds of leaves and undergrowth.

'They're going down to fetch water to wash your shirts,' said Jean Louis.

'Buckets of water, all the way from the river?' said Melkov. 'What a business.'

'Not buckets, large bamboos, four inches in diameter and two to three yards long – very good for carrying water. They walk slowly backwards into the river, lowering the bamboo between their legs to the angle where it fills up.' He caught his breath slightly and sat up. 'That's funny – they're quiet. *C'est curieux.*'

There was a piercing scream, then another. Jean Louis was out of his chair and moving like a sprinter off his chocks. All they heard him say before the black shadow dived off the terrace and their reflexes had them plunging after him was, *'Merde – crocodile!'* The track was just visible in the moonlight and they flung themselves down it, just able to see Jean Louis plunge into a group by the water's edge, a sobbing and moaning group which parted for him and left him for a moment a bending, then kneeling figure, his black and white check shirt distinctive, his back motionless as he did something with his hands.

Bradley, who had been just behind the nimble Melkov, then saw something which made him stop. He had no intention of stopping, there was nothing conscious in his sudden freezing. It just happened the moment his eye glimpsed a movement off to the left of the track, on slightly higher ground, perhaps a little less covered with vegetation and perhaps eight or less paces from the group of figures, most of whom were almost prostrate. But Bradley wasn't taking any of this in; what had imprinted itself on his eye was the raised arm and the knife. The posture of an arm about to throw a knife had been stamped in his mind in Vietnam; it had a certain immobile elegance about it, a frozen promise which moonlight exaggerated almost to beauty. He fired, and almost immediately heard a heavy crash which gurgled. He had forgotten that he was carrying the Colt, part of that grab a gun reflex of years before. He went forward quickly and fired again, this time at the back of the head.

Now there was suddenly more screaming and yelling, this time from the house, and Jean Louis shot past him shouting, 'Bravo, bravo,' followed by a hissing Melkov, automatic in hand

'*C'est Colombe, c'est Colombe.*' The shouts grew nearer as the three men raced up the path to the paved yard outside the house, where a crowd had gathered, a motley of *gisement* workers, women, and, of course, by this time, children. There was much shouting and pointing, and some people were lighting hurricane lamps.

'*Colombe – il est disparu – deux hommes, un camion peut-être, nous ne savons pas.*'

Jean Louis was shaking them one by one to get some sense out of them, then he held up his hands. '*Attention, attention.*' They could hear the grumbling murmur of a vehicle.

Jean Louis had grabbed the automatic from Melkov and jumped for the cab of his camionette before the other two had started to leap for the tail-board. They made it. Bradley couldn't remember when the back of a truck had been such misery. He and Melkov were like snooker balls, and the spare wheel a loose cannon which smashed them off any momentary handhold which they managed to grab on the sides or the tail-board. Eventually they clung together and let the spare wheel do its worst. The track was jeepable, but not at Jean Louis's present speed, and the truck swung over steep edges while the four-wheel drive clawed it back to a more or less centre line. It was brilliant driving but they were not gaining; that much they could judge from the flickering lights of the vehicle ahead, momentarily visible as their angle changed or they plunged down a slope.

Melkov started banging on the roof of the cab and shouting, 'Stop, stop,' and a stream of imprecations. He had somehow managed to lock his legs round the heavy spare wheel and they were therefore cannoning more slowly, although every bit as painfully. Bradley heard him shout, 'They will kill him if we get close. You stupid bastard, they will kill him. Let them go. Use your head, let them go.'

The camionette lurched to a halt and Jean Louis got out, holding the automatic. Bradley thought he would blow Melkov's head off, so black was the passion in the man's eyes and in the trembling of his body. The Russian walked slowly forward, and gently raising his right arm placed his hand just below Jean Louis's left ear and held it there motionless. It was man speaking to unreasoning animal fury. The eyes stopped flickering and the teeth bared. Jean Louis's head went back and a laugh of sheer relief bellowed into the moonlight.

'You are right, Russian bastard, you are right.' Two arms went round two shoulders. 'Colombe will lead them a dance, whatever they do to him, and he knows that I will get to the caves before them. Come on, we must grab some, how do you say? kit, and take the short route.'

'First I must look at that body,' said Melkov. 'How much time do we have by the short route?'

'We need all of six hours and with Colombe's directions they will need eight, so forty minutes from now we must start. You can examine the body while Alex and I put some things together. Yes, I too would like to know something about that man and thank you, Alex, for your good shooting.'

He was in high good humour again and Bradley began to think there had been no bullshit in Melkov's training on the human psyche.

Ten minutes later Melkov and Bradley were on the terrace examining, with hurricane lamps and torches, the now naked body of the would-be assassin. Despite many such post-mortems in Vietnam, Bradley found it revolting in its thoroughness. Melkov was minutely scrutinising the area of the huge exit wound on the chest and was no less meticulous over arms, legs, abdomen, crutch. The face was virtually blown away. He motioned to Bradley to pull the legs apart, then gave a satisfied grunt, pointing with the torch beam to the inside of the left groin. Bradley peered. all he could see was a small tattoo mark which looked somewhat like a wheelbarrow being pushed by a man. 'Enough,' said Melkov, 'I will explain on our journey.'

'Hurry, you two.' Jean Louis's voice came from behind. 'The truck is loaded, there is kit for both of you and here is coffee for the long hours; three jammed in front, I'm afraid, and we share the driving – OK? We'll make it by dawn and form a plan as we go.'

The moon was well up and Bradley saw jerricans strapped in the back and the spare wheel firmly moored. Jean Louis thrust a hunting rifle at him saying, 'There are clips at the back of the cab, but we may need it in a hurry, like your pistol.' And the grin was firmly back on his face.

'Tell about the tattoo, Sergei,' said Bradley once Jean Louis's gear-changing had simmered down a bit.

'This man was Spetsnatz; the tattoo doesn't say that, it says he was Blatnog Mir, a Russian criminal society. Most of them were in the Gulag, responsible for torture and liquidation of political prisoners. Spetsnatz recruited some of them from the Gulag but about a dozen or so deserted about two years ago and joined the Foreign Legion. It is *very* difficult to desert from Spetsnatz, but the Legion, which gives complete change of identity, is a good way. Then they deserted from the Legion and became entrepreneurs!' Melkov was shaking with laughter. 'You can't be two years in the Legion and not learn some French!'

Jean Louis growled in sympathy.

'I know about these men,' Melkov went on. 'We have been looking for them. Now, of course, they are working for Truong Chinh, and the man you shot would be the leader, I guess. That leaves three; they like four-man teams. They are rather special, the Blatnog, descendants of thieves from the Middle Ages. The wheelbarrow tattoo is of a Gulag prisoner wheeling stones,' he added inconsequentially. 'They will not be nice to Colombe.'

After three hours' skidding, twisting and diving for the outside edge of the track, which often enough seemed to hurl them back to some rough centre of gravity, they stopped for coffee and a plan. It took some hammering, that plan, because the major unknown centrepiece was, How much has Colombe told them?

'Oh, while we're talking, Jean Louis,' said Bradley, 'what the hell was happening on the river bank before we got there?'

'When the girls go down to the river with those bamboo poles I told you about, they are sometimes grabbed by a crocodile as they back into the water. They know the risk and they are very stupid about it. When I heard the scream I thought it was a crocodile. But when I found the girl, her throat had been cut.'

'So it was to draw us off in order to grab Colombe, and of course to kill you, Jean Louis,' said Bradley.

'Exactly. And having *not* killed Jean Louis – because

they have lost their leader they must know Jean Louis is alive – they must find and destroy the heroin; that would be the mental process, I guess,' said Melkov 'And we must finish them off.'

The plan had to be simple, and it was. They would not ambush the Blatnog near the inflatable, because that would be expected. The ambush must be *in* the cave, from a ledge close, but not too close, to that which housed the pile of double plastic sacks containing the heroin. The inflatable would just hold four, of which Colombe would be one. They would use injections to keep him conscious enough to lead them, but even he didn't know the exact ledge with the pile of sacks. Jean Louis was sure that, when the shooting started, Colombe would slide into the water, trusting his luck with the crocodiles.

'Why should he have any luck with the crocs?' asked Bradley.

'He might; they're funny creatures, and his black skin could help.'

'That's a nice way of telling *us* what to expect,' said Melkov, in the voice of a man for whom the unexpected always happens. 'Especially,' he added, 'as we're going to have to swim through them – am I right?'

Jean Louis nodded. They would swim about a quarter of a mile, towing the paddle-pool inflatable, which they had in the truck, loaded with their boots, helmets, Petzl lights, pistols and the hunting rifle. Their polyester and cotton boiler suits would be cached and they would wear swimming trunks.

'Just one more question about these goddam crocodiles,' said Bradley. 'Assuming they are there – and you tell us they *could* be because it's the dry season and they like the cave's humidity – and we don't stir them up on the way in, but Blatnog *do*, how do we cope on the way home?'

Melkov looked pleased; this was his question too.

'You shoot them in the mouth,' said Jean Louis.

The truck slugged its way through the night, the three men taking turns at the wheel, waking up Jean Louis for directions when the track divided, sleeping on each other's shoulders, too bumped-about and swaying to have much in the way of private thoughts.

Sergei did manage to ask one more question. 'How do you suppose the Blatnog arrived on the island, Jean Louis?'

'Up the Betsiboka river, I expect, by the same route as the heroin. In fact the drug-smuggler probably shipped them in!'

22

Dawn found them below the north-west facing cliffs of the Ankarana Massif, with the truck well hidden in a deep ravine, even though they were still a couple of miles from where Jean Louis expected Colombe to take the Blatnog.

Red-eyed and stiff, they did some stretching exercises and Jean Louis laid out the kit.

'I guess the boots will not be too comfortable,' he said, 'as I didn't know your sizes, but its only a two-mile walk.'

'You know the Marquis de Sade was a Frenchman, don't you, Sergei,' said Bradley as Jean Louis threw a boot at him.

They undressed and dressed again in swimming-trunks and the boiler suits and sun-hats. Jean Louis had thought of belts and sheath-knives, also pistol holsters and French Army water-bottles. There were even light packs for the helmets and lamps and the inflatable's gas-bottle. He slung the hunting rifle and Bradley the baby inflatable and they were off, picking their way across the *tsingy*, which was already beginning to heat up. Surplus clothing was slung in the back of the truck.

After three hours of mostly silent cursing they reached a large depression, and there below huge boulders was the river. They could also see the canvas-sheltered inflatable left by Jean Louis, conspicuous enough in the open, some three hundred yards away. So they were ahead of their prey. The thought of the water – albeit at over seventy degrees – spurred them on despite fatigue, and soon they were ready for it, boiler suits and sun-hats hidden, with the torturer's boots, under boulders. The baby inflatable was gassed up, weapons and water-bottles were loaded, and into the warm, dark, gently flowing water they went. In minutes they were in a vast cave which still had shafts of sunlight, and then all was dark except for Jean Louis's helmet lamp. The humidity made breathing difficult; all three men were now calling on their reserves of strength, and the prospect of a crocodile, or even a swoop by a leaf-nosed bat, did nothing for their imaginations.

Eventually, when even Melkov's training had been fully tested, they were heaving themselves on to a ledge covered in what Jean Louis explained was desiccated guano.

'Drink some water,' he said, 'and make yourselves comfortable. Don't shoot before I do,' he added, taking the Finnish Sako Vixen from its case.

Alex Bradley dangled his legs over the edge of the rock and practised drawing the Colt from its canvas holster. He didn't want to sit with it in his hand for fear that physical exhaustion would cause him to let it slip. He felt he might even drop off to sleep; after all, these Blatnog could run late – Jean Louis had spoken of a two-hour advantage. Bradley didn't like ambushes whoever the bad guys were. He'd set up plenty in Vietnam with John Vann, successful and unsuccessful, but he'd never got used to the idea – it was somehow un-American. He knew that was crazy thinking, but it always came back. These men would have automatic weapons; Jean Louis was going to let the range close;

surprise was their only advantage. More thoughts flickered through his mind.

Come on, Bradley, take a pull on yourself, you'll feel better when you see the black man slide into the water; at least he knows what to expect. But could he have warned them? No, because his only hope of staying alive is the surprise which lets him slip into the water. They would make him paddle, of course – no engine, of course no engine; Jean Louis wasn't going to leave them an engine, for God's sake.

His mind was in half turmoil, half unconsciousness; he slipped into a doze. He was woken by a click. Hell no it couldn't have been a click, it must have been some kind of tuned reflex – whatever that might mean – the click of Jean Louis's helmet light and an almost simultaneous crack from the Sako Vixen, followed by another. As he got off two shots from the Colt he could see the three men – or anyway two of them – leaning backwards to get their machine-pistols to an angle of fire, but Jean Louis's position of advantage on the ledge was too well chosen; and now, with all three helmet lights on and three weapons firing, they didn't stand a chance.

Bradley just caught sight of Colombe, crouching like an animal, an animal which had already accepted death, before he slipped into the water. He had not been rowing. Now the three other bodies were in the water, the inflatable was a crumble of rubber and slatted flooring, and there were darkening stains, getting steadily bigger, in the water. They sat and watched and waited and hoped for a sign of Colombe. Then out of range of the lights came a thrashing noise and the feeling, rather than the sound, of water being pushed away; then, still out of range because the bodies were drifting, a crunching noise of sickening contentment.

After an hour of searching from the inflatable the surface of the dark, slowly flowing water, Jean Louis said in a low voice, 'So – let's go.'

They found the Blatnog truck about a mile away on the Route Grim. There was a lot of blood in the back, which they scrubbed out with water and brushwood, but otherwise no trace of the occupants, despite a careful search by Melkov.

'The natives will write them off as crocodile-poachers,' said Jean Louis, 'which in a sense they were.'

After an hour's sleep in the shade of a tamarind tree, and a meal of bananas, chocolate and beer, they set off for the *gisement* and the sad faces which somehow knew already of Colombe's death.

23

'Of course they'll have another go, Archie boy, you realise that?' Brock had voiced no objection to a grilled Dover sole, which he was now washing down with a Sancerre rosé Forbes had thought might be a touch too delicate for the Ulster nose but which was proving a great success. They were in a cubicle in Wheeler's in Swallow Street, not completely secure, of course, but good enough for the staccato conversation which went with enjoying food. Forbes was host, thanks to Ansbach's very practical suggestion that there could be nothing wrong with 'keeping our CIA link in good working order'.

'Damn nice of you to give me lunch incidentally, I get very bored with clubs. But you haven't done much communicating lately, have you? I suppose there's been a touch of keep the old bugger at arm's length for a bit – eh?'

The eyes were twinkling now as the hand went out again for the glass (getting a bit gnarled, Forbes was thinking unkindly).

'Dangerous game, old fruit, dangerous game. I might want to tell you something, and if I rang Zulka in your absence, she'd probably see me off!'

He started laughing, as if he rather enjoyed the prospect, which Forbes knew that he did, because if he made Zulka angry enough on the telephone, she would have to have lunch with him to tell him she didn't really mean it.

'Getting down to business, Brock' – the Sancerre was disappearing faster than ever. I've given you all the Truong Chinh background, and the decision at the Moulin to send Alex to Madagascar –

'And Sergei – don't forget Sergei,' Brock interrupted with a chuckle. 'Get on with it,' he said.

'Sergei and Alex are now back from Madagascar, and Josel reports that some thugs tried to kill Jean Louis, which they failed to do; then they tried to find the heroin but were finished off by Sergei, Alex and Jean Louis. "Good for them", came the reaction, but who were these thugs? We assume they were sent by Truong Chinh – who had promised to wait for an answer.'

'Promised is a big word, Archie.'

'So what do you want me to do?' He tapped the bottle of red wine which had arrived with the Brie. 'This is excellent, and excellence always has a purpose.' And he sighed.

'Persuade your CIA chums to persuade their Asian desk to haul off Truong Chinh,' said Archie Forbes with a glimmer of hope in his voice.

Brock sighed again, heavily this time. 'Archie, I never tire of telling you that the CIA is riven with factions. Each one believes it has the ear, trust and confidence of the President and/or the Secretary of State, the National Security Advisor and above all, God Almighty. They thrive on going their own separate ways, in the belief, not always mistaken, that come the day, the President will pick the winning ticket from his hatband; the ticket which pulls in the most votes. the dream ticket, of course, is the one which pulls in the votes *and* gives the high-tech and defence industries what *they* want. They're mining a rich seam now called the defence programme, plus an even richer one to come, an absurdity called Star Wars; and they're looking ahead. They want a big propaganda coup to launch themselves into new big markets: Russia, East Europe, Asia. They don't want to believe in MIAs, it's the markets they're after. On balance, your *Erweckung* plan probably has the edge because American spending on the defence of Europe is very unpopular on Capitol Hill – ask Senator Glenn!'

'For God's sake stop calling it *my* plan, Brock. I'm your damned conscript, remember?'

They were walking now and Brock was swinging his umbrella ferrule at discarded paper on the Duke of York steps.

'You need a spike on the end for that job,' said an irritated Forbes.

'And you need one up your arse,' came the reply. 'Has it not crossed your tiny mind that, while that heroin is for the time being very safely hidden, another attempt on Jean Louis, this time successful, puts it virtually beyond the reach of man? Has it not also occurred to you that friend Chinh has by now probably identified the whole of your fun group (with the possible exception of A. Forbes) by the simple method of asking himself who are the close associates of Jean Louis's ex-wife, who lives in Paris and is an obvious possible link with a European narcotics pedlar? The housekeeper in Paris disappears from time to time to the Midi to the house where many hire-cars arrive for short visits – right?'

'Then why exclude me?' said Forbes peevishly.

'Oh, don't be offended, dear boy,' Brock said, giving Forbes a hug and drawing an odd look from a passer-by. 'They probably think you're just soppy about the girl – that's the way I'd play it, anyway, if I were you.'

They were passing Wellington Barracks and Forbes thought he noticed a stiffening of his companion's back. Fighting the last war? Our classic mistake? Could the old sod really know what he was about? he wondered. But the mellow voice resumed.

'I suggest, for safety's sake, that you move, say, half of the stuff to your safe house in Germany. My feeling – don't say I said so – is that the programme could be accelerated by the Kremlin. The head of the KGB is a very active and imaginative fellow called Mikhail Gorbachov, who seems to want to push ahead. Goodbye, old boy – thanks for lunch, hope it was worth it.'

With that he was gone, negotiating the island opposite the little shop and then off across the grass triangle beside Buckingham Palace. A spring in his step and – Forbes hadn't the slightest doubt – humming a little tune.

It was time to call Josel.

24

Josel was crisp and to the point – 'Be at the Moulin, if you possibly can, by lunch-time tomorrow. We have much to discuss.'

'Can you give me any more background?' he asked.

'No, I can't.' And click – she was gone.

Bradley fared no better, except that she added, 'You could call your Vietnamese friend.'

'I've never stopped trying,' said Bradley rather sulkily. 'Stupid cow,' he muttered, and tried again.

A man's voice answered 'Yes?'

'Van Cai, is that you?' There was a click and silence. Bradley was getting damn tired of clicks, and tried the number again.

'Yes?' It was the same voice.

'Can I speak with Monsieur Van Cai?' asked Bradley politely.

'Van Cai is dead,' said the voice. And then silence.

'Can you please tell me – ' Click.

It was very hot at the Moulin as they arrived between twelve and two in different stages of weariness after long hours of driving. Lunch was pâté of boar's liver with a salad, followed by goat's cheese. They ate lugubriously, in some anxiety; although Bradley and Melkov had given a faithful account of their adventures and the successful outcome, the chilling finality of

Bradley's telephone call to Van Cai's number seemed to leave a crackle of question marks in their minds which even the Château Simone was having difficulty in turning into words.

Why was he dead? Who had killed him? Why hadn't they waited for Bradley to get in touch? Could they have heard what had happened in the crocodile caves? Did Chinh know who was in this group? Jean Louis, of course, and Josel, naturally, and therefore, perhaps, her father?

Bradley turned to Josel. 'Your father is coming today, I imagine?'

'Yes, of course. My mother telephoned early this morning to confirm.'

'He is quite late,' said Melkov, looking at his watch. 'It doesn't take so long to get here from Munich.'

So they got on with their business, which was to discuss Brock's recommendation – almost more than a recommendation, in fact – to move half Jean Louis's cache of heroin to Germany as soon as practicable because the coming winter and spring could be, and probably would be, the critical period. There was no demur. When they had finished Willi remarked that he had telephoned Helmut the previous evening to suggest they might travel together, but that Helmut had said he wanted to visit the bank in Zurich on the way home. This added nothing to their knowledge and only seemed to increase Josel's sense of foreboding.

Bradley said he would have a quick swim then set off for the crucible factory in Grossalmerode to prepare them for a shipment of 'graphite'. He too felt ill at ease; it was obvious from Forbes's expression that he had realised that Bradley and Josel had arrived the previous evening. It was the look of a man who was expecting trouble, who might even welcome trouble.

The tension probably explained Josel's school-marmish behaviour. She was uncomfortable too. They were all uncomfortable.

Willi was examining his nails. Josel went up the stone steps to telephone her mother. She came back and said, 'He left at six o'clock.'

Bradley said his goodbyes, aware that his voice was sulky and that his face probably showed how much he wanted to grab Josel, race her down to his car and take her with him. Forbes's wave was barely civil; damn clever these Limeys, he thought, getting hostility into a wave. It was three o'clock.

They all swam, and Forbes, as he crawled up and down at top speed, asked himself how, at a time like this, he could only think about Josel's figure. *At a time like this*? What did that mean? Nothing had happened; Helmut was late, that's all. Dashka had said he left at six. He wouldn't stop to telephone, he wasn't that sort of man. So why the tension, what was the matter with everybody?

It was half past three. Bernice appeared on the steps, waving and miming telephone. Josel ran. God, thought Forbes, that girl moves beautifully. He, Melkov and Ansbach went on swimming, but it was desultory now. Josel appeared on the steps and beckoned. They climbed out, made their way to the terrace and sat down in towels and puddles.

'They've kidnapped him,' she said, and sat down as if the news had become a physical weight. Willi took her hand. Archie lent forward. 'What did she say, your mother?'

'She said they had just telephoned and told her that she could find him at Telouet in Morocco.'

'The Dar Glaoui,' said Forbes suddenly and unexpectedly. He got up. 'May I telephone your mother?'

'Of course.'

He held out his hand for the telephone number. Willi gave him a card and he was gone.

'Can you tell me what he said and how he said it?' Forbes asked when Dashka answered the telephone.

'Yes, I can,' she said in a clear controlled voice. A man telephoned last night after Helmut had gone to bed and said, "Please tell your husband to bring his passport tomorrow." That was all. I thought it was perhaps Sergei because the accent was rather strange, almost but not quite French. Anyhow, I forgot the whole thing because Helmut always has his passport in his briefcase. When the same voice rang ten minutes ago and said, "Telouet – en Maroc," I tried to ask, "Where? When? Why?" He hung up.' Now her voice was getting shaky.

'Try not to worry, Frau von Heimann, we are going straight there now. Willi will give you all the details later this afternoon ....' But the line was dead. Dashka's moment of bravery was over.

On his way back to the terrace he decided what he had meant by *going straight there now.*

'Willi,' he called out, 'if you could speak to the bank and tell them to foot the bill, we should be able to charter a plane at Avignon and be in Marrakech by midnight.'

He felt better; he was in command now, and action was the best therapy. He felt zest. Thank God bloody Bradley isn't here, he thought.

'Do you want me?' asked Sergei, looking up.

'No thanks, Sergei. I would love it, but you're a Soviet military attaché, remember – that could be awkward in a place like Morocco. I think Josel and I can cope,' he added, sounding humble for a moment and looking at the girl.

She nodded woodenly and said, 'I'll go and dress.'

For an hour or more Forbes and Willi flogged the telephone, and by five o'clock Josel and Forbes were on their way to Avignon airport, where they had chartered a Jetstream turboprop to fly to Marrakech. They had booked rooms at the Mamounia. He had called Brock, luckily finding him at home, and asked if he could persuade the embassy in Rabat to lend him some sort of weapon, 'a stalking rifle, if that's all they've got – I don't want to feel completely unprotected.' He had given Brock a brief account of their probable mission and listened, with what he thought was exemplary patience, to the explosions at the other end of the line.

'This is James Bond stuff, you idiot. No, it's worse than that, you've been reading Bulldog Drummond. I always knew you were an overgrown schoolboy. What do you imagine the embassy will think when they hear about a madman called Forbes setting off for Dar Glaoui with a stalking rifle?'

'Well, you *could* remind them that I once did an attachment with them on your behalf.'

There has been a long silence. 'All right, Forbes, you win.'

'Thanks, Brock, but on *no* account mention Dar Glauoi.'

He had looked up at that point and found Sergei grinning and holding out a large sheath knife.

At half past six they were airborne and enjoying, or at least Forbes was, a large glass of whisky. Josel looked numb. After a second glass of white wine he got her to talk a bit about what Bradley and Jean Louis had seen and done in Madagascar, but when she spoke about the caves she faltered, and Forbes guessed that Bradley had not said a great deal about how their mission had ended.

'They were marvellous, those two guys,' he said.

For a moment the dark brown eyes narrowed in suspicion, and then there was the hint of a smile. 'You English!' she said and put out a hand.

The stewardess brought omelettes, red wine and cheese, and as they finished eating they sat in wonder at the giant white-crested waves of the High Atlas under the sapphire blue of the southern sky at night.

On arrival at the Mamounia, Josel went straight up to bed while Forbes checked with the hall porter that the hire-car would be ready at 6 a.m., together with a simple picnic and bottles of water and brandy, and blankets for von Heimann, should he still be alive. Finally the man handed him a package, heavy for its size and so carefully wrapped it could have had British embassy stamped all over it.

'I had to sign for this, sir. Would you please do the same?'

Forbes asked for a glass of whisky to be brought to him by the pool, and walked out to enjoy the huge ramparts of the mountains. As he sat, the Smith & Wesson .38 on his lap, trying to wrench his mind from von Heimann, he thought that James Bond was better organised on the whole *and* even had quite a lot of fun. At least he would have been provided with a weapon which could hit a barn door at twenty yards. Well, perhaps there wouldn't be an ambush, perhaps Chinh's men would assume they had alerted the Moroccan police? Or perhaps they thought that the kidnapping of Helmut von Heimann would be a sufficient deterrent? But who did they think they were deterring? Who else was on their list, and how had they got there?

'Unanswerable questions,' Archie said to himself, 'always mean that it's time for bed.'

25

'The hand of Allah lies heavy upon Telouet.'
Negro Slave

Josel appeared calm and refreshed in the morning, sensibly dressed in khaki shirt and slacks and what looked strong, but not too heavy, boots. She had had time to pack some clothes; Forbes hadn't. He had grabbed a spare shirt from Willi and some extra socks from Sergei, plus a razor. He felt vaguely apprehensive and wished he were ten years younger. James Bond had faded.

'It's about two and a half hours' driving,' he said, 'would you do the first hour while I study the map?'

'Yes, and you can tell me more about this place, Telouet, and perhaps we can work out why they have taken my father there and what we might expect.'

The last words were in the rising pitch of a question and Forbes thought, I'm expecting an awful lot of this girl.

They set off, with Forbes fumbling with the map and the guidebook thoughtfully provided by the embassy. 'I'll start,' he said, 'by reading to you what Pliny said about one of the Atlas mountains: "Such is the most fabulous mountain in all Africa. Surrounded by sand, it lifts up towards heaven, rugged and barren on the side facing the ocean, but covered with thick shady forests and gushing streams on the side which faces Africa."'

'What does it say about Telouet?' she asked. 'I mean the guidebook, not Pliny' – this with a sideways glance.

He read on. ' "Telouet . . . in the upper valley on the Oued Immarene . . . the Dar Glaoui, former residence of Thami El Glaoui, Pasha of Marrakech, built towards the end of the nineteenth century and stands on a hill looking down on the Oued Immarene. It consists of a principal enclosure with several courtyards surrounded by crenellated walls which give a quite singular appearance to the whole structure." '

'Now tell me how *you* remember it?'

He was silent for some moments, pretending to be searching the guidebook but in reality thinking of Glaoui's dungeons 'from which no human being had ever emerged, alive or dead'. Helmut von Heimann would be dead, even if they found him. He was sure of that.

'Glaoui was a mediaeval-style baron who brought together the warring Atlas tribes and ruled Morocco for almost forty years within French hegemony. Telouet was his fortress, his kasbah in the Atlas, the source of his power and authority. He was ruthlessly civilised. Churchill admired him.'

'And de Gaulle?'

'I don't know about de Gaulle, but I know the French had every reason to be grateful to him.'

'What happened in the end?' she asked. She knew that he was temporising, putting off the difficult part of the conversation, and she felt rather grateful.

'Oh, he was discarded; he was a dagger and daggers are always discarded. Don't you have a word in French – *glaouisé*, meaning betrayed?'

'*Bien sûr*,' she answered unthinkingly.

'He died in 1956,' said Forbes, although she hadn't

asked. He pointed out a large jay-like roller bird sitting on the telegraph wire, with glorious light azure plumage and bright russet back; then, suddenly swooping on a grasshopper, it showed flashing blue wings edged with black.

Slowly they climbed into a mountain world of villages, poised, it seemed, for flight from some sharp promontory. The heat of the day was giving way to mountain coolness as more and more trees covered the red sandstone, ilex and thuya, firs and juniper. Forbes was explaining that Theophrastus had called thyine wood the *arbor vitae* when he felt her hand in his and heard her say very softly, 'He'll be dead, Archie, won't he – *if* we find him?'

'Yes,' he said in a matter-of-fact voice. 'Now watch out for the hairpin bends.' But he'd tightened his fingers round hers.

In Taddert they stopped and drank some mineral water while they watched village elders drinking mint tea and playing draughts. It was cool and pleasant, and they lingered, listening to the song of the blue rock thrushes and wondering in silence.

'You didn't tell me what you thought of this Glauoi kasbah,' she said. 'You were going to.'

'Yes – well, it's a ruin of a Xanadu, a mixture of ego and despotism. It reeks of power and ruthlessness. It is huge and crumbling but somehow it seems to be telling you its story, as if there was a heartbeat somewhere. Someone once called it a "tower of tragedy".'

He hesitated, it was *too* dark a picture he was painting. There was a long silence. She looked up at the red hills with their green shelves of crops. 'Is that why they're taking us there – because it's so frightening?'

Forbes took over the driving, and the hairpin bends took over from him. Soon they were on the Tizi

N'Tichka pass, and he concentrated on the road, although longing to look at the sheer drops on either side. The Wagnerian landscape of changing rock colours was in the literal sense breath-taking; it was a relief as well as an anti-climax to find the turning off to the left for Telouet.

As they bumped along the apology for a metalled road Josel asked, 'How much further?'

'About ten miles,' he said, and looked up at the 12,500 feet of the great Jebel Ghat ahead of them to the east.

Josel fell into a reverie, asking herself what lay ahead. Not just the kasbah, for she was beginning to come to terms with the thought of finding her father's dead body, nor the prospect of consoling her mother, nor nursing some feeling of guilt for having so strongly encouraged her father in what now seemed a wild venture. No, it was the sickening possibility that the whole of their team would be annihilated, one by one, and her father's dream, which was Willi's dream and the dream of the 'good ones', Juris Wolfmannis and Sergei, would die for ever. Isn't it curious, she thought, that men will die for a dream while women will make sacrifices for men's right to do so; the dream itself for them being a lesser thing. Perhaps not fair to Joan of Arc, she rebuked herself. Then the kasbah came into view, sitting on its plateau of desert scrub circled by the giant peaks of the Massif Central. It looked vast, and desolate, and unbelievably threatening. All it needs, she thought, are birds of prey – and I'll bet it's got those too.

Forbes stopped just outside the outer courtyard, pointing out a row of a dozen huge garages where Glaoui had kept his Bentleys and Rolls-Royces, and said he would find the guardian. He disappeared into what looked like an orchard, and emerged two or three minutes later with a youngish man whose clothes had vague military pretensions and who was carrying the most enormous ring of keys and studying with the immense care of total incomprehension a piece of paper which Forbes was stuffing under his dark, handsome nose.

'An ex-Spahi corporal,' said Forbes, 'and luckily he can't read or he would realise that a compliment slip from the British embassy doesn't give one access to a dog kennel. It's the royal arms which do the trick, though.'

The huge gates to the inner courtyard had been swung open now, and they advanced, wondering how they could search such a place, and already aware that their guide would be of little use. He was three paces behind them, clutching under his djellabah the vast sum in French francs which Forbes had pressed into his hand when first waking him from his siesta in the orchard.

'I've told him why we're here, that we've come to find your father who was kidnapped. But he won't be the slightest use to us. He hardly knows the place himself it's so vast, and nobody ever comes. The men who brought your father threatened to kill him, and he is too frightened even to describe them.'

'How *are* we going to search this awful place,' she said.

'God knows – just walk and walk and call and call. The ground floor is the best bet – above the dungeons.'

But it wasn't on the ground floor where they heard the faint answering call. It came, on a stone staircase, from a tiny oubliette let into the wall, invisible but for half a missing step. They must have climbed that staircase half a dozen times, Josel calling in a deliberately high pitch. They had tried to concentrate on the ground floor, but the courtyards and alleys and stair cases were all designed to lead to the great main reception rooms, which were all on the first floor, their intricately carved and painted yew-wood ceilings and cracking painted plasterwork dull with neglect.

The cry was of weakness and despair.

By looping Josel's scarf round a nearby broken window frame, they were able to locate from outside the building the approximate position of the staircase and there, beside a stone buttress and partially concealed by creeper, was a rusted iron grille some five feet from the ground. Forbes and the ex-corporal scoured for pieces of fallen masonry which they could wedge into the angle formed by the buttress and the wall and make a rough high step from which they could reach the grille. It had been recently disturbed and fixed back into position with some of the rusted iron spikes which lay among the fallen stonework. Once he was close enough, Forbes could see what looked like the bottom half of a trouser leg.

Helmut was unconscious by the time they got him out, which was just as well because the dungeon was incredibly small and their handling was inevitably rough.

It was Josel who had first seen the blood-soaked cloth round her father's eyes and dashed back to the car for their meagre first-aid kit; so she'd had two or three extra minutes to ask herself what to expect. They didn't help. When she saw the gouged eye sockets her whole body became a shivering gasp of horror.

The corporal disappeared in the direction of the main courtyard at prodigious speed, returning it seemed almost immediately with the roughest of simple hurdles on which they then carried Helmut, who was moaning slightly now. They managed to stretch him out awkwardly on the back seat of the car and Forbes cursed himself for not thinking of a station wagon, if there was such a thing for hire in Morocco.

He left Josel with her father and again quizzed the now friendly but still very frightened concierge. When did the men arrive? How did they travel? What did they look like? What did they say? They had arrived the previous afternoon by helicopter. They looked like Russians (how does one look like a Russian to an ex-Spahi, Forbes wondered, but he knew what the man was getting at). They said they were '*Deuxième Bureau*' and the prisoner was '*espion – très dangereux – un séjour de deux ou trois jours seulement. Ils parlaient une langue très brute.*' Yours isn't much better, thought Forbes unkindly, and as the man finished speaking he caught sight of a shovel lying on a heap of rubble. The man followed his glance and their eyes met for an instant. Forbes walked two paces, and picked up the shovel and put it in the boot of the car. The corporal gave an imperceptible nod, just enough to make Forbes wonder where he had seen active service.

Josel called out to him. She was standing beside the car, shading her eyes and looking at the sky above the whole mass of the kasbah, and straining, or so it seemed, to identify the birds of prey which were weaving their mesmerising patterns on the hard blue sky. There was total silence but for the cries of the vultures, ravens and kites, and the clacking of storks from their ragged and vulnerable-looking nests. How she could see anything Archie didn't know, for the tears were pouring down her cheeks.

They set out on their bumpy journey, Josel cradling her father's head, bathing his face as best she could and whispering in German. Every now and then Forbes thought there was a faint reply. It was hotter than ever and the track – for it was little better – looked and felt interminable.

After what seemed an hour Josel said, 'Please stop, Archie, I think he's dying.'

He stopped, and they lifted Helmut von Heimann out of the car and into some shade beside a shallow stream which ran across the road. They made him as comfortable as they could on the rugs, and Josel sat holding his hand.

It wasn't long before she looked up and said, 'He's gone, Archie, the poor darling . . . .'

The spade had been an instinctive precaution – his military training, perhaps. It was the vulture that decided him. Its huge wingspan had thrown a vast shadow as it had seemed to follow them. Don't be absurd, he was muttering now. He took a grip on himself.

'Josel, do you mind if we bury him here?'

'Here,' she said, her eyes widening in what began as horror and finished as a dull look of resignation. 'You mean because of . . . ?'

'I mean because we won't be allowed to leave the country unless we do.'

'Oh God – my mama.'

He didn't answer. He went and got the spade. It was a hellish job, but fortunately, below the track, where the stream twisted and turned round huge boulders, there were some patches of soft, almost marshy ground. Archie stripped to the waist, Josel to her bra, and they dug and pulled out stones for an hour or more. Finally, over a cairn of stones, Forbes said what he could remember of the burial service in English, and Josel said a German prayer. They set the milometer to record the distance, drank water and splashed a bit in the stream. The vulture had gone.

They drove in silence until the tower minaret of the Koutoubia mosque of Marrakech broke the skyline, then something made them look over their shoulders at the mountains. The sun was sinking and the snow on the high peaks was turning to blazing oranges and pinks. Perhaps it's their way of saluting him, Josel allowed herself to imagine.

It was straight into the pool when they arrived at the Mamounia, and then a long late siesta for Josel while Forbes telephoned and arranged a flight plan for Munich. Josel would go to her mother,and it was time he went to see Oberdorf. Then he walked into the Dj'mma El F'nea for an hour's prowl to see the snake-charmers, sword-swallowers and fire-eaters, and he watched the Cleuch boy dancers with their painted faces and clicking castanets, the performing monkeys, the fortune-tellers and the clowns. It all had so much noise, movement and colour he could feel the memory of von Heimann's wasted face slipping away. He bought himself a djellabah, partly to amuse Josel, mostly to replace his now torn and filthy trousers. He then called Willi Ansbach.

He consulted the head waiter about dinner and was persuaded to order mutton, 'cooked slowly in honey with raisins and almonds, nutmeg and thyme, myrtle and lavender, ash tree seeds and garlic, mint and stavesacre seed, roots of strapwort and locust beans'. Forbes suggested this was too rich for a hot evening, and the man pointed out that monsieur had had a very long day, also the herbs would make monsieur very amorous. Archie sighed, and ordered champagne.

Josel laughed and laughed at the djellabah — all he needed, she said, was some dark make-up. She was wearing a simple cotton dress of pale yellow, narrow at the waist, and large onyx earrings. Her hair, she said, was a mess, and Forbes was inclined to agree, but its dark, almost bronze, colour seemed to like the moonlight.

They drank champagne, then more champagne, then decided that they were ravenous and that the mélange of mutton and herbs was absolutely delicious, and so was the head waiter's choice of Moroccan red wine. Archie almost began to believe that the events of the day had never taken place. He ordered coffee and brandy by the swimming-pool.

'Why did they do that to my father, Archie?' she said suddenly, her chin cupped in her hands. 'Did they think he would tell them anything, or was it just to frighten us?'

'Both,' he said. 'They would have hoped that he would give them all our names *and* told them where the heroin is to be stored in Europe. Also, they would want him to live long enough to tell us what he'd said.'

'But they didn't know about Yugoslavia,' she said. 'That's what he kept saying to me in the car – "They didn't know about Yugoslavia."'

Forbes stared up at the Atlas snow. 'You mean that a man who could stick it out in winter for four days on a train axle, thinking what the partisans would do to him, wasn't going to break in the hands of Chinh's Blatnog thugs – if that's who they were?'

He could see the tear on her cheek and so he waited. It wasn't long before she turned to look at him, and her eyes had a questioning look – an I-know-it's-difficult-but-give-me-an-answer look.

'How long can *we* go on, Archie? There's Willi, you, me, Sergei, Alex and Jean Louis, and I have a mother too. Is it worth it? How much does it matter if the American soldiers stay in Germany? Would their removal really open the way to unification as Papa and Willi so passionately believe? And selfishly, yes selfishly, what am *I* doing in this crusade to save the soul of Germany? I joined Papa and Willi to escape those witches in Madagascar; they had wrecked my marriage and pursued me everywhere. I *saw* them everywhere. Also there was love and admiration for Papa and his feelings for Germany – born of his *Kampfgeist*, his fighting spirit. It was wonderful, it was heroic, but I am not wonderful, I am not heroic.' Her voice trailed.

Forbes had clapped his hands for more champagne. There was a long silence while Josel got up and walked by the side of the pool.

'Those birds today frightened me; they were everywhere I looked – they seemed to own the kasbah, they seemed to be the spirits of the dead. That huge vulture which appeared when we buried him, what was that? Am I going to be haunted again? Am I never to have a normal life? Is this why Chinh brought him here? Does he think he can hurt more with ghosts than with guns?'

As she finished the questions she stopped and, flinging her glass into the pool, dived in after it, whirling round on to her back. Her hair spread out on the water, and in the moonlight her body, through the clinging dress, was more seductive than nakedness could ever have been. Archie whispered 'Ophelia!' and, slipping out of his djellabah, dived.

26

Willi Ansbach met them at Munich airport. His round face was always cheerless, but this morning he looked as if the whole world had packed its bags and departed. Josel gave him a great hug and he brightened visibly.

'Your mama is at our house already, Josel, and there is of course a bed for you, and for you too, Archie; also plenty of my clothes which you can use' – this last as he looked unhappily at Forbes's djellabah. 'Alex and Sergei will arrive tomorrow – oh, and I have a separate car here for you, Archie, in case you want to go and make some business visits after we have finished talking, tomorrow, or the next day, perhaps? Josel, I would like to propose to you and your mother that I should go with her to Morocco as soon as possible. It would not be wise for you to go with her, because there could be some awkward questions from the authorities, I believe.'

Josel nodded her head slowly.

And so they had a quiet evening, a very quiet evening. Elli Ansbach's warm and smiling friendliness and her air of understanding everything and saying nothing was balm to Josel and Dashka, while Forbes and Ansbach discussed the practicalities of explaining von Heimann's death and immediate burial to the Moroccan police. It was not going to be easy.

Breakfast saw the arrival of Melkov and Bradley and

all their faces wore the look of bewildered loss. The *Erweckung* crusade had been from its birth von Heimann's vision, the vision of a united Germany which would bring peace to the whole of Europe, including Russia. 'The best of Bismarck and of Peter the Great', Dashka had often heard him say. The unspoken thought round that silent room was: What do we do now?

Josel broke the silence. 'They asked my father for all our names. Archie and I think that they wanted him to live long enough to tell us they had done so, that this would frighten us. It *has* frightened me.'

Sergei clicked with slight impatience. 'But, Josel, they already know who we are, except for Archie and me. The connection between Helmut and Willi has always been visible, Alex, by now, they must assume to have a closer connection with Jean Louis than some vague idea of a CIA link. The knife-thrower shot by the tall American – this must have filtered back.'

'And so it was to terrorise, and so with me it is succeeding,' said Josel obstinately.

Willi put his fingertips together, leant forward and said, 'I think we should hear from Dashka.'

Dashka's paleness under her still dark hair gave her an ethereal look. She put her hand on Josel's and looked at the others in turn, but quickly, as if she were making sure they were still there. She smiled at Melkov.

'What you meant to say was that it makes no difference, and you are right. Please let me go to Morocco tomorrow with Willi and I shall be happy that you are all doing everything that needs to be done.'

Ansbach and Melkov smiled their appreciation as Dashka rose to leave. Josel looked at Forbes and gave him a flicker of a smile.

They then reported their progress in a businesslike way. Bradley confirmed that the 'graphite' shipment would shortly reach Hamburg and that he had carefully briefed the crucible foreman in Grossalmerode. He would now prepare Strenca in Paris for a date some time in October, timing which his CIA colleagues in Washington had already agreed with Brockles Fitz-Herbert in London. He then said that he would scrap his plans to rent a house on the Wörthersee for the summer visit of 'Susannah and the kids'. He was looking at Josel as he said it, with a smile which she knew was supposed to mean 'so that we can spend time together'. He then went on to dot the i's with a reference to 'all our families now being at risk'.

Melkov gave what Forbes rather thought was a sniff. He said, 'I am happy with the month of October, Alex, for the start of our campaign, but please be very careful that Strenca is told as little as possible at this stage. I do not have to stress how vulnerable we all are until the heroin is safely in his hands.'

There was a nodding of heads.

Since it was now clear that Chinh knew of the Moulin's *raison d'être*, they agreed to use it no longer as a rendezvous. For the time being anyway there would be no more meetings. Once again eyes met across the table.

Elli produced an early and delicious lunch and Bradley and Melkov took their leave, Melkov waving away Forbes's offer to return his sheath knife. 'Keep it, Archie, it might bring you good luck!'

As Sergei spoke Forbes remembered the pistol. He telephoned Oberdorf's office, and then waved goodbye to the little group, which was planning Dashka's journey to Marrakech. He half wished he was going with them. Part of him felt that von Heimann might expect it of him – if he closed his eyes he could hear again that voice of the cold April night of thirty six years ago: 'I can't tell them not to shoot, you know'.

Hunyon Graf, Oberdorf's secretary, was a woman who suffered from perennial optimism. She never wavered in her belief that her boy-friend would one day marry her, despite what all observers saw as convincing evidence to the contrary. He was a ski-instructor, a very good-looking and successful one, who found Hunyon's ski-chalet in Kitzbühel an admirable place to entertain innumerable girl-friends of every nationality. Hunyon knew this. She also knew that she was not very good-looking and skied rather badly, but her optimism was bolstered by the confidence of being a very good cook and having the temperament for the waiting game. In Archie Forbes's eyes she had one other inestimable quality: she adored Archie Forbes.

'*Jawohl*, Herr Forbes.' Then she remembered to practise her English on him. 'Herr Oberdorf is delighted for you to have dinner with him, also I have reserved a room for you at the Vierjahreszeiten and, as well, I have booked your flight for London tomorrow afternoon after you have visited customers with Herr Oberdorf in the morning.' She was getting breathless. 'Now you have two hours to go shopping for the shirts and trousers you spoke about on the telephone.' This was said with a disapproving look at Willi's trousers which were straining at Forbes's shins. Her ski-instructor was always very smartly dressed. 'Oh yes, one more thing, Herr Forbes – your wife telephoned.' She was looking at him steadily now, and of course, beaming.

'Wonderful Hunyon, you think of everything. Now would you be very kind and put these samples in the safe? They are rather special and I shall need them on my next visit.' He handed her the pistol very carefully wrapped, first in a Mamounia hand-towel to soften the outline, then in some fine sacking he had obtained from the hall porter, and finally in the remnants of the Rabat embassy's package to give a spurious respectability to such circumstantial evidence of wrongdoing. He reflected that a djellabah was ideal for arms-smuggling – the Arab equivalent of a violin case!

'*Natürlich*, Herr Forbes. I will do it immediately,' and she disappeared.

Forbes thought about Zulka's telephone call. Zulka never telephoned; she knew better than that. He went and bought the shirts and trousers and, as an afterthought, a Tyrolean hand-embroidered apron for Zulka. Then he went to his hotel room and slept; it had been a gruelling forty eight hours. He hadn't returned the call.

Conversation with Oberdorf over dinner, and with the customers the following morning, was uneventful but satisfactory. Oberdorf always made a snide reference to Archie's 'other interests' but he never went too far, and, since it was good for his ego, he met the little hints about 'intelligence work' with a knowing look or a slightly theatrical lifting of the eyebrows. Thus the missing, but not forgotten, twenty four hours had formed a bond between them.

The house was stuffy and very silent. There was no sign of Zulka or of Ruffian, his black labrador. He found a note from Zulka on his desk, beside the whisky decanter. A note from Zulka in an *envelope*? Zulka didn't put notes in envelopes; there was no one to read them except him – Mrs Tomlinson came in the morning. He got some water, poured some whisky and settled into his chair with a faintly uneasy feeling at Ruffian's absence. The letter – it wasn't a note – seemed quite long.

Darling, I've gone to Washington. Guido is really ill with measles and Sophie badly wants some help. Scarlatti is being difficult as usual. I tried to telephone but no one knew where you were, except on the Continent somewhere. Brock, of course, was awfully funny and said *'Cherchez la femme.'* I could have killed him. But there's more to it than Guido and Sophie and bloody Scarlatti, Archie, much more. So much more that I don't believe we can go on together, so much that I don't know whether this letter will be ten pages or one. You are a fool, Archie. A lovable one and a forgivable one. You always have been and I have loved you partly because of it — I suspect *too much* because of it. In the early days it was wonderful to have a roller-coaster (I think you say?) marriage. There was so much to laugh about and so much to hope for. But now the laughter and the hoping is finished, the foolishness has gone on for too long. What I need — what we *both* need — is peace and calm and sensibleness and steady boring middle age. Not crusades, Archie, with or without beautiful girl partners; not cloaks and daggers with Brockles FitzHerbert and those Germans you like so much; and *not* endless worry about keeping the job, the job you really *have* to keep because otherwise we sit and look at unpaid bills and empty whisky bottles. I've gone on long enough. I hoped that loving you would help but it hasn't.

Zulka

PS Ruffian is with Mrs Tomlinson.'

He poured himself more whisky and thought of their

little ski-hotel in the Tyrol. They had called it 'The Blick' because it was the only house in the valley which had *no* view, which was why they had got it so cheaply. In every other way it was perfect and the struggle – even though they'd lost – had been wonderful, the 'roller-coaster', as Zulka had called it. He began to think of excuses and alibis for them both. He had been a *bloody* fool not to call back from Munich. She had got tensed up because of Scarlatti being bloody to Sophie. She would calm down and call from Washington. The grandchild would be better, and Zulka would have given their Italian son-in-law a good Slav broadside – memorable stuff, as he knew well. And *he* would have some memorable stuff for Brock; stupid fool, mischievous too – always a little too ready to stir things up between him and Zulka. Rather fancied her, of course, in his tucked-up bachelor way. Oh well, most of it *was* his own fault. He had taken forgiveness for granted, assumed that landing on one's feet was God-given and irreversible, that luck never ran out. Yes, Archie – you're a fool all right, a 55-year-old incorrigible idiot, and you'll soon become an even bigger one if you don't stop thinking of a moon-soaked pool and those timeless snows, he told himself. Then he took a long swallow and called Brock.

'I've got a lot to report and it's going to take some time to say it. Zulka is away and I'm in charge of the dog, so do you mind coming here? You'll have to face my cooking but I've got a decent claret.'

He wanted to call Josel in Paris, but that meant loss of self-respect. So he went to collect Ruffian from Mrs Tomlinson, who gave him what his mother had always called 'an old-fashioned look' as she fussed over the lead. He asked her if she could prepare some vegetables in the morning. He could see the question in her eyes about Zulka, so he quickly said, 'A rather important colleague,' and dragged Ruffian away.

Brockles FitzHerbert was genial; in my present mood, he needs to be, Forbes thought. The hangover had taken a firm hold and his temples were drumming a merry tune in defiance of his mood of self-destructive despair. One medicinal gin had had no effect, and the second, poured just before his guest's arrival, was making him belligerent.

'The good news, Archie boy, is that Washington are firm of purpose. You may say that requires a holy miracle, but it's true none the less. Your friend Sergei's chums in the KGB are of a like mind and time therefore could soon be of the essence.'

Forbes wished Brock wouldn't talk in clichés but managed a 'thank God for that', followed by a twisted grin. 'When you hear my report you'll need another drink,' he growled, as he handed over the Ulsterman's schooner of sherry.

They sat on the terrace for the story of Telouet and its overture of telephone calls. When they got to Dashka's firm resolve and the doubts which she had stilled, Brock let out a whistle of admiration.

'That's quite a lady, Archie that's quite a lady. I'll try to persuade our embassy to oil the wheels for her a bit in Morocco. Of course they'll assume he was a drug-smuggler and victim of a gang war, which is to our advantage. In a way true,' he added, not noticing Forbes's grimace at his tactlessness.

Forbes recharged the glasses. The drumming in his head was subsiding at last and he felt slightly less antagonistic towards his visitor. He led the way to the dining-room, where Mrs Tomlinson had set out Marks & Spencer's shepherd's pie, vegetables and brie. Forbes had uncorked an '86 Medoc, and they returned to their agenda, which was, broadly, action for Strenca and low profile for everyone else.

'Do bear in mind, Archie, that Strenca's network, when it receives the heroin from Grossalmerode and gets the signal, must work insidiously. We need a longish period of slow penetration in order to ensure that public opinion *gradually* becomes aware of what is happening. Water on stone, Archie, drip drip drip. That's what fuels indignation and resentment, that's what in turn will open the doors to the alternative solution to the Cold War. By the spring, I guess, there's every chance that the hard-liners on both sides will discover they've been outmanoeuvred, while both Europe and America wake up to the amazing discovery that both the economic division and the nuclear division of Europe is to become a memory. How's *your* enthusiasm these days, Archie, by the way?'

The sudden sharp question took Forbes by surprise; he had been gazing into his claret glass listening to Brock droning on, as he called it – 'poor old bugger, trying to convince himself,' he would have said to Zulka had she been around to listen.

Startled out of reverie, he said, 'Mine? Oh fine, Brock. Enthusiasm? That's an odd word. It's personal now; funny how great causes have to become personal before one really throws in one's lot. You can call it enthusiasm, call it what you like, it *matters* now; that's what makes the difference – it *matters*. Not that I need any lectures from you, FitzHerbert, on the subject of morale or conviction. I doubt if you've ever known what it feels like to be convinced of anything. You're a studier of form, you like to think you know which way the cat's going to jump, and if that means you've got to stir, then you'll stir. "Archie Forbes the womaniser" –

that's your line, just for the fun of causing trouble. And you talk to me about convictions.'

He paused. FitzHerbert – as he had been called – looked stunned. It wasn't the first time he'd heard harsh words from Archie Forbes, but never with such vehemence, such quivering indignation. A quiet lunch with Zulka (always look after the wives, had been his watchword) and a light-hearted reference to Josel Morsaing, and this was the result. The Irish blood in him wanted for a moment to spit fury, but Zulka's very absence brought him to earth – something could be, obviously was, seriously wrong.

'Sorry, old boy,' were the words he found. 'I've overstepped the mark.'

The two men stared at each other as the Médoc and the ticking of a clock did their work.

Forbes spoke slowly and thoughtfully. 'If Truong Chinh thinks he's put us out of business, that is good. From his viewpoint it would be a fair assumption and logically it should encourage him to press for a decision on the deal to return the American prisoners of war. Can you find out anything about this from your CIA friends? Put it another way, if both CIA projects, ours and theirs, are on their way to Reagan for decision, which one is he going to choose? You say that Washington is firm of purpose; what exactly does that mean if the President still has to choose?'

Brock drank his coffee and got up to go. 'Leave it with me, Archie. I take the point and will ask the question.'

Forbes watched the slightly stooping figure as it walked to the gate, and thought, Perhaps I was on the tough side, but mischief-maker he always was.

27

Forbes thought vaguely in terms of taking Ruffian for a long-overdue walk and then putting his feet up. He was smarting physically from the Atlas sun, (digging a grave stripped to the waist in eighty-five degrees had not come his way for thirty seven years), and emotionally from Zulka's letter, his hangover, and his outburst over lunch. But the cool shade of his garden and the rest of the Médoc won the contest, and only the insistent ring of the telephone brought him round.

Josel's voice was urgent, but his blurred mind for the first few moments could only think of the first time she had telephoned out of the blue. It seemed years ago. It had been a cool voice, not over-confident but quite assured in a surprisingly friendly way. It wasn't assured now. She spoke rapidly, using words and phrases she knew he would understand but which would be meaningless to anyone not aware of the background. He made her repeat some of the sentences as he dragged himself out of the alcoholic haze, and even managed to notice and admire her patience with him.

'I tried and tried to persuade him to discuss with Willi. I said that Willi is *simpatico* and not without some fears too, but he is so balanced and understands so well the historical pressures and is not just confused by feelings of loyalty for my papa.'

'So you think Alex's motive is fear – not ideology?'

'Yes, I think it is fear – fear for Susannah and his children, fear for me he says too. Yes and perhaps a little bit of *lack* of ideology, with strong feeling for those Vietnam prisoners, because he was so long in Vietnam, and not a great love for Europeans and especially not Germans.'

The Vietnam prisoners have got nothing to do with it, as Bradley well knows, Forbes thought.

'He is your lover, isn't he?' he said, with a casual brutality born of jealousy and alcohol. The silence was so long he thought the line had gone.

'Was,' came the answer, with surprising strength and coolness, and then the silence once more.

He tried to make his voice more sympathetic, less aggressive, less inquisitorial. 'What would you suggest I do?'

'Go and see him, Archie; persuade him, explain. If there were time I would say take Willi with you.'

'What do you mean, "if there were time"?'

'He's gone to meet them, Archie. He's leaving Paris tomorrow as soon as he contacts them by telephone. You've got to stop him, Archie. You used to have doubts yourself, you understand doubts. He will listen to you.'

'Where is he going?' he asked.

'To Giessen bei Frankfurt, the Hotel Jaegerhof.'

It was his turn for silence now. There had been entreaty in her voice; he wanted to think there had been something else as well, and then reminded himself that alcohol was the father and mother of sentiment.

'I'll do my best, Josel.' He knew that his voice carried no great conviction.

'Thank you, Archie dear.' And suddenly there was a heartening and longed-for warmth.

He roused himself and called Hunyon. There was

only just time to catch her before her office closed – it was 5.30 in Germany. They worked out the flight times and Forbes asked for the package of samples to be sent by special messenger and be put in the boot of the hire-car; he had no wish to bump into Chinh's men without at least a sporting chance.

Meanwhile, think of what you're going to say, he ordered himself. He had arranged to call Josel in the morning, and she had promised to ask Bradley when he planned to leave for Frankfurt. A talk with Willi on the telephone would lead to him offering to come to Giessen, but Forbes knew that while Bradley might listen to one man, he certainly would not give way to two. In any case, there were things he was going to have to say to Bradley which couldn't be said in front of a German.

What had got into the man? Was he just plumb scared? He had saved Jean Louis's life at a very ugly moment. He hadn't even seen the horror of von Heimann's face, and he'd seen plenty of horrors in Vietnam. Wife and children? Yes, they *were* vulnerable, and he hadn't had a family when he was in Vietnam. He was going to tell Chinh where he could find the heroin. *Die Erweckung* had been a nice idea, but now it had to be stopped, Bradley had said to Josel. And by the time I get there, thought Forbes, he will have arranged to meet Chinh.

After she had spoken to Archie Forbes, Josel thought again of her walk with Alex Bradley in the prim little Parc Monceau. They had lunched at La Marée, open despite its being late July, and the meal had been pleasant enough, although she had seen unease and tiredness in Bradley's eyes which hadn't been there at Kufstein. But then all her faculties at Kufstein had been blurred by the last indelible picture of her father's face.

Bradley had made all the arrangements at Grossalmerode and with Strenca in Paris, and he made her laugh at his account of persuading Strenca *not* to let his old French Army stalwarts from Indo-China in on the game.

'Yes,' he said in answer to her question, 'Strenca is totally secure.'

They had walked in silence while Josel thought about their picnic on the maquis beside the pool, and the Madagascar witches; how Bradley's passion had banished them for ever. Or almost for ever; there had been the moments, dreadful moments, at Telouet, and when they buried her father, when the birds had become the witches – witches which had stared at her from her father's absent eyes.

Bradley settled them both on a hard stone bench and said, 'You wouldn't mind *all* that much if the whole thing ended right here and now, would you?'

'What whole thing?' Her eyes searched his face for a sign that he knew she was acting dumb.

'The plan, the project, the scheme, the *Erweckung*, you Germans called it, didn't you?' His voice had become harsh, but only for a moment. Then came the persuasion – innocent people at risk, women and children, Chinh had all their names, Strenca's outfit was just fine, the best he'd come across, but no team was safer than its weakest link. She had been dead unhappy on her return from Morocco, her mother's bravery and example had been more than anyone could have hoped for, but on reflection it wouldn't and couldn't last.

On seeing that dead face, is what he means, Josel thought. And so it went on, until she said, 'What exactly are you proposing?'

'Oh, I'll simply get hold of Chinh and tell him where the stuff is stashed; I have traced the telephone number.'

They walked round for the twentieth time. Josel spoke of Willi Ansbach's feelings, Washington's feelings, how Sergei Melkov would take it. Archie Forbes, she admitted to herself, would not be a powerful argument – they didn't like each other – but she brought him in.

'Forbes,' he said. 'He had to be dragged into the team, didn't he? Had to be blackmailed by his own boss!' Bradley was laughing now. 'He'll dance for joy when he hears it's all over!'

She turned and looked at him then. His face had an expression of amused and hopeful happiness, but a lot of determination as well.

'You can call me, Josel. I'm at the Travellers', and I won't leave until after lunch tomorrow.'

'No, Alex, I shan't call you,' she had answered, before she turned and walked away and felt the first tears coursing down her cheeks.

She waited for Archie to call.

28

Forbes sat in the aircraft remembering all he could of his professional training. He knew he must be prepared to find Chinh's men possibly even *with* Bradley, or anyway not far away, either coming or going. He guessed that Bradley had asked for a rendezvous in order to barter safety for his family, Josel, Dashka and possibly Willi. He had some recollection of Giessen, as the big sub-components company in the town had once been a customer, and he remembered the whereabouts of the Jaegerhof. He drove slowly past and noticed the almost empty car-park – people were on holiday in the mountains or on the beaches – and, with a wry smile, the fire-escape. He parked a quarter of a mile away in a residential side-street where young people were arriving for some sort of party and pop music poured from open windows. Lovely for the neighbours, he thought. It was just past dusk.

The hotel porter looked ancient and somnolent – possibly a holiday relief – and simply said, '*Dreiundzwanzig*,' with a nod towards the stairs in reply to Forbes's 'Herr Bradley, *bitte?*'

Alex Bradley opened the bedroom door with a half-expecting-you grin and a 'Hi, Archie, I'm glad to see you – come on in.'

Forbes swung his bulky brief-case on to a side table

and set the duty-free airport bag gently on one of the two beds.

'Thought we might have a glass of malt together,' he said.

'Sure, great idea, glad you came. I hoped Josel would tell you I was here.'

'And that she'd tell me what's on your mind?' Forbes said.

'Sure, Archie, sure. Let's get the glasses into action.'

They drank some whisky and stared at the uninspiring carpet; the windows were wide open and Forbes could hear the pop music from where he'd left his car. His silence had something to do with not having rehearsed any opening remarks. He filled up the glasses and waited for Bradley.

'How much did Josel tell you?'

'Just that you had decided to call it a day.'

He glanced towards the open window, leaned forward and turned on the radio beside the bed. Then he settled himself in the only comfortable chair.

'Ah, wise man,' said Bradley, grinning. 'Well trained!'

'Well enough trained to know you've got a deal in mind. An escape route, perhaps, in exchange for information.' This didn't come out quite as a question, nor was he sure he had intended it to.

'No, no deal, Archie, just *out*. Perhaps you wouldn't understand because you English are just so full of grit, but I've had all that I can take of nastiness. I lived through a lot of nastiness in Vietnam, a good deal of it admittedly engineered by me, but that business in Madagascar the other day, that was my last throw. These Chinh boys, they will go the whole distance, but I can't. It's as simple as that – dead simple, Archie.'

'So you'll dump the whole team, me, even Josel?'

'Why not? She was all over the place about her father's death. She came in originally to please him and to unspook herself from Madagascar. It was never a heart-and-soul business for her. And you? For Pete's sake, Archie, we got you in a package deal, remember? You were the guy who worried about the morality of getting GIs hooked on heroin, no matter how good the cause.'

Forbes reached for the bottle of malt. 'And so is it moral support you're looking for, or is it a whitewash job for when you tell Washington some cock-and-bull story about the team breaking up?'

'A little bit of both, Archie boy, it's ninety per cent a John Vann type gamble. Vann and I took plenty of decisions which would never have got past Westmoreland, but we took them just the same and squared them away later. You must have done the same thing in your time? There's also another way of looking at it, and that's that it doesn't make sense any more. With Helmut dead, the German driving force isn't the same. The battle for the soul of Germany is what we talked about: reunification as absolution for the guilty Germans and some equally guilty Russians who are now "Kremlin liberals" and therefore knights in shining armour! Isn't that about it? Helmut was a great guy — "Cometh the hour, cometh the man" — but without him ....' Bradley spread his hands, not a gesture he looked particularly comfortable with, and lay back on the propped pillows.

'It's going to happen anyway, Archie' — this with a tired smile as if he were thinking he'd overdone the bit about von Heimann being another Bismarck in waiting.

Forbes did some more work on the malt. He was in dire need himself, and also thought it might bring out the sentimental streak so close to the surface in most Americans.

'You've worked it out quite well, Alex, and the most effective part of your theory is the grain of truth which you've pursued so energeticaly. Josel *did* have a nasty wobble of confidence. I *was* a reluctant conscript. Your Madagascar trip showed us all that we're up against something much nastier than anything in our experience, and Telouet was designed to do just that again, with the promise of again *and* again. Now you're holding out the hand of an alliance with Josel and me as both an alibi and a justification for ratting. It might help to clean your slate with Washington and even produce a backlash of credit if and when a Vietnam deal is signed and sealed, but the really important thing, the central fundamental motive, you forgot. You belittle the cause of the soul of Germany, and in a way you are right – another grain of truth – Germany of itself is *not* important enough, but nuclear war *is*. However tempted we are – and it happens, oh how it happens – we need only remember one thing: that as long as American forces stay in Western Europe and the Soviet economy continues to disintegrate, the Red Army and the Kremlin hard-liners have the huge temptation to take by force what otherwise calls for years of patient negotiation, not to mention the sacrifice of privilege and perquisites. You remember what Pushkin said: "The nature of the Russian rebellion is brutal and merciless. It knows no reason, no leaders." Then the Americans would use nuclear weapons. You forgot the nuclear horror, Alex, because of your Vietnam sentimentality. You are yourself a casualty of Vietnam.'

Bradley was grinning and mockingly clapping his hands. 'Very good Archie boy, very good indeed. Mrs Thatcher would be proud of you. Thanks but no thanks, I'll stick to my John Vann gamble, and I've got a sneaky feeling that once the deed is done – and that's tomorrow – you and Josel could change your minds. Come, let's have some of that malt.'

'No, that won't happen, Alex. You're wrong about that too,' and he got up and reached for the whisky. But his hand went past it, to his brief-case, and sprang the two clips in quick succession.

Bradley glanced up at the sound and, as Forbes swung round with the pistol in his hand, looked as if he was about to say something. But it would have been inaudible because Forbes had just turned up the volume knob on the radio a second before the first shot hit Bradley in the chest, the second, because of the angle, in the throat. Forbes knew he was dead because of the mixture of blood and foam from his mouth and the lolling tongue. But it was the look of surprise which stuck hard in his memory.

He wiped the glasses, the radio knob, having turned it down, and both door handles, moving with an unhurried speed which surprised him. Then it was a short nip down the corridor to the fire-escape and across the almost deserted car-park at a fast walk, the memory saying, Never run or turn your white face to look back.

The teen-age pop crowd were still buzzing in and out of their party when he reached his car; they seemed not very sober, he was happy to note.

In forty minutes he had joined the autobahn at Limburg, and by 7.30 in the morning he was checking in the hire-car at Charles de Gaulle airport, having had a Thermos of black coffee and an hour's sleep on the way. He called Josel and asked if he could come to breakfast.

29

He was shaking a bit when she opened the door of the flat but not so much that he couldn't produce a lopsided grin and an apologetic 'Coffee?'

She took him by the wrist, led him into the sitting-room and pushed him gently into an armchair with his back to the window. He sat staring into the fireplace, vaguely hearing the clatter of coffee cups. It was Sunday morning. He had forgotten it would be Sunday morning. He was thinking that mornings were going to be difficult from now on. Josel came in with a tray, looking how he wanted her to look and moving with a youthful quickness which made his limbs ache – perhaps with desire; he wasn't sure, and so he laughed. She looked startled for a moment and then laughed too, tucking in her skirt round her bare legs as she sat on the sofa and poured coffee and buttered his croissant.

'What happened, Archie?' The voice was calm.

He got up suddenly and took two paces to the window. 'I killed him.'

There was a clatter from the tray and he turned, but it was Josel coming quickly into his arms, 'You poor love.'

He looked down at the tear-moistened face and said, 'Death seems to travel with us, doesn't it, darling?'

They finished the coffee and made some more, then for Forbes it was two hours' sleep in the chair, followed by an omelette. Being Sunday, there was no Bernice, and the flat was full of a warm quietness; Paris was pausing for breath. Josel brought a bottle of champagne with the raspberries and whipped cream, and finally, teasing him about the roughness of his unshaven chin, led him into her bedroom, letting slip the wide-striped skirt as they went.

Later, over a second bottle of champagne and the hum of a gently reviving city, they got down to the business of deciding how and who they would tell of Bradley's death. Willi and Dashka were back from their nightmare trip to Morocco, where the authorities had been surprisingly helpful about returning her father's body to Germany – probably on account of anxiety about their tourist trade, as Willi had pointed out. Josel would go and see them both the following day. She would ask Willi to tell Sergei what had happened; also, she would tell Jean Louis by means of her bush telegraph. Willi they agreed, must be asked to take over both Grossalmerode and Strenca, and to tell Melkov to listen out, through the Kremlin grapevine, for the repercussions in Washington. They must all understand that Forbes could not be seen again on the Continent. In fact, they could count him out. He would resign from his company in September, having gone to Scotland for August, and give Zulka's visit to the States and the possible offer of a job there as his excuse.

It was then he told Josel about Zulka. They walked hand in hand to the métro. Archie told her she must stay with Elli and Willi for as long as possible. They even toyed with the idea that Bradley's death might somehow satiate Chinh's appetite for murder, but perhaps that was the champagne – and perhaps their feeling of happiness was the champagne too.

Paris métro entrances must have seen many such partings. Forbes made for the Gare du Nord and then the night ferry from Calais. The weight of his brief-case was a timely reminder of the pistol, which he dropped, as gently as possible, into the Channel, discovering at the same time the remains of the malt, which he must have scooped up in the last whirl round that surprised figure on the bed.

It was early morning when he banged on Mrs Tomlinson's door. He had managed to shave but, judging by her expression, his appearance left a lot to be desired. Ruffian's welcome, on the other hand, was different altogether.

30

Brock was affable. 'Come and have dinner at my flat,' he said. 'Come early, about 7 p.m., because I know you like a preprandial glass of sherry' – this last with a guffaw which was lost on Forbes, not least because he well knew that Brock himself never blanched at two seriously large dry martinis.

They were, in fact, already shaken when he arrived and looked round at the comfortable but sparsely furnished high-ceilinged sitting-room. It had bachelor stamped all over it: the curtains and lampshades, the hearthrug, the trophies from the Italian campaign, the photographs of an austere-looking matriarch and a chubby, beaming cleric all testified to an existence rather than a life. The room was a biographical footnote which said 'Brockles FitzHerbert lived here. He lived here without emotion, without feeling, almost without humour – that elixir of what is called home.'

But Brock was busy giving the lie to such a bleak message because he was chortling with an exuberance which Forbes felt betokened ill. Two martinis went down without Brock voicing more than affable enquiries about Zulka's welfare and the health of the Scarlatti grandchild in Washington. The good humour seemed more than ever out of place, but ponderous jollity was nearly always, with FitzHerbert, the precursor of unpleasant news which he was reluctant to impart. Forbes had his own contribution to make but he waited – and downed a third martini.

'You remember you asked me to check with Washington on their degree of enthusiasm for your project as opposed to Chinh's feelers for a Vietnam deal?' Forbes noticed the 'your'. 'Well, it's zero, Archie boy, it's zero. I don't know how that hits you, but it sure knocked me sideways.' Those damned Americanisms again.

Some sort of gust of awful humour, a parody of Brock's exuberance, was beginning to shake Forbes, but he stifled it and managed to say, 'Do you mind explaining?' at the very moment the Filipino housekeeper announced dinner.

There was small talk, a marvellous soufflé followed by lamb cutlets and a '75 Pomerol; Brock waved in the cheese, and they were left with the silence which precedes an answer.

'Explain please, Brock.'

'You remember Gordievski?' Forbes nodded.

'You're not supposed to know about Gordievski, you realise that? You're a damned irregular, Archie. There are things I shouldn't tell you.'

Forbes nodded again, and thought of something which perhaps he now wouldn't tell Brock.

'Well, Gordievski is in Moscow Centre, and he reports the Kremlin is in a state of panic. Apparently they have convinced themselves that the US is planning to launch a surprise nuclear attack. They have ordered the KGB and the GRU to co-operate in an intensive intelligence-gathering operation on the *assumption* that such an attack will be launched within six months.' He held up his hand. 'I'm as sceptical as you are – we are all as sceptical as you are – but the clinching, the so-called irrefutable piece of intelligence, is the address given recently by General Kryuchkov, head of the KGB's First Chief Directorate, to his senior officers. His instructions had come *direct* from the Politburo, which had referred to the US development and siting of new weapon systems for a sudden attack; weapons such as the Trident II, the Pershing II and, of course, Cruise missiles on the ground in Europe. There is *genuine* fear in the Kremlin, Archie – that's the first thing. The rest of the message is that your scheme, because it would be seen as the precursor to an attack, goes on the back burner *at best.*' (There was that 'your' again.) 'So you're dead in the water, Archie. Dead in the water.'

They were back in the sitting-room by now and Forbes had a glass of brandy in his hand.

'I'm dead in the water all right, Brock, but not for the reason you think. What I came to tell you was that I've just killed Bradley, your CIA link, for trying to sell the pass. You won't find that easy to explain to Washington, but I expect you'll have a bloody good try.'

He'd emptied his glass and was now busy filling it again. He didn't think Brock would mind the lapse of manners and he was right – the older man looked as if a bitter wind had scoured his ineffable smugness. The expression on his face was not surprise; he seemed to be struggling to make it look like surprise. Forbes told him in detail what had happened and finished by saying, 'So unless the German police get after me, you won't hear any more of me. I shall take my leave in August and resign from my job when I get back.'

He was still trying to digest what Brock had said. His own bombshell had, in a sense, been delivered to give him time to register and comprehend the other. He tried some disciplined questions to assist the process.

'Why does Washington think that the sight of GIs in Europe hitting drugs will frighten the Kremlin?'

'Because they would interpret the clamour in America for the withdrawal of troops as convincing evidence of a planned nuclear attack.'

'Why have the US hard-liners suddenly achieved the ascendancy when all *our* evidence is to the contrary. What happened to the Kirkpatrick school? Is this the Chinh deal finally queering our pitch?

They went on like this until the brandy was finished and Brock was flapping his hands. Forbes remembered to ask when Sergei would know the Washington decision. 'Forty-eight hours from now.' was the reply. They talked on again after that, but Forbes said no to more brandy – a taxi was the answer.

He looked hard at the old man standing on the doorstep – he *was* an old man now, the bravado had gone – and reminded him of his promise to persuade his CIA chums to use their influence, such as it was, to call off Chinh's murder gang.

'It's capitulation of a sort, but *maybe* there'll be a sting in the tail.'

'What do you mean by that?' Brock's face was showing agitation.

'I haven't the slightest idea. It's your brandy speaking, I expect.'

He was in the back of the cab now, pulling down the window and saying, 'Thank you.' Thank you for what? rose to his lips as he slid back on the seat and faintly heard the parting words – 'I shall miss you, Archie boy,' trailing after the gear change.

Funnily enough, you old sod, I believe you really will.

31

Archie Forbes called Kufstein early in the morning and asked Elli if he could speak to Josel. She came to the telephone, and he said, 'I'm afraid I've got to ask you to come to London. It's very important and I can't explain on the telephone.'

'Yes, of course I will come. I will call you in half an hour with the flight number – oh, and I have told my mother, Elli and Willi what happened in Giessen, Archie. They all understand.'

'But not yet Sergei?'

'No, not yet Sergei.'

Melkov's going to get two surprises in one, he said to himself as he waited for the telephone to ring.

She came through the Customs exit smiling and waving, and he wished with all his heart that they could walk across to a departing flight and go just anywhere. They sat down on a neglected-looking seat near the main exit and looked at each other, taking in, as if measuring against some mental picture, each other's tilt of head, curve of lip and above all, eyes. They smiled and then they laughed.

'It must be damned important,' she said.

'It is,' he answered.

She looked down at her overnight bag.

'No,' he said, 'more's the pity. You've got to go

straight back – it's *that* important.'

'Well, get on with it then,' she chided him, and they laughed again.

Josel took his news quite calmly. It was a shock, an unpleasant, unfair and unexpected *coup de grâce*, but it was the end of the fairy-tale world in which she seemed to have been living for too long, from which, when she was honest with herself, she had wanted to escape. She felt pain for her father, for Juris, for Willi, and above all for Archie, but none for herself. She could see that Archie intended to treat Brock's dénouement with assumed casualness and pretended relief, and so she played her part accordingly.

'You want me to tell Willi and Sergei, of course?'

'Willi, yes, but Sergei no, because Brock said that he will know by tomorrow from his KGB source. But you should get them together as soon as possible and ask them . . . .' He stopped. 'What the hell's the use of me asking questions or sending messages? They'll have to make up their own minds. They know damn well that the panic brigade will melt away when Brezhnev goes, also that both the heroin and the money are not in any danger. With those two assets and Strenca, they can set things in motion whenever the climate changes.'

He was making light of it all.

'How many people,' she asked 'could be anxious to kill them now?'

She said 'them', but of course Forbes knew she was thinking 'us', and 'us' of course included Dashka who, she had explained, would spend the rest of the summer in the mountains with Elli and Willi. He hesitated and then laughed.

'I was bright enough to tell Brock to ask his CIA friends to cool off Chinh – to send him some sort of 'don't bother with them now' message *if* his Vietnam deal is now taking shape, but I was too dumb to think that those very same CIA friends could want us *all* dead and telling no tales; the same applies to the KGB, I suppose, if they get frightened enough.'

'How horribly sure is your Brock that Gordievski has got it right, that there really *is* this thing he calls Operation Ryan?'

'He is horribly sure, and even surer that Sergei will confirm that Ryan is the anonym for RAKETNO-YADERNOYE NAPADENIE (Nuclear Missile Attack) (he fumbled the words) and it is *the* prime example of Soviet paranoia, the fear of the West. It is a vast strategic gathering of intelligence on non-existent US and NATO plans to launch a nuclear first strike. Juri Andropov has set the whole thing in motion and the general atmosphere is heightened by Jaruzelski's efforts to control what looks like a workers' revolution in Poland by Lech Walesa. But eventually of course the hysteria will subside.'

Sergei and Willi will still have their three great strengths – time, the money and the "graphite", not to mention Jean Louis with the strategic reserve. I *didn't* say that to Brock.'

She smiled and held his hand. 'What is *your* great strength?' she asked.

'You,' he answered, and was rewarded with a blush. She had forgotten that she could blush and saw that he was laughing.

'I *meant* how will you occupy yourself?'

'Walking the Scottish hills and waiting for you to join me. I shall take my typewriter and record all that has happened, and why it happened and why it didn't happen or hasn't *yet* happened; most important of all, how it can *still* happen.'

They had drunk coffee and walked outside to get

some air, which was mostly exhaust fumes, and now they were eating hamburgers and drinking lager and, for some extraordinary reason, laughing. Josel was wearing a short red cotton dress with a narrow studded leather belt. Forbes teased her and said she must have dyed her hair, but the answer was, 'It's the mountain sun, it has always done that to my hair – *Du wunderschönes Alpenland!*'

He fell silent and thought for a moment of Zulka. She put her hand in his and he said, 'You'll come to Scotland, won't you?'

'Yes, darling Archie, I will come to Scotland, but time, Archie, I need some time – *so* much has happened.'

Then she remembered to give him the malt whisky from her overnight bag and the envelope with the German newspaper cuttings on the death of Alex Bradley. It was time for her to go, so they walked slowly and with increasing reluctance towards the departure gate.

'Your father was wrong about one thing, Josel – it was never a "battle for the soul of Germany". It *is* a battle for the soul and the survival of Western Europe, but in people's minds Western Europe has no identity, certainly not yet, no music, no romance, no banners, no barricades. These are the things which are missing. These are the things people used to die for. In fact, Sergei might tell you that the Red Army would invoke just these ancient sentiments if it should try to crush West Germany – the desperate cry of Mother Russia which has saved them so often.'

'Are you making a speech, darling, or saying *au revoir* to me?'

They were both laughing again – was it a secret relief that the ordeal appeared to be over, or was it just happiness? The final parting was as swift as they could bring themselves to make it – 'The Kenmore Hotel, just leave a message with the Kenmore Hotel. I've given you the number' – and she was gone. He stood and watched the receding figure, returning her wave and asking himself was it only four months since he'd first met a pretty girl in St James's Park and then seen her off at London Airport? It was the only time since he had first met Zulka that love was inescapable, that Forbes the philanderer, the never-quite-grown-up Archie Forbes who couldn't resist a well-turned head or ankle, had gone for ever. He would even be patient, waiting on those Scottish hills.

He had telephoned Kenmore and arranged for Mrs Finlayson to prepare a bed-sitting-room for him in the bothy. He had escaped there once or twice before when he had made Zulka really angry – angry enough to throw him out, in fact – and he knew that walking, solitude and writing would between them heal the violent memories. He knew well how Josel felt when she said, 'Time, Archie, time.'

So with Ruffian in the hatchback of his ancient Golf he made an early start, leaving a telephone number with Mrs Tomlinson should, for some reason, Zulka call. He knew she was in good hands. She adored their daughter Sophie, and Scarlatti, although bloody by any standard, was at least rich. In the car he thought of money and how little there would be once his job ended – his pathetic pension and perhaps something from the book he was going to write – a bit tricky that, with the German police very interested in the whereabouts of someone who killed Bradley. Perhaps Sergei would be able to help with some sort of false trail – assassination is, of course, the occupational hazard of the CIA. Did he regret killing Bradley? NO, emphatically no, he did not. Did he regret anything? Again, no, but perhaps after several days on the hills above Kenmore *some* regret would surface. Time for a stop now, out with Ruffian, out with the Thermos and then a short kip, he decided. The road to the north was always a fast road.

Mrs Finlayson settled him in with a high tea the like of which he had forgotten existed, and then, standing in the doorway of the comfortable, spacious room at the back of the bothy she gently quizzed him.

'You'll be spending your time on the hill, I would imagine, like you did on previous occasions?'

The lilt in her voice was reassuring him that this was no idle curiosity but simple concern for his welfare.

'That is correct, Mrs Finlayson, and then hitting away at my typewriter keys in the evenings. Tell me, are they planning to drive the grouse in a few days' time?'

'Not yet awhile, Mr Forbes, not yet awhile. The birds are that scarce this season after the bad spring. Later, perhaps, they'll be out, I shouldn't wonder, but the keepers will be keeping a sharp eye and I imagine they will be expecting the likes of you to keep to the tracks and the high tops whenever possible.'

The next days were heaven. He took his packed lunch and some whisky in a flask and walked, or lay in the heather, for eight to ten hours. He had remembered his cromack and his field-glasses, and while he looked for birds – and especially the big ones in some vague hope of exorcising the memories of the seven-foot bearded vultures, the lammergeyers, of the Atlas – his mind was constantly busy ravelling and unravelling what he was going to bash out on the typewriter in the evening.

Just as the days were spent tousling his mind with all

the facts and theories surrounding the dramas of the past four months, so were the evenings behind the typewriter flooded with the colours, the shadows, the light, the clouds, the mist and the movement of his walking hours. Never had the loch sparkled with so much magic; seldom could he find a memory which compared with the endless unfolding of hill and sky. Whisky introduced an element of competition – rather happy, if distracting, competition – and once or twice Mrs Finlayson had to tip him gently into bed.

To his surprise, his story took less time to write than he had imagined; it virtually told itself, it was so fresh in the memory. Fiction, of course, he kept reminding himself. No similarity with any characters etc. But at least the *aficionados* would understand what had really happened *and* what was about to happen – oh yes, most certainly yes! It was at this stage that he would fill his glass and let the colour of the day flood back into his mind. He posted each morning to his bank what he had written the evening before.

All he really wanted was for the telephone to ring. He knew it would.

Josel and Elli and Dashka were breakfasting on the terrace and looking respectfully at the mountains, respectfully because Elli had suggested a picnic and a walk, and coming from Elli that meant an energetic day. Josel thought it would be good practice for Scotland. Dashka gave a happy smile.

Willi came with the post. He handed an envelope to Josel and sat down to untangle a periodical from its wrapper. Josel paid no attention to the typed foolscap envelope until Willi said gently, 'It's from London, Josel.'

She opened the envelope and stared uncomprehendingly at a newspaper cutting.

Tragic Death on Grouse Moor

A lone walker was found dead yesterday just above a line of grouse butts near Loch Tay. He had been killed by a single shot from a stalking rifle, said police. Captain Archie Forbes of London . . . .

The print dissolved before her eyes. She heard herself say, 'I thought they killed grouse with shotguns?'

'Yes,' said Willi, holding out his hand for the cutting, 'they do.'

But Josel heard nothing; all she could see were birds of prey.

32

Josel stood in the doorway of Pasinka and remembered. She had no memories of her own, they were all second-hand from grandmother Josel, absorbed at the age of five, but none the less sharp and clear.

She loved the large flagstoned hall with its immense fireplace and the two staircases, one with oak balusters leading to the first-floor drawing-room, and the other, narrow and spiral, up the tower. The tower with its tiny bedrooms off the staircase and the large four-windowed room at the top which had been sometimes bedroom and sometimes study, and the stone steps leading to the small door onto the battlements.

Pasinka – the Gatehouse – had survived everything from the Battle of the White Mountain, through several centuries, through Nazi occupation, through perhaps the harshest of the East European Communist regimes, and now had entered the safe haven of democracy and rightful ownership. 'Or so one hopes,' Josel murmured.

It was now early 1994 and she was only too well aware of the ominous signs that, for many of the peoples liberated from Communism, democracy was proving bitter medicine.

She was the rightful and restored owner of the whole of her grandmother's estate on the edge of what had been the Sudetenland. It was in fairly good repair because the Czech Government had in 1948 handed over the castle to 'the Artists of Bohemia', and they had looked after it tolerably well. A colony of artists usually includes some artisans who, whatever their politics, resent any neglect of the work of fellow craftsmen of earlier centuries. So she had imagined, and so it had proved. The gatehouse, the park, the woods and, to an extent, the farms, were enough for Gordon and her to look after as more or less absentee landlords, and so she had left the artists undisturbed in the castle.

Gordon's wealth had, of course, played its part in all their decisions – as had his intense interest in everything East European. Bohemia – Eastern Europe? How grandmother Josel would have scoffed at the idea!

But then, she often asked herself, had she married Gordon for his money, or because of his sheer niceness – or was it because she couldn't stop thinking of Archie Forbes?

She put some more logs on the fire and went up to the tower room to make sure it was ready for Willi and Elli Ansbach, who were coming for the weekend. There was no *need* to wonder, she thought; her life was balanced and happy, with two young sons and a husband whose only fault was his niceness – what a terrible thing to say, even to oneself – and she laughed as she drew curtains and settled down to wait for Gordon to get back from Moscow. The fire glowed, Pasinka was peaceful – there was just that haunting, mocking memory of a single rifle-shot on a Scottish hill.

Gordon Ellsworth had been a New England playboy until he was thirty, when his father in desperation shippped him out to Seattle to run the family lumber and construction business. In Los Angeles he met and married a 'starlet', who took him for every kind of ride and dumped him, half-full of drugs, in exchange for a lot of money, in the divorce court.

He then set out for Paris, for one last fling, and there met Josel, who seemed, in the eyes of the battered and no longer so young American, the personification of European culture and sophistication. Also, he discerned in her somehow a quality of timelessness. Paris's perennial magic had done the rest.

Gordon had mixed feelings about his very demanding Moscow business trips; they gave him both huge frustration and great satisfaction. His construction empire was big enough and strong enough to cope with the perverse horrors of the Russian longing for everything to happen tomorrow, at the same time as they enjoyed the sardonic humour of delay. He had now gained access to what he called the top brass, and never hesitated to use it. They in turn used Gordon as a channel of communication with Washington.

Gordon's teams of supervisors were in charge of the construction of the housing estates planned for Red Army soldiers returning to Russia from garrison duty in what had been East Germany. He had other projects as well, but this was the one which filled the hopes and expectations of Yeltsin's ministers. They were greedy for success – partly because it would be a show-piece and partly because, having extracted money from Chancellor Kohl to finance the project, they had every intention of extracting more with which to build the factories where the demobilised soldiers could be employed.

They were, of course, oblivious to the dramatic failure in Poland, after World War II, of the programme to provide jobs for war-widows. The factories had been hopelessly badly located and produced goods which no one wanted. There was another, they hoped temporary, difficulty. Local Russian peasants, living in pathetic hovels, were bitterly resenting what seemed such luxurious housing for soldiers who had done nothing in East Germany except 'live off the fat of the land'.

But none of this was Gordon's concern as an industrialist working in partnership with the Civic Union, however dismayed he might be as a liberally minded American.

Returning now from what had been, in all respects except one, a routine visit, he stretched out his long legs in the aircraft and prepared to do homework. He wished he was going skiing, the snow in the Alps was perfect for early March – goddam! Willi was actually coming *from* the Tyrol! Well, perhaps he and Josel could slip away after the weekend for a couple of days in the Riesengebirge.

In the car from Prague airport to Pasinka he did rather more serious thinking. What he had just been told in Moscow took some believing, however impeccable the source. It took so *much* believing that some form of corroboration was essential if it was not to join all the other fantastic stories in his private Arabian nights collection. Willi? Well, Willi Ansbach was a great man on the grape-vine, but he had little access to Western intelligence these days. *Western* intelligence – what *was* he thinking? They would be the *last* people; hadn't Boris Yeltsin said, 'And don't go to the CIA, for a check, Gordon. You might as well ask Santa Claus!' And then had come that hoarse, rumbling laugh. Even so, thought Gordon, even so . . . .

When he got to the house, Josel was watering an azalea for the Ansbach's bedroom. She was wearing a kaftan, and when he kissed her he said, 'that looks like an omen,' and enjoyed the puzzled look on her face. So then he had to explain what he had been told, and discuss the implications for Europe as a whole, especially Germany. They talked into the night, and Josel, of course, guessed the source of Gordon's information, although the name was never mentioned.

Josel lay back on the long sofa by the fire. Its glow lighted the Slav cheek bones and the now tousled hair. At forty two she had lost none of her looks, although perhaps there was a calmness about her expression which took away some of the youthfulness of the early years of their marriage. Memories often show themselves on faces, he reminded himself, and he thought for a moment of the Atlas Mountains. He loved her for a whole heap of reasons, but the combination of gentleness and courage always came top; her unshakable belief in the basic fairness and decency of human nature. She perfectly accepted that leadership could call for sacrifice, but believed that it could also require an element of ruthlessness. One weakness, he knew, was her sometimes uncritical admiration for a ruthless streak in others.

'Come on, Gordon.' The voice from the sofa was slightly husky from slivovic. 'You're day-dreaming, and what's more, in all this time you haven't told me what Yeltsin and his KGB pal actually expect you to *do*.'

'I never mentioned Yeltsin.' There was an edge to his voice.

'No, but you might just as well have done, darling. Now it's getting late, so spill the beans, as they said in the old movies; he wants you to ask Clinton for help, doesn't he?'

Gordon gave a huge snort of laughter. He had enjoyed, in his long-winded American way, painting the background, explaining how well-informed Moscow was about Germany and what they had called 'the new virus': the combination of economic recession with ethnic revisionism, inflation, the flood of refugees, and now political instability in Germany itself, where riots were beginning to threaten the sheet-anchor of Europe's economy. Finally had come the bombshell from Deniksenko, the KGB former hard-liner who had only recently defected *to* Yeltsin.

'But bombshells on their own are not enough,' Josel said. 'Of course a defector delivers a bombshell; he must to justify his defection, but apart from "Is it true?" someone has to say, "what do *we do* about it?" I can easily believe that the Red Army hard-liners are in cahoots with Saddam – it makes sense. But for Yeltsin to pull you in for a briefing by Denisenko and nothing else, makes no sense at all. So I'll tell you what he wants – not that you haven't known it all along, but you've waffled around, my darling, because you think it'll scare the daylights out of me!' Her eyes were sparkling. 'Well, you're right, it does, but we might still have to do it just the same. They want us to pick up where we left off in '81 and do *something* which will shake the Germans *and* the Yanks out of their goddam complacency, something which will make Slick Willie not just *want* to help Yeltsin but *have* to help him if Russia and Germany are not both to fall apart with the rest of Europe not that far behind! Come on, old darling, let's tumble into bed where I can hug you for minding so much about the ghosts of my past!'

33

The Ansbach's arrived early enough for Willi and Gordon to go down to the lake and shoot some duck. It was late afternoon with swiftly changing light; a sky of torn green silk with a biting wind which kept the birds coming. Severely tested, their skills just managed to produce that glow of satisfaction which precedes hot baths, malt whisky and the conversation on which both men had been brooding. Willi looked all of his seventy five years and his facial expression, never one of unbridled cheerfulness, almost justified the phrase 'sunk in gloom'. But the eyes still had their humour and vitality and his voice the sharpness of live wit.

'Suppose, Gordon, you give me an appreciation of the situation, as we were taught in the Wehrmacht.' He stretched out long legs to the fire.

'I'll do better,' said Gordon, 'I'll give you Denisenko's appreciation and you can cross-examine me as if I were him!'

The two men knew they had some two hours before supper. They also knew that the wives would join them, so much would have to be repeated, but the process would sharpen all their wits.

'Well, here goes,' said Gordon. 'Denisenko's appreciation in my language, and no interruptions please. Yeltsin is still in bad shape politically, under increasing threat from his Fascist hard line wing as the Russian economy lurches through this appalling winter of discontent, cold and despair, plus inflation of Weimar proportions. The privatisation programme has collapsed in ridicule. In Germany the neo-Nazi riots show Kohl's inability to control unrest, and efforts to restrict the flow of refugees have met with little success. Kohl receives meagre sympathy or understanding from his European colleagues, who are still in a swamp called Maastricht.

'The West, and especially America, *must* understand that Eastern Europe and the Balkans now have a new virus with which to infect the whole Continent, a devil's concoction of recession, ethnic passions masquerading as nationalism, and tides of refugees. It would be fair to say that the *whole* of Europe is now reeling from the consequences of ending the Cold War – its forty-year-old insurance policy of peace and stability. You have a new US President who is preoccupied with a domestic economy which has been much neglected and burdened by winding down defence programmes, huge deficits and fears of still more "high-tech" unemployment as large corporations seek to put their new investment into Mexico. In the US, most references to the Balkans, the erstwhile Soviet Union republics, Russia, even Germany, are met with mutterings of "Vietnam", "quagmire", "body-bags" and "our boys". From where Clinton sits, neither Mitterand nor Major, and certainly not Kohl, look a good long-term bet. What is needed is a new and immense Marshall Plan, but of that there is not the slightest chance unless and until US public opinion is moved by either fear or compassion.'

'How do we bring that about? By administering any day now, a shock of seismic proportions which I will tell you about, but, as it is so far without proof and therefore invisible, it will have no credibility. In consequence there must be an overture, a visible panic-rousing horror which is instantly credible and can be played fortissimo by the media to the audiences of Western Europe and America. Panic must grip their throats.'

'This is beginning to sound all very Russian,' muttered Willi.

Gordon reproached him with a glance. He was into the part now; it was the ex KGB man who was speaking. The wives had slipped silently into the room and were listening with amazement. He went on. 'And so to the centre-piece. Rogue right-wing elements in the Red Army have reached an accord with Saddam. I need not spell out the implications. Their nostalgia for the power they enjoyed in the Cold War, and their disgust at Russia's failing experiments with democracy have led them to an alliance which they are confident will enable them to regain their ascendancy. It is cold horror. I helped to negotiate it. It is the reason for my defection. You must take this information yourself to Clinton; no other channel will carry conviction.

And the overture? The visible shock? That must be in Germany – an immense escalation of the neo-Nazi riots which will show Germany to be what it is, the tinder-box of Europe, from where panic hits out through every television screen in Europe and America and destroys the lethargy and wishful thinking of the West – and so becomes the concoctor of the only antidote for Europe's death wish. And the *blame* for these riots must be laid at the door of the Red Army's extremists.'

Gordon was exhausted, and looked it. Someone recharged his glass.

Willi spoke, trying to keep the disbelief out of his voice. 'And who's going to conduct the overture?'

'We are' said Gordon, and his voice shook a little.

They gave up then and had dinner – roast venison with a decent Hungarian red wine. They all knew better than to continue the discussion before bed, but in reply to Willi's question Gordon said, 'Denisenko knows that we have, cached in Germany, a large amount of heroin, and suggests we could use it to fuel the anti-Nazi riots.'

'For that we would need a Che Guevara', said Willi gloomily.

In the morning sunshine, with a glorious hoar frost on the trees, they walked and talked round Josel's demesne. They stumbled through frozen ditches and climbed over fences with broken stiles, and the peaceful smiles of the odd peasants they met told them all they needed – that 'Prague Spring' was finally a reality. 'Let's hold on to it this time,' the faces said.

Willi brushed the frost from his sleeves as they got back to Pasinka and, without looking at anyone in particular, said, 'If you can convince Clinton, I will provide our Che Guevara – but hurry, because Easter is the crucial time and the neo-Nazis *are* organised. That I can promise you.'

Josel gripped Gordon's hand and whispered, 'You *will* tell me, what *exactly* this Che is going to do?'

Gordon thought he knew only too well.

34

After lunch Willi and Gordon talked, recognising that what they were about to tackle was going to call for every ounce of judgement and energy they possessed. As they talked themselves into clarity, the tasks they saw for themselves took shape, and then each questioned the other on the detail of how they should handle every stage.

The contrast between the two men could hardly have been greater. Willi's face showed his seventy five years of poor health; the eyes and mouth were putting up a fight against lassitude, and the overall impression was that of a man asking himself, 'Just what am I taking on?'

Gordon, on the other hand, was a picture of 52-year-old energy. Fair hair and blue eyes gave him a Scandinavian look, and his trim, fit figure radiated New England energy. He wondered what kept Willi going. Was it deep conviction, loyalty to Helmut, love of Josel, or that peculiarly German sense of obligation – that Hitler's debt must somehow be repaid? Willi's role was crucial. He must handle this man he called 'Che Guevara', he must provide the heroin without revealing its hiding-place, and he must ensure that media reaction to, and coverage of, the riots attributed them to the intervention of Red Army extremists – massive tasks for one man, however experienced and dedicated.

They slogged on, both well aware that whether Willi took even the first step would depend on White House reaction to the Yeltsin/Denisenko–bombshell.

In the morning they set off early in two cars. The plan was to lunch in the Riesengebirge, after which Willi and Elli would visit Dresden on their way home; something they had long wanted to do. It was a magical walk in brilliant sunshine along the Polish frontier to the ski-hotel. Deep virgin snow made them all pink-faced – even Willi – and puffing. They stopped quite often to gaze at the ever-widening view of mountains above and dark forests below, part of its enchantment being the reminder that here was a corner of Europe unscarred and unchanged since the Hapsburg empire.

They lunched in blazing sunshine on the hotel terrace, watching the skiers in rather sombre mood as the questions and answers of yesterday filtered through their minds. Josel now knew exactly how Willi was going to use the heroin and, for all her great conviction, felt a shudder as she visualised Easter in the great cities of what had been East Germany.

'What's the name of your revolutionary, Willi?' asked Gordon as they were all taking leave.

'Carl Heinz' said Willi, fixing Gordon with a look which said *leave all this to me*. 'I know him well, he worked for me for a time on the journal. You won't be disappointed; in fact, I suspect he may even exceed your fond hopes.'

This last comment came with a smile which on any other face would have been mischievous. Gordon thought, he still likes to take the mickey out of a Yank.

Once on the road home Josel let herself rip. 'You were a *great* Denisenko, Gordon – you got right into the part – but who *is* this guy and why does he carry such guns with Yeltsin, and with you, for that matter?'

Josel's Americanism, delivered with her French accent, was as ever music to his ear, and he laughed with the enjoyment of getting rid of tedious explanation (dear Willi *was* long-winded) and getting down to nuts and bolts.

She went on, 'How can we handle anything so big? In '81 our "struggle for the soul of Germany" came to nothing because Reagan pulled the rug; now we are embarking on rescue for the "soul of Europe", is that right? Then we had allies, now we have Denisenko. Tell me I'm dreaming, Gordon, tell me Europe's got to find another Sir Galahad – I'm not as brave as I was! And why, for God's sake, *should* a new Marshall Plan succeed? Russia has been the despair of everyone since Peter the Great.'

Gordon glanced sideways, smiled and said something about the New World coming to the rescue of the old. Then he took her gently through the arguments for responding to Yeltsin's plea – for plea it was – and supporting the idea of crisis intervention by both fair means *and* foul.

'The world is nowadays only roused by crisis, visible understandable crisis, like riots in Germany. Words like "recession" and a statistic like 600,000 refugees arriving in one year are meaningless. They provoke no feeling. Blood on the streets, as shown by the media, *becomes* public opinion, witness Boris Yeltsin on his tank. To tell them that the Red Army "baddies" have a deal with Saddam is a yawn – bread-and-butter stuff from the CIA – but show them on telly the collapse of law and order in German cities and it stirs that fear only just dormant, the nightmare scenario of Germany slipping back sixty years.

'A new vast Marshall Plan *will* work because it must be based on investment in Russia's vast mineral and oil reserves. As the US proved in the 19th century, if you move the right people on to huge natural resources you get the American Dream!'

Josel found her hand in his and, smiling told him to get on with his driving. Gordon squeezed the hand. 'Now tell me about Denisenko.' Her voice was crisp and businesslike.

'There's not a lot to tell. He was the original hardliner – KGB right or wrong his credo – and so he fell out with Gorbie when Gorbie wooed the West and, in Denisenko's book, deserted the East European soviets. But Denisenko is first and last a patriot and his discovery of the Red Army/Saddam pact took him straight down the road to Damascus. He was head of the First Chief Directorate i.e. foreign intelligence and, even more significant, he was close to Khomeini when he was top KGB man in Iran. So when *he* is convinced of a Red Army–Saddam deal it's got to be for real.'

'But you're still checking?'

'You bet – I'll see Bob Scholey at Heathrow on my way to Washington.'

'One more question, darling, and then I'll shut up. OK, so there's a deal with Saddam, horrible implications of every kind, but what does this new Red Army alliance actually have to *do* to bring the US to understand an *immediate* need for a Marshall Plan?'

'Honey, it doesn't have to *do* anything, it just has to be seen to take the blame – unfairly, of course – for what Willi and Carl Heinz are going to trigger at Easter and high summer – riots big enough to make us all sick with fear.'

35

Bob Scholey paced round the lobby of the Forte hotel at Heathrow looking at notices, people, goldfish, newspaper headlines and occasionally a clock. He was an active man and waiting for people to appear always made him restless; perhaps today was a good excuse for restlessness because he could not, for the life of him, figure out why Gordon Ellsworth should want to see him so urgently. Yes, it *had* happened before. Gordon had summoned him at short notice to meetings in a dozen different capitals but *always* with an explanation, however brief. Time enough always to collect his thoughts, do some homework even, but this summons was different, out of character; strange.

Bob was that rarish animal in the construction industry – a freelance engineer. Freelance because he enjoyed it, it gave him immense variety and it was lucrative; also it fitted well with his background. Bob's father had been a Corporal of Horse in the Household Cavalry when they helped to liberate Iraq from Rashid Ali in the summer of 1941. An enterprising soldier in more senses that one, he had 'liberated' Bob's mother, who was later put to death. Bob's appearance – swarthy and dark-eyed – was on his side, and he had survived a strange and instructive upbringing; instructive in the sense that he learnt, with his foster-mother's milk, how to 'dodge the column', 'stay ahead of the game', expressions he thought his father would have approved of. But Bob had inherited something else – the concept of fair dos. If a man played straight with you, you played straight with him, and Gordon Ellsworth was in that category. He had done jobs for Gordon of many kinds, some very difficult, not to say tricky, but they had come out right in the end. Gordon was a man you could trust.

Only a very few minutes later he was feeling sorely tempted to revise such a hard-won opinion, but he clenched his teeth in a grin as Gordon unfolded Denisenko's story.

'I never took you for a sucker, Gee, but I think someone's taking you for one now.' Gordon waved a hand. 'All right, I'll shut up and listen but I wasn't brought up in the land of 1,001 nights not to smell – OK, OK, you just go on to the end, if there *is* an end,' and the chuckle was close to a guffaw.

When Gordon had finished and Bob had subsided into thoughtfulness, they ordered lager and sandwiches and munched in silence. It was the silence of disbelief; both men were now wondering what substance there could be in such an ominous and strange alliance. Could even Saddam risk the frail and virtually negative support he could still look for in the Arab world? Could the Red Army – extremists, certainly – throw away the last shreds of respectability it had gained since the Berlin wall came down? Deals yes, there would always be deals, arms must be bought and sold; the Caucasus was vulnerable to Islamic influence, was it not? But an alliance? With bilateral obligations? Public knowledge in course of time? And hysterical reaction a copper-bottomed certainty?

'OK, Gee,' said Bob eventually, 'leave it to me – but if I give you the answer you seem to want to hear, you might just bear in mind that *this* time the old joke about what happens to me if my sources are blown is not a joke any more. One whiff of a connection between me and the rather nasty mechanics of checking your story, and Engineer Scholey is found – or rather not found – floating face down in the Tigris. I may have *access*, Gee, but Madam Access can be a tricky bitch, so just remember.'

Gordon felt a heel, and from the twinkle in Bob's eye it could just be the thought gave him pleasure. They parted.

36

Gordon was at home in Washington, DC. He often wondered why that was, because politics had no appeal for him whatever. He had inherited from his father an indifference towards the motives of politicians; he judged their actions and their plans with the yardstick of *cui bono*, and where he believed he could see a long-term benefit to his business and to the U S of A, he would try his darnedest. Too simple by half? Probably yes, but it seemed to work. In the field of really big long-term construction programmes a degree or two of over-simplification seemed to be the right formula. It had worked well with Reagan and Bush, so why not with the new boy? He could but try. So he'd sent the message into the White House: 'Boris Yeltsin wants me to discuss with you a construction deal bigger than anything you, he or I have ever thought of.'

Gordon Ellsworth wasn't an arrogant man – he'd made too many early mistakes for that – but he'd got used to being listened to on the subject of Europe, and, in Washington's eyes, Josel's German and Czech blood was a useful enhancer of prestige. So it came as no great surprise that he found himself, two evenings later, in the upstairs sitting-room of the White House (was there still a whiff of Jackie Kennedy somewhere in the décor?) with a glass of malt whisky and two very attentive listeners. He had spiked the message with 'there is, of course, an element of blackmail about all this'. There had been questions, many questions, but it didn't take all that long – to his pleasant surprise.

'You're having this checked at the Iraq end, you say, but however good that check, the only real proof is when the trouble starts – correct, Gordon?' He was standing by the elevator now and his hand was being shaken with a warmth which brought the laughter in the voice tingling into his fingers. 'Take care the CIA doesn't get a whiff of any of this deal Gordon, or we'll have another Iran–Contra on our hands.'

He followed the security man back to his car, trying to remember Reagan's instructions to Ollie North, or was it Nelson's signal at Copenhagen? He preferred the latter.

On the plane to Seattle the following day he again reminded himself that there were never fewer than three US foreign policies at any one time, their progenitors being the White House, the Pentagon and the State Department. Could he really believe that the joke made standing by the elevator was in fact the go-ahead? It had better be, Gordon said to himself, because I'm going to act on it.

Was this the boy scout in him suddenly taking charge? Or had Helmut's original vision for Germany and now for Europe so filled his mind as to become the Holy Grail? Or was there an element of jealousy of Archie Forbes? Was he subconsciously vowing to outshine him? Well, that hardly made sense, because Archie, by all accounts, even Josel's, had been lukewarm at best and had probably even considered sabotage.

The stewardess came round with more coffee, which

he declined. He abandoned his search for a motive and went to sleep.

37

Josel scratched around in the little panelled study in Pasinka for the telephone codes which would – or might – reach out to Jean Louis in his Malgache *gisement* and defy the fitful behaviour of his radio telephone. She had rehearsed what she was going to say; it must be simple. She and Jean Louis had kept in touch. He was godfather to Franz, her elder boy, and they had last met in New York when he was visiting a graphite customer in New Jersey. He had grown more like his father, heavier in the shoulders, and there was grey in the fine dark hair. He had the look of the *colon*, a sort of wariness which seemed to ask why civilisation was so unnecessarily complicated. He had taken trouble with Franz, remembering Christmas and birthdays with knives and woodcarvings – fearsome sometimes – from Madagascar.

It was early morning, so radio interference was slight and she got it all said in quick, competent sentences. Was he planning to visit Grossalmerode in the near future on a routine visit to the crucible manufacturers, and if so would he join them at Pasinka for Easter?

Bien sûr, most certainly he would.

Would he perhaps add two weeks to his visit, one week to give some help to Willi and one week to ski with the boys in the High Tatra?

The radio crackle, now warming up as the sun rose,

did nothing to subdue his laughter. 'I haven't skied since I was in the French Army – *mais oui, oui, bien sûr, et j'arriverai chez vous pour Pâques!*' His laughter almost drowned the crackle. Josel hadn't had to explain what 'helping Willi' meant. They had remained friends, ill-assorted brothers of different ages, was how she always saw them in her mind. Besides, they were guardians of the 'graphite'; it had never been given to Strenca thanks to Operation Ryan, only Willi and Jean Louis knew the hiding-place to which it had been moved after the stand-down of 1981. Somebody might have thought that Archie had also known; and she frowned.

She felt a lot happier at the prospect of Jean Louis coming to help what was fast becoming a complex situation. *If* the White House gave the nod, Gordon would have to brief Yeltsin, keeping all the 'usual channels' completely in the dark. Willi would bring Carl Heinz as quickly as possible to Pasinka, and then those awful final decisions would be taken. Thank God for Jean Louis and the High Tatra mountains. She longed for Gordon to call.

Gordon's voice from Seattle was jubilant. 'You remember I spoke about lingering doubts,' he said. 'Well, they're all but resolved. I had a call early this morning which in effect said that the message had sunk in, and contingency planning had started. That's fast work, Josel, and it means I can make the other leg.'

She longed to know what 'all but' meant, as well as what the lingering doubts had been; the 'other leg', she knew, meant Yeltsin. She felt cheered and at the same time appalled at the hugeness of their project; they were turning Germany into some sort of arena for gladiators.

Of course, she reminded herself, there is still Bob Scholey. He could turn up at any moment and tell them there was no such thing as a Saddam–Red Army pact, saying that it was just another of the endless stream of canards which flow through the so-called intelligence channels, designed to provoke yet more careless talk and maintain the tensions. Rumours which were the bastard sons of every bazaar.

Get out, she thought, and walk – watch the ducks swinging low over the frozen lake as the light fails and they look for open water, let the conifers do their job of looking ghostly against the night sky, think of Jean Louis's laughter and the excited faces of the boys, now so nearly on their way.

'Or in other words,' she said aloud, 'be a sensible mother and wife.' Gordon would go direct to Moscow, and how long would that all take? Damn – she was fretting again. She never used to. For a moment she thought of Sergei Melkov – wishing he was still on the team. But at the height of the Operation Ryan flap he had been quietly removed, much too quietly they had thought.

38

Collecting his thoughts in an aircraft was therapy for Gordon, and if sleep intervened the process was usually enhanced, so flying via London to Moscow gave him perfect conditions for what the business schools call 'balanced reappraisal'. He thought first of Nixon's remark about Yeltsin – 'our best friend in the race between the new democracies and the old despots in new clothes'. Clinton would think like that too, he decided. And what about the paranoia in both Europe and the US about the future role of Germany? Assuming that Willi's wild card, Carl Heinz Winterhalter, succeeded in raising tension in Germany to fever pitch and hanging the noose round the necks of the old despots in the Red army, would Yeltsin keep his nerve and embark with the US on the rescue plan, or would Russian anathema for deals with the West take him down the same road as Gorbie? Back to Yeltsin again; all reasoning took one back to Boris.

He yawned, 'so here goes,' he muttered, waiting for the rumble of the undercarriage, the formalities, and the taxi to the Metropole Hotel.

His message was a simple one. If, as a consequence of the Red Army–Sadam link, the situation in Russia and/or Germany began to look, or even become, threatening to the peace of Europe, the US would launch an economic rescue plan of immense proportions on a very long-term basis. Security for loans would require that Russian's mineral, gemstone and oil wealth be pledged as assets, thus stabilising the currency. Implementation would be in the hands of Yeltsin and the US President alone, and for practical purposes – i.e. the approval of the US Congress – the turmoil would have to be so great that the decision would be of equivalent status to a declaration of war.

Gordon sighed and gasped simultaneously as the cold air hit him with the opening of the taxi door. There was still Bob Scholey, he reminded himself, almost with a feeling of relief.

He called Josel and had a banal chat about the flight and the weather. He could never completely get rid of the feeling that hotel bedroom chandeliers still nursed unrepentant bugs.

His meeting with Yeltsin and Denisenko was fixed for two days later, so Gordon decided to spend twenty four hours in St Petersburg and then mooch around Moscow before the meeting. It was a long time since he's seen anything of Russia except hotels, offices and construction sites.

Moscow station was straight out of *Doctor Zhivago*; only the steam was missing. Gloom became virtual darkness as the station confines closed in on him, full of human noise and smells as people shuffled, heaving burdens.

Gordon's taxi-driver hired two large men to carry and protect his suitcase, illustrating vividly in dumb wambo how otherwise he would never see it again. Diesel locomotives certainly, but otherwise the train was vintage – a lavish and very overheated vintage. Like everyone else on that train he drank vodka and slept like a child.

It was still early light when the train crept past the

tiny houses on the outskirts of St Petersburg, so Gordon told his taxi-driver to take him straight to the Neva river knowing that the ice and the bridges and the two great rostral columns of the original port looked their best in low sunlight. They stopped by the river wall for photographs and for the black-market boys to emerge stealthily. Gordon bought fur caps for Josel and the boys. Then it was breakfast at the Hotel St Petersburg, followed by the taxi-driver's idea of a guided tour of palaces, canals, Falconet's statue of Peter the Great, St Isaac's Cathedral and, after lunch, the Russian Museum.

Lunch was bortsch with vodka, followed by a freshwater fish. It was a good restaurant, judging not by the food but by the Mafia-looking types in expensive suits. He had had dealings with them in the past and found them unpleasant but effective. It was all too easy to accept them as part of the landscape.

The Russian Museum in Carl Rossi's Milchailovsky Palace was a different world. He stood or wandered enchanted. the snow, sleighs and sky of Kustodiev's *Maslenitsa* were painted with its bustle of winter activity and energy just one year before the Revolution, when the United States was about to join the war and Russia was about to leave. Boris Yeltsin might well have stood in front of Vasnetsov's *The Hero at the Crossroads* with its beckoning skulls and bird of prey?

Driving to the airport he had only two thoughts – how ridiculously American to think you can 'do' St Petersburg in one day, and, if St Petersburg tells you anything it is that Russia is a country worth saving. This time the attempt must succeed.

39

Boris Yeltsin was not, to Gordon's mind, looking like a man of destiny, nor did his first words dispel anxiety – 'You are looking at another Mikhail Gorbachev!' But they were followed by a twinkle and, a little later, a rumbling laugh.

The face was tired and the hands no longer motionless. 'Your president is really going to save Russia from the hands of despots, or can the West still not forgive Stalin?'

Gordon took a deep breath. This was not going to be easy. Both their countries loved drama, he knew well, but drama was the most treacherous ally in delicate manoeuvres. Silence became his temporary refuge as he watched his face being carefully studied. 'I still have enemies who want to have me out,' the big man said, 'and the Red Army, backed by Iraq's power for mischief, would then make puppets of them.' "No deals with the West" would be the populist cry, "Russia needs firm, independent Government" – in other words dictatorship with the face of democracy. October 1917 all over again.' The voice was becoming harsher. 'Do you want that? Does Europe want that?'

'There is, of course, a beautiful irony in their solution, which you will appreciate.' The tone was becoming sarcastic. 'The new dictatorship would do an economic deal with Germany, a very favourable deal for Russia because the threats they have to offer are very persuasive – riots in German cities activated by Red Army special forces, ultimately civil war, with NATO therefore forbidden to intervene.' The smile was becoming less menacing and humour was creeping into the voice. 'Now – there you have it, cards on the table, isn't that what you Americans always ask for?'

Yes, thought Gordon, cards on the table; the chessmen could still be somewhere else.

'The tragedy,' he then heard his host say quietly almost as if to himself, 'is that it would be economic salvation but political death.' 'It is time,' he resumed, 'that the US is giving Russia aid, massive useful, helpful aid, and if we had a political life span of ten years, or even perhaps five years, in which to breed the virus of democracy into our institutions, it might be enough. But the enemies of democracy would like to give me, at the most, months and possibly less. Please remember that, after World War II, Germany was given years in which to create her economic miracle, and so the foundations of democracy were laid without too much difficulty. I can see from the expression on your face that you need no lessons in Russian history!'

Which means, of course, thought Gordon, that he believes the US Administration certainly does, and a lesson in propaganda warfare as well. To the perception of Yeltsin in his present predicament, the necessary aid programme not only had to be of gargantuan proportions, but mounted simultaneously with a message to the world which would have struck with awe those who heard the Sermon on the Mount.

He groped for words. 'Mr President,' and he tried to make his voice sound jocular, 'if we were standing in the middle of a park – '

He was interrupted by a roar. 'Microphones! Microphones! I should have known – you Americans think only of microphones! To the roof then, in the cold February wind you can tell me. Bring vodka,' he shouted, and a minute later they stood on the roof beside a parapet, while the security men edged nervously out of earshot as their master directed. Denisenko was already pouring vodka into mugs.

'It is simple enough really,' said Gordon apologetically. 'For the US President a crisis in Germany such as you describe must outweigh, *apparently* outweigh, all other considerations. Then, and only then, can he tell the world that to rescue Germany – that is, in fact, Western Europe – he must rescue Russia as well. He must be able to explain that only the rescue of Russia makes the rescue of Germany possible. That should be simple enough, even for American voters.'

Gordon felt a huge arm round his shoulders and the mug of vodka pressed firmly against his lips.

40

Two nights after Gordon's arrival in Moscow Josel was devoutly hoping he would call, not least because Bob Scholey had telephoned from Rome saying that he hoped he could meet Gordon in Vienna. He had sounded not quite his usual cheerful self and refused to give a date for a meeting, just saying he would call again. She was just about to call Gordon's hotel and leave a message asking for news when Scholey called again.

'Tell Gee,' he said, 'I'll be at your house late Friday,' and rang off. So Bob was in trouble – people only behaved like that when they were in trouble; Josel began to feel the memories of 1981 stealing back and allowed herself a quick shudder.

She knew she couldn't and mustn't affect Gordon's timing in any way, but she thought a garbled message – which would certainly be even *more* garbled by the time he got it – would do the trick.

It worked. Gordon came on the line rather testily and said, 'What's all this about neighbours wanting to shoot duck?'

'Not *neighbours*, darling, it's just Bob.'

'Bob,' he said, after a long silence. 'OK, fine, tell him I'll look forward to seeing him. I can let you have a flight number in the morning.'

So Josel had to be content; it was Wednesday

evening. On Friday she sent Gordon's driver to the airport with a note explaining – or rather *not* explaining – Bob's telephone calls.

Gordon appeared at dusk and came into the house grinning and saying, 'He'll be too late to flight duck if he doesn't appear pronto,' and they heard the sound of a car.

Bob Scholey leapt out shouting apologies, and whatever irritation they had felt vanished as they led him into the house, listening to a jumble of explanations which, once he had a glass of whisky in his hand, condensed themselves to a single sentence – 'I think I've got a tail.' He slopped a little of his whisky and dabbed at his trousers with a handkerchief.

'How come?' said Gordon.

'Two men at Rome airport.'

'When?' said Gordon.

'When I arrived from Baghdad; that's why I called Josel and said I would come here. I think I've shaken them.'

'But you're not sure?'

'No, dammit, I'm *not* sure, and *if* I've ballsed it up I could have brought them on to you – bloody idiot not to drop the whole thing and go on to London.' He swallowed the rest of his whisky and stared at Gordon, as if asking for agreement.

Gordon filled his glass and said, 'If they're anywhere in this neighbourhood we'll hear about it by morning. Strangers are always noticed in this part of the country, and I'm assuming your friends must be Iraqis – correct?'

'Sure, Gee, they're Iraqis, but not very noticeable as such. It's time I calmed down and told you what I've learnt. It's good and bad, Gee, it's both good and bad.' The whisky was steadying him and the humour was coming back into his voice and eyes.

'They've got a pact all right, the Red Army and Saddam, and of course it's nuclear weapons for Iraq as you would expect, but what the Red Army gets in exchange is not so crystal clear.'

'Are your sources quite certain – put it simply, how would they know?'

'How would they know?' And Bob laughed, his old happy laugh, the one he liked to tease the Yanks with. 'Because my "sources" have to prepare the nuclear weapon sites, that's all. They got me in on preparing the site for the Supergun, that's why I know them so well. I couldn't very well tell you about that at the time, Gee – it might have embarrassed you,' and off he went again into his now infectious laughter. 'Well I don't know what the Red Army expect to get out of this deal, but it will sure scare the hell out of the US – that's for certain.'

Gordon filled his whisky glass and took him up to his room. He didn't think the hard-liners of the Red Army would have much difficulty in making use of their pact, and scaring the US Administration would be high on their list.

Bob had a happy evening, forgetting – or anyway seeming to – the tail at Rome airport. He talked about his sons, one of whom had joined the British Army and was at present in Northern Ireland. 'He'll make a good soldier; he's a corporal and the men like him, that means they won't let you down. Northern Ireland? Well, it's a bit of old-fashioned British Imperialism in a way. The best sort, I mean, preventing the natives from cutting each other to ribbons.'

Josel asked about his wife.

'Oh, she's a happy lady – Scots girl, you know. they understand about husbands who wander all over the world; it's in their history.' They talked and laughed and then stopped to look at the moon because Josel always left the curtains open when the moon was full. Moonlight on dark trees was rather like life itself.

Bob Scholey left after a late breakfast, heading back for Vienna by Prague and the frontier post at Snoimo.

'Are you happy now, Gee?' he said, 'because I can't do more, if there *was* a tail it's because I've pushed my luck, and they may just have *wanted* me to spot it so as to warn me off. But go carefully, Gee, go carefully, you're just the kind of guy Saddam would like to see dog- knotted!' Now he was laughing and waving as he drove away.

'Salt of the earth,' Josel heard Gordon murmur.

By lunch-time they had done all their telephoning, bar Jean Louis, giving March 17 as the date for the meeting at Pasinka; Willi would include Carl Heinz. Jean Louis would call, Josel knew, as soon as his dates were firm for his European trip. It was action now, that was clear from the little she'd so far heard about Gordon's Moscow mission. Nasty, brutal action which could, as always, so easily go wrong.

41

Carl Heniz Winterhalter was the product of post-war disillusion, too much education and parents who adored him for the wrong reasons. Also he had an Irish mother, so no amount of education had been able to do more than cover his passions with a cold veneer. His father had been a student architect when he joined the German Army and was sent to the Russian front in 1943. He had spent the next seven years in a Russian prison camp, returning to the Rhineland unimpaired except for a bitter resentment for Nazi Germany and all that it had inflicted on his country. Marriage had brought out a kind nature to balance his acerbic mind, and Carl Heinz had epitomised, to his father, all he thought post-war Germany could and should become. He had therefore been amazed when his son, half-way through his law studies, had announced he was off to spend five years in the Foreign Legion.

His mother was distraught; explanation there seemed to be none. Girls? Yes, there had been plenty of girls, but always ships passing; there was a coolness, some thought coldness, about the man which the girls said reminded them of the English. 'Irish,' he would then say sharply, passion for a moment sparking, and they would peel with laughter because German girls know about Irish blood – 'You Irish are like the Poles, full of untrustworthy charm!'

Carl Heinz would scowl and his mother would remind him that the Irish have a sense of humour. 'And a sense of injustice,' was the invariable reply. He was good-looking in a dark, almost Byronic way, strongly built but with graceful movements which concealed it. He had worked for Willi Ansbach for a time as a freelance journalist; a political column had been his aim but Willi had hesitated to give him the free rein he longed for. 'You are basically a Communist,' he would say, and Carl Heinz's answer had invariable been, 'No, No, Willi, I am a left-wing English Socialist,' and after much coffee and laughter they would let it go at that.

The Foreign Legion had been an escape from restlessness and a way of learning about men of his own age who came from strange backgrounds which they wanted to lose and forget – or did they? That puzzled him; he couldn't understand why people should want to lose their background. *His* background had forged all his thoughts and many of his intentions, he felt, and he wanted to be a social animal, an agent for change, and how could you understand other people's backgrounds and history except by studying your own?

The Kolwezi raid in 1978 to rescue European residents from the Katangan rebels had fired his imagination as a young man with his idealism unimpaired, and the performance of the Legion's parachute battalion seemed to call directly for him to show that he too had such qualities. From the first step, to the tough commando school in the old Mont Louis fortress in Andorra, and thence to the parachute course at Calvi, he had felt nothing but exhiliration. Then in '83 the job became peace-keeping with the Green Berets in Beirut under sniping and shellfire. More than anything else he learnt the strength of comradeship, something which he realised would never leave him.

When Carl Heinz walked into the hall at Pasinka with Willi, Josel felt there was a warmth about him, a warmth which had been absent from Willi's description, and she wondered if this was the male instinct, almost predatory, which made an animal manipulate its own personality in order to lull or coerce others. She mistrusted it but enjoyed it to the full; the man was witty and attractive and well-informed. He would be good company, and whatever it was about him which was slightly sinister did nothing to diminish his charm.

Men would follow him.

42

By lunch-time on 17 March they were all assembled except for Jean Louis, who had been delayed by his crucible manufacturers in Grossalmerode.

It was clear – to Gordon's surprise – that Willi's briefing of Carl Heinz had been very thorough indeed, and so, with coffee, Gordon asked him to outline his plan of campaign, which he did with a quite startling clarity and an almost patronising attitude to questions. His posture was one of total confidence, and Gordon for one found himself flogging his brain for ideas on which to quiz this surprising young man. He caught Willi's eye and saw that he at least was thoroughly enjoying the performance – his subdued twinkies speaking volumes.

Then Josel's cook announced Jean Louis, who walked into the hall and exploded with affection. His pleasure at being with them all spilt over to Carl Heinz – the new boy, the stranger upon whom so much depended.

Gordon first gave a summary of his Washington and Moscow conversations, taking care not to dramatise or exaggerate, as he felt inhibited rather by the presence of the young stranger. He then made Carl Heinz go through his plan again from A to Z, and Jean Louis entered into the spirit of inquisition by cross-examining Carl Heinz on points of detail and on his beliefs, all in a far from Parisian French, which, to Josel's enjoyment, Carl Heinz found difficult to follow. But as the afternoon wore on and they broke up into twos and threes, it was evident that Jean Louis and Carl Heinz were beginning to enjoy each other's company, and, with supper anecdotes began to flow about life in the Legion and on the crocodile rivers of Madagascar.

'When does Carl Heinz take over the "special graphite", Jean Louis?' asked Gordon after supper.

'Immediately we leave here. Willi and I will take Carl Heinz to the little sheds near Düsseldorf. We will unlock them for him and leave him with the keys. For the sake of your good health, Willi has never told you about these sheds. They are part of an old business selling fluxes and other foundry materials, including, of course, graphite, which Willi bought some years ago as a safe haven, as I think you say, for the drugs, which naturally could not remain at Grossalmerode indefinitely, and, of course, because of Operation Ryan were not handed over to Strenca. There is no one there – not even a caretaker – who could be interested in some sacks of graphite.' Willi smiled at Josel as she nodded approval.

'Telephone, Gordon,' she said as she picked it up and inclined her head for him to go into the small study. It was the London office.

Gordon sat down at his desk and looked at his notes, then picked up the receiver and said, 'Hello, Dick,' to Dick Scourfield, who was on a routine call. 'Anything top of your list?'

'Well yes, Gordon, and not a nice one at all.' The voice went quieter. 'Bob Scholey's dead, Gordon, blown up in a car somewhere in Austria. Hey, Gordon are you there – are you hearing me – place called Snoimo. I'm damned sorry, he was a good pal of yours, I know.'

'OK, Dick, I hear you – details later, I'll call you back.'

Scourfield tried to say, 'We have no details,' but the line was dead. Gordon walked stiffly back to the hall and to his place on the sofa beside Josel, who looked up and saw a man without expression, just eyes which seemed to be seeing something in another place, far away.

He fumbled for her hand and in a steady but very quiet voice said, 'It's bad news, I'm afraid, but before I tell you I must fill you in some more background. When Jean Louis got here this afternoon I gave you the rundown on my Washington trip and on my Moscow trip. That rundown contained the essentials, and the essentials are not changed in any way – but,' and here he looked searchingly at the attentive faces, 'we've just lost a member of the team. Bob Scholey has been murdered.'

'Bob Scholey had checked for me the accuracy of the report that Iraq had a deal with the Red Army; there was no need to tell you that. Bob was a man with his wits about him who knew how to use what he called "Madam Access" in Iraq; his connections were impeccable and had never failed him, even in the Gulf war; there was no need to tell you that. He left here five days ago in a hire-car he'd picked up in Vienna. When he arrived he said he'd suspected a tail at Rome airport but thought he'd shaken them off. Well, this is the bit that matters to all of us, so please hoist it in carefully. The car blew up on the Austrian side of Snoimo, the frontier post, and my guess is that the timing device had been set wrongly by twenty four hours. My guess is they *meant* to set it to blow *before* Scholey got here because they knew what he was going to tell us.'

He paused, and Josel, seeing the look of slight bewilderment on the faces of his listeners, began to realise that Gordon's tenseness and his curious way of telling them what had happened was simply because such a dramatic death was completely foreign to him; such things didn't happen in his world. To Willi, Jean Louis and Carl Heinz it was the violence which they knew was inseparable from what they had decided to do; it was just the first casualty, that was all. Josel squeezed Gordon's hand even harder and said, 'If his tail knew he was coming here and intended to kill him before he could tell us what we wanted to know, they wouldn't now bother to keep a watch on this house and its visitors. So, while Gordon and I will have to watch our step, the rest of you should be in the clear.'

Willi smiled. Willi always smiled when things like that were said. Gordon knew why she had interjected and smiled too.

Jean Louis said, 'I can't see what there is to be happy about, one might almost think you were English.'

Carl Heinz thought that extremely funny and cackled, 'English? By God – yes of course!'

The spell was broken. The chill was gone.

Josel looked at Carl Heinz and said very gently, 'So that we all perfectly understand every move, could you take us through your action plan just once more in case Scholey's death makes any of us think of something?' Her eyes were fastened on him because she wanted to sense any awareness on his part that Gordon wasn't quite the hard American businessman the world had always seen. She had just begun to suspect that her own role could be changing and she felt horror mixing with determination as she wondered if Carl Heinz would accept her turning into a boss figure.

He smiled, and it was the smile which acknowledged, faintly but adequately, that he would learn to respect, as well as charm, this lady. '*Natürlich*,' he said, acknowledging German as her first language, and embarked with care and precision on the action plan he had agreed in detail with Willi and Jean Louis.

First; his response to neo-Nazi riots at Easter, would be deliberately amateurish, ensuring that the immigrants be seen to be victims and the media suitably horrified.

Next; they would reinforce the immigrants, possibly with mercenary Afghan veterans available for hire from a dozen Soviet garrison towns, and supply them with small arms from the Riga black market and drugs from the cache in the Ruhr.

Third; they would arrange for some two or three German ex-legionnaires to infiltrate the neo-Nazis with both small arms and drugs, while Willi started to persuade the media that Germany was drifting towards civil war. Always assuming that police sympathy with the neo-Nazis kept their intervention to a minimum, conditions would then be ideal for Red Army hard-liners, real *or* phoney, to intervene to 'rescue' the immigrants.

The consequences ought then to be the chaos which would justify the intervention of Washington and Moscow. The German Government, facing dismissal by voters in the forth-coming election, would fiddle with indecision, reluctant to call upon the Bundeswehr (still mutinous from defence cuts) while pleading with Yeltsin to arrest the Red Army hard-line generals, which, of course, he will then, and only then, be ready and strong enough to do. Strong enough, that is, provided that the US simultaneously stuns the world with an economic rescue programme of an immensity which has so far not even been contemplated.

'And don't for one moment forget,' interrupted Gordon with abrupt forcefulness, 'that what tips the scales in the US is the knowledge that Saddam is getting – will have got – nuclear weapons from the Red Army. Even the ghosts of Vietnam quail before *that* threat.

'And speaking of ghosts,' added Josel quietly, 'Kohl will realise, just too late, that a Communist uprising, aided and abetted by the Red Army, was the very spectre feared by Hitler. I suppose we all realise,' she added more thoughtfully, 'that we are starting a civil war in Germany largely because Europe couldn't find the guts to deal with the lethal fragmentation of Yugoslavia; their decision being to let Europe sink noisily and bloodily back into the Middle Ages but armed with the weapons of extinction.'

They all looked at each other, each thinking in his, or her, own way – 'What an assorted crew we are, and how visibly, with the exception of Carl Heinz, unfitted for the task we have so arrogantly assumed?'

The afternoon light was failing and the fire murmured invitingly, but Carl Heinz and Jean Louis made for the heavy oak door, clearly bent on air, exercise and more talk. The glances they exchanged were companionable, and Josel felt happy. These two men will work well together, she thought; they are just different enough. And Willi? Well, Willi is just paternal enough and hardened enough in the fire of the *Erweckung* to handle impetuousness. She caught Gordon's eye and saw he was reading her mind.

At supper they discussed their movements. Josel and Gordon were off to Santa Barbara before the weekend, returning with the boys just before Easter. Willi and Jean Louis would leave early the next morning for the Ruhr, there to inspect the 'graphite'. Carl Heinz would leave for Dresden, where he would make his headquarters and where he knew of a lodging.

Supper brought a calmness, if not a familiarity, to their relationships, something which had been lacking, not between any two of them – save perhaps Gordon and Carl Heinz – but overall, as if there were still rough corners to rub off. But the fire, the powerful venison stew and great beakers of Hungarian wine soon had their effect, and the tenseness of conspiracy gave way.

Carl Heinz fetched his guitar and soon the room was filled with Tyrolean songs, and even Gordon got red-faced and reasonably in tune with the yodel of *Du Wunderschönes Alpenland* . . . . Then Jean Louis – as they sat in the candle-light – suddenly remembered the words of *Chevalier de la Table Ronde* and so of course Carl Heinz had to learn the tune. They were happy when they went to bed, 'happier than they had any right to be' – as Gordon said to Josel as she turned the light out. The thought of Easter was filling their minds.

In the morning Carl Heinz lingered over coffee and then took his leave. He was keen to know their movements so that he could call them from his Dresden suburb of Gorbitz and give them some idea of what to expect in the media.

'It will be cryptic,' he added, 'because the Verfassungsschutz are very good at phone-tapping and I can't be certain they'll never get my number, however many times I move, and that will be often!' This was said with a grin which was meant to be nonchalant, but it somehow gave him a crafty look, and when he added, looking at Josel over Gordon's shoulder, 'So if you want to know more you'd better pay me a visit,' she felt the shiver which is somewhere between fear and anticipation.

She now didn't feel she was going to like this man, but he certainly had some fascination and he was aware of it. So much was evident from the stories he'd told the previous evening about the Legion, stories not *designed* to put himself in a good light but which somehow gave the impression that he saw himself as a man whom others found easy to follow. There was a mocking tone sometimes which, she had felt, was saying, 'Go on, find objections, but in the end you'll do it my way.' She had laughed as she thought of the song, and caught Gordon smiling. She loved to see Gordon smiling.

43

Carl Heinz stretched himself out on the narrow bed in the basement flat in Gorbitz and started to go through his list of telephone numbers, making notes on how best to get his message across to the select few he had already contacted. They were all his legionnaire buddies, including the caretaker of this block of flats, who was the leader of a group of Dresden caretakers. Other basement flats would be at Carl Heinz's disposal when he needed to avoid the attentions of the police. Nothing was to be left to chance in planning and organising the 'overture' to the chaos which was to engulf the cities of Germany.

Carl Heinz looked at the clean but dingy little room with its stucco on concrete walls and the small window through which light penetrated from the bars of a grating. There was a scullery, a lavatory, and a door leading to the lift beside a narrow stone staircase. It was typical of East Germany, and the cultured side of his nature hated it. For Carl Heinz – like almost all human beings – was two people. There was the dreamer whose Irish blood told him great stories of spirits which could fill a man's mind and change his destiny, bringing with them a fatalism, an acceptance – comforting sometimes, more often frightening. Then there was his Teutonic self, which demanded that ambiton be satisfied, however ruthless the means, however great the cost. He didn't like either of these two selves and vainly hoped they would cancel each other out and leave him to paint or to write, or to walk in the Himalayas and find undiscovered plants, leaving human beings to their hugely enjoyed vices.

And this venture? It called for almost nothing except organisational skills, leadership and ruthless ego. He had them in abundance; he could summon chaos and then perhaps chaos would summon him. To politics perhaps and power? Then it would be a final goodbye to plants and poetry, and to those Irish ghosts.

He thought about his co-conspirators and in particular about Josel. The men, Willi and Jean Louis, who had been hardened in the different and difficult worlds of World War II and Madagascar, were easy enough to understand, and their qualifications for the task were unmistakable. Gordon was a horse of a different colour (to use one of his mother's expressions); his background of the international construction industry was completely alien to Carl Heinz. He had no idea what sort of personality it created. All he had seen so far was the wobble over the death of Scholey which Josel had so quickly and faultlessly balanced and corrected.

And Josel? Well, Josel was *une autre chose*. At first sight she looked the part, the Americanised wife of a copy-book, Ivy League American; her voice had not lost the charm of Paris and her clothes suggested the English country with a whiff, in the evening, of the Avenue *Montaigne*. But most important was the absence of sophistication, either Parisian or transatlantic. Josel's naturalness had sailed through, it seemed, an amazingly complicated life, marred by tragedy but now apparently serene. Yes, there were anxious doubts, but her motives triumphed over them, as they had so swiftly coped with Gordon's confusion.

Her father's death was, of course, the mainspring of her desire to see the sort of Germany he had so longed to help build. German idealism spurred on by Slav temperament – that was Josel, and without her there would be no team. Without her, Willi would have faded quietly away into retirement, while Jean Louis, despite a *colon's* passion for his mother country, would nevertheless have let it burn itself out in the bewitching somnolence of Madagascar.

And himself? The demon of introspection never gives up! Well, perhaps the law and a rich wife would have quietened his Irish quest for rebellion and danger. Success could, and should, mean politics – Germany's answer to *Jöerg Haider* of Austria whose right wing charisma was having dramatic effect. A pale and democratic imitation of Hitler? He was thirty two, the perfect age, and cometh the hour, he let himself wonder as he thought for a moment of de Gaulle.

'You are day-dreaming, Winterhalter,' he said aloud as he drove his mind back to the present.

First, Easter; it was already March 19 and he had much to do, firstly by telephone, all in a jargon code he had built up with his ex-Legion friends. In fact, despite Willi's express instruction to do no such thing, he had given the most trusted five of his old comrades a briefing. Now he would bring them up to date but leave the precise details for Easter Sunday to his closest and most reliable comrade, Hans (known as *'Die Kopf'* because of his huge head), a man of Bavarian charm and Prussian meticulousness. They would fix a rendez-vous for Carl Heinz to run through the programme and hand over two sniper rifles (Barrett Light Fifty semi-automatics) which lay in their cases under his bed. He gave them a wistful look – he was no slouch himself at up to 400 yards; next time, perhaps? He would now call

Willi and make sure he gave the media the tip off; Hans would alert the Nazis. A peaceful Easter Sunday? It was sad in a way. How many *agents provocateurs* would think so?

44

On Tuesday, March 29, Josel, Gordon and the boys all arrived at Pasinka from California. Jean Louis also appeared, having done his rounds of visits to the crucible manufacturers in Europe and the US. It was an annual trip and always left him with the huge feeling of relief that he lived in none of the so-called civilised countries. He was bursting with good humour and Franz and Tom gave him what they called 'a hero's welcome', which consisted of a fierce attack from all angles with the heaviest cushions they could find. Boots and skis were got out and checked, measured and tried on; every conceivable item of clothing got the same treatment, sometimes leading to fractious disagreement which Josel and Jean Louis skilfully neutralised. The house was warm with companionship. How lucky I've been, thought Josel and Gordon grinned at her across a tangle of arms and legs trying on new ski-pants.

By early morning they'd gone, promising to telephone safe arrival in the mountain village, all with great merriment. Josel reminded herself that she and Gordon could have been of the party, except for her promise to Carl Heinz that she would be firmly beside the telephone for his first report on Easter Sunday. So she disappeared into her greenhouse and Gordon got on with his homework. Another trip to Russia was due to start on the Tuesday after Easter and, like Josel, he was on tenterhooks for Easter Sunday. It was going to be a long weekend.

But the sun shone and so they worked in the garden together, and the telephone didn't ring except to say the snow was wonderful and that Jean Louis had fallen more times than Thomas. The blossom was glorious. Sunday dawned and, after church they watched the television news and, yes, there had been a demonstration in Dresden. Some bus-loads of immigrants had marched across the Augustus bridge carrying banners saying '*Heimatland ist Deutschland*', and had almost reached the Frauenkirche when they were attacked by skinheads with swastika arm bands. The scuffle looked ominous; no police appeared, but the buses followed closely and, despite a fierce exchange of blows with pick helves, the immigrants remounted the vehicles rather quickly. The episode faded into a commentary with the verdict that, as a potential riot, it had been a damp squib.

'Not quite what I'd expected from Carl Heinz,' said Gordon, looking somehow pleased and dissatisfied at the same time. 'That won't exactly set the Elbe on fire, will it?'

'I don't know what I expected,' she said, 'but drama certainly – perhaps we're being simple, perhaps that was just the bait. Riots have to have victims, but they also have to have guilt, and so far we have neither; I have a feeling that we have only seen Act I.'

So back they went to gardening, pruning some shrubs, planting others, longing for that telephone call – doubtless just as Carl Heinz intended, thought Josel, as she vented her impatience on a forsythia.

But the evening and the next morning passed in silence until the radio announced there had been midnight rioting in Gorbitz and, as it did so, Carl Heinz drove through the courtyard gates with what might have been called a flourish.

'It worked,' he said, getting out. 'They came after us and set the school on fire, so we shot two with sniper rifles *and* the media got the full picture. Now things will really start to happen.'

'Any police?' asked Josel.

'Yes, but very late and not enough.'

'I'd like to see it,' she said.

'There's nothing to see,' he answered in a bland, not-taking-you-too-seriously voice.

'Yes there is,' she answered. 'There are people's faces; they say everything.'

'Well, perhaps – '

'No, Carl Heinz, not perhaps, *now*. Let's go now while they're still taking in what happened, and what is perhaps going to happen.'

'You're serious,' he said in a wondering tone. 'You want to go now to Gorbitz and take a look – '

'Yes, and smell,' she interrupted. 'You can tell a lot from the smell.'

He suddenly remembered, not for the first time, that Josel was not the pampered wife of an American tycoon but a woman who had seen – known – the rough side of life, in Madagascar, in the Atlas mountains with a tortured and dying father. He smiled – a little feebly – and opened the door of his car. Josel was giving Gordon a goodbye hug as thanks for his benign smile.

They drove to a parking lot near the Augustus bridge where Carl Heinz had left his Trabant.

'My Gorbitz vehicle' he explained. 'I'm supposed to be a freelance journalist, and they seem to like that. It's odd the way journalists are accepted by simple people as if they were part of a priesthood.'

'Some priesthood,' said Josel, but there was a tease in her voice.

They had talked all the way from Pasinka, she about her father and the plan which had been foiled by Reagan, and he about his ambitions and his attempts to explain them to himself. 'I'm introspective like most Germans, and it is dangerous as well as stupid.'

'My Slav blood protects me from that particular risk,' she said in a voice of assumed solemnity, and they both laughed.

'Were you in love with Archie Forbes?' he asked suddenly, his hands paying great attention to the steering-wheel and his eyes fixed on the road.

'Yes,' she answered, 'I was.' The hint of warning in her voice was either unnoticed or ignored.

'His Englishness, perhaps?' This time the voice had a lightness in it, a little too obviously introduced.

'The first thing all Germans should try to learn, if they want to grow up, is that the English are not in *fact* in any way superior, they just seem so.'

'Ah.' It was hardly an exclamation, more a gesture of submission.

They drove in silence for some time. Carl Heinz was right, there was nothing to see in Gorbitz. One does not drive eighty miles to look at tenement buildings built of concrete, washing lines and a burnt-out, or almost burnt-out school. But Josel was right too because there stood clusters of immigrants, men, women, children, and their faces, apparently without expression, seemed to consist wholly of watchful eyes; eyes which said things and asked questions at the same time. There were smells too: newly washed clothes, tobacco, some clinging sweetness, whiffs of alcohol. They stared, the people, because they knew that, despite her jeans and denim gardening jacket, here was a visitor to the zoo who was going to be disappointed with the animals. They wouldn't sniff or paw the air or look interested or hopeful, not these animals, especially after last night they wouldn't.

But they'd reckoned without Josel. She had no Turkish, but bits and pieces of their other languages she managed to conjure up – her Polish ancestors had lived in the Ukraine, so that helped with place names. She told them she had been partly brought up by a grandmother who had been a refugee from Bohemia in 1948, and been so homesick she had gone back to live alone in one room in Prague.

They started to move into a semicircle and one or two young fingers were plucking gently at her jacket. There was now some humour breaking through the hitherto expressionless faces.

'What will happen now?' a man asked. 'Two of them were shot.'

'You may have to fight,' said Carl Heinz, whose admiration for Josel's simple niceness was warming his voice.

'What with?' asked a woman with a gesture of despondency.

'We'll fight,' said a little man with astonishingly wide-apart eyes. 'You are a newspaper man, you ask your powerful friends for weapons.' There was a growl of approval from most of the group; the young boys had eyes and smiles wide with excitement. Carl Heinz said nothing.

Josel said in English, 'The thought of fighting brings such happiness – reality is so often different.' She was shaking hands now, hands that were warm and firm in their grasp, and saying goodbyes. There were words like 'come again' and 'we'll do what we must', as if they were acknowledging leadership. She could feel a tear pricking so she said, 'bloody hypocrite' aloud three times.

Carl Heinz made coffee in his bare underground cell and tipped some schnapps into it. Josel thanked him and, looking round, said 'What no pictures, photographs of girls – anonymity, I suppose?'

'Yes.' He liked her coolness and quickness and he'd especially liked her way with the gathering of immigrants. She was the genuine article, Josel, he thought. Pity she'd married that Ivy League American; it was a waste. She had good German blood in her veins.

On the way home they discussed his plan for the first of May. Carl Heinz was proposing to 'light the fuse? – as he put it – in Rostock. The town was hypersensitive because of the earlier riots, and the media should therefore react swiftly and probably hysterically.

First he and his Legionnaires would form a cadre of volunteers from among the Rostock immigrants. They would prepare them for a Nazi attack and arm them with the sniper rifles, two or three Kalasnikovs and some grenades. The Nazi grape-vine would be fed the intelligence that some mercenaries (ex-Red Army) had been hired by an unidentified Communist group which intended, on the first of May, to provoke the local Nazis.

'All this, of course,' said Carl Heinz, 'is no more than broad outline. The important thing is, that after the battle, for battle it will be, the media will be told that the mercenaries were in fact Red Army Special Forces. They are indistinguishable, one need hardly say. After a couple more riots we can reveal the Iraq–Red Army deal and all hell should break loose. At last the Americans will take Europe seriously, or see Germany go down the pan with Russia close behind. I hope you'll forgive my Americanisms,' he added with a sly smile.

'So the Iraq–Red Army deal is the master-stroke,' said Josel. 'I could almost believe you had negotiated it yourself!'

They both laughed and, Carl Heinz thought again, no wonder so many men had found her irresistible.

45

That evening they sat long over the fire. Gordon had asked a raft of questions, most of them political, and seemed satisfied with the answers. He had talked a lot about the German economy, the effect of the recession on German industry and its dependence on Russian gas supplies, not to mention Russia's huge foreign debt to German banks.

'To paint the gloomy picture, he said, 'one must see the German and Russian economies as interdependent; the collapse of one spells crisis for the other. Your first of May scenario is a catalyst for political crisis in Germany with talk of civil war. The presumption *must* be that publication of the Red Army deal with Iraq, plus Red Army involvement in Germany's Nazi riots, will bring America to its senses, and to the economic rescue with an aid programme on a hitherto undreamt-of scale. But just let us remember that only last year Russia's government almost fell to pieces, civil war was a well-discussed and seemingly inevitable nightmare and the United States' present economic rescue plan is a goddam damp squib! 'Why couldn't that happen again?'

'You're right, of course', said Carl Heinz. 'Last year Yeltsin called upon Russia to save herself by her own exertions. It was achieved by calling the hard-liners' bluff. That can't happen again, *this* time the world will see the *whole* nightmare. It will see that a partnership between Red Army hard-liners and a nuclear Iraq can lead to a deal which would be the economic enslavement of Germany, and *that* threat will be enough to waken the US; for them a nuclear Iraq is the mother of all nightmares! Russia and America,' he went on, 'are still suspicious of each other – the Cold War legacy – and the only thing which can kill that suspicion is cold genuine fear.'

'Do you still believe,' said Josel, 'that Rostock won't pull in the Germans' federal anti-terrorist force?'

'You mean the Grenzschutzgruppe 9?' he said.

'Yes, I think they will be sent in, but too late. Remember that our government is always pandering to the right, and the police reflect it; they say the police are unable to snatch a Molotov cocktail from a twelve-year-old! There are practically no arrests when the Nazis demonstrate, even with brownshirts and Hitler salutes.'

Stretched out in his chair, Carl Heinz's dark, handsome face – perhaps more striking than handsome – seemed to reflect some of the light from the fire, and for a moment it looked as if he were about to put his fingertips together, a movement he rather hastily abandoned.

'I need help,' he said, 'in two ways. Before I can cash in the "graphite", as we politely call it, I need some money and in order to set in motion the "graphite" deal I need some assistance. Can you, Gordon, let me have some money on account, and could you, Josel, give me some help?' The voice had a ring of innocence as well as confidence and Josel found herself admiring the excellent timing.

'Of course,' said Gordon. 'How much?'

'Half-a-million,' came the reply, and Josel received a warm and welcoming smile. Her own smile was coloured by wondering why he'd said nothing in the car.

'What help do you want from me, Carl Heinz?'

He took a deep breath which sounded rather deliberate. 'Before I can do this deal I need someone to break the ice. someone who can introduce the package to the arms-dealers and then quietly fade away, leaving the heavy part of the transaction to Willi. I mean "heavy" in the literal sense.'

She saw that Gordon was looking anxious, so she gave him her I-can-handle-this smile. 'Spell it out, Carl Heinz. Tell me *exactly* what you want me to do, and why me. Then I'll give my answer.'

'Of course, Josel, and its very simple. If you, Gordon and the boys are leaving here for the US as soon as Gordon gets back from Moscow, you could perhaps spend a few days in Paris. I guess the boys would love that. I could arrange for the arms-dealers to meet you there once, just perhaps twice. You would tell them that heroin, pure heroin, is already *in* Germany and immediately available in exchange for arms as to seventy per cent of its value, with the balance in dollars. No bargaining is possible. They would be invited to inspect a sample and, at that meeting, a list of the required weapons would be handed over and the sum of money specified. All this, plus the arrangements for hand-overs, would be for Willi. Nothing more would be asked of you.'

She laughed, this time with enjoyment. 'You've still got to tell me why *I* should see these men rather than you or Willi, or even Jean Louis!'

He managed to look slightly abashed and said, 'There are three reasons, Josel. First, Willi is not the right man for the first encounter, he *might* be drawn into discussing details. Second, it is always helpful, when dealing with these people, for there to be *two* principals; it slightly confuses them and so they become less confident.' (He almost said 'aggressive' but thought better of it.) Third and *most* important, they will be impressed.'

Josel saw Gordon nodding his head. 'OK, Carl Heinz – you're on. Tell us when you want us in Paris.' As she spoke she was asking herself the reason for her reluctance – was it nerves, or was it a feeling that Carl Heinz was trying something on? To embroil her in some way?

That she attracted him she had little doubt, and as for herself she was prepared to admit that she found him 'interesting' – a word she knew with many meanings. Perhaps it was because of a kind of sophisticated gaucheness about him, an anxiety to impress without appearing to try. But so what? If he wanted to embroil her it wasn't unreasonable, and she wanted to help; she already felt like an onlooker, a captive audience.

'Today is the fourth. Could you make it today week?' Carl Heinz asked. 'That would give us almost three weeks to prepare for the first of May, which is just enough – how is that for you Gordon?'

'Fine by me' he said. 'I'll make some reservations.'

'And so will I!' said Carl Heinz, looking happily at Josel.

'What are these people like?' she asked.

'I don't know much about them, except that they are Russian, they come from Yaroslavl and one of them's a woman.'

46

Josel sat nervously sipping tomato juice in the Ritz bar on the Rue Cambon. It was noon and she was dressed as she might to meet a maiden aunt, a somewhat racy maiden aunt, perhaps, but maiden aunt none the less. She wore a dark skirt, a white shirt with an amber necklace, and a sleeveless loden jacket with brass buttons. The bar was empty and she felt conspicuous, wishing that Gordon or Jean Louis had hung around for a bit. But Carl Heinz's instructions had been explicit and she reminded herself that she was not without experience of delicate missions; how Archie would have laughed at her predicament. Damn Archie, he always came into her mind at moments like these, moments of uncertainty.

In the end, after much discussion, the whole family (Jean Louis was very much recognised as family) had piled into the aeroplane for Paris and the Hôtel Suède on the Left Bank. Jean Louis had argued that he could be useful sitting in on the debriefing with Carl Heinz and Josel. He might then be of some help to Willi, who would be taking on the heavy end of the deal. The boys were ecstatic.

A waiter came over to ask if *Madame* was expecting two guests. She got up to greet the two strange figures advancing across the still almost empty room. Strange, that is, for the Ritz Bar. They wore heavy-looking suits and had fur caps tucked under their arms; they bowed slightly and introduced themselves in heavily accented English. It was only on shaking hands that Josel could be sure that one of them was a women, and that was partly because of a whiff of a very expensive scent. They sat down. The waiter appeared. They ordered vodka. Josel felt she should put them at their ease with small talk, but the man put up his hand in a polite but silencing gesture.

'When and where do we inspect samples?' he said, in a soft and rather kindly voice, as if he were speaking to a slightly retarded member of his own family.

Josel could only scuffle in her handbag, like a schoolgirl with a message, for the piece of paper which had Willi's name and telephone number. The woman smiled a friendly-looking smile from what Josel saw as a not very friendly face. It was Asiatic-looking, with dark parchment skin under dyed straw hair. The eyes were almost invisible.

Then came the wholly unexpected – 'You will, of course, be at the rendezvous yourself on the Wednesday in order to effect the introductions?' The stilted English was slow in sinking in, so Josel's *'aber natürlich'* came out before she realised what Carl Heinz had let her in for, and how natural it was.

She smiled and nodded, more schoolgirl than ever as her hand was seized and clasped by each of them in turn. Now the vodka glasses were raised and emptied with a muffled salute, and they were on their feet and shaking hands again for taking leave. The man, she noticed was fairly tall, heavily built and wearing a quite beautiful white silk shirt under a heavy tweed suit – bought in Edinburgh, Josel's flapping mind suddenly and wildly suggested.

'*Bis Mittwoch*', said the woman – that smile again –

and they were gone. It was still only a quarter past twelve so she walked up the Rue St Honoré the better to think out the implications of a rendezvous with drug-smugglers in probably some remote part of Germany. At the same time she laughed at herself for being shocked; was not their own project *much* more shocking than a little straightforward arms-for-drugs deal? Curious how respectable she had managed to become! And what else was Carl Heinz going to propose when she met him for lunch? She wouldn't underestimate him again.

They lunched sedately in the Ritz dining-room – 'always safe from prying eyes in boring places,' said Carl Heinz presumptuously, clearly hugely enjoying himself. He had everything at his fingertips. The rendezvous was to be near the turn-off from the main road to Gummersbach, less than an hour's drive from Cologne airport, where he would meet Josel and Jean Louis on Wednesday morning from their flight from Paris. Then he would get her back in time for a Paris flight to connect with the Los Angeles one out of Charles de Gaulle for which she, Gordon and the boys had reservations.

Willi would, of course, go direct to the rendezvous. Jean Louis was important because he could provide the provenance of the heroin.

'You take a lot for granted don't you?' Josel said.

'I call it thinking things through,' came the reply, with what she would have called a smirk. 'Time is short, we've only got, from next Wednesday, seventeen days to the first of May. Mind you, shortage of time is a blessing in one way; it keeps everyone on their toes and helps hold the lid on security – not that we want all *that* security.' He laughed. 'The Nazis have got to know in good time!'

He was het up, she could see that, and it made her feel uneasy. They'd only had half a bottle of white wine, but his eyes had a sparkle – or perhaps a glint? – which she hadn't seen before. His clothes made him very much the English gentleman lunching at the Ritz – blue pin-stripe suit, Jermyn Street shirt and dark suede shoes; how Archie would have laughed. *Damn Archie, he hovers about far too much.*

Gordon, Jean Louis and the boys came tumbling back into the hotel at around six, having 'done' the Eiffel Tower and Notre-Dame, and called breathlessly for soft drinks, hard drinks and sticky cakes. They all talked at once, but Josel managed to take Gordon quietly through the Wednesday programme, which made him gasp a bit. He offered to come with her, but she said, 'It would upset the balance,' and he settled for that, adding, 'I guess my balance is in a fine upset already.' But he looked happy because he was proud of her. Josel decided to enjoy Tuesday at least.

Tuesday was perfect weather, so they all went on the river and Jean Louis tried to tell the boys something about the history of Paris. He failed, but the boys loved him for trying and managed to ask one or two sensible questions. Then a visit to Les Invalides and, of course, second-hand bookstalls. But it was early to bed for everyone; although Carl Heinz came to supper he disappeared soon after to stay with a Legionnaire friend.

Wednesday was faultless. Carl Heinz escorted Josel throughout; a hire-car from Cologne airport took them and Jean Louis to the rendezvous some fifteen minutes before Willi appeared in his old Range Rover. There was just time to agree on how to conduct the business before the Russians appeared in a large Mercedes.

Everyone shook hands, clasped hands, and drank vodka produced by Willi. They stood in the biting east wind, not talking, looking at a wonderful backdrop of heavily wooded hills which seemed to shout 'spring' at them in defiance of the cold.

With the vodka bottle soon empty, the Russians were escorted by Willi and Jean Louis to the Range Rover – more handshakes, *Wiedersehen* – and Josel found herself back in the hire-car, heading for Cologne airport with the heater full on.

She laughed despite her irritation. 'You do love to be dramatic! I expect you can't help it but I don't believe for one moment that it was necessary for me to meet your Russian friends in Paris, still less for me to be here this morning, but never mind, they seem to have got off to a good start and, after all, with the heroin already *inside* Germany, it's a wonderful deal for both sides. When will you know the result?'

They drove some way in silence. Oh dear, she thought, I've made him feel small.

'I am not offended by your remarks' he said suddenly, reading her mind. 'You just don't understand that those dealers live permanently in a world of blackmail, double-cross and murder. They assume that any deal will have to run the gauntlet of a dozen dirty tricks, and that takes time – and we don't have time. By meeting you *and* seeing you again today they know they have a guarantee – *no* dirty tricks. They can see you for what you are, and that's enough. And is that flattering enough?' he added caustically.

'Very flattering,' she said, 'but let's not kid ourselves – you *do* love dramatising!'

The rest of the hour's journey was spent checking and rechecking the sequence of the preparations for Rostock. Josel asked many questions, about getting the weapons to the immigrant cadres, security, the role of Carl Heinz's Legionnaire buddies, the handling of the media by Willi and how and when Gordon would liaise with Moscow. All ground which they had gone over a dozen times at Pasinka but, leaving for California, she wanted to be doubly – trebly – sure. He answered patiently.

'Tell me about your Legion buddies,' she said. 'They must all be close friends, I mean really close friends who will do anything for you; who are they and where do they come from?'

He said, 'It's a pity this journey isn't four hours or I could explain them to you!' He was teasing now and she enjoyed it. 'Yes, they are great buddies; yes, they will do a lot for me, partly because they need excitement, and they miss the comradeship of the Legion; they all live in what was East Germany, and while not criminals they are not exactly law-abiding citizens. In the Legion they were self-made outcasts, so they know how these genuine outcasts, the immigrants, feel. Last but not least, they hate these young neo-Nazi thugs because they despise them.'

They were getting near the airport now and she suddenly felt she wanted to say something kind to him. 'Carl Heniz, you know we couldn't do this without you and you *are* appreciated, even if in our anxious moments we find fault. It's letting off steam really.' And she leant across to give him a warm and rather smudgy kiss on the cheek. As she did so, and saw his head turn slightly, the look of longing in his eyes told her that, but for the steering-wheel, he would have put his arms round her.

47

The boys settled quickly in the jumbo once they had worked out how to watch the film, so Gordon and Josel were able to bring each other up to date. In the case of Gordon this mostly consisted of rolling his eyes in the direction of the stewardesses and whispering, 'It's all pretty grim out there, I'll tell you when we get home,' Josel on the other hand gave him a blow-by-blow account, only leaving out Carl Heinz's calf-like glowering in the car. He asked a lot of questions until Josel had to turn her attention to the boys, who were beginning to hang around.

First thing in the morning they were all in the pool. As Josel ploughed up and down, she shrugged off some of her misgivings. She had meant what she'd said to Carl Heinz, but his eyes had undermined her confidence; they had seemed either too dull or too bright. Willi had been, as always, utterly dependable and wonderfully sure of himself, but Jean Louis, mentally and physically the toughest of the team, had now to go back to Madagascar, and that left the project – especially Rostock – wholly on the shoulders of Carl Heinz and his Legion buddies.

Come, come, she said to herself, Carl Heinz is tough enough, he thrives on risk, danger is like a drug for him. Drug? Drug? Why had she used, or rather thought, that word? No certainly not, the man was a tough professional ex-soldier, natural leader, of course there's tension, that's the word, *tension*, leadership tension, that's what it is. Then came the fleeting reminder that he seemed to be potty about her and she smiled. *That won't do him any harm*, she thought.

'Talking to ourself, are we?' called Gordon as he flashed past in the opposite direction. 'Time we had coffee, I guess.'

Over coffee, with the boys still in the pool, he told her about the atmosphere in Moscow. 'It's really grim, honey, not yet horrendous, but grim. The US relief programme isn't effective to any noticeable extent, and inflation rages on. The riots in Germany have got to tip the scales and make the US realise the full horror of a recidivist Russia and a disintegrating Germany both happening *at the same time*!'

His voice had a hardness she hadn't heard before. 'Are you happy that Boris can and will grab those hard-line generals the minute the Iraqi deal is pushed at the media?'

'Yes, I am, and I'm also happy that when Citizen America sees Saddam with nuclear weapons he and she will give the President all the backing he needs for the mother of a Marshall Plan.'

They were both smiling now, partly because the boys were out of the pool and wading into the cookies and orange juice. The sun shone.

48

By the April 29 Josel was back at Pasinka, having delivered the boys to their English school. Gordon was somewhere in the Persian Gulf and due to turn up in a day or two. She'd heard nothing since she had parted from Carl Heinz at Cologne airport, and the media, having yelled blue murder after the Easter riot, had drifted off in search of blood-curdling incidents in Bosnia and Africa.

No news is of course good news, she muttered to herself as she went about domestic chores. Well, OK, she would give Willi a ring why not?

Willi's mood was calm and confident. All consignments had moved according to plan, thanks to Jean Louis on the one hand, and Hans 'die Kopf' on the other. 'Almost too good to be true' was his comment, and Josel fervently agreed while wishing he hadn't said it.

'The media? Yes the media are primed; not an easy thing to do, because it had to be done by leak or they suspect a plot – and how right they would be,' said Willi with a noisy chuckle. Jean Louis had left for Madagascar but would reappear shortly 'to help tidy things up'. 'But what he could mean by that I can't imagine,' he added with another chuckle.

So, Josel decided, gardening with a radio by her side was all that was left for her to do. But her mind played on; even the therapy of pruning roses had little effect, and odd scraps of her last conversation with Carl Heinz kept pushing their way in.

They had discussed Communism over lunch at Cologne airport. He asserted that there was nothing inherently wicked about Communism, it was merely socialism taken to extremes. 'Take Lenin's economic policy, for example,' he said. 'It was based on building successful small businesses, the concept of vast state enterprises came later.

'Private enterprise took a lot of stamping out; for example Jean Louis knows of a foreign owned crucible factory in St Petersburg which traded successfully until 1927. But so what Carl Heinz? What are you trying to say?'

'Simply that socialism can live side by side with capitalism in the Western world, that for example a socialist government in Germany need not inspire fears of another Weimar, or justify a swing to the right, as some politicians would have us believe. To the contrary, a socialist government is more likely to cure Germany's two fundamental weaknesses, the failure to curb immigration and to assimilate the *Ausländer*.'

He continued in the same vein until Josel felt compelled to ask, 'What has all this got to do with us?'

'Nothing,' came the reply, 'except that if I go into politics it will be to help the *Ausländer*; Europe so far has failed to realise that Germany today is for the refugees from East Europe and the Balkans what America was for Continental Europe in the last century – "Give me your huddled masses . . ."' he started to quote.

'And if you're branded Communist?' she asked, 'you won't mind?' It was meant to sound like a tease but came out as a challenge.

'Not in the least – for a good cause one must always be prepared to fight,' was his reply.

As the secateurs did their careful work on the climbing roses, she let her mind wander through uncharted paths, all of which had 'what if' on their blurred signs. Carl Heinz as an ambitious politician? The man who had saved Germany from economic collapse, political collapse perhaps, architect of her partnership with Russia, might make a huge appeal to German voters sickened by Kohl's failure to cope with the political and economic consequences of unbridled immigration.

'*Ausländer* are now 7.3 per cent of the population, and only when their status is rationalised will they live at peace with "German stock".' Those had been his closing words.

So let's assume he has ambitions above and beyond the immediate rescue of Germany, she thought as her mind drifted down another byway. That simply means that success can breed success; it's no concern of ours. And what if Herr Winterhalter claims leadership of *Ausländer* throughout Germany as a result of Rostock's success? *Still* no concern of ours. (The secateurs closed firmly on a thick spur.) And should Rostock prove a little *too* successful and launch its leader as an inspired rabble-rouser who had no intention of pausing in his stride? The very stability they sought to ensure could be swept away. Only someone unbalanced? Aye, but there's the rub. Carl Heinz could *be* unbalanced, could he not? Those eyes could be a little too blue? With plenty of Saxon blood of her own, Josel nevertheless had always been sensitive to 'blueness', as her mother called it; the English, for example, always seemed to avoid having eyes of hardened light blue. The short ladder creaked ominously and she came down to earth, in both senses, with a start. All this rambling means, you stupid girl, is that you're going to have to go to Rostock to have a look for yourself, and she gathered herself up to make preparations.

There was plenty of time; she wouldn't leave until the morning of May Day itself, and she wouldn't tell anyone even if she could. Gordon was not due to call in before the late evening of the first of May, although by then the media might not have fully reacted and so early on the second of May was more likely. She couldn't leave a message with Marlene, her cook-housekeeper, because she only spoke Czech. Well, she would have to risk letting Gordon worry.

It was a hellish drive, she well knew, and that meant large flasks of coffee and soup, brandy and plenty of tapes – Mozart for preference; also perhaps Gordon's twelve-bore – it might frighten someone if it didn't frighten her too much first. A couple of rugs and a first-aid kit went in too, and by six o'clock on May Day morning the BMW was well on its way. It was fine and warm. She had put on light blue jeans, a striped jersey and an old yachting cap, and hoped she might look like someone off a boat, a common enough sight, she imagined, in a Baltic port. The drive, lovely to begin with, became boring once past Dresden, but painless and fast. Mozart was the perfect companion.

It was about one o'clock when she reached the car park in Rostock, from where she walked, past the Kröpeliner Tor to Wallanlagen park. There she could see, near a bronze statue of a seated woman, a fair-sized crowd of men, women and children, and there was the sound of music. She drew nearer and saw a band platform on which young men in Turkish dress were dancing to pipes. It was an elegant, attractive performance, and drew applause. Then there was singing, followed by a magician for the children, who drew closer and closer to him until they began to suspect his magic and yelled with laughter. Josel, in her sailor's outfit, seemed innocuous enough to any of the women who looked at her, and she settled down to watch; listening was to no avail as the crowd was predominantly Turkish, apart from what looked like Balkan Muslims with different headgear.

There were speeches and clapping and good humour. A few young German-looking youths hovered round the edges of the crowd, but there was no sign of threatening behaviour despite the circular cloth patches sewn on to their denim jackets with their black eagles and the words 'Proud to be German'. Josel wondered about them, and wandered closer in the hope of hearing scraps of conversation, but they seemed strangely silent and when one or two of them eyed her she drifted away again.

Eventually food appeared on tricycles – kebabs and sticky Turkish delight. Josel went in search of coffee but had no success. Exchanging remarks about the weather with a young man, she asked if there would be any more May Day celebrations and he said, 'Yes, of course, this evening in the Sports House.' Then, looking curiously at her, added, 'And where are you from?'

'Oh, from a boat,' she said, hoping that her nautical appearance would stand up to scrutiny.

'Must be a very smart boat,' said another young man with a friendly grin.

She said goodbye and made for her car and the coffee thermos. The crowd, at least those with very young children, were drifting away, and she guessed it would be sundown before they took themselves to the Sports

House. However, to be better informed and to pass the time, she set out for the Universitätplatz and the Meerschaum milk bar.

The pavement tables meant being rather noticeable, so she went inside and tucked herself behind a corner table and ordered coffee, wurst and a newspaper. The paper had little to say about May Day in Rostock, simply that the *Ausländer* would have a 'children's party' in the park, and an evening meeting with a guest speaker. Provocative enough, she thought, and wondered whether Willi's skills had reached out as far as Mecklenburg.

She lifted the paper to turn and fold back the pages, and realised that someone had pulled out a chair and sat down at her table. As she brought the paper down she found herself looking into a face which had a smart black beret perched over tawny hair and sloe-black eyes. Lower down there was a smile.

'Who are you and what are you doing here?' said a voice with a Bavarian accent.

'I might well ask the same question,' retorted Josel, feeling her face break into a smile, which was clearly interpreted as a welcome because the young woman was signalling to a waitress for coffee.

'I'm Gisela, a reporter from Frankfurt she said.

'And I'm Josel, just a rubber-necking American,' said Josel.

'Your German is too good for that,' said Gisela, 'but let's skip the interrogation and get to the nitty-gritty, as you say in the States.'

They both laughed.

'It's a curious set-up, isn't it?' said Gisela; 'here are the immigrants, who know full well the risks, having fun and games in the park, *and* announcing an evening meeting with a guest speaker, while the young Nazi *Chaotiker* do nothing about it.'

'Yes,' said Josel, 'it's strange, and what do you make of those two over there?' – gently moving her head to indicate two young men sitting, it seemed in silence, at a table on the other side of the room.

The girl squinted carefully and said, 'Baltic types from further east, I would say.'

'Not Russian, perhaps?' said Josel, an idea beginning to form itself in her mind.

'Russian? – what would they be doing here except off a ship, and those two aren't sailors. What *are* you getting at? There's enough edginess in this town already.' Gisela's voice was full of humour but her eyes were sharper than ever. 'I could believe you were CIA or something, except they're too dumb to have someone like you on board.'

Their laughter this time was that of growing confidence. They ordered more coffee.

The two young men, meanwhile, had got up, pulled on woolly caps of indeterminate shape and walked briskly out to the *platz*.

'Russian mercenaries perhaps,' said Josel, 'here to protect the immigrants from Nazi thugs?'

'Are you kidding?' said Gisela. 'Because if you aren't then you know something I ought to know, but which you're not going to tell me – am I right?'

'Sort of,' said Josel, and then quickly asked, 'What was your briefing in Frankfurt?'

'Oh, just that my editor swears the Nazi thugs are organised, so go to Rostock, where there's some kind of immigrant rally, and see if there's any sign of genuine brownshirt stuff, as opposed to the usual gang which likes to shout for the benefit of the media. Tonight the meeting is going to be addressed by some ex-Foreign Legion chap so that could be their chance, I guess.'

'And the *Ausländer* might just be ready for them, I suppose,' said Josel.

'What do you mean – you suppose? That's the second time you've dropped that hint, so now let's hear the rest of it; are you saying that the Sports House is going to be stuffed with Commie thugs from Russia, and if you are, where does your information come from?' The black eyes had lost their twinkle and were fixed on Josel's face.

'I am not going to tell you any more because I can't,' she answered. 'All I will say is that if you haven't got cameramen up here, then call them; you won't regret it.' Willi's briefing, she was thinking, hasn't quite reached its mark.

'OK,' said Gisela, 'I'll do it. It's late in the day, they'll have to use helicopters and they'll murder me if its a damp squib, but I reckon you aren't phoney and I'll take a chance. After the Gorbitz affair at Easter,' she went on, 'when two Nazis got shot, we reckoned things would quieten down for a while – you know *reculer pour mieux sauter*, that sort of thing; it often happens that way. Mind you, there are enough media men here to keep the editors happy, but they're *not* expecting a shoot-out. I'll get on the wires, and then let's go and look at the Baltic. I've always wanted to do that.'

Josel was beginning to think her journey might have been worthwhile.

They went to the beach and hired deck-chairs. It was still warm enough to sit in the sun; in fact it was warm enough for Gisela suddenly to whip off trousers and shirt and dash into the sea in a tiny striped bikini. Panting and gasping as she wrenched a towel from her backpack, she explained that her boy-friend had bet her she wouldn't do it. 'I'll make him give you lunch in

Frankfurt, Josel,' she said, roaring with laughter and dancing to keep warm.

Then they returned to the car and drank coffee laced with brandy. 'I don't think they'll get going before nine o'clock,' said Gisela, 'but I "cased the joint" this morning and I know where we can position ourselves so as to keep an eye on what's happening inside and outside. But we'll need this stuff, its marvellous' She pointed at the thermos. 'Can we meet at the café at around 8.30, and meanwhile I'll hang about for the helicopter if you'll drop me in the *platz*. They were partners now; this could be fun.

After dropping Gisela, Josel sat in her car on the parking lot and checked the equipment she would take with her – sheath knife, camera and first-aid kit, all strapped to her waist and concealed by a three-quarter-length very light cape. She could feel Gordon's disapproval.

They parked the car about a hundred yards from the Sports House and crept into Gisela's vantage point behind the dustbins. The stench was awful but there was a narrow window through which they could see the interior of what seemed to be a large hall with no ceiling. There were what looked like platforms round the top windows. Josel guessed the platforms were used in conjunction with the climbing ropes she could see looped beside them. There were four, two on each side of the hall, and each had a low canvas screen round three sides. They saw a rostrum and rows of plastic chairs, with wooden benches down the sides. There were three double doors, each with a pair of stewards both inside and out. The hall was filling up with men, women and teenagers and Carl Heinz was sitting on the platform on the right of a burly Ukrainian Josel guessed was the chairman.

When the hall had filled up the chairman made his introductory speech which, despite the fact that she couldn't hear it, gave every sign of being dull and boring. At last Carl Heinz was on his feet and, judging by his gestures, had launched full tilt into his theme, modelling himself, she guessed, on the body language of Haider, the charismatic Austrian he so admired. He had spoken for about seven minutes and, judging by their faces, was holding his audience in rapt attention, when Josel began to notice the several groups of figures on the edges of the open space which surrounded the hall. From her vantage-point she could see the ground on both sides of the building for quite a distance before the angle of the walls cut it off. But she could not see if the stewards were still outside the doors or if they had slipped inside.

Quite suddenly all the windows were shattered by what must have been a mixture of stick- and smoke-grenades. There were loud explosions and huge belches of smoke inside the building, and appalling screams as people tried to fling themselves to the floor despite the chairs. Smoke then blotted out all vision, while the screams grew louder as more grenades exploded. The doors must then have been thrown open because she heard shouted commands and saw some dazed-looking people stumbling into the open. Figures were retreating now from the windows, and she could see some Nazi arm bands.

It was then that she heard the first shots from what must have been machine-pistols. They came in rapid succession and seemed to combine a crack with a thump. She could see bodies falling as the retreat turned into a rout. The shooting was evidently coming from the top windows, because the people streaming out of the hall were quite clearly not in the line of fire. Her throat filled with the horror of the spectacle at the same time as she wondered where Gisela had placed her cameras.

Already the fire sirens were sounding and the *whoop-whoop* of the ambulances could be heard in the distance, and the beacons on speeding police cars were joining in the chorus. The shooting had stopped now and the smoke inside the hall was clearing as she saw six men jump down from the window platforms. They wore dark-coloured denims, but she could just glimpse the insignia on an arm band which one of them seemed deliberately to discard. As they reached the doors at the far end of the hall, a police van with siren blaring and beacon flashing drew up. The side doors opened and all six men vanished inside as the driver threw the vehicle forward and away.

Gisela, white-faced in the glare of headlamps, was clutching Josel's hand, and was only just able to wave her press card at an advancing policeman, shouting, 'Red Cross' as Josel unhooked her first-aid kit and they dashed into the hall to do what they could for the wounded.

Some emergency lighting had come on and police were using fire extinguishers which made clouds of steam and smoke, so it was difficult to find people's wounds leave alone dress them, but the two women slapped on dressings and prayed for the paramedics to take over.

Suddenly Josel felt herself grabbed by the shoulder and turned her head to see a caricature of Carl Heinz's face; it was ashen white, cadaverous and rather bloody, with pin-points for pupils.

'For God's sake get me out of here,' he said, and then

she saw that the sleeve covering his right arm was soaked in blood.

She managed to rip the cloth with her knife and tore the shirt-sleeve with her hands to expose the wound, which was bleeding freely. Gisela joined her, and between them they managed to apply a tourniquet and a dressing. Carl Heinz, even allowing for the demonic lighting, looked on the point of collapse.

'I'll get your car, give me the keys,' said Gisela, and Josel dug in her pocket for them. 'I'll be outside that door in three minutes; my press pass will get me through the police.' Then she vanished.

Paramedics were everywhere now, so Josel half dragged, half steered the wounded man to the space behind the open door. Almost simultaneously the BMW appeared, horn sounding, headlamps blazing, and Carl Heinz was levered and pulled into the back seat. Gisela pushed her face and a business card through the driver's window, saying, 'Bloody well telephone me, Josel. I want to know a *lot* more about this,' and Josel found an arm band being stuffed under her nose. She lost no more time; seconds later the car, with its large press pass on the windscreen, was scything through the police cordons.

From the sound of his breathing, she guessed that Carl Heinz had passed out, and only when he was aroused by his own moaning did she stop to make him more comfortable and give him water. Several times she saw to his comfort. There was no interest in her passenger at the Czech frontier, and Carl Heinz was again out for the count when she reached Pasinka at daylight.

How she managed to get him on to the sofa in the hall she never afterwards remembered; too busy with the telephone and making coffee even to wonder how the wounded arm had taken the long and, on the hill roads, bumpy journey.

The doctor looked quizzically at Josel. 'A hunting accident, I presume?' he said, and she nodded, neither of them being disposed to touch on details such as hunting what?

The doctor and Marlene between them managed to get Carl Heinz to the lavatory and then to one of the spare bedrooms. Dr Weiss was a Sudeten German who had managed to get back into his old home. He was a punctilious, cautious man, and when he came downstairs he spoke firmly to Josel, having often cared for her boys.

'Mrs Ellsworth, you will have to look after your guest with great care. It is a nasty wound and I am unable to give him a sedative because it is evident that he has been taking some powerful narcotic.'

'Thank you, doctor. I suspect I'm the one who needs the sedative!'

She slept for more than ten hours, and when she woke it was early Tuesday and the telephone had been clamouring.

49

Gordon had telephoned to say he would call from Moscow as soon as he got there from Cairo – that much he had managed to convey to Marlene. Willi had telephoned and wanted her to call him, which Josel promptly did.

The media, Willi said, were in an uproar. There had been no reporters allowed in the hall, but the immigrant spokesmen had made much of Carl Heinz's speech and the TV commentators had left nothing to the imagination – a communist Hitler had appeared in Rostock and after a rabble-rousing anti-Nazi speech had unleashed Red Army Special Force Commandos on the Nazi thugs who had first attacked the building with fire-bombs and hand-grenades. Casualties heavy on both sides: at least twenty Nazis dead. Police now searching for Carl Heinz Winterhalter. Was the Red Army trying to cause civil unrest in Germany? – and more in the same vein.

Willi was delighted, and asked when would they know the reaction in Moscow and how soon would the Kremlin announce the Red Army–Iraqi deal.

'Hold everything, Willi, I'll call you back – oh just one thing: I assume it was the arm bands which identified the so-called Special Forces?'

'Yes, and some are saying how clumsy of them to give themselves away like that!

'Willi, we should *not* be talking like this, can you come here, there is much to discuss.'

'Yes, of course,' he answered. 'Tomorrow at noon I'll be with you.'

Damn, she thought, putting down the telephone. If the Verfassungsschutz are on the ball, they'll quickly find out that media briefing is coming from Willi and tap his telephone.

Gordon called from Moscow to say he'd arrived. 'I'll know something by tonight,' he said, 'and I'll call you to say whether the "wedding" has been arranged or postponed. How was your trip, honey. Did you have any kind of a bumpy ride?

'I had *every* kind of a bumpy ride, my sweet, *and* it's not over yet – and *that'll* teach you to talk in riddles.'

His laughter gave her the feeling he was optimistic about the 'wedding'.

She went to look at Carl Heinz and found him still asleep and breathing heavily, but a better colour. His backpack was beside his bed where the doctor had put it. Carl Heinz must have rummaged in it, because one zip was open and she could see what looked like a sponge-bag, and then as she moved her head the sunlight from the window caught a black metal stub with a hole in it. She lifted the machine-pistol by its strap and placed it carefully on the top shelf in the clothes cupboard, covering it with a spare pillow.

Next she telephoned Gisela. Knowing how openly journalists talk on the telephone, she started by saying in a low voice that Carl Heinz was in the room. 'OK, I get it,' came the reply. 'We'll watch our words. I know that you will have a lot to tell me when we meet,' she went on, 'but for the moment I just want to say that the media is in an uproar *and* there's more fuss – political fuss – to come. The Red Army has got some explaining to do, and so has your friend. Come to that, you've got some explaining to do too, but I won't harass you, I'm too pleased with my story.'

'What's in your story?' asked Josel.

'Oh, the whole works, but especially the arm band and what it means, the political implications – all of them, *and* that speech!'

Her voice had a ring of triumph, as if she approved of all Carl Heinz had said. Perhaps she does, thought Josel.

'Oh yes, *and* the photographs, they are terrific – from half-way up a lamp standard; he should have been riddled with bullets!'

'Listen, Gisela,' she interrupted, 'you sound pleased, but this time tomorrow you could be even more happy when I give you a call.' She put down the instrument. Gisela's version of the 'wedding' would carry more weight than most.

Marlene came in, rolling her eyes and pointing upstairs. 'The gentleman is awake.'

'Good, let's go and see to his arm.'

The wound was quite swollen and bruised, as well as being a nasty-looking hole from which Dr Weiss had removed the piece of shrapnel, but the owner of the arm, despite an alarming pallor, seemed lively enough. He was impatient for Marlene to go and, when she finally did so, he looked at Josel with a glimmer of a smile.

'It was a success, wasn't it?' he said.

'Yes it was a great success.' And she told him about the media reaction, and emphasised there was more to come.

'Wonderful,' he said. 'Now I can plan my next appearance.

'We can discuss,' she said very severely, 'what needs to be done when we hear from Gordon in Moscow. In the meantime, get some sleep and come downstairs for supper. I think you're well enough for that.'

She didn't think anything of the kind, she simply hoped that getting him out of bed would induce some sort of normality. His pallor, the sharp intensity of his eyes, some rambling in his speech, all made her wonder just what 'narcotic', (the doctor's word) he had been taking; quite possibly some of Jean Louis' heroin, but if so for how long? He wasn't paying any attention to what she was saying. His eyes were fixed on her as if to compel her attention, but first to silence her.

'Josel, may I have a radio and a television, also a telephone? I would like very much to hear the reactions and opinions of the outside world so that I can plan my next speech; a tape recorder would also be helpful.' This was said with great courtesy as if to imply, *I'm not sick or dotty, so please take me absolutely seriously.* So that is what she did, and minutes later was fumbling with plugs and adaptors in different corners of the room.

She had never experienced a stranger relationship with any man; it was part sister, part mother, part accomplice – oh yes, and lover too, because she had often seen the look in his eyes which said *I need more, what we have between us is not enough.* A look which at once sought approval and demanded respect for the dominant partner – a look which also managed to show much more than affection. Josel was always slow to recognise passion – it had too many ghosts.

He appeared downstairs at about seven o'clock and, over a glass of Gordon's malt whisky, quizzed Josel on what she'd heard from Willi about media reaction to the events of Sunday. She gave him a report as best as she could remember and found herself referring more than once to the comments on the excellence of his speech.

'Did Willi mention the absence of the antiterrorist brigade, the Grenzschutzgruppe, and the late arrival of the police?'

'Yes, and he said there had been much to the effect that the Government is frightened lest tough action against the neo-Nazis should lost votes to the right-wing parties.' 'And what about Gerhard Frey's Deutsche Volksunion?' he asked.

' "At last the Red Army shows its hand" was apparently their mildest comment,' she said.

'Anything else of significance?'

'Well yes – much talk of emergency measures to control immigration, and one Culture Ministry official has spoken about the situation having a similarity to Weimar. What is it you are fishing for?' she asked.

'Comment on my speech, of course, no matter how mangled, he answered with a smile, a hopeful smile, she thought. But why not? He had evidently done well in the eyes of the media, aroused interest – 'a Communist Hitler' was, in his mind, flattering. He was greedy for more, and she thought of Gisela's enthusiasm. But somehow she couldn't quite muster praise of her own. She hadn't heard the speech herself, nor had anyone except the people in the hall.

Josel paused while she poured a drink for herself. 'There's not much more to say; the journalists have interviewed people who were in the audience, of course, but the reactions and impressions were all general, there was nothing specific, according to Willi, except 'a Communist Hitler".'

'But you've been listening and watching, so what have *you* gleaned? *My* feeling' she said, 'is that the attack drove everything except self-preservation out of their minds.'

'Well, we'll soon put that right,' he muttered,

helping himself to more whisky. The smile had gone now.

Josel watched the glass as he gulped it down. What do whisky and heroin do to each other? she wondered; too late now to ask Dr Weiss. He was speaking. 'As you say, I have listened and watched, and I think absorbed, the media reaction which usually becomes the public reaction, or more accurately it becomes two opposing public reactions. *One* will prevail, and that must be *my* vision for Germany. To ensure popular support for my policy I have a plan, and you, Josel, will appreciate how it also becomes *your* plan, the plan which you and your father saw first as a vision.

Listen carefully, Josel, because you and I are both essential to the task of making the vision reality.'

Josel put on an attentive expression and longed for Gordon to call. With luck, he would report that the Kremlin had acted, the generals were under arrest, the world was aware of the Iraq deal, the plot to destabilise Germany, and the massive US economic rescue programme for Russia.

'The next demonstration of Germany's new spirit,' he began, will be in Eberswalde on Thursday. Hans and Frick are there now, making arrangements.' He chuckled.

'Why Eberswalde? you may ask. Because the first neo-Nazi atrocity was committed there when a young Angolan immigrant worker was beaten to death in the street. The townspeople walked by on the other side, but today they are full of shame. The murder was in November 1990, and we go there on Thursday to ask the people to salute the memory and show solidarity with Rostock. In my speech I shall tell them of the vision of Bismarck and how it is the destiny of Germany to be the keystone of the European arch. I shall remind them that three times Germany tried to fulfil her destiny by force of arms, has paid tenfold for her mistakes, and could now pay the ultimate price of civil war.'

Josel repressed a sigh and thought, He's talking to immigrants, people who know nothing of German history. But an idea was forming itself in her mind and she refilled his glass with whisky.

'I shall tell them,' he went on, 'how, with new leadership, Germany can now take her place in an economic partnership with Russia, in a new European entity of enormous economic strength, something for which the great leaders of the last three centuries, Frederick the Great, Peter the Great, Napoleon and Bismarck, had strived, sometimes unknowingly'.

As Josel gathered up a dog lead in preparation for an evening walk, she knew what the next sentence would be, and sure enough the words came from the now trance-like features – 'So it falls now to me, Carl Heinz Winterhalter, to lead this great nation to its final destiny, a Germany respected but not feared, shaking off its pathetic government of ditherers, and ready to forge Europe's future.'

'Carl Heinz,' Josel whispered softly, 'I am going to take Benes for a walk in the woods. I will make you an omelette when I get back.'

There was no answer; eyes firmly fixed on the fire, he continued with his speech.

50

Josel drove a short distance in her car and then took Benes into the woods. She was hoping that Gordon would not call in her absence; Marlene might give Carl Heinz the telephone and God knows what he would say. At least Gordon would realise that all was not plain sailing at Pasinka.

The wood she'd chosen, a mixed coppice of oak, beech, ash and chestnut, had been planted by grandmother Josel's father-in-law and was now at its best. The warm evening sunlight came gently through branches decorously showing early leaf, and fell on the carpet of bluebells, primroses and cowslips. It was almost a shame to let Benes rampage.

She forced her mind to make a careful analysis and told it firmly to back-pedal on what her instinct had been whispering since Carl Heinz had first come downstairs. One thing at least was clear: he couldn't be allowed to go anywhere, least of all to Eberswalde, whatever preparations he might have made. Another piece of common sense would be to assume, for the moment, that Gordon's call would be to say that the Kremlin had *not* yet reached a decision. In that case Eberswalde might – in fact would – still be necessary; properly orchestrated, of course, and not, in his present condition, by Carl Heinz. Then that instinct, or rather impulse, reared its head again – she longed to go herself! Her Czech blood, she supposed, was clamouring for action, a feeling of guilt, perhaps, because the Czechs had done so little when war had raged all around them.

So go to Eberswalde, Josel, the impulse was crying. Be the centre-piece, make sure the lesson of Rostock is driven home into those hearts and minds in Russia and America. But could she? The answer was a plain and simple no. The press would identify her immediately, and through Gordon the Washington and Moscow connections would be laid bare; the whole scheme would unravel in less than twenty four hours – unthinkable. But then who?

Benes! Come here, damn you,' she shouted as the dog shot after a rabbit. He had been trained not to hunt – but then why shouldn't he? His namesake had chased enough hares in 1947's wretched months before he'd kissed the Communist ring. Her laughter revived her imagination and she shouted, 'Gisela, of course! She's the answer!' and in the same breath, 'Eberswalde is going to happen anyway, Hans and Frick are there right now fixing it.'

Breathless, almost forgetting the reprieved Benes, she dashed for the car. The dog raced after her, snorting, thinking it a game. The woods had performed their magic for him, anyway.

Carl Heinz was asleep by the fire. The whisky decanter had done its job. Marlene's apprehensive eyes came round the dining-room door.

'It's all right, Marlene, you can have a quiet evening. I will make an omelette for Herr Winterhalter when he wakes up.'

The door closed with a soft click of relief. Although a child of the revolution who had seen and heard plenty in her day, Marlene was noticeably apprehensive and uneasy with this particular house guest; perhaps some Bohemian ghost was resenting his presence. But Josel had no time for such thoughts as she nipped upstairs to her bedroom telephone.

'Hi Gisela, it's Josel.'

'Hi Josel, how are you?'

'I'm fine, Gisela, and I've got important things to tell you.'

'OK, shoot.'

'You know I can't tell you on the phone, you'll have to come here.'

'Are you out of your mind? Do you imagine that I sit here on my fanny waiting for you to call and say you have important things to tell and I must drop everything and come to *Bohemia*?'

Josel took a deep breath; she'd allowed her voice to be too imperative. She managed a laugh. 'It's worse than that, Gisela. When you've heard what I've got to tell you, I'll ask you to go to Eberswalde on Thursday, and when you know why, wild horses won't stop you going.

'You kid me not?'

'I kid you not,' she answered, wondering why they spoke American rather than German, and slang at that.

'Tell me how to find you and I'll be there Wednesday evening, and Josel . . .'

'Yes?'

'. . . find a nice doctor in that God-forsaken place of yours and get him to give you something to calm you down. You sound like Maggie Thatcher on a high. I'll call you in the morning with my map and pencil out. '

'Fine – and don't forget to warn the camera crews.' The click was a sharp one but she knew all was well.

Next she telephoned Willi and explained as best she

could – which wasn't very well – why she didn't now want him to appear in the morning. She blamed it on complications with Carl Heinz's wound and Gordon not having pinned down Moscow, but she felt she sounded half-hearted, and the disappointment in Willi's voice was unmistakable. He was, after all, the oldest ally – and sometimes had a way of showing it.

When she got back to the hall, Carl Heinz was pacing up and down, brow furrowed but otherwise, apart from the wounded arm and shoulder, a picture of alertness and concentration. Heroin, she guessed with a sinking heart, and then checked herself brutally with the thought, probably just as well.

'I must have your attention,' he said. 'I must go through the instructions with you.'

'The instructions?' she said dumbly.

'Yes – as I told you already, Hans and Frick are now in Eberswalde, and tomorrow I shall go through with them in detail on the telephone the arrangements for Thursday. This evening I must discuss all this with you; it is important.'

She didn't ask why because she knew only too well.

'Also,' he went on, 'you must hear my master plan for a series of meetings in six cities. From what we know about media reaction to Rostock, the atmosphere is changing and I must take my message to the people.'

'Talking of changing, Carl Heinz, I must do just that – I'll be down in about half an hour to make that omelette.'

'I will do the same,' he said briskly, pouring more whisky into his glass.

Josel visualised hearing the whole of Carl Heinz's speech over dinner and thought she would do something for her morale. So, after a bath, she came downstairs in brick-red linen trousers, black suede shoes and a white cashmere turtle-neck jersey with a long gold chain. Carl Heinz must have had similar thoughts, she reckoned, because he had somehow got himself into a suit of blue serge, double-breasted almost to his chin. It was reminiscent of a cadet uniform in a pre-1914 photograph, except for a white polo-neck instead of a winged collar. He's a good-looking devil, she thought, with just that streak of cruelty which fascinates so many girls – and *what* an odd couple we must look, she thought as Carl Heinz heaved logs on to the fire with one hand.

She got out a bottle of Gordon's best burgundy. She had no idea how whisky, burgundy and heroin might affect him, but she thought she had better find out because, if her plan was going to work, the following evening would be crucial. Oh yes, and she must get Dr Weiss to dress that wound in the morning.

It would be a busy day.

Sure enough, over the burgundy and a powerful local cheese, he launched into *the* speech, until Josel tapped sharply with her coffee spoon and said, 'Enough, Carl Heinz, I've heard all that; now tell me about your programme *after* Eberswalde.'

He was looking a bit glassy now and the corners of his mouth had a curious droop, but, after a huge gulp of wine, he began.

'In Germany today the mood of the man in the street is *Politik–verdrossenheit* – the word for apathy, disgruntlement and contempt – call it a yearning for leadership. Without leadership – and remember it is only months before the elections, always a vulnerable period – Germany could drift into a Communist and Red Army-inspired uprising designed to crush the neo-Nazis; that is the danger. For Germany to be without leadership is, as history has proved, the greatest peril for Europe.

'I can provide that leadership; Germans love charisma and I have charisma. That I proved at Rostock. I have been listening to the radio, and it is clear that I am recognised as Germany's *Jöerg Haider*. I must now organise meetings in all the most sensitive places; after Eberswalde it will be Mölln and then Sachsenhausen, where they fire-bombed the site of the old concentration camp. I have aroused decent Germans; I shall appeal to them to crush the resurgent neo-Nazi spirit. Before the elections I shall be the acknowledged leader. He paused 'And you, Josel, must be at my side.'

His voice, she noticed, was no longer full of emotion. It was cold, if anything, and matched the conviction in his eyes which remained steadily on Josel's face as he felt for her hand across the table. She didn't withdraw it, but she brought a firm edge to her voice as she said, 'Carl Heinz – you've got to come back to earth, you must rejoin *us*. You have set off on some journey of your own which has got nothing to do with the present. Germany is *not* looking for a *Jöerg Haider* and, if she found one, it would scare the world from its wits. Haider suits Austria, perhaps; but Austria is unimportant and can be ignored despite history; history which seems to be mesmerising you.'

She went on. 'What Germany needs is an economic partnership with Russia, sponsored by America; and *without* that partnership peace in Europe is impossible, without that partnership Russia will disintegrate and there will be a tidal wave of refugees. That tidal wave would engulf Germany; we have already seen the horrible consequences of the present immigration rules – just imagine the numbers trebling at least. No, what Germany needs is a fright, a fright big enough to bring swift change in the immigration laws, in the franchise, a fright which reminds them, in all its pain, of Weimar, and makes them leap at the opportunity of a partnership with the US to bring the Russian economy into Western Europe.

'They must fight off the trauma of East Germany and accept the next vast economic challenge of Russia.' She gasped for breath. 'but as a democracy, dear friend, not as a spectre from the past – which is what you would be.' She was gently withdrawing her hand.

Carl Heinz's face was wearing a patient expression. 'There are two flaws in your programme, my darling,' he said. 'First, Germany's history proves that she can never take tough decisions without strong leadership, and so democracy must, as the Americans say, go on the back burner. Second, we already *have* the new Weimar crisis, but this time it is immigration rather than inflation, and you can be sure the one will swiftly bring the other. And remember, Josel dear, that democracies can never recognise a crisis – even under their noses. And remember too, that where Europe and trade are concerned (especially European economic programmes) the Americans can never be trusted; they dislike us, and they're jealous of our history.'

As she wondered how long she could go on bashing her head against this wall of obsession, Marlene came in, looking dishevelled in a dressing-gown, to call her to the telephone. She filled Carl Heinz's glass with wine and went up to her room.

Yes, at last it was Gordon, and he had a secure line. He was brusque and to the point.

'Honey, I just don't know what our friend thinks he's up to but this "Commie Hitler" business has turned everyone right off, both here and in Washington. A punch-up between neo-Nazis and immigrants with

Black Berets wading in on behalf of the maverick Red Army generals is fine; it spells civil unrest and calls for the democratic cavalry, but a "Commie Hitler" means the *end* of democracy, and the US would have none of it. All bets will be off.'

'I'm talking to him now,' she answered, 'and I'm saying it all.'

'Talking isn't enough, honey. He's got to be stopped, my love, and *you're* going to have to do it – and pronto.'

With that there was a buzz and a click and then Gordon's voice saying, 'Hell, I've lost my safe line.'

She wondered as she went back to the dining-room whether the someone who'd cut that secure line had not wanted any argument.

Carl Heinz looked up and raised his glass. 'Gordon, I suppose – and I salute him. When he hears the reaction to my speech on Thursday he will know that our campaign is well and truly launched. Then it's a matter of getting ready for the elections – I have arms, drugs, men and money, and all will be used to good effect. By Friday morning the media will be calling me Germany's *Jöerg Haider*!'

'Just pause a moment and tell me one thing, Carl Heinz. How will you explain the Black Beret arm bands at Rostock? The media are making a big fuss about them. They came to the rescue of the immigrants, remember, and killed a lot of neo-Nazis very quickly and efficiently. We have now to explain to the media that they were Boris Pugo's Black Beret commandos, sent by Red Army generals out to create civil unrest in Germany. So that makes Red Army thugs your allies; how does Germany's *Jöerg Haider* explain that?' She was speaking now very patiently, as to a child.

'Black Berets? They weren't Black Berets, they were the local Turks trained by my men, Hans and Frick.'

'And the arm bands?'

'Planted by the Nazis,' he said without a flicker of hesitation.

'You mean that's what you're going to say *now*?'

He nodded slowly and thoughtfully as though she had made a valuable suggestion.

Marlene had shuffled in with a tray of coffee while Josel was on the telephone. She picked it up, saying, 'I think we'll have this by the fire,' and moved into the hall with its peaceful and welcoming warmth.

51

They helped each other put logs on the fire, he determined not to let his wound affect him and she equally firm about not giving it a chance to cause more trouble; she was already expecting reproaches from Dr Weiss in the morning.

Carl Heinz showed that he felt himself at home by helping himself to brandy from the drinks tray and settling himself beside her on the big leather sofa. Perhaps he'll drop off, she thought; otherwise, it's going to be a long evening. She looked at the taut figure – probably the wound was hurting – and wondered why she found him attractive. He was good-looking – the Irish blood had seen to that – and he used the blue eyes and dark lashes with delightful unsophisticated skill; but the charm was somewhere else. In his movements, perhaps, which were quick and at the same time peaceful; or the way he moved his head to look haughtily or quizzically, sometimes intensely.

But beyond the physical there was some curious bond between them and she knew now what it was. A love of risk and adventure had come to her, perhaps from some ancestral quirk, or just from the post-war circumstances in which she'd grown up, and which had found their first real outlet in marrying Jean Louis. Then, joining her father and Willi, going in search of Archie, even the nightmare of Glaoui's castle, they all belonged to that indefinable world of 'I'll be damned if I don't'. And here once again was that invitation. Hell – she'd just resisted it in her walk in the wood with Benes, and now Carl Heinz was going to dangle something insanely more risky.

Gordon had said, 'He's got to be stopped, *you're* going to have to do it.' Yes, she could stop him from going to Eberswalde – but after that? Here was a man with a fixation supported by guns, drugs, some loyal and ruthless henchmen, and the most powerful bewitchment of all, the acclaim of the media – a seduction from which few men escape. After Eberswalde? Could she cajole (or seduce?) him away from his egomania, assuming of course that the White House and the Kremlin were still dragging their feet? Or would he have so damaged German democracy in the eyes of the US that they would consign the whole endeavour to the dustbin of 'well – we tried'? What *was* her influence, if any, on this would-be Hitler?

'You're a fool, Carl Heinz,' she said, 'if you are planning to model yourself on an Austrian tinpot Hitler-in-waiting. Even if – as you claim – the German people might like the idea disillusioned as they are, the rest of the world would reject you utterly, and the golden opportunity of a New Deal for Germany *with* Eastern Europe would vanish like a puff of smoke. Haven't you the imagination to see that the vision Roosevelt had for the States in the thirties will look like a whim compared with the programme which you are now trying to wreck?'

He stood up. Even in the firelight she could see that his eyes were now dull. All he said was, 'Come to Eberswalde, Josel. Come to Eberswalde.' The words came slurring out and she turned him gently towards the stairs.

'No, I won't do that,' she said, 'but we'll see how it goes and then perhaps.'

As she helped him up the stairs, feeling the weight increase as he leant more heavily, she wondered what the hell she meant by 'then perhaps'. Did she imagine she could wean him from his crazy ambition, bring him safely back to democracy, make him understand the hopeless enormity of his ideas? Was this what was making her say and think 'and then perhaps'? Or was it something else which had got muddled in and was causing strange gyrations in her mind? Was the wild streak in her nature finally at rest, or was she longing to recapture, even for a moment, the wild spirit which had sent her out to waylay Archie Forbes all those lifetimes ago?

At last they reached the top of the stairs and she tried to turn him towards the door of his room. As she pushed carefully at the unwounded shoulder, he managed somehow to grip her firmly by the waist and quite gently turned her for their lips to meet. The kiss was passionate and rough, but somehow under the roughness there was a curious gentleness to which she longed to respond. But there came a gasp of pain and, with a suddenness which belied both drink and wound, he was gone.

Her hesitation was the merest splinter of time, but when it was over she found herself in her room staring out of a window which looked down on what was left of the moat. The waters rippled slightly under the breeze and the vanishing moon, and in them for a moment she caught sight of Carl Heinz's face, half pleading, half amused. A look which seemed to say, *We aren't finished yet, you know – you and I.*

She found some sleep at last, but the thoughts which darkened it were not dreams.

Josel woke up longing to talk to Gordon. There was no sign of her turbulent guest, so she sent Marlene up with orange juice, croissants and coffee, and telephoned Dr Weiss.

Then the telephone finally rang, and after long pauses, clicks and horrendous crackling it was Jean Louis.

'Darling,' he said 'I can't be with you, I can't get back to Europe. I've been a bloody fool – you remember the Betsiboka river and the Mozambique channel? Well, I took some customers there to see the sharks fight the crocodiles, I was careless and got nipped by a shark – damn stupid, not serious but can't travel. Terribly sorry.' And then amidst more crackles and clicks he was gone.

'Oh God,' she said aloud, 'now I really am on my own.'

Carl Heinz came to – you couldn't call it waking – at about eleven and drank some cold coffee. His wound was throbbing and so was his head, but his mind was clear enough to start making notes for his conversation with Hans and Frick and preparing his excuses for keeping the doctor satisfied with his progress – if progress it was. Any suggestion of hospital and he was off. Truth to tell, he felt bloody awful.

Sure enough, Weiss appeared at noon, and after careful examination of the wound asked bluntly what drug he had been taking. He searched Carl Heinz's arm for needle marks and, when he got no answer, said, 'I can only stop you by moving you to hospital, which I shall do tomorrow. In the meantime I cannot give you antibiotics or even sleeping-pills, and you will find alcohol a poor substitute. Yes, you can smile, Herr Winterhalter, but I believe that the hospital disciplines will have the last laugh. He was folding up the blood-pressure arm band. 'And I have a feeling that there may be other disciplines in store for you also. Until tomorrow then' – and he was gone.

'He could be going to inform the police that I'm here – or more likely he's just giving me a warning,' muttered Carl Heinz as he padded across the room to the wardrobe and rummaged for the hypodermic and the packet of needles. The Foreign Legion curriculum had not covered dangerous drugs, but some knowledge it had been impossible not to acquire, and anyway there were only twenty-four hours to go.

When Josel came up with soup and a salad on a tray, he only wanted to talk with bustling enthusiasm about the final instructions for Hans and Frick when they reported by telephone.

Neither of them mentioned the doctor's visit or spoke of the previous evening. The speech he would deliver tomorrow had taken over his whole mind, and even his body had responded with a burst of energy as he paced up and down in Gordon's dressing-gown, using both hands for oratorical gestures, until Josel quietly slipped away. It was after three when he came downstairs, still in the dressing-gown, and demanded sleeping-pills.

'I've been through everything with Hans and Frick; all the preparations are made and now I must have some sleep. I must leave at five in the morning, and I'll be no use at all without sleep – last night was a disaster.'

She winced but sped off to Gordon's medicine cupboard, saying, 'I'll bring them up,' remembering sharply, as she said so, the doctor's warning.

'And sleeping-pills you shall have,' she said to herself with the cold realization that he must be knocked out for fifteen hours at least. She took up the pills with an extra bottle of mineral water, and received detailed instructions for the morning – which boiled down to an alarm clock and a flask of coffee.

He was back in bed and looking at her with a puzzled expression. 'You could so easily come, you know.'

She laughed and put three pills in his hand. 'All you really want is a gangster's moll, and *that* can wait for another day.' She bit her tongue, wishing she had left the words unsaid. 'Now, come swallow up and I'll draw the curtains.'

He said no more. She closed the curtains and then the door.

52

It was about seven when Gisela Schreiber arrived, complaining loudly but with good humour about the last lap of the journey – 'No wonder that Chamberlain said "It's a far-off country of which we know little." You take some finding.'

Josel had just been to make sure that Carl Heinz was fast asleep, and to switch off his alarm – an act of treachery which left a guilt which no amount of reasoning could still. So pushing Gisela into a chair by the fire with a large glass of whisky was a welcome distraction from the pangs of conscience which she knew would get much worse as tomorrow dawned. Gordon's sleeping-pills were blockbusters, to be used only after a series of transatlantic flights.

'If you can stay awake after that drive,' she started, 'I'll tell you the whole story.'

'Keep filling this glass,' said Gisela, 'and you can make it the story of your life!'

'Which is almost what it is,' came the sobering reply.

By midnight and after a marvellous stew complete with dumplings – cooked by Marlene, whose spirits seemed to have revived – everything had been told, and every question, with almost no exceptions, answered. Gisela had said at one point, stabbing with a fork speared on a dumpling, 'You're only telling me all this because you want me to do something, and curiously enough – I surprise myself – I'll give you a blank cheque. I'm normally cautious about wives of tycoons, but with you I'll take a chance. So come clean, what is it?'

'I want you to tell the world about the Red Army–Iraq deal'.

'After tomorrow?'

'After tomorrow.'

'And you want me to say that Iraq, is planning a nuclear strike on Kuwait, using Red Army weapons?'

'Yes.'

'When they get them?'

'Yes – as soon as they get them.'

'Why does tomorrow matter? I know we're expecting a series of neo-Nazi riots, but what's special about tomorrow?'

'OK,' Gisela went on, 'it *was* going to be Carl Heinz offering himself as Führer-in-waiting, ready for the December elections, as protector of the Reich from neo-Nazis, Commies, immigrants and recession – but what happens now?'

'What happens now,' answered Josel rather sharply, 'is what was always going to happen, except there will be no Carl Heinz.'

'Tomorrow has to be the curtain-raiser for your revelation of the Iraq deal, and that revelation has to hit the world between the eyes. The impact has to make the Kremlin *act*; there can be *no* pussyfooting, *none* of that beloved jargon – "We're examining the options." It's action *now*, Gisela, or Carl Heinz will get back on his podium and blow the whole thing.'

'I think I've got the picture,' came in a calm steady voice.

Josel went on: 'I don't have the details but the meeting will open in the *platz* at around two o'clock.

Neo-Nazis are expected in large numbers, certainly armed, and out to avenge Rostock. Carl Heinz's grapevine is emphatic about that. It will be a large meeting because Hans and Frick are also bus-ing Turkish women from Berlin. Willi is making sure the media will be there in large numbers.'

'And you're making even more sure!' said Gisela good-humouredly. 'And so with every one expecting a riot, virtually stage-managed, our antiterrorist Federal boys, the Grenzschutzgruppe 9, will be somewhere nearby?'

'Yes,' said Josel, 'but there's no knowing whether they will intervene before Carl Heinz's Black Berets hit back at the neo-Nazis.'

'And you want me in the thick of it, don't you – that's about right, isn't it, Josel, with my camera crews hanging from the lamp-posts!'

'That's about right!'

The two women laughed and got up to fill their glasses.

'So Carl Heinz doesn't mind using Red Army thugs to help make him a "Commie Hitler"?'

'No,' said Josel 'he reckons the ends justify the means.'

'And it suits us well enough.' Gisela came back.

'Very well indeed, as long as you hit the world with the Iraq nuclear deal; that's the frightener, the one which gets the US to stop thinking about Vietnam!'

It was five o'clock when Gordon called; he'd had trouble getting a secure line. She brought him up to date and warned him there was absolutely no way that anything could be changed.

'Except, of course, your instruction to Gisela to blow the Iraq deal; my friends here might not like that one.'

'Not even that one, Gordon. Gisela's already left for

Eberswalde.' It's a lie for your own good, she said quickly under her breath as his silence began to lengthen.

'Jesus, that'll shake 'em.' The words came at last. She heaved a sigh of relief, which he heard, and it made him laugh. 'Where are you going to be, honey?'

'Right here, glued to the telly, waiting for the Führer to wake up and be mad as hell.'

She took Gisela coffee. The reporter was up and ready to go, dressed in workaday jeans and sweater, with tape recorders and cameras making her look like a Christmas tree. She was very good-humoured, her sloe-black eyes twinkling at Josel and with her red hair carefully pulled back behind the ears with a satin ribbon she looked action journalism to her fingertips. They drank the coffee together and then peeked in at the heavy-breathing and grunting figure under its duvet which was Carl Heinz.

'He'll kill you,' said Gisela.

She waved Gisela off and telephoned Willi.

'Just two things, Willi. I've stopped Carl Heinz from going to Eberswalde, partly on Gordon's instructions, but mainly because he's far from well. I can't tell you any more on the telephone; it's difficult here at the moment but I'm better on my own. There's nothing you could do to help.

'The other thing is that I've briefed Gisela, who's on her way there now, to blow the whole story of the deal. It will have dramatic impact if *she* does it, although it steals your thunder, I know. The important thing now is to provoke a decision; delay could be lethal.'

'I'm sure you know best, Josel, but do please keep in touch.'

The voice sounded tired and dispirited and she thought. What a way to treat one's best and closest ally – hell.

53

Before setting out in the car with Benes for a walk which she intended should last all morning – she had no wish to be the recipient of Carl Heinz's first outburst – she gave Marlene instructions to take up a flask of coffee as soon as she heard him wake, and a noisy waking she guessed that would be. She made the coffee and dissolved two more sleeping-pills in it in a gamble that they might send him off again before the media hit him. She drove for half an hour to where she could walk in open, gently rolling country, with sheep grazing and Benes pretending to chase hares. It reminded her of the Hoch Sauerland in Westphalia where they used to go for her school holidays.

She examined her conscience without great enthusiasm. Perhaps unwittingly she had given Carl Heinz some encouragement? Yes – he had lost touch with reality but so, in a way, had the whole of Europe. It had been the height of folly not to appreciate – perhaps not immediately but certainly early on – that the collapse of Communism must bring horrors in its wake, and that Germany, the geographic and economic centre of the Continent, must become the magnet for the forces of chaos and envy. Since unification, Germany was drifting back to the world of Weimar, and that legacy was once again presenting the grim scenario – recession, immigration and inflation, all versus democracy.

Yes, she *had* encouraged Carl Heinz; they had all encouraged him – without him they were a bunch of has-beens who had tried to take on too much. And if they *could* snatch victory despite Carl Heinz's defection, by revealing the Iraq deal with the Red Army generals, it would be a supreme irony. Collaboration on a big scale must save both Russia and Germany from years of ethnic and economic turmoil, and the United States would at last find her peace dividend in vast new outlets for her technology.

Benes was drinking noisily from a stream, so she stopped and wondered how much of this self-examination was simply a matter of preparing alibis for Carl Heinz's storm of resentment and recrimination when he discovered that for him she had torpedoed Eberswalde.

'Back home, Benes,' she said abruptly, 'and let's face the music.'

Marlene reported no sign of life from Herr Winterhalter, so Josel composed herself for a simple luncheon beside the radio.

By two o'clock the commentators in Eberswalde were in full spate, describing the scene in the *platz*, with the buses arriving from Berlin with their cargoes of Turkish women, the banners saluting Rostock, the police still few in number, and of course the platform with the chairman on his podium. It was time to move to the television set and she settled down beside it in sickening anticipation.

Herr Pfaff, the chairman, on his feet behind the cluster of microphones, was well into his speech – a mixture of rather soppy hand-wringing for the victims of Rostock, embracing both sides in his sympathy, and rousing calls to Germans to welcome and accept the new citizens now being blatantly attacked 'by recidivists in our midst'. Not an easy text, she thought, and he wasn't having much effect on his audience, judging by the commentator's remarks. Carl Heinz would have roused them by now, said another twinge of conscience.

As if answering her thought a hand came quietly over her shoulder and turned off the radio, his voice murmuring politely, 'Do you think we might listen upstairs, it's so sunny.'

'Yes, of course,' she said, 'I'll bring up some coffee.'

'I've moved into the tower bedroom, I hope that's all right,' came his voice from the stairs as she went into the kitchen, wondering with an awful premonition what this calmness could mean.

'I came up here because of the view,' he said, as she arrived with the tray.

'The view, yes of course, it's lovely, especially on a day like this.'

His voice became more earnest. 'I have sent for Hans and Frick and I can see from here anyone arriving, and that's important because the Grenzschutzgruppe could persuade the Czech police to arrest me, and I won't be safe from that until Hans and Frick get here. Yes, you can see everything from these windows,' he said, glancing at the four embrasures which between them covered the whole garden round the house. She saw he'd brought up the television and the radio, together with his belongings, and had been lying on the bed. 'Let's sit and listen,' he said, moving the small sofa.

They sat side by side without speaking, like children who have quarrelled and don't know how to make it up. She knew he hadn't had any lunch so she'd put biscuits, apples and brandy on the tray. She began to feel the afternoon was going to last for ever.

They watched and listened, sometimes television,

sometimes switching to radio, where the commentary was more sober. It was like opera on a huge stage. Josel felt she could have written the score herself, everything was so predictable – horrifyingly predictable.

First the rather luke-warm crowd of immigrants, with women in the majority, then the cameras caught some shadowy figures with placards on the edge of the *platz*. The placards moved closer, watched by a thin screen of police. There was another five minutes of the chairman's speech, and then a group of some twelve or fifteen men threw down their placards and rushed the podium, shouting slogans and waving cudgels. This onslaught was attacked by the police from behind, when immediately another posse wearing swastika arm bands charged from the side-streets by the *platz*. They appeared to be carrying weapons, and there were shots, mostly it seemed in the air. The crowd was thinning rapidly as they were now being fired on by machine-pistols, while the police screen, heavily outnumbered, withdrew, throwing smoke-grenades.

The neo-Nazis were by now on the podium belabouring with their heavy sticks those who had stood their ground. Now came another hubbub on the edge of the *platz*, and through the thick smoke came about twenty men in fatigues, wearing arm bands on which could be glimpsed a pattern of red and black. They were moving in an echelon towards the neo-Nazis; the crowd had thinned and almost vanished, apart from the writhing and ominously still figures on the ground. The new arrivals were pausing, firing machine-pistols and then advancing once more. The TV cameras were obscured by the smoke as the fusillade of shots increased. Then came another intervention; the cameras switched again to the edge of the *platz*, where heavily armed men with helmets, visors and flak jackets were dismounting, without fuss it seemed, from large trucks. 'Grenzschutzgruppe 9,' said Carl Heinz in an undertone.

Then the cameras were again obscured by smoke, leaving only a view from a helicopter of a smoke-filled *platz*, while the radio commentary was inaudible in the echoing gunfire. Carl Heinz was drinking brandy now, she noticed, as she managed to find another radio channel on which a commentator was discussing the riot with a former leader of the Social Democrats.

'Can you explain what is going on?' she asked.

'Well, it is really quite simple. The meeting was planned as a mark of respect for the Rostock victims, and the neo-Nazis decided to make it their revenge, only to find themselves once again confronted by Black Berets, sent presumably by hard-line Red Army generals who want to promote civil unrest in Germany in front of our elections.'

'But what are these Black Berets and who were the heavily armoured squads we saw arriving just now in buses?'

'The Black Berets are MVD troops controlled by hard-liner General Boris Pugo and commanded by General Shatalin, an Afghan veteran. They are trained to suppress public disorder and are known to be politically reliable, as the phrase goes. The last arrivals must have been 'Grenzschutsgruppe 9', sent in by the Federal Government to restore order, and almost too late, I would hazard a guess.'

'But what could be the motive behind the Red Army trouble-making?' the commentator persisted.

'The German Government is in a very weak position before the elections. It has not coped successfully with recession or immigration, nor as yet with these neo-Nazi riots. Voters are very sensitive on these matters;

they bring back the memories *and* the consequences of the Weimar Republic. That is the nightmare.'

'So you think a weak government could be forced into a deal with the Red Army?'

'Yes, it is possible; and don't forget there are still more than two hundred thousand Soviet troops in our eastern provinces!'

Josel switched off and looked at Carl Heinz. He was smiling. 'They need me more than ever now,' he said. 'Your stupid idea of keeping me away from Eberswalde with those damned sleeping-pills has had the opposite effect – Germany *needs* a leader. She must stand on her own feet, my next meeting will tip the scales – you'll see.' He gulped more brandy.

Josel was searching channels again and this time she found London where the BBC was interviewing 'an American expert on the German political scene'. It sounded like a well-meaning waffle and she was just about to switch off when the announcer intervened and said, 'I have an important news flash from Moscow; it reports that President Yeltsin has ordered the arrest of six Red Army generals. It seems they are accused of conspiring against the state by attempting to negotiate the supply to Iraq of nuclear weapons, and attempting to cause civil unrest in Germany by sending special forces to take part in, and ferment, the recent riots in German cities.'

Carl Heinz was pacing up and down the room, his hands spread out in a gesture of repudiation, while Josel restrained a nod of satisfaction. So Gordon *had* persuaded them to jump the gun? The White House *must* have agreed, and of course the German Government.

The BBC announcer seemed to be following her thoughts – 'We have just heard from Berlin and from

Washington that there will shortly be a joint communiqué from the Russian, German and US Governments which will set out the framework for a programme of economic measures on a scale hitherto unimagined.'

Then followed questions and answers which were at best half-guesses in an atmosphere characterised by exclamations such as 'it beggars belief', and, 'how was all this put together?' – not to mention 'the nightmare prospect of Saddam with nuclear weapons would be enough to concentrate any number of minds in Washington'.

Josel was spellbound and longed to go on listening but, forcing herself to concentrate on the atmosphere in the room, she said, 'It looks like we've won through.' The words came out with what she knew to be an apprehensive smile.

'Grandiose schemes involving the Americans never work out,' he said. 'Look at the Gulf war. The Russian people are too suspicious and the Germans are nothing without strong government – a leader! And a leader they are going to have. As soon as Hans and Frick arrive, we can leave for Gorbitz and plan my next meeting; missing Eberswalde will be like coming back from the dead – always a good thing to do.' He grinned.

The BBC chose that moment to say, 'What news is there of Herr Winterhalter, who caused such a furore with his Rostock speech? The German media were greatly impressed and spoke of him as "an up-and-coming politician". I expect we'll hear more of him.'

'You most certainly will, my dear lady, and very soon, what's more,' said Carl Heinz, laughing happily and pouring more brandy.

Josel switched on the television again. The shooting

had stopped and the *platz* was empty save for ambulances, paramedics, casualties, and some men of Grenzschutzgruppe 9 visibly on the alert for any recurrence of the battle. How many casualties? she wondered; what price had been paid here for saving democracy, and how safe was it now? Must there be more riots as Carl Heinz intended? They had stopped him from going to Eberswalde, but what about next time? Full of drugs and alcohol, what was he capable of?

His ex-Legion followers must have been among those Black Beret thugs. Unless the New Deal just revealed, obviously at Gordon's instigation, could be quickly implemented, enormous damage could still be done, and talk of media admiration for Carl Heinz was a nightmare.

With hindsight, of course, it was blazingly obvious that much of his original plan had been dangerously over-ambitious and wildly improbable. What of feeding heroin to the neo-Nazis? The whole group should have recoiled at the suggestion. If only *some* seed of doubt about Carl Heinz had been sown – *damn* hindsight.

The commentators on television were now speculating about the size and nature of the New Deal, and one said it would 'make Roosevelt's efforts look like chicken-feed'. Another suggested that George Soros could be involved,and a third was stressing that it couldn't come fast enough if it was going to save German democracy from what he called 'a sickening encore of the thirties'. They were all agreed that the prospect of Iraq having nuclear weapons must have been the decisive factor for the United States.

While all these thoughts from outside, plus many of her own, were churning their way through her now muddled mind, she was vaguely aware of Carl Heinz packing his holdall, and she glimpsed the machine-pistol which she had tried to hide in the wardrobe. He put on a light duffle coat.

Josel was beginning to feel frightened. She cursed herself for it, because fear, she knew, communicates itself. Up to now she had seen Carl Heinz as a passionate eccentric with an over-developed sense of drama. An Irish mother who dreamed dreams and a father who had never escaped mentally from his Russian prison camp, combined with an over-educated intelligence and very un-Germanic good looks, had produced rare qualities of strength and courage, hampered by an unswerving sense of righteousness. Dangerous mixtures at any time but, in the present circumstances, they were pushing him, she thought, to the limits of reason.

The radio broke in; she had nervously fiddled with the knobs. 'And now,' the voice said, 'we will talk to Gisela Schreiber, the well-known political correspondent, who witnessed the whole riot at close quarters and seems to have got pushed about a bit at some stage. Are you all right now, Gisela? I believe you tried to interview some of the Black Berets before they were finally arrested by the anti-terrorist brigade?'

'Yes I did,' came the reply, 'but without much success, except to be convinced that they were in fact MVD special forces.'

'And you are in no doubt that their taking part in riots in Germany (they were, of course, also at Rostock), coupled with the Iraq–Red Army nuclear deal, completely justifies President Yeltsin's decision to arrest six Red Army generals?'

'Oh absolutely, and now of course, the German Government can have no excuse for feebleness in dealing with these riots.'

'And you believe they *will* be tough?'

'Yes, I do.' Here Gisela's voice took on a slightly hesitant note. 'Although there is *some* feeling in Germany that Carl Heinz Winterhalter, who made the famous Rostock speech, could be politically a force to be reckoned with.'

Josel heard the hiss of breath caught sharply, but she didn't look up, she was busy collecting the coffee tray. 'I will make some more,' she said quietly as she slipped through the door and down the narrow winding stone staircase, past the tiny turret bathroom, noticing how difficult it had become to stop her hands from shaking and the tray from slipping out of their grasp.

He had fallen in love with her – genuinely she thought, although its roots lay in his hunger for drama – and that came almost as a flash of comfort and a feeling of protection. But no – something had changed; the cumulative effect of heroin and alcohol feeding on his fanatical righteousness? With hands and mind trembling and coffee cups rattling on the narrow and now gloomy spiral, she was relieved to reach the solid kitchen floor, but only for moments; Marlene was gibbering something about the telephone.

'All the instruments are dead, madam.'

Josel stared at her, wondering how she had come to find out, but before she could speak she heard Carl Heinz on the staircase, moving slowly from the sound, and with something bumping against the stone wall.

He appeared, humping his holdall in his good hand, with the other tucked inside his duffle coat. He put the holdall on the stone floor, and, holding out a piece of rope attached to the handle, he said to Josel, 'Help me get this to the car.' Bemused, she took the rope and, pulling the holdall, moved towards the front door. Then the other hand emerged from the duffle coat, holding an automatic pistol. 'Yes, darling. I've cut the telephone. We can't have any more meddling.'

Marlene screamed and slammed the kitchen door.

'Willi has just arrived,' he said, 'so we must leave at once for Gorbitz; there isn't time to wait for Hans and Frick, and Willi might not like it.' He laughed. 'You're coming with me to Gorbitz and you must tell Willi not to interfere.' As he spoke there was a loud knock on the front door. 'Open it, and remember what I said.'

She moved towards the door, pulling the holdall, and flung it wide open to reveal Willi, all smiles and hugs of affection. He couldn't see Carl Heinz in the darkness of the hall after the brilliant daylight so there were moments of 'How lovely to see you!' and 'What a surprise!' and Willi started to say, 'I was getting worried about you,' when Josel cut in sharply – to force his attention – 'Carl Heinz says that I am to go with him to Gorbitz to prepare for the *next* meeting at Mölln and that you are not to interfere in any way.'

Her face said the opposite, her expression was that of sick horror – *Do something, Willi, do anything* it was saying, as he stood, mouth wide open, watching the approach of the automatic pistol and the smiling face behind it.

'You see, Willi, Germany is going to have her leader; a strong leader is all she ever understands. I have the guns, the men and the money, but I need Josel as well. You can spare her now, Willi, so just help her with that bag to my car.'

The strange procession moved across the courtyard to the car, and only when Willi found himself slamming the door on Josel in the passenger seat did his mind begin to grapple with what he'd heard and seen. Carl Heinz was turning the car now, preparatory to setting off down the 200-yard drive, and Willi was gaping at him, incapable of movement but with one screaming thought inside his head: *the hunting rifle and the tower.* They were photographs, not words, talking pictures, saying louder and louder, *Move, man, move.* In his Range Rover was the hunting rifle. It virtually lived there because he so often went out after roe-deer and sometimes even *gamsbok.* It was part of life, always had been.

So as the car went gingerly down the twisting drive, Carl Heinz obviously encumbered by his wounded shoulder, Willi sprinted for the rifle and cartridge belt and, grabbing them, made for the tower. He had slept in the tower bedroom and knew there were only ten more stone steps beyond it to the roof. It was simply a question of speed and then aim. The car would have to pause when it turned into the public road. How long for, Oh God, how long for?

His shoes had rubber soles and that was good, but keeping the rifle upright to avoid touching the stone walls in their narrow confines slowed him. His breath was coming in great gasps, the years were telling, and the blood pounding in his ears blotted out the radio – still switched on – from which praise was being lavished on the 'brilliant collaboration between Washington, Berlin and Moscow which has averted European nightmare'.

Willi pounded on, taking his nightmare with him.

Between the door at the top of the stair, happily open, and the parapet, he managed to get a cartridge into the breech before virtually sliding on his knees into a firing position. For a moment he thought he couldn't grip the rifle firmly enough to take aim. Open sights it had to be, the telescope would have taken an age to fix. Yes, there was the car. It had turned already into the minor road, but was pausing for some reason, a bicyclist perhaps or just gear-lever trouble? Damn – now it was moving and all he could fix on was Carl Heinz's shoulder. 'Imagine it's a slow-moving beast,' he said, half aloud, as he squeezed the trigger. *'Gott verflucht* – a gasp, and then a surge of relief which took him into a sort of shaky lope with which he managed somehow to negotiate the stairs, still holding the rifle, and then more soberly the drive.

Josel was out of the car now, waving, but as he approached she got in again and seemed to be struggling with the front seats. He could see Carl Heinz, stretched out awkwardly between the flattened driver's seat and the back of the car, blood pouring from a high shoulder wound which Josel was trying somehow to staunch with a scarf.

As Carl Heinz's body slumped away from Josel's struggling hands, Willi leant over him through the driver's window and managed to half-hear some words.

'He's gone, Josel,' Willi told her.

'What did he say?'

Willi hesitated and fumbled for words. 'Something from a song, an old song, Marlene Dietrich, I think – about flowers'.

'Sag mir wo die Blumen sind', she whispered.

They looked across at each other, two original partners in the seemingly hopeless mission, and no words came.

Then through the tears and sobs he just heard –

'A single shot – oh . . . *God!*'

The sobs turned the last word into a sort of echo, and Willi wasn't sure who the tears were for.